DATE DUE

The
Healer's
Keep

Also by Victoria Hanley

THE SEER AND THE SWORD

The Healer's Keep

A companion book to
The Seer and the Sword

Victoria Hanley

Holiday House / New York

Acknowledgments

Thanks go to:

My daughter, Rose, who read at least six versions of this story, and gave enthusiastic encouragement as well as on-the-mark criticism; my son, Emrys, for his wise questions and suggestions; my husband, Tim, for believing in good outcomes; my mother, Ane, for helping me through; and my father, Tim, who read the manuscript with an engineer's eye.

All of the following people have read various drafts of this book or portions thereof; each has provided valuable commentary and encouragement: my sisters Bridget and Peggy, Bonnie Callison (thanks for the coffee and conversation too!), Mary Ann Fisher, Bella Pearson, Ben Sharpe, Cynthia Torp, and the members of Colorado Word Weavers: Carol Berg, Krista Brakhage, Virginia Cross, Linda Kinsel, and Shirley Wilsey. Special thanks to Hannah Mahoney.

Thanks also to Sophie Hicks, for representing me, and to Trina Schart Hyman, magnificent artist. Immoderate gratitude goes to the two editors of *The Healer's Keep*—David Fickling and Regina Griffin. Thank you for your perceptive insight!

Library of Congress Cataloging-in-Publication Data
Hanley, Victoria.
The Healer's Keep / Victoria Hanley.—1st ed.
p. cm.
Summary: When the Healer's Keep is attacked by dark forces, Princess Sara and the foreigner Dorjan join forces with the slave girl Maeve and freeman Jasper to defend it.
ISBN 0-8234-1760-3 (hardcover)
[1. Fantasy.] I. Title.

PZ7.H196358 He 2002
[Fic]—dc21   2002017107

To my parents,
Tim and Ane

THE EASTERN KINGDOMS

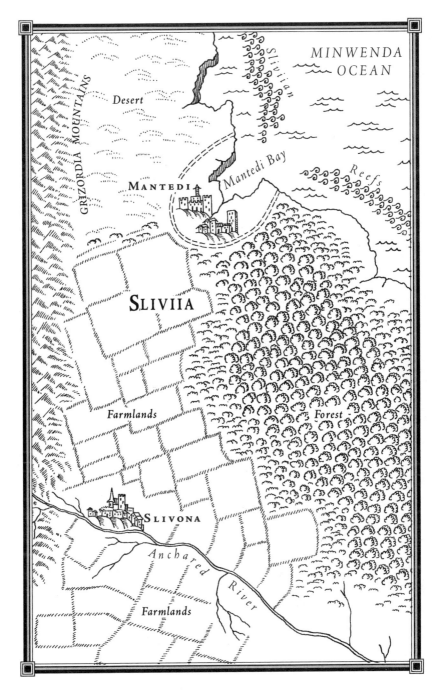

SLIVIIA

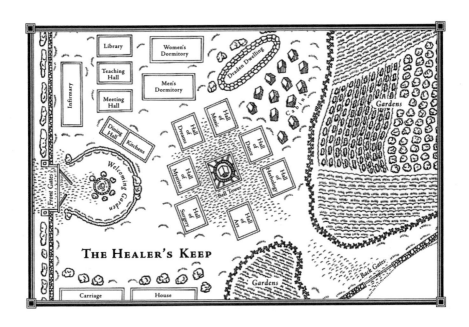

THE HEALER'S KEEP

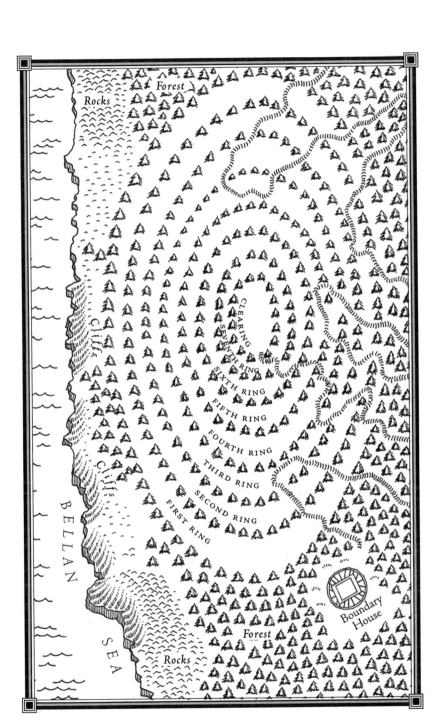

THE SEVEN SACRED RINGS

Contents

Part One

Sliviia

Chapter 1

Maeve sank onto a narrow bench in the back room of Lord Indol's bathhouse. The hard boards did little to comfort her aching body, but she would be off her feet for a few short moments. She sat quietly, watching steam rise from the enormous kettles on an iron range nearby.

Orlo came through the door, yelling for more hot water. But when did Orlo not yell? It was one of the sounds Maeve had grown used to, like splashing water and hissing kettles. Orlo wasn't cruel; he even looked the other way when Maeve stole moments in the ornamental courtyard, sitting in a sunny corner behind tall potted plants, out of sight of Lord Indol's guests. The guests might admire the fountain—carved stone fish spraying water into a clean pool of pink and red tile—but Maeve thought the golden sunshine more beautiful. Her mother had told her that without sunshine, she would grow up stunted like so many of the other bath-house slaves. Perhaps there was magic in the sun's rays; though she wasn't very tall, Maeve's proportions were what they should be—as men told her every day. She tried to avoid their eyes, hiding under drab shifts and ragged scarves, but still they noticed her.

"Maeve!" Orlo called. "High lord waiting in the corner compartment."

Maeve drooped. She tugged at her damp shift. *A lord.* Ladies were easier; they were often kind, complimenting her indulgently as she rubbed scented oils over their backs. Lords made rough remarks, telling her it was a pity they couldn't meet her among the sentesans.

Adjusting the ugly scarf that never quite hid all her hair, Maeve let her bare feet guide her into the guest area. Here, underground fires kept the granite floor warm—Lord Indol's visitors must never feel a chill. Colorful tile work lined the walls, matching the great tubs where people bathed. At the far end of the guest area, beyond the baths, were the compartments where lords and ladies could receive a massage if they wished. Maeve wondered if the lord waiting there would be someone she knew.

The light of the single lantern showed a stranger, wearing the customary silk loincloth of the bathhouse. The way the man lounged on the padded table reminded Maeve of the lizards that sometimes crawled over the wall into the courtyard. They would lie so still, they seemed to be part of the wall; when they moved, they were quicker than the bugs they caught.

Maeve's stomach tightened. "Good evening, sir," she said. "I am Maeve, here to serve you."

The lord propped himself on an elbow. "Maeve." He stared at her with eyes the color of steel. "And what is an unmarked girl doing in a bathhouse?"

Born into slavery, Maeve didn't know why her face was still unscarred when custom decreed she be cut by the time she was five. For years, she'd dreaded being called into the presence of her master, Lord Indol, afraid the day of marking had come, as it had for every other child in the bathhouse. Afraid of Lord Indol's *patrier*, the razor-sharp, double-edged knife of the privileged man. Every common slave in Sliviia received a slash mark on each cheek and one in the middle of the forehead. Crescents at the temples were Lord Indol's individual mark. Scars that named skills were put close to the ears or down the neck: a three-pronged mark for a cook, crisscrossing lines for a weaver, five slashes for a bathhouse masseuse.

Lord Indol had summoned her twice a year ever since she could remember, but he had never cut her. Instead, he had asked her in his reedy voice whether she knew the name of her father, and watched her closely when she told him no. Maeve's mother—once known as Lila the Fair—had been born a high lady but was condemned to slavery by her own father, Lord Hering. Why? He had promised his daughter to a noble Sliviite captain, but Lila had loved a different man instead—a man whose name she refused to tell.

Normally, only the nobility and lowborn free kept the smooth faces they were born with. But slave girls who gave promise of future beauty were also allowed to pass their fifth birthdays without being cut. If that beauty bore out, they received sentesan scars the day they turned fifteen: two lines circling each wrist, permanent bracelets condemning them to unspeakable lives. Because Maeve's owner, Lord Indol, had never cut her, Maeve feared he intended to make her a sentesan.

I'm seventeen, and still unscarred. Lord Indol had never tested her abilities, never sent her to train in the kitchens or gardens or in the sewing room, where her mother worked, never told her what he planned for her. When she asked Orlo, the slave who had risen to be master of the bathhouse, why she wasn't marked, he said he didn't know. Maeve was glad she served under Orlo instead of under the house matrons, who resented her smooth skin—they would cut her themselves, except that only lords could wield a patrier.

And now a man whose name she didn't know was looking at her as though she half belonged to him. Wishing she could tell him to close his mouth and shut his eyes, Maeve said, "Lord Indol considers me fit to serve here."

"What a lovely voice you have. Do you sing?"

"No, sir." Maeve hoped he couldn't tell she was lying.

The man looked from her to his patrier, which lay on a shelf close to the table. The patrier was the only weapon allowed in a bathhouse, an emblem of privilege the lords never relinquished. Maeve's face grew hot. A patrier was not to be used in a bathhouse. Why was he looking at her that way?

She ought to say something, any of the hundred soothing things Orlo had taught her. Instead she waited silently while the lord's smile faded. "You were sent here to rub my back," he said. "Proceed." He stretched out on the table, his broad back waiting for her touch.

Maeve dipped her hands in patchouli-scented oil and laid them on his back. As soon as she touched him, she felt as if she had fallen into a cold, gray bog.

Her hands often told her things about the people she touched. A tingle would begin in her palms, and she would *know*. She *knew* that Lady Loren's smiling face concealed great fear, *knew* Lord Meche was lying when he pretended to be a generous patron of the arts. The first time her hands had led her into someone else's mind, it had startled and worried her. But she'd come to accept this *knowing*: it helped her to stay out of trouble. And if Lady Loren covered her fear with a smile, or Lord Meche was really a miser, what of it?

But this man chilled and frightened her. Nausea roiled through her; she drew her hands away.

His head came up. His fingers grabbed her wrist, pulling hard. "What's the matter with you?"

"I'm sorry, sir. Perhaps another masseuse. There are many far better than me."

He twisted her wrist. His eyes impaled her, sharp as a patrier and very nearly the same color. His nostrils flared. "I never thought to find one such as you in a private bath-house," he said.

"Such as me?"

"Others may have missed it, girl. I see better than most."

Maeve wanted to ask what he meant, but her tongue felt numb. She tried to avoid his scrutiny but found she couldn't turn her head, couldn't even close her eyes, which seemed to obey his will instead of her own. She descended into the darkness of his pupils, down, down, into shivering blankness, a place of gray shadows.

Abruptly, he let go of her wrist. "I don't want others," he said. "Proceed."

What choice did she have? A high lord, here at her master's invitation—Lord Indol, his host, would have promised him a luxurious bath and massage. The lords were very exacting in their code, and if this one complained, what would be the price of Lord Indol's honor? God knew it was never the wealthy who paid it.

Though tendrils of steam surrounded her, Maeve shivered. She coated her hands in oil once more.

A boy, perhaps eight years old, darted behind the curtain where Maeve worked. He carried fresh towels, pleasantly scented with rose. Evan, the new child. His lowborn free parents had died, and heaven help the orphan in Sliviia. Losing both mother and father was a misfortune that often ended in slavery if the orphan's relatives could not afford to feed him.

In keeping with his free birth, Evan was still unmarked around the face and neck. Lord Indol kept a strict schedule for markings—setting aside only one morning in the month for it. Other lords ran their households differently, Maeve knew, adding scars at whim until the necks of their slaves no longer looked human, the skin full of patchy whorls. Lord Indol did not seem to relish cutting. Even so, Evan's sad day would soon come.

When Evan put the towels down on a ledge beside the table, the scent of roses calmed Maeve's churning stomach. *Roses—that's wrong. Gentlemen prefer patchouli or cedarwood, even the scent of bergamot.* Maeve tried to signal Evan with her eyes. *Get away. Not safe.* He only smiled, shaking his head at the curtain as if she played a game.

The man on the table got to his feet in one sudden motion. Without a word, he grabbed his patrier. He snatched Evan by the smock. As he jerked the boy forward, Maeve saw their eyes lock; Evan's gaze wide and helpless before the lord's penetrating stare. The patrier sliced Evan's face, deep enough to scar him for life.

Marking him.

Maeve fled, crying for Orlo.

Orlo moved fast, but very carefully. He knew his place. Lord Morlen had overstepped, marking another lord's slave in a private bathhouse. Nevertheless, it was dangerous to approach any lord holding a patrier, and Lord Morlen was not just any lord.

Curse him for disrupting the peace here, Orlo thought. Most lords would not dare to flaunt the law so openly, but Morlen would never be found at fault. No one would gainsay this man, who was said to be richer than Emperor Dolen himself.

Pulling aside the compartment's curtain, Orlo saw Lord Morlen's knife poised over Evan's forehead. The child wailed, blood pouring from his cheeks.

"My lord!" Orlo tried to bring the proper note of humility while still making himself heard.

Morlen looked up. "What is it?"

"My lord, I'm sorry you were offended, but that is Lord Indol's new slave you are cutting."

"I hope your place is worth a great deal to you," Lord Morlen said. He released Evan, flinging him carelessly to the floor. "The boy needs better training."

Orlo's heart thudded so hard, he knew it could be seen through the walls of his chest. "Apologies, Lord." He hoped Morlen would leave without causing more trouble.

Evan sat groping his face, whimpering. Maeve knelt beside him, cradling him while Orlo stanched his wounds. A curious slave or two peered in, but they scattered when they caught sight of Lord Morlen wiping his patrier.

Maeve huddled on the warm floor, holding Evan.

"Is the girl new also?" she heard.

"Maeve was born into Lord Indol's household, Lord Morlen," Orlo answered.

Lord Morlen! Maeve tightened her hold on the boy. Orlo might have warned her. The slaves told stories of Lord Morlen's riches and of his cruelty. It was said he could drive his enemies to madness without ever laying a hand on them. Maeve wanted to jump up, run away, go anywhere at all, so long as it was far from Lord Morlen. But he was between her and the curtain now.

"Why isn't she marked?" Morlen asked.

"I don't know, sir. I was never told," Orlo said.

"I will make a formal application to buy her. The boy, too."

Buy her! *No, no, Lord Indol will never sell me,* Maeve told herself, silencing the scream that wanted to erupt from her insides and tear across the bathhouse.

"Lord Indol has received many offers for her," Orlo answered.

"Indeed? You talk as if I had asked your opinion, oaf. Now give me a robe."

Orlo helped him into a silk robe and handed him his patrier. Lord Morlen strode away. Maeve shuddered as she tried to console Evan, murmuring comfort she didn't feel. She looked at the pattern of red and pink tile in the wall, then at Orlo's jowly face, white under black stubble. She stroked Evan's hair, remembering Lord Morlen's gaze, the way her eyes had stayed open when she wanted them closed, the clammy gray sickness when she had touched his skin. "Orlo, you said Lord Indol has had other offers for me?" He nodded; she saw his chest jumping as his heart beat. "But what if Lord Morlen offers him more than the others?"

Orlo's head shook back and forth. "If Lord Indol had made you a sentesan, the income to his household from his fellow lords could have ransomed an emperor. No, I doubt gold is his object in your case. But they say that when Lord Morlen sets his mind on something, he doesn't turn aside."

"Then I must beg Lord Indol, Orlo—beg him not to sell me." Orlo looked doubtful. "Let me have a bath and a clean shift?"

She saw tears misting Orlo's eyes as he nodded.

Lila knew she was dying. Often these days, swirling fields of stars interrupted her sight. Sometimes she wished the stars would stay and guide her to the next world. But then she would think of Maeve, her precious daughter, and go on with her work, the never-ending chore she'd done for so many years, transforming heaps of cloth into garments for Lord Indol and his family.

All I have left . . . my daughter and my memories of her father. Maeve, with her exquisite singing voice that Lord Indol will never hear. Cabis, who sailed away and didn't return.

Once, Lila had dreamed of escape to a better life across the ocean. Now she could hardly cross the sewing room, and her tiny needle was heavy to lift. She sighed softly. A tear slid down her face, spotting the dark satin she sewed. The tear surprised her; she had thought herself past weeping.

For weeks, as she toiled over gowns and shirts, Lila had planned what to say to her daughter. Maeve must escape slavery. The time was right; Maeve's secret gown was complete at last. Sewing it had taken nearly a year. Lila had filched thread and needles and purposely cut gowns too large so she could pick up the scraps when the silk needed to be trimmed. She had said she thought too much blue was being worn in Lord Indol's household, knowing that Matron

Hilda, always spiteful, would order still more bolts of blue silk. Then Lila had allowed all of her infirmities to show and pretended that her mind was fading along with her body.

No one suspects the poor weakling, sewing in the corner. Tonight I must tell Maeve. It can't wait any longer.

The shadows of evening slanted across the floor of the sewing room, releasing the slaves from another day of work. Grudgingly, Matron Hilda signaled that the women could leave. Lila put away her needle and dragged her small body up the stairs.

My life is ebbing from me. Low tide, and it will never be high again.

At length she reached the door to the garret she shared with Maeve. Slipping inside, she fell onto her thin mattress. Maeve wasn't there. Lila groped for strength, counting each breath, waiting for her daughter.

Maeve bathed quickly in the tepid water of the wretched pool reserved for the bathhouse slaves. Once she was clean, she asked after Evan. Orlo had sent the boy to bed in Lord Indol's orphan slave house.

Maeve crossed the summer garden between the bath-house and mansion. She hurried up the broad stairs, expecting to be challenged by the matrons who were usually in the hallways. But the place was silent. Another flight. No one. She found the door to Lord Indol's study. Still no one.

Her chest hurt as she paused outside the door. She knocked. No one answered. Emboldened by her terror of Morlen, she turned the knob. The door gave.

Maeve's bare feet sank into thick carpet as she stepped into the room. No slaves bustled about, yet this was the time of evening when Lord Indol took his pipe and brandy. She looked around, smelling tobacco. Shelves along two walls held many leather-bound books. Another wall backed a row of wooden chests and cupboards. Heavy furniture sat before an unlit hearth—a fire would not be needed this evening; the summer heat lingered in the air. Oil lamps warmed the twilight coming through east windows. A polished oak table held a brandy decanter beside two goblets—her master must be expecting a guest. What if that guest were Lord Morlen?

Maeve heard men talking in the hallway. Her legs trembled as she searched the room for a place to hide. She opened a tall cupboard in a dim corner. Brandy bottles filled it.

The study's doorknob clicked as it turned. The cupboard slanted across the corner, not quite tight. Ducking behind it, Maeve wedged herself between the cupboard and the wall, where no light shone.

Chapter 2

Lord Indol often thought with satisfaction that his study fit him well. Paneled walls, quality books, well-set furniture, and luxurious carpets—all these properly conveyed to others just what sort of lord he was. The sort who—like Emperor Dolen—valued the proud culture of Sliviia, who understood art and etiquette. A lord of standing, whose hospitality was famous.

Sitting now before the wide hearth, Indol turned to Lord Morlen, his guest, a different sort of lord. One he detested. Indol wondered how it would feel to be hated and feared as Morlen was, by everyone from slaves to the elite classes—even, it was whispered, hated and feared by the emperor himself. Perhaps Lord Morlen did not realize how hated he was—and if he knew, perhaps it did not trouble him.

Morlen didn't live in Slivona and mixed very little with the emperor's court. Though rich beyond the reach of other lords, he didn't see fit to maintain a household in the capital, nor was he a patron of the arts. He let it be known that he actually preferred Mantedi, that seamy northern port through which all the sea trade in Sliviia must pass. Regrettably, Sliviia's shoreline was almost completely hemmed in by spiny reefs, except for Mantedi Bay.

Footsteps approached her corner; she pressed closer to the wall. She feared that Lord Morlen would sniff her out, as a bloodhound finds the hunted. But she heard Lord Morlen's voice from across the room—it was Lord Indol who came so near her. He seemed to be unlocking one of the chests she'd seen pushed against the wall. A lid creaked open, then fell again with a thud. Maeve's breath came in rapid, silent pants.

Lord Indol's tread moved away. "A pleasure, Lord Morlen."

The door opened, then closed after the two men. Maeve freed herself from the cramped corner. Her legs ached but she ignored the pain, scrambling along the row of chests, feeling the wood with her hands, reaching with her mind for traces of Lord Indol.

Here, the *knowing* told her. *This chest*. Maeve tried the lid. Locked. She lay back, pressing her feet against the rim of the lid. She braced herself against the floor with her arms, pushing hard against the wood. With a loud crunching sound, the edge of the lid splintered.

She reached inside the chest and found a soft bag. She could feel large coins through the leather. Her price.

If anyone saw the ruined chest, an alarm would be cried. With shaking hands, Maeve took a weaving that covered a nearby chest and patted it down over the broken one. She picked up the splinters that had flown wide, putting them into the leather bag of coins, praying that the slave who straightened this room tonight would be too tired to examine things closely.

She had to get away. But how, without being seen? The mansion's halls must have been deserted because no one wanted Lord Morlen's notice. Soon everything would return

Indol disliked Mantedi. Along with thousands of shipbuilders and sailors and untold numbers of slaves, Mantedi harbored great nests of the lowborn free. Only the free would work Mantedi's filthy coal mines. Slaves put to work in mines often gave up, quickly dying. But the lowborn free held on to their pathetic notions of freedom—and lived. How they could call themselves *free*—with their short lives contained by Mantedi's thick walls—Indol couldn't fathom. Here in Slivona, free farmers, merchants, artisans, and carriage drivers at least had some reason for their pride.

It was said that most of the people in Mantedi worked for Morlen whether they knew it or not—even the members of the emperor's navy. Morlen had vast holdings in the desert west of Mantedi, too, though why he cared to own such worthless expanses of sand no one knew and no one dared ask.

His enterprises always seem to flourish, Indol thought, concealing his envy as he poured brandy, incensed that all his household slaves seemed to have vanished. He was forced to pretend it was his own choice to have an entirely private meeting with Morlen. And though Indol despised the superstitious fancies of slaves, he knew what was whispered about Morlen. "*When he looks into your eyes, he knows your thoughts.*" "*If he looks into your eyes, he can haunt your dreams ever after.*" Nonsense, to be sure, but Indol found himself avoiding Morlen's harsh glance.

Negotiations were going badly. Morlen had recently acquired the merchant pier in Mantedi that Indol used to bring wines into Sliviia. *I ought to have bought a Mantedi pier ten years ago.* Not only was Morlen raising the pier fees, but he'd also made it plain he expected to buy some of Indol's slaves.

"Very well, Lord Morlen," Indol said. "Since you insist upon Maeve, I accept your offer of fifty delans, and you may have Evan in the bargain."

"You forced me to bid an exorbitant amount, sir, to indulge my fancy."

"You must have taken *quite* a fancy to her." Indol's stomach pained him. He tried to rub it surreptitiously.

"What were *you* saving her for, Lord Indol? Going to make her a sentesan?"

"I could never reconcile myself to the idea of Lord Hering's granddaughter as a sentesan." Indol didn't want to admit how much the girl's ancestry had troubled him. He had thought, from time to time, about bringing her into the nobility when she came of age. But Lord Hering would be grossly offended; he had made it plain that he never wanted to see or hear from his daughter or her child again. And Lord Hering was close to the emperor. So Indol had left Maeve to labor in his bathhouse, where she would be treated well and kept from harm.

I tried to put her out of my mind, and now it's too late to help her.

Morlen looked interested. "A lord's granddaughter?"

"Yes. Her mother is Lord Hering's daughter."

"Indeed? What became of the mother?"

Lord Indol shifted uncomfortably in his chair. "Her father marred her face and sent her into slavery. I bought her as an act of charity, for I once knew her as Lila the Fair." Indol wished he understood how to guard his thoughts. And his tongue. He had not meant to tell Morlen about Lila.

"Marred her face? She must have committed a grave transgression. Did she have a lover then?" Indol nodded. "Does Maeve resemble her mother?"

"Lila's beauty is entirely gone now. Maeve's fea[tures] resemble what her mother's used to be, though Lila wa[s] as milk, while Maeve, as you've seen, has golden skin. A[nd of] course Maeve's eyes . . . very unusual."

"Indeed. The father?"

"Her parentage is unknown."

Morlen's gray eyes narrowed. "The girl doesn't kno[w] her father is?"

Indol shook his head. "Lila refused to tell anyone."

"Surely, a mother would tell her daughter?" Morle[n's] lips stretched over white teeth. "Now that you've agr[eed to] sell her, perhaps I will find out what you could not."

Indol nodded wearily, wishing he could take ba[ck the] sale. "I'll have my clerk draw up the parchments tomor[row]."

"Tonight."

"My dear sir, have another brandy. I invite you [to stay] until morning." Indol felt he would choke on the word[s].

"Thank you. I accept your hospitality, but I req[uire the] parchments tonight so I may depart with my proper[ty.] I have a long journey ahead."

"As you please." Indol suppressed his loathi[ng and] tried to fix his mind on the rare foreign wines an[d the] ary fifty delans would bring. It was, in truth, an ex[orbitant] price.

Lord Indol's clerk had come and gone. Now the so[und of] quill on parchment told Maeve the two men wer[e signing] the document that would transfer ownership of [her.] Goblets clinked as they toasted each other; she [heard the] chink of coins.

to normal. She must go immediately, before the house slaves and matrons came back.

She stuffed the stolen bag awkwardly into her shift. It fell to her waist, stopped by the rope that belted her. Folding her arms over the lump, she hurried out of the room.

Lila often wished her daughter could have seen her original face, the one she'd had when she'd been known as Lila the Fair. The only parts of that face left unscathed now were her eyes. One tangled scar united her cheeks, forehead, and chin—she had seen it herself, for Lord Hering had shown her a mirror to punish her further. All because she had chosen love, and because she would not name her child's father.

Until now.

Maeve knelt on her pallet in the silk skirts of the gown Lila had made. It fit well. "How did you know, Mother, that tonight would change everything?" She looked down at the soft folds of the dress. Tears leaked from her eyes. "I have something to show you." She rummaged in her blanket and produced a gold piece. "I have fifty of these," she said, her lovely voice trembling. "Surely that will be enough for us to get away."

Lila wondered if she were seeing things. "Fifty delans?"

"My price." Maeve lifted her chin.

"But how—?"

"I stole it. Lord Indol sold me. To Lord Morlen."

"Lord Morlen," Lila whispered. Suddenly, her veins seemed to hold a torrent too heavy for her heart to move. "Sold to Lord Morlen? Did you meet him face-to-face, then?"

"Yes. Only today."

God give me the strength to tell her. "Listen closely, Maeve. Your father's name was Cabis Denon." *At last, the words I've guarded against my heart for eighteen years!*

Maeve's silk rustled as she gathered Lila into an embrace. "Mother!"

Lila held her daughter close, then drew back to look at her. "Your eyes are just like his, Maeve. Many babies are born with that color—I used to call it endless blue. Very few keep it. He did. And you have."

Maeve took a long, slow breath, then let it out in a great sigh.

"There's more," Lila said. "Your father was from a Dreamwen family."

"Dreamwen? But—"

"I know. I taught you that Dreamwens were only myths. I said so to protect you, and him, for you couldn't tell Lord Indol what you didn't know. The Dreamwens are quite real, Maeve. Before Sliviia was overrun by the corrupt men who now call themselves lords, Dreamwens were highly valued. They have profound powers, though not all in the line carry the gift."

"The gift?"

"The gift of travel through the inner worlds, walking in dreams. An adept Dreamwen can visit other realms, can aid the dying, can heal the minds of the living. But without training, even if the gift is there, it remains dormant." Lila heard her own voice as though it rippled from far off, as if she spoke from under deep water. She must hurry. "When the lords took over, the Dreamwens were hunted down. Almost all were killed, though a few managed to hide among the lowborn free. No, don't try to talk." Lila raised a hand as Maeve opened her mouth to speak. "Your father was the grandson of the last great Dreamwen, the only son of an only daughter. His mother was gifted and trained by her father, but she hid her powers, living among the free. Cabis told me her name—Marina. I never found where she lived, or I would have run to her. . . ."

Lila paused, reaching for Maeve's hand. "Your father couldn't walk in dreams, but Marina taught him the Dreamwen lore. He told me—the Dreamwen gift sometimes skips a generation, and when it does, it grows stronger. That means *you* may be a Dreamwen, Maeve."

Maeve had always had vivid dreams, but Lila had never known what they meant. Having Maeve as a daughter was like being mother to a great artist but having no idea of how to draw—left without paints or canvas or anyone to learn from.

"Cabis was conscripted into the Sliviite navy and sent east for the great invasion of Glavenrell. He never knew I was pregnant and he never came back. I believe I would feel it if he were dead. He may still be alive, living in Glavenrell, or in one of the other free kingdoms across the ocean. You must go to Mantedi Bay, Maeve, cross the Minwenda Ocean, and leave Sliviia. See if you can find Cabis—"

"But—you're coming with me."

"Maeve, death is a blessing I seek. It's come for me, and I've turned it back because I wanted to see you one more time. Now that I see you, nothing can hold me in this world." *My darling child. God must watch over her now.* "No, don't try to change my mind. Listen.

"Because he was lowborn free, only Cabis's wrists were scarred when they conscripted him. But he marked *himself*. If he didn't come back, I was to sail after him and look for the man with a star on his chest."

Lila lay quiet, seeing a faraway picture of the rich, lovely young woman she had been, and the freeman who had carved his body for love of her. A man with brown skin and eyes of deepest blue.

"With the delans, you can hire a carriage. The gown will let you pass for one of the rich. But before you sleep again, there is something you must do. . . ."

"Before I sleep again?" Maeve squeezed Lila's hand, her fingers trembling.

"Alas, there were Dreamwens who fell under the sway of evil. The Ebrowens—they can invade the dreams of any-one whose eyes they've looked into even once. Inside the dreamer's mind, they can learn everything the dreamer knows." Lila shuddered. "I'm thankful my father scorned the notion of Ebrowens. An Ebrowen could have entered my dreams and learned Cabis Denon's name."

She gathered her breath. *I must tell her.* "I was always care-ful to avoid anyone with Ebrowen eyes."

"Ebrowen eyes?"

"Cabis told me a secret: no matter what eye color Dreamwens are born with, once they fall to evil and become Ebrowens, their eyes will be the color of steel. It's said that if you look at them, you will feel the Shadow King they serve. And when they are looking into your eyes, they can know your thoughts and control your soul." Lila saw the fear rush into Maeve. She wanted to take it away, but now wasn't the time for soothing words. Only one thing could help her daughter. "And now you've met Lord Morlen. You know the tales of him, Maeve. He's an Ebrowen. You must protect yourself."

"But how?" The question came out in a terrified whisper.

"Cabis gave me a family treasure. The Dreamwen Stone."

"Dreamwen Stone?"

"A jewel made by Dreamwens. It can protect you from Morlen." Lila paused. "It was so long ago. I thought I would never forget and yet it's dim to me now, but . . . I know the bearer of the Stone cannot be invaded by an Ebrowen." Lila wanted to press Maeve's hand, but her body wouldn't answer her thought. "I wish I could tell you more, my love, but the mists are upon me. And you must go."

"Go where?" Maeve's voice broke in a way it hadn't since she was a small child.

Lila could no longer see her daughter. Instead she saw a peaceful sky lit by floating stars. She made herself keep talking. "The Dreamwen jewel is disguised as a simple brown stone. Cabis told me to guard it. He said if there were ever a question of its being taken, I must bury it, to keep it safe.

"I knew that once my pregnancy was discovered, everything would be taken from me. I crept out of my father's mansion in the last week of my freedom.

"There's a narrow track north of Lord Hering's estate," Lila went on. "Travel down it until you come to a rock that looks like the head of a lynx. Behind that rock, walk two hundred paces due north to a young oak. At the base of the oak is a small boulder shot through with red veins.

"I wrapped the Dreamwen Stone in green satin and buried it beneath that boulder."

Matron Jill rubbed the sleep from her eyes. Never a moment's peace—her charges finally all quiet, and now that clanging bell. She hurried to the main door of the orphan house. A young woman stood outside, dressed finer than any of Lord Indol's family, and everyone knew he had the best seamstresses in Slivona, except for the emperor. Where could she be from? All elegance and beauty in the middle of the night.

Something familiar about her, but Matron Jill didn't know what. Jill wanted to kick the sheen out of the blue silk gown the young lady wore. She curtsied instead. "What can I do for you, ma'am?"

"I've come to fetch the boy."

"Boy? What boy?"

"Evan. The one Lord Morlen's bought."

"Come in, lady. Come in." So Morlen had paid for cutting Evan, the new orphan—there'd been talk he would. Matron Jill offered a shabby chair. The lady looked at it with contempt.

"Lord Morlen doesn't like to wait."

"Sorry, my lady. I'll be quick." Matron Jill bustled toward the long room that held rows of cots.

Bandages covered much of Evan's face. She had given him a strong dose of valerian. Too much of a bother to tend to the young ones with a first cut; easier to make them sleep. But now she couldn't wake him—when she shook him, he only mumbled and turned. The matron bundled the boy into his blanket.

The young woman took him—her arms were surprisingly strong. She held him as if he might spoil her gown. Matron Jill opened the door.

Chapter 3

As usual, Orlo began his duties well before dawn, seeing to it that the bathhouse was in order. Full kettles were set to heat, spotless towels freshly scented, all the tile work scrubbed and shining. Slaves went about their work stolidly, as if this were only one more day. But Orlo paced. Neither Maeve nor Evan had come in with the dawn. The word among the slaves said they'd been sold to Lord Morlen.

Foolish to allow myself to love Maeve as if she were my daughter. She had to leave eventually. But I didn't get the chance to say farewell.

The front doors of the bathhouse, built thick and solid to hold in heat, crashed open. Lord Morlen strode through them, dressed for traveling. He carried a scroll with the seal of Lord Indol, and beside him stood Lord Indol's clerk, looking sleepy.

"I've been told the slaves known as Maeve and Evan were to be found here at dawn," he said. "Lord Indol's clerk will verify they are now my property. Bring them to me."

"Maeve?" Orlo said, confused. "But she—isn't she with you? She didn't come in this morning. I thought—"

"Find her and bring her to me."

Orlo's lungs struggled as he hurried out a small side door. He ran for Maeve and Lila's room. He took the stairs two at a time. He knocked loudly on the garret door, didn't wait for an answer before going in.

A tiny window in the garret shed dim light over two pallets on the floor. One pallet was empty. On the other lay Maeve's mother, the monstrously scarred daughter of Lord Hering.

"Lila, where's Maeve? She's late to the bathhouse." Lila didn't speak. "Lila? Where's your daughter?"

She didn't answer, and Orlo knew he wasn't going to persuade her to tell him anything. He almost fell down the stairs in his rush to report to Lord Morlen.

The bathhouse had emptied—all the other slaves must have slunk away. Orlo stood on the granite floor, sweating as steam curled around him. "She isn't in her bed, Lord Morlen. If her mother knows where she is, she didn't say."

"You think the mother knows?"

"I . . . couldn't say, sir."

"You must. Does she know?"

"She didn't say," Orlo repeated, his pounding heart making his body shake.

"Take me to her."

Orlo led the way to where Lila lay on her simple pallet. The wedge of window opened a pathway of sun across her head. "Orlo?" she said.

"It's Lord Morlen, your daughter's new master," Morlen said.

Lila stared at the window. "My daughter has no master now."

Morlen drew his patrier. He held it up against dancing motes of dust. "This patrier will be *your* master if you don't tell me where she is."

Lila laughed faintly. "You surely don't believe you can frighten *me* with a patrier?"

"Look at me, woman."

She went on looking toward the window. "Do you want to find your way through my eyes to my soul, Morlen? It's too late for that." A hideous grimace that might once have been a smile creased her scars. "Where I'm going, you can never follow. And where Maeve has gone, you'll never discover."

Lila's breath left her so lightly that it took Orlo a few moments to realize she was gone. He bent to her. In death, her eyes shone with triumph.

Orlo knelt in Lord Indol's study, Lord Morlen standing over him. Matron Jill knelt, too, her pudgy face bright pink, her eyes red. She made smothered, hiccuping sounds as Lord Indol questioned her about Maeve.

"You've done enough, woman, without filling my ears with your sniveling. How could you give a slave to another slave?"

"Lord Indol, I swear, sir, no one would have known her. Such a gown, and her hair done high, and she talked like a fine lady."

Wearing a gown? Maeve? Orlo would have liked to see that. And talking like the highborn? He'd never known her to do so, but after all, her mother had once lived as a wealthy lady.

"A runaway *and* a thief. A girl with much more daring than you gave her credit for." Morlen's tones were admiring.

"But aside from Maeve, Lord Indol, your household is filled with fools."

"Orlo, why didn't you report instantly when Maeve and Evan were absent from their duties?" Lord Indol demanded.

"I heard they'd been sold, my lord. I thought they'd been taken by their new master."

"And you took the rumor of slaves to be the truth?"

Orlo wished he'd been born with the blessing of a steady heart. He wanted to shout that of course he'd taken the rumor of slaves, for who else would tell him anything?

"You failed in your duty to me," Lord Indol said.

"I'm sorry, my lord. I didn't know." Orlo's knees hurt. The bathhouse needed his attention. And he wanted to crawl into a corner and pray for Maeve, the one slave he'd loved like a daughter.

Lord Morlen pointed to the cowering Jill. "This matron said the girl wore a fine silk gown. Where did a *slave* get such a dress?"

Lord Indol's thin face puckered like fruit left too long in the sun. "Her mother was a seamstress. She must have made the gown and hidden it."

"This is a house of lenience, Lord Indol. Your matrons have only the minimal scars. Your sewing slaves are unsupervised—an entire gown was made with no one knowing of it. Curse the woman for dying."

Lord Indol coughed. "Even if she had lived, Lila could never be forced to say anything. She would not have told you where to begin looking for Maeve."

"It would not have needed force," Lord Morlen said. "Merely a night of dreaming—and a visitor in those dreams."

Orlo's heart thumped so fiercely, he feared Lord Morlen would hear it. *The tales are true, then.*

Lord Indol seemed to have lost the use of his tongue.

"No matter," Lord Morlen said, looking as if he enjoyed the fear on his host's face. "Tonight I can visit the dreams of Maeve herself. And until then, I will enlist Emperor Dolen's soldiers to shut down all commerce in delans and sweep the city. If she isn't found by nightfall, I *will* know where she is tomorrow morning."

Chapter 4

When Jasper Thorntree took old Thom's night carriage route, his first passenger was a noble, besotted with wine, who wanted to be taken to one of the rich neighborhoods. Jasper watched him stagger through his door, then drove on.

Street lanterns revealed a hurrying figure in billowing skirts. Curious, Jasper drove slowly, wondering why a lady would be out alone past midnight.

When Jasper came abreast of her, she hailed him. He stopped. She wasn't alone after all; she carried a sleeping boy. Her face in the light of his carriage's lantern was young and smooth. The boy had bandages on his face. *Fresh marks, yet she carries him tenderly. Rich. I'll never understand their ways.*

Breathlessly, with the accents of the highborn, she commanded Jasper to take her to Lord Hering's estate, then drive past it to a point she'd show him. Well, that was a length to go. It would mean he got no other fares that night, and he said as much.

"I can pay," she answered. Her voice was as pretty as her hair. Jasper found himself wanting her to talk longer, but she simply stood waiting for his answer.

Puzzled, Jasper looked at her. He'd seen plenty of dresses, never one like what she wore. As if someone had sewn together the best silk from a hundred different bolts of blue. The scarf she carried was frayed. No doubt he could gain some lord's favor by reporting this fare.

But Jasper wanted none of their favor. It was enough that he'd survived six years without being taken for a slave. Keeping out of slavery, after being orphaned at twelve, had meant pretending he had no wits so the lords wouldn't want him. Staying free meant he would never tell the lords anything they wanted to know.

"Get in," he said.

Another odd thing—as she climbed into the carriage, he caught a glimpse of her feet under the long, full skirt. No shoes. Not the first time, either; those feet were callused.

Evan woke to pain in his face. A pretty lady held his head in her lap—it was Maeve, but dressed in a gown, and with her hair done high.

"You're awake?" she asked, whispering.

He sat slowly, feeling his bandages. Were they inside a carriage? He heard a rumble of wheels. "Where we going?" he whispered back.

"We're running away."

"From that bad lord?"

"Yes. He bought us. So we had to run."

Evan nodded. They did have to run; he was a very bad man. "How did you get gold?" he asked. It took gold to get carriages and to have good clothes.

"Stole it. That man was going to steal our lives away from us. So I took his gold away from him."

"How did you take it?" Evan looked at her with awe. "He's strong." The boy remembered the way the bad lord had thrown him around like he was nothing.

"I was lucky, Evan."

"My face hurts."

"I wish it didn't. You're very brave." She looked like she was trying not to cry. Evan decided not to talk about his face again. He leaned carefully against her shoulder, so his cut cheek didn't touch anything. "Don't go back to sleep," she said. "We need to keep each other awake now."

Jasper stretched his legs as they neared Lord Hering's estate. His fare had urged him to get there before dawn. "Can't," he'd told her. "Too far." The sun was full up now. Other carriages, and single riders, too, shared the road with him. He continued past the Hering manor as she had asked. Craning her head out the window, the girl waved him onto a narrow, overgrown track. When they got to an odd rock formation that reminded Jasper of a great cat, she signaled a stop. Jasper jumped from the box to help his passengers.

The girl stood in the dirt holding her slave's hand, for all the world as if she were his sister, except that their coloring didn't match and his bandages told of being marked. Her tired eyes were an unusual shade—reminding Jasper of the dark blue glass that held perfumes at the market—set off by gold skin and deep gold hair. Pretty she was, very pretty.

"You want me to leave you *here?*" He gestured at the dirt and the weeds and the saplings crowding the edge of the track.

She nodded. Her dress stood out like a banner. "Which way is north?"

He pointed. She turned herself that way and seemed to be trying to fix it in her mind. Then she faced him again. "How do I tell an oak tree?"

"You mean to say you don't know an oak?"

"Would I ask you if I knew?"

A number of oak seedlings were scattered among the maple and birch at the side of the track. Jasper plucked one of them and gave it to her. "All oak have leaves shaped like these. You see?"

"Thank you." She rummaged in her shabby scarf, handing him a thick coin.

"A delan! That's far too much. I don't have the besaets to trade you out."

"Keep it. I have nothing less."

"For that, you could hire and feed me for a year!" he said.

"So much?" She looked doubtful.

"So much. I'll wait beyond the bend, Miss, carry you back if you like."

"I don't want to go back," she said, lifting her chin.

Jasper considered. He had to get the rig back to Thom and give the poor horse a rest. This rich girl, with her fine gown and her dirty feet, had no more claim on him. She'd likely quarreled with her family, running off as so many had done before her. Probably wanted to escape a betrothal— weren't all girls silly about marriage?

With a whole delan, he could get new wheels for Thom's carriage, buy a buggy and horse for himself, have any food he wanted. In all his eighteen years, chance had let him survive. No more. Now chance was giving him a leg up. He wasn't going to argue.

"Please yourself," Jasper said, and climbed onto the driver's box.

Maeve had never stayed awake for a day and a night and a morning. Weariness dragged at her body, while her mind jangled in fear. She must not let herself sleep until she found the Dreamwen Stone. Lord Morlen was an Ebrowen, Lila had said, and if he entered Maeve's dreams, he would know where she was and what she meant to do.

Evan's hand in hers reminded her that taking the boy along exposed her to further danger. If Morlen could invade her dreams, he could do the same with Evan. Last night, Evan had slept unaware of their escape; Morlen might have visited him and learned nothing that would give away what she had done. But today? Tonight? And all the nights ahead?

As they went two hundred paces into dense woods, she tried to spot landmarks. Lila had said to find a young oak, but what was young for a tree? The last time Lila had visited this place was when she was newly pregnant. That would have been eighteen years ago. How big would a young oak grow in eighteen years? To Maeve, the terrain seemed a jumble of vines, bushes, large trees, and hardy saplings.

She went back to the lynx rock and took her bearings again. She aimed herself carefully in the direction the carriage driver had said was north.

She counted off the paces. Imagining herself matching her mother's stride, Maeve could almost see the young woman Lila had been: face unmarked, sneaking out of her father's mansion to bury her beloved's treasure.

Maeve *had* to find Cabis's last gift to her mother, the Dreamwen legacy. *My legacy now.*

In front of her was a good-sized tree, with large full leaves the same shape as those of the seedling she clutched. Dozens of shrubs and weeds pushed up beside the oak.

"Look for a stick, Evan, would you? To dig with."

Twigs scratched her arms as she pawed through underbrush, looking for a rock with red veins.

There, hidden by foliage. She parted leaves and grasses, exposing a small boulder. She knelt next to it. Veins of red ran across its surface.

Evan brought a gnarled stick with a sharp end. Together, they dug and pushed. The boulder was well embedded, but at last they heaved it to one side. Maeve set the stick to the earth again, digging in the dark soil.

Threads of green satin! She got her hands around a stony object wrapped in the threads. It came forth decked in dirt, trailing tendrils of roots. She brushed away the last bits of satin that clung to it, revealing a simple, smooth brown stone, naturally rounded, fitting easily into her palm. It looked ordinary, but it didn't feel ordinary. Soft, somehow, and Maeve felt a coil of warmth from it, traveling up her arm and into her chest. A radiant melody hummed through her heart—a song she'd never heard before, but which seemed familiar.

"You're happy?" Evan asked, and she realized she was smiling.

"I'm happy because this stone is something my mother wanted me to have, and now we've found it. It has magic in it and will help keep us safe." She wanted her words to be true. She *must* find a way to protect Evan's dreams, too.

She extended the Stone to him. He touched it with a finger. "Hold it," she urged. He took it. "Does it seem to sing?" she asked.

"No." His eyes showed puzzlement. "Does it sing to you?"

She ruffled his dark hair. "Yes."

He handed it back to her. Tearing a strip from the tattered shift she wore underneath the blue silk gown, Maeve tied the Dreamwen Stone around her neck.

Jasper wrapped the gold delan in a rag and stashed it in the toe of his left shoe. He wore his shoes large, often using them to transport what he didn't want noticed.

He picked up a fare on his way back to Slivona. Full of new prosperity, he was going to give the man, whose clothes were threadbare, a free lift, but thought better of it. His years on the street had taught him that anything out of the ordinary might call unwanted attention.

His fare asked to be left off at one of the lesser squares in Slivona. Jasper pulled up beside a hitching post. As he accepted payment, a soldier approached. Jasper took one look at the soldier's doublet, made of gray and black leather sewn into stripes. *Zind!* He looked down, forcing his jaw to go slack. Looking simpleminded was the best defense he'd found against the zind, elite mercenaries who had long served the emperor.

A large glove, each finger either gray or black, banded with steel knuckles, took the reins from Jasper's hands. "Step down," the soldier told him.

The free called zind *stripers,* and only a man who wished for death would disobey their orders. The striper hitched Jasper's reins to the nearby post, then climbed inside the buggy, lifting worn seat cushions, peering closely as if Jasper might have hidden something in the old carriage. When he was done looking, the zind turned to Jasper.

"Were you out taking fares during the night, driver?"

"Aye." Jasper squinted at the stones lining the square, pretending his wits were too dim for speed.

"Show me your scroll."

Jasper brought out his precious freedom scroll. The zind glanced over it and gave it back. "Now your wallet."

Jasper handed over the shabby leather pouch. It held a handful of besaets. If the striper wanted to keep it, Jasper wouldn't fight him for it. The zind carried a short black axe and a long steel knife; Jasper had nothing but naked fists.

"We're looking for a pair of escaped slaves," the zind said, returning the wallet. "If you see a young woman with gold skin and hair, and a boy with new marks on his face, report to a zind or Lord Morlen. Reward of two delans."

Lord Morlen! But zind carried the emperor's banner. Jasper's glance flicked to the soldier's face. The zind scars were in place, a double stripe from forehead to jaw. And the emperor's crest at the temples.

"Lord Morlen?" Jasper squinted harder, as if lords and their names were beyond the reach of his mind.

"The runaways belong to him. The girl's seventeen, wearing a blue silk gown, and has no marks."

Jasper nodded, mumbling, pretending to try to remember, staring at the zind's gray leather boots, waiting, praying for him to be gone.

The boots moved away. Jasper hauled himself up to the driver's box, hiding his thoughts behind a vacant stare. *A young woman with gold hair and skin, in a blue gown, and a boy with fresh marks.* Escaping slaves! But how did she talk like the highborn, then, and where had she gotten the dress?

Slave. It would explain a few things: her bare feet, the way she treated the boy as if she cared. And she didn't know the exact value of a delan. A slave wouldn't know, unless she were a house matron, and Jasper would bet his last besaet that the girl in the blue dress wasn't a house matron.

Why Lord Hering's woodland? Everyone knew runaways headed for Mantedi, the only port in Sliviia, where all ships from traders to the emperor's navy had berth. If you wanted to leave Sliviia, Mantedi was the place to aim for.

As the carriage rattled through narrow streets, the tired girl in the blue dress kept drifting across Jasper's mind. He saw her standing in the dirt, telling him to keep the gold piece. *"I don't want to go back."*

Small wonder she didn't want to go back. Owned by Lord Morlen, and stripers looking for her. Jasper shuddered.

He drove on to Thom's. The old man had a bundle of hay ready, and water, for the horse. Jasper handed him the entire fare from his last passenger. He hadn't changed the delan yet. He'd have to go to Farley for that. "Thom, have you heard about Lord Morlen putting stripers in his pay?"

Thom grunted, brushing a fly from one of his thin shoulders. "You met them on the road? They've been here, too, warning all the carriage-drivers not to take delans for pay." Thom sniggered. "Not once in all my years have I been paid with a delan. But you can't tell stripers anything. The word is that Morlen's hired a battalion of zind to help him roust some runaways. With the emperor's blessing."

No delans. Jasper helped himself to bread and cheese but had trouble swallowing his food. He flopped down on a cot. Sleep wouldn't come. A lovely voice haunted him. *"I don't want to go back."*

Jasper wondered what sort of slave she'd been, to have such an odd look about her, as if she'd seen everything and nothing. And how was it she didn't have marks? He turned, then tossed the other way. Why had it chanced to be him, of all the men she might have fallen in with? Many would have reported her for less than two delans. Well, he wouldn't. So maybe she was lucky. Maybe luck would take care of her.

He gave up on sleep and decided to get his delan changed. He walked a familiar network of alleys to Farley's store, a place scarcely less dilapidated than Thom's shack. As far as the emperor's tax collector knew, Farley sold an assortment of whatever was to hand: shoes that had seen better days but weren't too down-at-heel, shawls knit with poor yarn, pipes and low-grade tobacco, even sour wine when he could get it. But in the back room of his store, he made loans to freemen down on their luck and changed money for those in need of it.

When Jasper showed him the delan, Farley whistled softly, then checked the front of his store to be sure they were alone. "Where did you get this?" He stroked the coin with greasy hands.

Jasper shrugged. "Can you change it?"

Farley rolled his tongue around inside his mouth. "I can change it, my friend, but I'm taking my life in my hands moving a delan through Slivona. Or haven't you heard? Lord

Morlen has stripers in his pay. First thing they did was close all commerce in delans."

Jasper shrugged again. "A ban against delans won't last forever, as well you know."

Farley tapped his fingers together, pursing his lips. "I'll give you a quarter the value, paid in besaets, tomorrow."

"Bad bargain," Jasper said. "I'll say yes if you give me the besaets now." There would still be enough there to get a cab of his own, a good horse, a harness, and have some left over.

Farley took the delan and gave him a hundred besaets.

Jasper left Farley's and went straight to the horse market. He nosed about, choosing carefully. He bought a friendly mare. She had mild eyes and spirit enough to step lively. He named her Fortune, for luck. He drove a meaner trade than he needed to on the harness, haggling like a poor freeman who'd hoarded his last besaet. No need to call attention to his newfound wealth.

He got the buggy he'd had his eye on. Sturdy, with thick cushions. He should be happy, with his own horse and rig. Instead, anxious feelings stole his appetite. He worried about the girl putting herself in the way of Lord Morlen's stripers. He exchanged a besaet for some loaves at a bakery, hoping the smell of fresh bread would make him want to eat, but it didn't.

Why care if she got away? Because he himself had barely escaped slavery time and again? She must be a rare one to have brought the boy along. Would've been easier to slip away by herself—always easier to care for one than for two.

The sun was low as he headed out. He decided to spend the night on the far side of Slivona at a carriage corner where he wasn't known. When he got there, stripers cluttered the place, poking into carriages, repeating descriptions of the runaways. "*Girl, seventeen, unmarked, wearing a blue gown. Young boy with fresh marks. If you see either, report to a zind or Lord Morlen. Reward.*"

Maeve and Evan found a stream running through the woods. Maeve wasn't used to bathing in such cold water, but it served to keep her awake while she thought about how to keep Lord Morlen out of Evan's dreams. If the Dreamwen Stone could protect her, surely she could protect the boy. But how?

She rinsed the silk dress. She held the damp cloth against her cheek. She dared not wear it again, not until she and Evan crossed the Minwenda Ocean. The matron of Lord Indol's orphan house would remember it. Or the carriage driver; he had a clear eye. What if someone asked him if he'd seen a blue gown?

Lila had given Maeve two sewing needles, stuck in a swatch of cotton. Now Maeve used one of them to take out the threads in her shift that identified her as Lord Indol's property. She hated to wear it, but what else could she do?

Trees hung toward the stream, trailing sunlight, peaceful and green. Maeve had never seen nature up close. She was grateful to the day for being warm and to the trees for hiding her and Evan. But what about tomorrow?

They had to find food. Find their way across the Minwenda Ocean. To get a ship, they would need to go north and east, making for Mantedi. Now that she had the Dreamwen Stone, they could go back to Slivona and hire a carriage. The carriage driver had said that only one coin would feed him and buy his carriage for a year. Maeve had forty-nine more coins the same as the one she had given him. But other than gold, all they had with them were ragged slave clothes and the splendid dress she must not wear.

When she took off Evan's bandages, his cuts seemed to be festering. Maeve had seen the signs often enough: angry red swelling and oozing. He winced and his eyes watered when she bathed his face. He sat at the edge of the water, drooping and quiet, while she wrung out the bandages. She twisted the thin cloth with all her strength, trying to ease her raging sadness when she thought of how this dear child had been made a slave. *Mutilated.* She began to remove Lord Indol's threads from Evan's smock. *I wish I could burn all the threads from all the lords in Sliviia in one great bonfire, then throw their patriers on the blaze and watch them melt.*

"Do you know anything about the woods, Evan?"

"Before, I lived in the woods sometimes. My poppa taught me to fish."

Before. Maeve understood him. *Before he became an orphan. Before being a slave in Lord Indol's bathhouse. Before being marked by Lord Morlen.*

"I'm lucky to have you with me. I've never been to the woods."

When the clothes and bandages were dry, they went on, making their way slowly through dense woods lining the stream.

Sunset brought a chill to the air. Their empty bellies made the cold worse. As it grew dark, they made a nest of tall weeds, huddling together for warmth, pillowing their heads on the folded silk dress. Maeve heard the soft, brilliant hum of the Dreamwen Stone next to her heart. *"The bearer of the Stone cannot be invaded by an Ebrowen,"* Lila had promised.

Somehow, I must guard Evan's dreams.

Part Two

The Healer's Keep

Chapter 5

Torina, queen of Archeld and Bellandra, arrived at the Healer's Keep dressed as a peasant. Her oldest daughter, Saravelda, sixteen years of age, had been identified as healing-gifted. Sara would study at the Keep, Bellandra's famous school for healers. Because she didn't want the other students to know she was a princess, she and her mother traveled in disguise.

Torina had been surprised when Ellowen Bazin, healer scout for the Keep, had reported that Sara had strong healing gifts. *If Sara is truly a natural healer, why does she behave like a natural fighter? A fighter from the warrior line of Archeld. More like her grandfather Kareed than her kind father, Landen.*

Politely, Torina had protested that perhaps Ellowen Bazin was mistaken.

Bazin, a quiet man with bony hands, shook his head. "There is no mistake here, my queen." He handed her a parchment tied with silver string. "It's not for me to name her specific gift, Your Majesty. That must be formally done by Ellowen Renaiya, who lives at the Healer's Keep. I can only tell you that your daughter would be welcome there. I leave you with a list of the healing gifts."

Torina had read the parchment with Saravelda looking over her shoulder:

Gifts Accepted for Study at the Healer's Keep

Avien—Healer-Artist

Lyren—Healer-Musician

Mystive—Essence Intuitive

Phytosen—Herbalist

Sangiv—Bone Setter and Bloodless Surgeon

Trian—Healer-Dancer

Genoven—Healer of Dreams

Firan—Spirit Warrior

"I'll learn to dance like the Trians!" Sara had stood on her toes excitedly. She quickly dismissed all the other gifts. "Healer of Dreams—I wonder what *that* is. Must they hold the hands of children having nightmares?"

True, Saravelda had always moved with irrepressible grace, seeming to dance even as she learned to walk. And when the Trians came to the palace to perform, the princess tagged after them devotedly. But the famous dancers were unfailingly serene, while Sara seemed the embodiment of turbulence. *A turbulent healer.* Torina smiled to herself. "You're certain you'll be named a dancer?" she said, teasing. "No interest in herbology?"

"If the Ellowens set me to counting out leaves and roots," Sara had answered with a laugh, "no one who came to me for healing would get well."

Now here they were, not far from the Healer's Keep, on the day appointed for arrival. Captain Andris, King Landen's most trusted soldier, had dressed in ordinary clothes and escorted them on an uneventful journey.

Torina took leave of the soldier. "Thank you, Andris. I'll meet you at the inn in Tanyen tomorrow morning."

The big man nodded and turned his horse.

"Which way?" Sara asked. Her thick brown hair had broken free of its ribbon to stream out under her broad hat. Her red peasant shirt and plain muslin skirt suited her, Torina thought.

The queen pointed to the smaller of two roads. The larger way was a wide avenue, gravel-paved, lined with imposing trees. "The big road leads to the Keep's infirmary," she said. "We've been directed to the private gate on the other side."

They turned onto the more humble road, little more than a track, edged with large trees to its left. On the right, great tufts of summer grasses pushed against a tall stone wall. The smell of the sea had stayed with them throughout their journey, for they had taken coastal roads. Now its sharp salt scent was laced with the aromas of fragrant herbs.

At the end of the road Torina and Sara dismounted. A tall young man stood quietly before a set of scrolled iron gates. Torina eyed him curiously. His odd squashed hat was like those she had seen among the people of Emmendae, the harsh land north of Glavenrell. His rough-spun shirt bunched and pulled across his wide shoulders and came up short at the wrists. His pants, too short for his long legs, showed a wide margin of brown skin at the ankles. A worn bag lay at his feet.

When Torina's gaze met his, she was startled by eyes the color of a clear sky at dusk. "Good day, I'm Nina," she said, regretting the deception. "Meet my daughter Sara."

"Dorjan," he said. He shook hands first with Torina, then with Sara.

"Are the gates locked?" Sara asked.

Dorjan nodded. Looking through the gates, Torina saw expanses of well-planted beds and recognized several herbs, lavender and sage among them. Behind the herb gardens, forests grew along rising ridges that ended in crags high above. West of the gardens, a path led up a gentle hill; the stones paving the pathway sparkled with a glint of pink. *Rose quartz?* Beyond the hill, Torina saw the tops of several stately buildings. A bell tower rose higher than the rest. The bells shone as though made of pure silver.

There was a sound of wheels on dirt and the jingle of a harness. A carriage pulled up. Though covered with dust, its paint was fresh, its top made of new leather. Matched horses wore a jaunty orange harness.

The driver jumped down to open the door for his passenger. A young man stepped forth, smiling as soon as his head was free of the carriage. "Thank you, Garen, for bringing me here," he said to the driver. "Now let me have my luggage, and be off. It's time for me to become a humble student." He chuckled. Garen handed him two well-tooled bags, which he set gingerly in the dirt.

The driver climbed back on the box, turned the horses in the track, and drove away.

"Good evening, good evening!" The young man stepped forward. He kissed Torina's hand. "Sorry about the dust, madam. Let me introduce myself. Bern, here to study at the Healer's Keep. Draden-gifted."

Torina swallowed uncomfortably, feeling a sinking inside herself, and wondering why. Surely it could have nothing to do with this charming young man?

His features looked as if a sculptor had taken great care with them—generous lips, even teeth, high cheekbones, high forehead. His skin could have been cut from cream-colored silk. Pale eyes sparkled earnestly.

"I didn't realize there was a Draden gift," she said.

"Oh, yes. It's distinct from the healing gifts—it wouldn't be on your list." He chuckled again. Torina felt unaccountably stung by his authoritative air. "It takes a particular set of abilities to administer the Draden duties and enforce the laws of the Keep. Dradens have been here as long as healers have. Healers might be the soul of the Keep, but it's the Dradens who let the healers function."

"Let them function?"

"Yes, madam. Healers teach and heal. Dradens do all the rest. I assure you, the scouts look just as diligently for Dradens as they do for Lyrens or Aviens."

"Then your gift is already named?"

"There's only one Draden gift," he said breezily. "But I await Ellowen Renaiya's formal decree. I hear she's a remarkable Mystive."

Mystive. Essence Intuitive. But just what does that mean?

"A Mystive can recognize the other gifts," Bern went on, just as if she'd spoken her question aloud. "The scouts are all Mystives, of course, though most are not as adept as Ellowen Renaiya." He smiled. "But as to more important matters"—he gestured at Saravelda—"is this your daughter?"

"Yes. Meet Sara."

Torina watched Bern clasp Sara's hand in both of his. "Please tell me you're Draden-gifted, too," he said admiringly.

Sara smiled. "I want to learn to dance like the Trians."

Bern bowed over her hand. "You certainly have the grace for it."

Torina turned to Dorjan, who stood looking on. "Are you healing-gifted?"

"So they tell me."

"From Emmendae?"

Dorjan nodded, putting a hand on the gate's latch. He shook it a little.

"Sealed," Bern said. "Only an Ellowen can open the seal of another Ellowen." He winked at Sara.

"You know quite a bit about the Keep, Bern," Torina said, pressing the latch to see for herself how it felt. An invisible force held it immovable.

"I'm Chief Draden Hester's nephew," he answered. "Draden gifts have been found in my family since Bellandra established the Keep."

"I don't see a bell," Sara said. "How will they know we've come?"

"The bells are on the welcoming side of the Keep, near the infirmary. They don't encourage visitors at this gate," Bern said. "Ah, but someone approaches."

Someone did. A white-haired man in silvery robes, looking as if he'd bathed in moonlight. He moved with such a spring in his step that Torina thought perhaps his hair had gone white prematurely. But then, Ellowens were famous for staying young even into advanced age.

"Welcome to the Healer's Keep," he said, opening the gate by touching it. "I am Ellowen Mayn." He heard their introductions, neither smiling nor frowning.

Inside the gate, a young man came to take the horses.

"Dra Jem will see your animals stabled," Ellowen Mayn said, "while I guide you into the Keep."

He led them past the gardens, down the neat walkway lined with polished flagstones. *Rose quartz indeed.* Craftsmanship at its finest. Had the healers laid these flagstones? Or was it, Torina wondered, the Dradens?

With every step, the uneasiness she had felt on arrival intensified. She wanted to take out her seer's crystal there and then, but to do so would be a terrible breach of protocol. As soon as she was alone, she would ask for a vision.

The others trooped forward, apparently undisturbed. As the group crested the small hill, the Keep's buildings lay before them. Torina counted seven imposing halls, arranged in a circle around the bell tower she had seen from the gate. The halls gleamed, as though the marble blocks that formed their walls had been hewn only days ago. Yet, the queen knew that the Healer's Keep was ancient; older even than the royal line of Bellandra's king, her husband, Landen. Beyond the circle, other buildings of the Keep could be seen.

"These are the halls where we teach healing," Ellowen Mayn told them as they reached the nearest one. "Each hall is for a separate discipline. This one, closest to the gardens, is where we teach herbology and distill medicines." Torina glanced at her daughter. Sara wrinkled her nose slightly, but didn't say anything.

As they passed halls where music and art were studied, they met students on the pathways. All wore simple, undyed muslin—long tunics over light trousers. Torina saw no difference in the way males and females dressed, though the young women had braids while the young men had short hair. Everyone gave the same greeting: "Health," and all moved sedately, as if their steps had been measured to be sure they were neither too short nor too long. Torina could not imagine her daughter saying "Health" and walking like the others.

Ellowen Mayn showed them the rest of the halls. He displayed neither pride nor humility when he told them he was a Sangiv and taught bloodless surgery and bone-setting.

Beyond the halls of healing stood several large buildings, for dining and studying, and two vine-covered dormitories: one for young men, one for young women. The dormitory windows were small, the doors wide. Ellowen Mayn invited the students to set their bags inside. "Rooms are prepared for you; your names are on your doors." He nodded to Torina. "You will have a place in the visitor's quarters of the infirmary tonight, ma'am."

Ma'am. How refreshing. I must remember to travel as a commoner more often.

While the young people found their rooms, Torina stood with Ellowen Mayn, trying to quell the sense of danger murmuring through her. She had heard that Sangivs were very perceptive. Did he know her thoughts?

"It's a joyous day when new students arrive," the healer said.

"Do they arrive often?"

"Several every month. Not as often as the realm has need for, though since King Landen has ordered scouting in all kingdoms, we will have more, I trust. Dorjan, the young man from Emmendae, is our first foreign student."

Torina caught herself before she spoke like the proud wife of King Landen. "When will these students have their gifts named and begin classes?" she said instead.

"They receive their first lectures tomorrow. Ellowen Renaiya will name their gifts soon."

Torina looked back at the wide circle of healing halls and then to the trees that began not far away. She noticed a domed structure, a little smaller than the halls, set off by itself among the trees. Its stained glass windows seemed cut from precious jewels, the colors unusually pure. "That building there," she said, pointing. "What discipline is studied there?" *And why didn't you take us past it?*

"That is the Boundary House, ma'am. Only Ellowens enter there, and the Dradens who clean."

"What does it mean, the Boundary House?"

"I can't explain it to you, I'm sorry. It's part of the work we do here."

"Perhaps you'll explain the titles you use? Dra, Draden . . . Ellowen?"

"*Dra* designates a Draden in training. When the healing-gifted begin to study, they're called novices. As they advance, they're known as Lowens. A new Lowen has trained for several years and is able to begin the work of healing others. A fully ranked Lowen is a proficient healer."

"And an Ellowen?"

He hesitated. "Ellowens have experienced Ellowenity."

"Ellowenity?"

"The love that unites us all."

When she didn't speak, he went on quietly. "Ellowenity cannot be taught, though it can be prepared for."

"Then not everyone can attain it?"

"Everyone can. Not everyone does."

Chapter 6

Hester, Chief Draden of the Healer's Keep, stood beside the well-swept hearth of the council room, brimming with rage. The upstart queen of Bellandra, Torina, daughter of the hated invader Kareed, had formally requested to meet with the Keep's Council. Under protocol, she could not be refused, though any other parent of a student would be prevented from speaking.

Fuming in her best robes, Hester frowned at Ellowen Renaiya. How such a weakling had become a member of the Keep's Council, Hester would never understand. Renaiya had served for only three months, since the death of the venerable Ellowen Tays—now *there* had been a well-spoken woman.

Across from Ellowen Renaiya stood Ellowen Desak, renowned First Avien, nearly bald, his skin smooth as a youngster's, his perpetual smile driving Hester to distraction. Neither Ellowen seemed fazed by having to obey the queen's summons. No bother to them. But then, why should the great Ellowens be bothered? It was not they who administered the Keep, not they who made sure that meals were served and students clothed and the infirmary scheduled and the grounds seen to and all the buildings cleaned each day. No, that work fell to the Dradens.

The meeting time had arrived. The queen would have no cause to complain about her reception—the council room was spotless as always, everything harmoniously placed. Fresh flowers, arranged by Avien students, decked the tables; rich paintings adorned the walls.

Their guest was heard in the foyer, speaking with Dra Jem. She entered without him, closing the door behind her. Hester stared. The queen of Bellandra wore a dingy blouse and skirt with a matching scarf over her head. As she approached the Council, she drew off the scarf, revealing a crown of braided red hair. No jewelry, no silk, nothing to dignify her station or enhance her rather pretty features. Hester almost expected her to curtsy.

But the queen did not go that far. "Good evening," she said. "Thank you for meeting with me."

Hester curtsied bitterly.

"You must excuse my dress," the queen said. "As the king's letter made known, our daughter wishes to conceal her royalty while she lives among you. You three Council members will be the only ones who know that Sara is Princess Saravelda."

Hester nodded grimly, ready for battle. No doubt the queen meant to ask that her daughter be named to a particular healing gift. "We give you greeting, Queen Torina," she said, gesturing to the four chairs gathered behind her. "Please, if you would, be seated."

They took their chairs; the queen began to talk. "I don't call you together out of curiosity or courtesy, nor am I here to discuss my daughter."

Surprised, Hester frowned, then changed the frown to a smile. "What is it you want with us, Your Highness?"

"As you may know, I am what you call gifted, though not in healing."

Go ahead. Proclaim yourself the Great Seer. We know that your father, King Kareed of Archeld, stole Bellandra's crystal when he brought war to this peaceful land.

The queen took a breath. "When I entered this place, I had premonitions of danger, yet when I looked for a vision, none was granted me."

Desak shook his head benevolently. The old man always managed to look as if he were granting favors, even when refusing them. "I'm sorry, my queen. I thought that you, being a seer, would know that you'll see no visions while you are here. Nor will you see visions of the Keep once you have left."

"How is that possible?" Spots of color, red as her hair, appeared on the queen's cheeks.

"We Ellowens put forth what we call Invisibility here. Reinforcing that Invisibility is as much a part of our training as setting seals on our gates."

"And what, precisely, is Invisibility?"

"A field of protection that guards us from outside interference." Desak's smile was like a father's to his child. Normally that expression infuriated Hester, but just now she enjoyed it. "The Single Invisibility affects all seers," he said, "and makes *everyone* perceive the Keep to be less powerful than it actually is." Desak put his two index fingers together, a favorite gesture when he lectured; Hester watched with satisfaction as he patronized the queen. "The Invisibility can be deepened, my queen," he went on. "When Archeld invaded Bellandra, the Great Seer Marla warned us. We set a *Double* Invisibility, which kept us entirely hidden from the armies of Archeld. Soldiers searched for us for nearly ten years, wanting to press our healers into the service of brutality." *Soldiers of Archeld, commanded by your father, Kareed, and his successor, Vesputo.* "But they never found us. When they looked at the walls of the Keep, they saw only long-dead ruins."

"You missed training a generation of healers," the queen said levelly. "Perhaps you went too far."

"We protected the Keep," Desak answered. "Our ways live on."

"Then you keep Invisibility in place at all times? You Ellowens do this?"

"Yes, my queen. Only the single Invisibility now, of course."

"I see." The queen spoke mildly. "Will you lift your Invisibility so I may see what danger threatens you?"

"Certainly not!" Hester broke in. It fell to the Dradens to uphold the laws of the Keep. As Chief Draden, Hester had full authority in this matter. "Our law says we may not, my queen, not for anyone."

Ellowen Renaiya shifted in her chair. "Just this once," she pleaded, "won't do any harm. She might be able to tell us what has taken our—"

"No." Hester frowned at Renaiya. "This is a Draden decision, Ellowen." She raised a hand to the queen. "The Healer's Keep obeys its own ancient laws. We bow to no one for governance." *That includes the king, and it certainly includes a false queen, with pretensions of being the Great Seer.* "We have been here longer than the royal line of Bellandra."

"I hope," the queen said, "that you are not refusing to hear me because you hold me accountable for the actions taken by my father when I was a child of nine? You wouldn't want to prevent me from giving you a timely warning."

"Indeed not," Hester said. "The law is quite clear."

Queen Torina rose to her feet. "No doubt your position is supported by *ancient* law. But what if I could tell you something important—*today?*"

"The law is clear," Hester repeated, standing also. "And was clear before you were born, Your Majesty."

"What if this matter is of importance to those now living and yet to be born? For though I cannot see *what* is wrong, I know it's serious."

"If so, the healers will know it," Hester answered.

The queen looked from Hester to Renaiya to Desak. "Have you not heard, Draden Hester, that a rigid mind is far worse than the unbending rule it defends?"

"No, madam. Who said such a thing?"

"Your queen." Torina took up her scarf. Then, with an abrupt farewell, she turned her back and swept through the door.

Renaiya darted from her chair, as though she meant to chase down the queen. Hester stepped in front of the small woman. "Let her leave."

"But she—"

"She's gone. You disappoint me, Ellowen, allowing a barbarian like her to shake your peace."

"She's the *queen*, Draden. The wife of our rightful king," Renaiya said.

"What leader asks his people to honor the daughter of the man who once conquered Bellandra? Torina might be our queen now, but she has always been Kareed's daughter." Hester watched her words rip through Renaiya. The invasion of Bellandra had taken Renaiya's husband and left her pathetically frail. Gifted, yes—everyone acknowledged that Ellowen Renaiya was an unsurpassed Mystive. But weak.

She often had to ask for entire days of contemplation or she, an Ellowen, would fall ill! "And," Hester rushed on, "what king lets his homeland become part of a conqueror's realm?"

"What if she's right, Draden?" Renaiya was quite pale. "I, too, have felt that something is wrong here."

"Perhaps *your* powers are failing, Ellowen."

"We can't ignore the disappearance of the Tezzarines!"

"Why do you drag forth those birds when you get the fidgets over your failures?" Hester replied. The Chief Draden didn't understand why the Ellowens mooned over their precious Tezzarines. *After all, they're only birds. Birds sometimes fly away.*

Hester had only seen the Tezzarines from far away, circling in lofty splendor. Magnificent they were, yes—quite beautiful, with their pearly wings catching the sunlight. But Hester didn't know, and didn't care to know, the bond of an Ellowen with a Tezzarine. "Aren't you healers trained to accept what happens around you?"

Renaiya looked as if she might start to cry. Desak patted her thin shoulder. "My dear Renaiya," he said, "fear never leads to the truth."

"Quite right," Hester said. "Now, do either of you wish for tea? Dra Jem is prepared to serve us."

Torina stood by the narrow window in Sara's dormitory. *Why is the Keep designed like a monastery?* Sara's rustic bed was covered with drab blankets tucked severely under its mattress. A simple chest of drawers, a desk for studying, a shelf for books, a basin for washing, a small mirror, and a supply of candles—that was all. Though Sara's natural tastes were not lavish, she was used to far more comfort than this.

Yet Sara hadn't been complaining about her room; she'd been arguing with her mother. Torina had described her sense of danger and her treatment by the Council. She wanted Sara to leave the Keep; Sara was adamant she would stay and learn to dance like a Trian.

Torina looked at her daughter, fixing Sara's picture in her mind: large restless eyes, delicate skin softening her forceful face, the way she fidgeted like a healthy colt ready to run. "Sara," she said, "perhaps *you* can find what the danger is."

"Me! I'm no seer."

"You don't need to be. Just look about you, notice all you can."

"But I don't feel anything wrong. How will I know what to look for?"

"Look for everything. And if your heart tells you to leave this place, listen to it." Torina held out a small pouch filled with gold. "The means to come home if you need to."

The following morning, Ellowen Mayn looked over the book-lined room in the teaching hall, where the Keep's incoming novices had reported to him for their first lecture at the Keep. In addition to teaching bloodless surgery and bone-setting, Mayn had the responsibility of giving untried students the foundation they would need to join the regular classes. The new students, sitting at wooden desks, each wore a scrubbed, fresh look that Mayn recognized from his decades of teaching: the eagerness of the beginner. That look would vanish once they'd spent a month or two in study.

One of the Dradens had been through this room before the novices arrived, to remove any traces of dust, to set forth parchment and quills, and to infuse the air with sage, the scent most helpful to students.

Surprisingly, Bern, Draden Hester's nephew, had presented himself along with Sara and Dorjan. The Draden-gifted seldom evinced much interest in healing. But then, Bern's gift had not yet been formally named—it was possible that another talent hid beside his family's well-known Draden gifts. And no harm would come from his listening to a lecture.

The three of them made an interesting group. Sara's feet danced beneath the desk, while her lively glance roved across the bookshelves. Her brown hair looked as if a child learning to braid had tried to weave it into plaits without success. Odd. Most young women would know how to make a neat braid. Her face was strong, her skin dainty. Dorjan sat to one side of her, a little too tall for his desk, a little too long for his Keep tunic. His black hair had been chopped short, but not quite evenly, as if he'd cut it himself with a knife. Eyes of an unusual deep blue regarded Mayn with an expression the Bloodless Surgeon couldn't quite define. *He looks as if he already suspects that Truth has a painful point and will stick him, as a needle will pin a moth.*

Draden Hester's handsome nephew sat on the other side of Sara, behaving like a normal youngster, winking at her, flattering her.

Mayn cleared his throat. "We will begin with a lesson about *gen*. Dip your quills." Mayn observed the separate habits displayed by his students. Sara dipped with a flourish, neglecting to wipe the excess ink, so that it spattered on her parchment. Dorjan barely seemed to pay attention to his pen, yet marked his page with clean strokes. And Bern's letters crowded into one another, but he wasted no ink.

"Gen is the name given to that precious, mysterious principle that en*ge*nders life," Mayn said, spreading his arms. "Everyone has personal gen. When strong and harmonious, it inspires happiness and health. Cultivating gen is something all healers learn to do, no matter what their gift. Much of what we do here is based upon enhancing gen."

Three pens scratched across parchment as he continued. "Think of gen as the blood of the spirit. It flows through us and animates us as long as we live. Health results from abundant gen."

The students were silent for a moment before Sara asked, "Is gen always good?"

Mayn hadn't intended to speak about the more advanced aspects of this lesson today. "No," he said. "Gen can be corrupted. That's why only those selected by Mystives are permitted to study here, for all healers learn methods for enhancing their gen."

"Corrupted how?" Sara asked.

Mayn paced, looking out the window of the study room to the gardens beyond. He stopped in front of Sara's desk. "Do you know any powerful men or women, Sara?"

"Yes, sir." She looked down, flushing slightly.

"And are they good?"

"Yes."

"Suppose they were *not* good?"

She chewed her lip a little. "I suppose they could do great harm."

"And why is that?"

"Because people follow them."

"Precisely. Powerful people have followers. When gen is elevated, it creates power. How that power is used depends upon the person who wields it. Like a weapon, it can be used to protect and defend or to kill and destroy. There are those who use their gen for selfish ends." Mayn paused, wondering if he should say something about the Ebromal. He decided against it. There would be time in a future class to discuss the Ebromal way. "Here at the Keep," he continued, "we use our gen to help."

He clapped his hands. "Now for an exercise in the control of gen," he said briskly. "Stand up." Chairs scraped; the students rose. Mayn beckoned them to the front of the room. He arranged the three of them and himself to stand in a square formation. Sara was diagonally across from him, Bern on his right, and Dorjan on his left.

"Close your eyes," he told them. "Breathe slowly, and let your breath carry you into the center of yourself." He waited for the students' breath to become slow and even. "Now breathe in, and hold the air. Imagine a silver sun shining inside your belly. That sun is the symbol of your gen."

Mayn opened his wisdom eye, gratified to see luminous spheres expanding in both Sara and Dorjan. Nothing changed in Bern, though Mayn noticed that Bern had an unusually large store of personal gen.

"Make the silver sun shine more brightly," he instructed. Dorjan and Sara did so. "As you breathe out, reach your rays across the room to me."

Bern's gen stayed in normal channels; that was to be expected. The Draden-gifted didn't rely on heightened gen to perform their duties. But Mayn watched in astonishment as a solid beam of Dorjan's gen extended toward him. The beam reached him and held steady. Seconds later, bursts of bright silver shot from Sara, bouncing exuberantly around the room.

"Breathe in again," Mayn said, "and pull your gen back into yourself, but don't let it fade—let it fill your body."

Dorjan's gen moved with a finesse few Lowens could equal; Mayn watched as silver light filled up the young man's form. Sara's gen stopped ricocheting around the room; it began rushing up and down her frame instead.

Mayn was amazed by Dorjan's skill. As for Sara, what she lacked in control she made up in intensity. At last, two students worthy of all that the Keep had to teach.

Wanting to find out how much Sara and Dorjan were capable of, Mayn decided to lead them in a more advanced technique. "Breathe normally for a few moments, feeling the warmth of your silver sun." He watched delightedly as they did what he'd instructed. "Now reach out again with your gen, toward the person across from you. When you feel your gen touch, let the two edges merge."

Dorjan's gen brightened, moving out toward Bern, while Sara's power spilled out of her in aimless profusion.

But as the silver light from Dorjan touched Bern's field, Dorjan recoiled and his gen dropped back. His eyes flew open for an instant. Puzzled, Mayn looked to Bern, wondering what had made Dorjan stop the blend. Had Dorjan sensed something? Perhaps Mayn should examine Bern himself. But wasn't that for Ellowen Renaiya to do? She would be scrutinizing the new students in her own way— she might be doing so even now. Renaiya was so adept that the novices would not need to be present in order for her to name their gifts.

Mayn brushed aside the question of Bern, his attention taken by Dorjan and Sara. They were now facing each other, eyes closed. A bloom of silver surged from her, met by a radiant crest from him. Where they met, Dorjan's gen blended with Sara's as though he'd practiced blending for years.

Convinced that Sara and Dorjan were both extraordinarily gifted, Mayn decided he'd need to use great care in training them. It wouldn't do to continue the experiment in blending now, without laying a better groundwork. "Pull your gen back into yourselves, and let your breath return to normal," Mayn said. The blend between Dorjan and Sara flickered, died down. "Now open your eyes."

Bern yawned. "Interesting lesson, Ellowen."

"What happened, Ellowen Mayn?" Sara may as well have been jumping up and down. *Like a child given cake for the first time, asking, "What is this?"*

"We'll resume the lesson another day," Mayn answered. "Class dismissed." He watched them gather their parchments. "Dorjan, please remain with me after the others have left."

Dorjan pretended not to notice Sara's curious glance as she and Bern left the room. He faced Ellowen Mayn, waiting. The teacher's dark eyes seemed gentle, but why had he asked him to stay?

"Dorjan, it appears you've already had training?"

Dorjan nodded, wondering how much he should say.

"Who taught you?"

"My father, sir."

Ellowen Mayn looked puzzled. "I don't understand. The Mystive who scouted you didn't report a gifted father trained in the uses of gen."

"He's not . . . that is, he didn't call it gen."

"No? What did he call it?"

A pause.

"If you have a secret, I can keep it," Ellowen Mayn said.

Dorjan sighed. "Do you know anything about the Dreamwens, sir?"

"Indeed, yes. Sliviian mystics. Why do you ask?"

"The Dreamwen gift runs in my family. My father doesn't have it, but he must have given it to me. His mother and his grandfather were both Dreamwens; they taught him the Dreamwen lore, made him memorize it."

"And your father taught you." Ellowen Mayn looked interested.

"Yes, sir. I have most of the lore memorized."

"And because you're gifted, you could practice based on the lore you learned." Ellowen Mayn nodded. "Our scout felt the gift and sent you here. Tell me, what are the traits of a Dreamwen?"

"Walking in dreams. It's said a Dreamwen can heal the mind of another."

"And you? Can you walk in dreams? Have you tried to heal the mind of another?"

"I walk in dreams, yes." Dorjan hoped he didn't sound arrogant, laying claim to the skill he'd practiced since he'd been a child. "I learned to meet my grandmother in dreams. She guided me through the realms. As for healing the mind of another, I've tried. I'm here in the Healer's Keep for more guidance."

"Your grandmother lives with you also?"

"No, sir. She's in Sliviia."

"Sliviia." Ellowen Mayn's bright gaze nearly overwhelmed Dorjan. "Tell me, did you receive a list of healing gifts?"

"Yes, sir."

"And which one do you believe you'll be named to?"

"The Genoven gift seemed most likely, sir."

"Healer of Dreams," Ellowen Mayn murmured. Dorjan didn't understand why the Ellowen seemed full of excitement.

"Yes, sir."

"Your father taught you well, Dorjan. You could be—" He broke off, clasping his hands. "Within a day or two, your gift will be named by Ellowen Renaiya. Until then, please don't discuss what we've said here with anyone."

"I didn't expect to, sir."

"And my word is good. I'll say nothing."

Bewildered by the Ellowen's manner, Dorjan stood quietly.

"One more thing, Dorjan."

"Yes, sir?"

"What does the word *wen* mean to you?"

"It means 'spirit,' sir."

Dorjan was completely puzzled to see Ellowen Mayn rubbing his hands together at this answer.

Chapter 7

From far away, the bird looked like a raven. Large, black, imposing. But as it flapped closer, Sara knew it was no raven: the wingspan wider than should be possible, a huge darkness filling her sight. Its gray eyes fixed on her, seeming to pick her out as prey.

She heard her own breath, ragged and rapid. Her legs felt tired and feeble. The bird's fiercely beating wings would overtake her easily.

A tall young man darted toward her, arms waving. *Dorjan?* "Wake!" he yelled. "Wake." She thought he would run straight into her; he didn't slow. He reached her, ramming a finger against her forehead.

She fell out of bed.

The floor of her bedroom at the Keep shone in the gleam of moonlight coming through the window. Sara rubbed her forehead and got to her knees, reaching for bed and blankets. She clutched the blankets, her fingers stiff. She felt as if the bird of her nightmare still hovered near, ready to seize her.

She heard a rasping sigh coming from the other side of her room. A figure in a long nightshirt crouched against the far wall. *Dorjan.* A sheen of sweat covered him; his deep eyes blinked as though he didn't see her. How had he broken through Ellowen Renaiya's seal? Separation between the sexes during the hours of darkness was strict at the Keep. Yet here was Dorjan in her room, well before dawn.

"Thank you," Sara said. He didn't answer. She crept onto the bed. When she looked at the wall where Dorjan had been, he wasn't there. She scrambled over her rumpled blankets, scanning the room. She poked under the bed. *Gone.*

The window was much too narrow for Dorjan's shoulders; Sara didn't understand where he could have gone. She went out into the hallway. Carefully spaced lanterns lit her way to the dormitory door. Not a sound beyond her own hasty steps broke the quiet. She tried the outer door. The seal held.

Returning to bed, she gathered her blankets close, staring at the moonlight. Had she made it all up, about Dorjan being in her room?

She remembered Ellowen Desak's lesson from that afternoon. *"If you look only for what you already know, you will miss your most important discoveries."* Sara thought Desak a pompous, tiresome man. She doubted *he'd* had a new thought in fifty years. Not like Ellowen Mayn, who was interesting.

She lay wakeful, gazing at the place where Dorjan had appeared.

Sara wandered between sleeping and waking. Each time she got close to sleep, she felt the dark bird waiting for her and would blink her eyes open again. When the Keep's bells began to peal, she was slow in rising, slow to dress. She tried for long minutes to fashion her hair into a braid; her mirror told her decidedly that she had failed again.

She arrived at the dining hall to find Dra Jem posted beside the doors. He greeted her, reminding her that no one would be allowed in now that the meal had begun. Sara trailed after him to the kitchen, where he gave her a piece of bread and butter and a cup of water. "You will join the other students in the Hall of Herbology this morning," he told her, pointing.

Shoving bread and butter into her mouth, Sara walked to the Herb Hall to wait. Soon more students arrived, the girls' hair neatly braided. Dorjan found a place near her in the back of the room; she didn't see Bern.

She leaned toward Dorjan. "What happened over the night?" she whispered.

"I don't know," he whispered back.

"But you were—"

Sara stopped as the teacher strode to the head of the room. "For those of you who haven't met me, my name is Lowen Camber, Herbalist." The woman's voice was so gravelly, Sara expected her to spit pebbles when she cleared her throat. Her Lowen robes covered her like a tarpaulin draped over a hedge. When she clapped her hands, it was as if she banged two stones together. "All students, including novices, will visit the forest this morning," she said. "If you don't yet have your herbology book, come here."

Sara looked at Dorjan. He shrugged. They both rose, making their way up to the front of the room. Lowen Camber handed each of them a leather-bound book, worn about the edges, thick as Sara's wrist. "This morning you'll be gathering wild herbs," she said, addressing the class.

"But I'm sure I'm not Phytosen-gifted," Sara said. "I wouldn't know what to look for."

Lowen Camber stared. "Even the lowest ranking novice must learn the plants commonly used for healing, no matter which gift you may be named to," she said, slatey eyes snapping. "Please take your seat."

Cheeks hot, Sara followed Dorjan back to her desk. She opened the book, resentfully turning pages filled with drawings of leaves, roots, and flowers. She wanted to learn to dance like a Trian, not pore over plants.

Lowen Camber droned on, directing them to pages showing herbs they were likely to find in the forest at this time. Then each student was issued a basket.

"Return with your basket before the luncheon bell," Lowen Camber ordered. "You will spend the afternoon with Ellowen Mayn, learning basic bone-setting." Her gaze found Sara. "Another skill *every* student at the Keep must learn."

Sara wanted to roll her eyes. Herbs and bone-setting were equally unexciting. When would she visit the Hall of Dance? Crowding out the door beside Dorjan, she wondered where Bern was today. Probably attending some Draden function.

The students started for the forest, treading shining quartz pathways. "I'm going as far as I can get and still be back by bells," Dorjan said. "Would you like to come with me?"

Sara nodded, taking extra steps to stay even with him. "So tell me what happened," she said.

"Wait." Dorjan didn't follow the rest of the students into the forest by way of the path. Instead he headed west, ducking into the trees at a spot away from the others. Sara ducked after him. Dorjan moved as if he knew where he was going. Odd. Hadn't they both arrived at the Keep on the same day? Sara hadn't had time to explore. She'd wanted to see the trees that the healers called sacred—ancient plant-ings infused with wards and seals. Ellowen Mayn had said there were seven rings of these trees among the forests of the great Keep, each ring contained within the others. No one who was not a sanctioned member of the Keep would be able to step past even the first ring. Students might go as far as the fifth. Lowens the sixth. But until the attainment of Ellowenity, with all the enhancements of gen that it brought, the seventh ring would be impossible to breach.

Sara had tried to understand what *Ellowenity* meant, but the Ellowens were vague when they spoke about it. "*Ellowenity connects us with all life. . . . Ellowenity enhances our gen for service to others. . . .*"

Sara couldn't picture Lowen Camber feeling something as mystical as Ellowenity. *What's it like to be the only teacher at the Healer's Keep who isn't an Ellowen?*

The wooded ground sloped gently upward; Dorjan walked so fast, she panted as she tried to keep up. Soon she could see the first band of sacred trees. Huge trees standing next to each other—any one of their trunks would have made fifty of Sara's width. Massive branches screened the summer sun into cool shade.

Dorjan stepped past two great trees without hesitation. As Sara slid between the enormous trunks, she felt a slight pull, as if she broke through thousands of spiderwebs woven together. But nothing was there.

"Wait," she called softly. Dorjan turned. "Stop a minute," she said. "I want to know what happened. How did you get past the dormitory seals? Why were you in my room?"

Leaning against an ancient tree, Dorjan seemed to belong in this forest. "Why did we share a dream?" he answered.

"Then you remember? The bird?"

"It would be difficult to miss."

"I don't understand," she said. "How did you—"

"Walk with me?" he asked. He didn't wait for an answer, just turned and began walking again. Sara hurried after him, wanting to shout questions at his back. But the peace here felt as though it shouldn't be marred, so she kept quiet.

Dorjan continued through smaller trees, heading upward in the direction of the sea. He passed out of the first sacred ring as it crossed their paths again on the western side of where they'd walked. He led the way out of the woods onto a rocky ledge overlooking the Bellan Sea. Sitting on the rock, his legs hung over its edge. He motioned Sara to sit beside him.

Swinging her legs high above the sea felt good. Sara took up a pebble, warm from the sunshine. She flung it, watching it arc from her hand over the water, landing with a tiny splash far below. "Tell me now, about the night?"

"You were there, too. What can I tell you?" His eyes reminded her of lapis lazuli embedded in rare wood.

"I know what I saw. I don't know what *you* saw."

He folded his hands across his knees. "I saw the bird ready to take you. I yelled for you to wake. Then I was in your room. Then I was back in my bed."

Sara shivered. Dorjan had been in her dream! Did he go through her dream into her room? Impossible.

The sky began to spin, mixing with the sea, spinning more, merging with the ground. Even the rock underneath her seemed unsteady. As she groped for something solid, Dorjan's warm rough hands pulled her away from the edge.

"Sara," he said. "Sara."

She gathered herself, waiting until the world righted itself, aware of Dorjan rubbing her hands. "Sorry, Dorjan. I don't know . . ." *I don't know anything!*

Gently, he let go of her hands. "It's all right," he said. "I don't know either. What happened with that dream hasn't happened to me before." He looked across the Bellan Sea, and for a moment he seemed utterly foreign and remote, much more foreign than growing up in Emmendae could have made him—as if he'd traveled past the rim of the world and seen things Sara couldn't have imagined. But then he looked back at her. "Shall we gather the herbs?" he said. "We'll need to return before our bone-setting lesson."

Ellowen Renaiya closed the door to one of the rooms in the Hall of Mystives. Within its walls she would contemplate the gifts of the newly arrived novices.

Sunlight, softened by muslin curtains, illuminated a soothing arrangement of flowers; the air had been infused with rosemary, a scent conducive to clear thought. Renaiya seated herself at the little table that held the flowers. She hoped Dorjan would turn out to be Mystive-gifted—she enjoyed training new Mystives. *There aren't enough of us.* All the others scouted the kingdoms for new students, leaving Renaiya to brave Hester alone.

Renaiya sighed, almost wishing her talent were less. Any Mystive could perceive the existence of gifts, but Renaiya's specialty—naming those gifts—took more talent.

She turned her attention first to Dorjan, the young man at the center of controversy—the first healer novice ever scouted who had not a trace of Bellandran blood in his ancestry. As an outsider, he was an object of contempt to the Keep's Dradens.

Dradens! They still exasperated Renaiya, though she'd lived at the Keep since she was fifteen, a span of thirty years. Chief Draden Hester had strenuously opposed letting Dorjan study at the Keep. If there had been a lawful way to stop him, Renaiya felt sure Hester would have found it. But the Ellowens had authority over student matters and they had stood firm—the Keep needed more students, even if those students were brought in from outside Bellandra.

Genoven.

Renaiya calmed herself, recalling the words of her mentor, Ellowen Tays. *"It's the Dradens who bear the weight of the world for us so that we may be free to heal."* So it was. So it would always be.

She recited the Mystive's prayer. *Help me to lay aside everything but the truth.*

She envisioned Dorjan in her mind's eye: dark blue eyes, rangy bones, long hands and feet. Sixteen for only a month and already tall. How much more would he grow?

Renaiya let her awareness drift clear of his appearance. Closing her eyes, she searched his colors. *Deep, and very vital. The young man has recently expended great amounts of energy.* She wondered what he'd expended it on. Her concentration broke, and she found herself thinking of Queen Torina's warning. If only Hester had allowed the Invisibility to be lifted. Queen Torina's status as Great Seer might be questioned by some and scorned by others, but she *did* have Marla's crystal. Perhaps something was very wrong at the Keep. Renaiya knew she herself wasn't in full health: Was something draining her strength?

Perhaps I'm losing my powers.

She bowed her head, returning to contemplation upon Dorjan's essence. *What is the gift?*

Genoven.

Her eyes popped open. She nearly laughed. Somehow she'd let herself get lost in a flight of fancy. Genoven! That gift hadn't been seen at the Keep since well before Kareed invaded. Though Renaiya had been meticulously trained by Ellowen Tays to identify all the gifts, there had never been a need to name a Genoven.

She shut her eyes. *Help me to lay aside everything but the truth.*

This time when the answer came she rose from her chair to pace the room. The Dradens were having trouble accepting that an outsider might be gifted at all. If the first outsider scouted surpassed every Bellandran for generations, how would she tell them? *Hester will want me dismissed from the Council.*

Renaiya sat again, forcing herself to be composed. Over and over she asked for Dorjan's gift. Always the same answer. *Genoven.*

A Genoven could do what no other healer could: heal those whose minds were deranged. Genovens learned to cure terrible fears and racking melancholy. They could even lead the way from outright madness into clarity and calm. They walked in dreams, and dreamed in daylight.

Renaiya noticed that her hands were clenched. She slowly uncurled each finger, breathing deeply. Hester wouldn't be happy, but Hester couldn't change the truth. Wasn't it cause for celebration, to have a Genoven to teach? Every Ellowen would play a part in Dorjan's training.

*It would be celebrated if he were Bellandran. A gift is a gift. I will
be glad.*

Renaiya longed for a peer to consult with, but there was
no one. She must attend to the other two novices.

First Sara, who moved so gracefully. *Unfair, unfair. Granddaughter of Kareed, the aggressor who destroyed Bellandra's peace.
No gifts should come to any of his seed, not ever.* Renaiya's breath
came short and sharp. *Why doesn't the Ellowenity last forever?
At the moment of attainment, all is plain—the unity of life, the
love animating all things—and now, my hands shake with defiling
emotions.*

Renaiya prayed for release from grief and anger, prayed
to touch Ellowenity. *Help me to lay aside everything but the
truth.* She waited until she felt tranquility flowing through
her soul before asking for Sara's gift.

The answer came clearly. *Firan. Spirit Warrior.*

Renaiya jumped to her feet. She pounded on the table.
The vase toppled, spilling water and flowers. She righted the
vase, cramming blossoms back into it, where they
reproached her, bedraggled and thirsty. Never mind. A Dra
would come in later and clean the mess; no one would speak
of it.

Firan. It couldn't be. It simply couldn't be. In centuries,
had there been a Firan identified? No. Ellowen Tays had
even talked about removing Firan from the roster of healing
gifts. No one could explain why Spirit Warrior had been
included among healing gifts in the first place—a Firan
didn't heal anyone.

*I must be wrong. Over the years, Tays and I named dozens of
Lyrens, Phytosens, Aviens, Sangivs, and Trians. Not one Genoven.
And even our predecessors never named a Firan.*

Sara comes from a warrior line, her intuition whispered. *Granddaughter of Kareed the Invader. Daughter of Landen, who has made a return to the days when all Bellandrans learned the arts of war.* Renaiya also remembered the way Queen Torina, the girl's mother, had confronted Hester.

Sitting down, Renaiya asked again for entrance to Saravelda's heart.

The girl has no idea of her gift. This enormous power she carries lies dormant. She believes she's Trian-gifted. I could name her a Trian and no one would ever have to know.

She decided to put Sara out of her mind. She would sense into Bern now, and go back to Sara when her confusion had passed. Naming Bern's gift would be simple. Hester would wear smiles for a month when her nephew began training as a Dra—perhaps he would follow in her footsteps and rise to Chief Draden.

Renaiya's thoughts rested for a moment on the young man's earnest eyes and well-combed hair. What excellent bones he had. Perfect beauty. Perfect manners.

Too perfect. Renaiya had been trained to follow human flaws to the core of another's being. She loved the small defects that defined each person as real. There was something unlikely about Bern, something unreal, like finding a polished gem within a mine.

She should name him and be done with it; all his signs pointed to Draden gifts. Hadn't members of his family helped administer the Keep for generations upon generations?

But she must complete the ritual. *Help me to lay aside everything but the truth.*

Bern's heart appeared dutiful—a bit shallow and arrogant, but that was normal for the Draden-gifted. Fighting the urge to skip the remaining steps of a naming, Renaiya attached her awareness to Bern's essence.

It was like falling when expecting even ground.

Renaiya gasped. Her hand flew out, knocking the vase over again. This time she didn't pick it up.

Charmal. A Charmal in the Healer's Keep. Bern has already constructed a false mask. Young as he is, someone has trained him in the intricacies of deception.

Charmal. The Charmer. Gifted with insight, yet having no conscience. A Charmal sees into others, bends others to his will.

Renaiya looked at the ruined flower arrangement, wondering if she had gone mad. *Three novices. Three unheard-of designations, and one of them doesn't belong in the Keep at all.*

The bells announcing midday startled her. She realized she'd spent hours in contemplation. It was her duty to preside over the dining hall while the students took their meal. She fumbled to her feet. She left the Hall of Mystives, heading for the dining hall. Dra Jem bowed her in. Renaiya set a weak seal on the door and went to the small table reserved for the presiding Ellowen.

She felt unmoved by the artful flower arrangements, snowy tablecloths, delicate china. She watched the students, three in particular, more narrowly than she had watched in many years.

As form required, students kept silent during the meal. At the table in front of Renaiya, Dorjan and Sara sat next to each other. Bern sat across from Sara, between Jeanne, a promising Phytosen novice, and Lorel, who had been named Lyren-gifted. Both girls had joined the Keep the previous month.

Renaiya expanded her awareness toward Sara and Dorjan. Were a Genoven and a Firan indeed sitting before her? Her stomach dropped. Dorjan seemed to be performing a blend—with Sara. And the girl's gen met his warmly, though with little control.

Renaiya's body ached. She rubbed her eyes. Blending was an advanced practice and Dorjan was untrained. Or was he?

When Dras had cleared the tables, the students might do as they wished. Conversation began with a low murmur. Renaiya watched Bern reach across the table, touching Sara's wrist. "I missed seeing you at breakfast."

Sara laughed. "I missed seeing food at breakfast."

Bern chuckled. "Where were you?"

"Late."

"Please don't be late ever again," Bern said, smiling his charming smile. "Not seeing you takes away all my peace."

Dorjan dropped the blend with Sara. He sat tall, staring narrowly at Bern. "Takes your peace? When did you have any peace to be taken?" he asked, and Renaiya heard contempt in his quiet tones.

Slicing through a Charmal's web? Is Dorjan stronger than all my skill?

Bern rose. He smiled, winking at Sara, ignoring Dorjan. "We'll talk again, you and I," he told her. Sara looked askance at the two young men as Bern moved away.

Ellowen Tays's teachings resounded in Renaiya's mind. "*Going against a Charmal will earn you his hatred. He'll work ceaselessly to bring about your undoing. Charmals make frightful enemies, yet there's nothing else to be done. For if you give in to one, he will take all your power.*"

Exhausted after having eaten only a few bites, Ellowen Renaiya left the hall. Her head throbbed with confusion. She felt unable to clear her thoughts. How could she possibly appear before Draden Hester and Ellowen Desak in such a state?

Seeking out Dra Jem, she formally postponed until the following evening the meeting that would name the three novices.

Sara woke early, filled with a pressing sense of darkness. She looked out her window, somehow relieved to see dawn breaking, though it brought only a pale puff of light to the sky—didn't penetrate a thick mist shrouding the ground.

She knew the locks were unsealed quite early. Feeling restless, she slipped into her simple novice clothes. She didn't see any other students as she left the dormitory.

Walking fast, she crossed the gardens outside her window and headed for the trees. Before long she had passed through the first sacred ring. Birds, hidden in the fog, called eerily as she sat on a rock beside a wild glade. She liked being away, for a short while, from the heavy rituals and rules of the school. She wondered if she and Dorjan and Bern would have their gifts named today. *If Ellowen Renaiya is truly the great Mystive everyone says she is, she'll name me Trian-gifted.*

She heard someone approaching. When Ellowen Renaiya appeared in the glade nearby, she looked like a ghost in her silvery robes. Sara's first thought was that the Ellowen had been spying on her.

But Renaiya didn't seem to notice anything around her. Her robes fluttered as she paced the damp ground; her mousy hair straggled around her face. "What do I do?" she said, speaking to herself. She lifted her arms in an imploring way. Then she sank down on the damp ground cover of the glade, lay back, and didn't move.

Sara jumped from her rock. She knelt next to the Ellowen, picking up a cold hand to rub it.

Renaiya flinched, hazel eyes opening wide. "Sara? What are you doing here?"

"I woke early."

"But what are you *doing* here?"

"Are you all right?"

The Ellowen sat up. "There's nothing wrong with me that a little solitude won't cure."

Sara rocked back on her heels. "Why do you dislike me?"

"Dislike—"

"You know about me, don't you? You know who I am."

"As a member of the Keep's Council, I had to know. I wish I didn't."

"You wish? Why?"

Ellowen Renaiya was nearly as white as the mist rising from the ground. "It's just that I suffered so much by the actions of your grandfather."

"That's nothing to do with me. I wasn't born then." Sara's tone had the edge she'd been warned about countless times. *But she's wrong to blame me.*

"Nothing, and everything. The truth is, I wish things could be as they once were."

"Because Bellandra was perfect before Archeld conquered?" Sara tried to hold back her anger; it poured out anyway. "Admit the rest of the truth, Ellowen. Bellandra was defenseless because of too many years of empty ritual—just as you have here at the Keep!"

She got to her feet and stomped off, face burning. She had done it again—spit on what someone stood for. What was she doing in the Healer's Keep? *I've never healed anything, only made things worse.*

She blundered down the trail, wondering what her parents would say if she were dismissed from the Keep before her gift was even named.

"Good morning, Sara." Bern's friendly face appeared out of the mist. He put a hand on her arm. "You're crying. What's the matter?"

She wanted to shake off his hand and hurry away. She almost did, but her head felt suddenly foggy, like the air. She hesitated. "I just insulted—" She stopped. She didn't know Bern well enough for secrets. And Dorjan didn't like him.

"Insulted? Whatever it is, it can't be serious." He stuffed a hand in his pocket and brought out what looked like a silk handkerchief. "Not regulation Healer's Keep, I know," he said, winking, "but very handy." He handed her the handkerchief. She hastily wiped her eyes.

She had a great urge to tell Bern everything, to spill out her entire life, all her weak points and secrets, her ambitions and desires. "Bern, if I tell you—"

He took her hand. Where his palm touched hers, a current of heat warmed her. Were they exchanging gen? Sara wavered, her head aching.

He slid an arm around her, squeezing her shoulder; she didn't pull away. He lifted her face with gentle fingers. "Please don't cry." He bent and kissed her tears. Slow and warm, his mouth traveled down her cheek, kissing. She didn't resist as he drew her near, so near that she felt the planes of his body pressing against hers, felt herself fitting against him as if they'd been formed for each other. So this was what it was like to be kissed, truly kissed!

Sara wasn't crying anymore. The incident with Ellowen Renaiya faded as she and Bern twined themselves together, wrapped in fog, defying the cool morning with their heat. She didn't want to think of anything else—she only wanted to meet Bern's delicious strength with her own, mouth on mouth, hand to hand.

The sound of bells clamored intrusively. Bern stopped kissing. "Hungry, my lovely Sara?"

She didn't feel hungry, not for food. She wanted to go on tasting his lips. But she let him take her hand and lead her. And when they reached the walkways where other students might see them, and Bern dropped her hand, she said nothing of how much she wanted to keep touching him.

She saw Dorjan but ignored him. You could never tell what he was thinking behind those remote eyes, nothing like Bern's eyes, which were open and cheerful. Dorjan would never understand what she felt for Bern.

Part Three

Journey

Chapter 8

Maeve knew she was searching for Evan but didn't know where she was. She walked through gray hallways filled with gray doors. Even the light here had a gray cast. When she brushed against the walls, they felt as cold as frozen metal. Deriding whispers followed her, jumbled over one another in a continuous hiss. *"Poor girl doesn't know where she's going." "No, never has known." "She doesn't know what to do unless someone's telling her." "She's lost."*

When Maeve turned, there was no one there, only the dull floors, cramped ceilings, and cold walls. *"Lost, lost, lost."* She wanted to tell them they were wrong, but she *was* lost.

As she walked, a young man appeared in front of her. She didn't see a place he could have come from, yet there he was. When he saw her, he gasped. "The Dreamwen Stone," he whispered. "You have the Dreamwen Stone?"

Maeve looked down. The Stone she wore began to glow with golden light. She felt warmed, as if its light had the power to overcome the gray surroundings. She touched it, and heard the Dreamwen song.

"How did you know?" she asked the young man.

Close up, he was taller than she, much taller. Brown skin, and fathomless blue eyes. "I've heard it described," he said.

"It's been missing for so long—and now I meet it in a dream while searching the halls of the Shadow King?"

"Dream?" She looked around. The walls appeared quite solid in the cold, flat light. *Dreaming!* "I need to find Evan before the Ebrowen does."

"You're looking for a friend? But if your search brought you here," the young man said, "doesn't that mean the Ebrowen has already taken your friend?"

Here? She didn't want to ask what he meant. "I don't know," she said. He seemed to understand so much more than she did. "I don't know."

"Is the Ebrowen looking for more dreamers, or only your friend?"

She put both hands around the Dreamwen Stone. "He wants me, too . . . but I have the Stone. My mother said the Ebrowen couldn't find me while I had it. Tell me it's true?"

"You don't know?" He looked bewildered.

"I only dug up the Stone this morning," she said.

"This morning! Who told you where it was?"

"My mother." She wanted to explain everything to him, but she pictured Evan being questioned by Lord Morlen, and urgency overwhelmed her. "I don't know anything more," she said. "Please—help me find Evan."

"Of course." He pointed. "That way. We'll look for him in the rooms." He hurried forward.

They opened gray doors, peered into gray empty rooms. The whispers began again, a cloud of scorn following them. "*Lost, lost, lost.*" Did the young man hear what Maeve heard? She felt too tired to ask him. How long had she been in these hallways? Each step seemed an effort. Shouldn't it be easy to walk through a dream? Shouldn't she be able to run, even fly if she wished?

She laid her hand on another door. "Here," she said. "I think Evan is here."

The young man opened the door to another gray room. On a bench lay Evan, ashen-faced except for two red marks on his cheeks. When Maeve rushed in and sat next to him, he didn't move, only stared with wide eyes. "Evan," she said. "Did Lord Morlen bring you here?" He didn't answer.

"We must leave," the young man said, "before the Ebrowen comes back." He picked up Evan, holding him over one shoulder. "Hurry."

She followed him into the cold corridors. She heard more whispers. "*Rest. Rest is what you need.*" "*You're tired. You can leave later, after you rest.*" "*There's no hurry.*" She saw shadowy women, and men too, smiling to her, beckoning.

Carrying Evan, the young man nearly ran through the halls. "Remember why you came here," he urged. She did her utmost to remember. *Evan.* As she strove to keep up with the young man, her lungs felt as if they were slowly freezing. She wanted only to rest. How did he know where to go? These corridors were all alike, long and gray and cold.

Another hallway. This one dead-ended in a wide door. She couldn't see any knob or handle on it. Trapped. She stopped, twisting back, facing the shadows that followed. Beyond the shadows, someone was coming toward her. A man, moving fast as a lizard, steely eyes cold as these halls. *Morlen.*

Maeve spun around. She tore after the young man. He had reached the door. He spoke a word she didn't know, and the door swung open. Maeve rushed through the opening. She heard the door close. She fell and lay on her back facing the sky.

The stars were nearer, brighter than they should be. Evan lay beside her in soft meadow grass. She didn't know this place, didn't recognize the close, bright stars above. She heard again the quiet beauty of the Dreamwen song; it seemed to sing the music that kept the stars alight. When she sat up and looked for the door they had come through, it was gone.

"Morlen . . . ," she said. "Did Morlen . . ."

The young man next to her patted her arm. "Ebrowens are barred from here. We're in the Meadows of Wen. You're safe from him here. More safe than any other place in all the realms."

"But how did he find me? I thought an Ebrowen couldn't invade my dreams as long as I had the Dreamwen Stone."

He raised his eyebrows. "He didn't invade your dream. You went into his."

She didn't understand. "What about tomorrow? What about Evan? How will I keep him safe?"

"No one has taught you?" he said gently.

"Nothing—I only know Lord Morlen is an Ebrowen."

He nodded. "But you have the Dreamwen Stone." He looked as if a hundred questions stood on his lips. "May I use the Stone?" he asked.

He had guided her through the gray hallways, taken Evan from Lord Morlen's dream lair. She was glad to give him the Dreamwen Stone. The young man moved to kneel by Evan, who still lay on the silver grass. "Close your eyes," he said softly. Evan obeyed.

The young man laid the Stone on Evan's forehead. "By the light of Wen, let the Dreamwen Stone erase the trace set by the Ebrowen." For a moment, the Stone glowed, pouring golden light over Evan's face. Evan breathed evenly, eyes closed.

"Is he asleep?" she asked.

"You and I are asleep," he reminded her. "He sleeps more deeply. No Ebrowen can visit his dreams now unless one of them looks into his eyes again while he's awake." He handed her the Stone.

"But—where are we? Who are you? Can we stay here?"

"We can stay as long as we sleep."

"Then we'll wake up in Sliviia?" Maeve didn't want to leave this place, where peace was so thick it touched her like a kind hand, where the stars were so close, shedding generous silver over the meadow.

He leaned toward her, peering at her, his eyes very near. "Sliviia," he said, and then he was gone, the bright air closing over the space where he had been.

"Wait!" Maeve called. She had so many questions for him. Who was he? Where did he come from? She hadn't gotten his name. But there was no answer, only starlight shimmering around her.

Maeve turned to Evan. She put her hands over the cuts on his face. The skin on his cheeks felt cold like the halls they had left. She gazed at the near, shining stars, asking for their gift of fire. They surely had fire to spare? She only needed a little.

Her hands on Evan's cheeks grew warm as she guided the starfire into his face. She listened to the Dreamwen Stone and began humming its song to the boy.

Dorjan woke shivering. He jumped from his bed, running through the silent halls of the dormitory. At the door, Ellowen Renaiya's seal held him. He sent his gen against the seal, banishing it. When he pushed again, the door opened and he ran into the night. He stood beneath the moon, hands stretched to the stars. The stars! If only he could pull himself up with their light and travel to the girl he'd seen in his dreams.

Sliviia.

And she had the Dreamwen Stone. Cabis had told his son that he'd left the Stone behind in Sliviia, left it with someone he loved. The girl in the dream said she'd dug it up yesterday, that her mother had told her where it was. *Her mother. She buried it. When buried, its powers go dormant.*

Could this girl be my sister? Her eyes in the dream were like my father's. And like mine.

No, she can't be. She doesn't look much older than I. And if Cabis had fathered a child in Sliviia, he surely would have spoken of it.

But perhaps he didn't know.

Sister, Dorjan's mind insisted.

And to meet by chance in a dream, to both be in the halls of the Shadow King on the same night, for different reasons. . . .

Soft footsteps moved near Dorjan. Ellowen Renaiya. She put a small hand on his arm. "Dorjan? How did you get outside the seal?"

He sank to the ground, holding his head, wanting her to go away, wondering why she was here in the middle of the night. His anguish mounted as he remembered the dreaming girl who'd searched doggedly for a child, the force of her love leading her to brave the halls of the Shadow King's empire.

Shadow King. Dorjan couldn't forget how he himself had come to be in those hallways. "Ellowen, why is the Shadow King attacking the Healer's Keep?"

"Shadow King," she whispered, tremors passing over her shoulders. "What do you know of the Shadow King? What have you seen?"

Dorjan wondered whether to tell her. Ellowen Mayn had asked him to keep quiet about his background until his gift was named.

"Dorjan? Why do you say the Shadow King is attacking the Keep?"

"I went looking for the dark birds that visit the dreams of those who sleep here, and ended up in the halls of the Shadow King."

"Went looking." She stared at him as if he were a dragon or a krenen or some other mythical beast. "I was right about you," she said. "Genoven."

Dorjan pressed his hands to his eyes. Ellowen Renaiya grabbed his wrists, kneeling in front of him, making him look at her. "Dorjan, you're gifted in a way none of us is. You can walk in dreams, and dream in daylight. Heal sorrow and madness. No one here can do what you were born for, though we have the knowledge to train you."

"I don't understand. None of you is a Genoven?"

"Not for a hundred years, Dorjan. But our wisdom still holds the knowledge that will benefit your gift."

"Walking in dreams isn't something I need to be trained for. I do it now," he said wearily. "I want to learn how to heal the mind of another."

Sara woke dazed, a sickening dream hovering around the borders of her mind. What was it? She stretched, trying to remember. The dark bird again?

The daylight streaming in reminded her that she was happy, happier than she'd ever been. In a few minutes, she'd see Bern again. Today, the two of them planned to slip away together: he had something to show her. When she had asked him what it was, he'd smiled and kissed her, telling her it was a secret, a secret she'd enjoy.

Eagerly, she got up. When she moved into the early morning, she rejoiced in the beauty of the day. Clear skies, but not blazingly hot. And there was Bern in the garden, true to his word, waiting for her beside the fountain.

Someone bumped into her. Dorjan. His eyes were unfathomable as ever, nothing like Bern's frank expression. He stood in her way. "Sara. I need to tell you—"

"Another time, Dorjan."

"Please."

Sara glanced ahead at Bern. He waved. "Another time." Whatever Dorjan wanted to tell her could wait. She hurried to the fountain and Bern's welcoming grin.

Sara followed Bern along a wide path that led through the Keep's forest. He still refused to tell her what he wanted to show her, winking and shaking his head when she asked.

When they came to the first sacred ring of trees, he asked for her hand. "Since I'm not a student of healing, the rings won't let me through without you." Sara tugged his hand gently as she stepped past the ring. She felt only a small resistance as she drew him through.

As the path became steeper, the occasional bells of the Keep grew fainter and fainter, muted by the trees. Warm scents of leaves and earth perfumed the air; late flowers clustered in patches on the forest floor. They talked as they went deeper into the forest. Bern asked Sara all about herself; she told him everything, glad to put aside restraint. When she revealed that she was really Princess Saravelda, and that her mother had asked her to find what was wrong at the Keep, she felt a twinge. But why should she have secrets from Bern?

Sara felt as fresh when they passed the fifth sacred ring as she had when they set out. Each time they came to another of the rings, Bern would take her hand. The trees didn't seem to object. Every now and then a break in the thick foliage let them look down at the Keep. Its stately buildings were so far below now, they looked like toys Sara and her sister Dreeana had once played with.

"We're coming to the sixth ring," she said as they approached another band of great trees. "We can't go past it without being Lowens or Ellowens."

"So they've told you," Bern said. He stroked her hair. "But maybe they were only trying to see if you're obedient."

"You think it's nothing but a rule?"

"Try it," he urged, leaning in to kiss her close to her ear.

Sara put a hand on the bark of the tree nearest the path. It felt so . . . wise. She walked slowly into the gap between two trees. She felt a firm density in the air.

He gave her a fond smile. "Remember what that old foozle, Mayn, started to teach us on our first day—about how to control gen?"

Sara respected Mayn. She didn't quite like hearing him called a foozle. But she nodded—of course she remembered. She'd been practicing ever since.

"Put your gen through the seal," Bern said.

Is it wrong to try? Sara wondered. The Ellowens never said the students *must* not go beyond the sixth ring, only that they *could* not.

She closed her eyes, gathered her gen, and sent it forward. Encountering the seal, she felt as if she pushed against a piece of thick cloth. She sent more gen into the obstruction and imagined the cloth unraveling.

The seal gave way.

"I knew you could do it!" Bern said, hand on her shoulder. He stepped after her through the narrow gap. For a moment, Sara felt a terrible weariness cover her. But when he let go and stood beside her, the sudden fatigue went away.

"Won't you tell me, now, what we're doing here?" she asked.

"Almost there." He led on, moving so fast she fell behind.

There were fewer trees in this part of the forest. More rocks and wild ground cover, the path overgrown in many places. Sara felt somewhat awed, though she wasn't sure why. Was it the air? It certainly smelled wondrously pure.

Ahead, Bern stopped. "There it is," he said. "The seventh ring."

They had come to the final band of ancient trees—the last ring within all the rings. Sara craned her neck to see the tops of the branches.

"They say no one can go past the seventh ring before attaining Ellowenity," Bern said. He winked at her. The wink seemed out of place.

"You don't mean to say you believe I could go past this one, too?"

"Of course. Ellowen seals can't contain you. Here, take my hand. Love overcomes all, doesn't it?" He squeezed her palm. "We have the power of love, don't we?"

Sara felt very warm inside. "Yes."

"What could be the harm in trying?" he said. "If it's true that you can't go past this ring, all that will happen is nothing."

"I suppose you're right."

"Go on. Try." He let go of her hand and gave her a light push toward the space between two trees.

Sara advanced. When she put out a hand, she felt the powerful weave of a strong seal; it seemed stronger than the nightly seal on the Keep's dormitories.

"Try," Bern said.

Shutting her eyes again, she envisioned the silver sun in her belly. She waited until it pulsed with radiance. She imagined the radiance forming into a bright knife with a sharp edge that could cut through the seal.

A hand shoved against her shoulder. Sara stumbled forward, opening her eyes.

Through. I'm through the seventh ring.

She heard Bern crowing, "You did it!" She looked around her.

The leaves of nearby trees shimmered as if coated with a layer of fine pearl. A tingle rippled through her body and a hum throbbed in the air. A hum, but she wasn't sure it came through her ears. It seemed tuned to her heartstrings in a way that made her want to sing, wail, whisper, cry, and shout.

She turned to Bern, eager to see what he made of these remarkable surroundings. But something odd was happening to Bern. Though the corners of his lips turned up in a smile, he seemed to sneer. His eyes held no love.

"What is it?" he asked.

Sara peered at him. Had the Ellowens contrived a price for breaking through their last sacred ring? A spell to make Bern appear like an evil deceiver? "We mustn't let them turn us against each other," she said.

He sneered again. "We're close now, to what I wanted to show you." He turned on his heel.

Sara followed, vowing not to let the healers hoodwink her. She knew the real Bern. No one was going to take him away from her by making him look like something he wasn't.

There was no path here, and Bern didn't seem quite sure of the way. Finally, he waved her through a veil of branches. "There!"

The surrounding hum intensified as Sara entered a vast clearing. In the middle of the clearing was a giant cage, in the cage a bird the color of pearl. It flapped its wings at their approach; its wingspan was twice the length of a tall man. Its feathers reflected the sun into thousands of rainbow shimmers.

"That's what we came for," Bern said. "A Tezzarine."

Sara felt as if she should tiptoe. Slowly, she went forward and lay her face against the cage. As the bird looked back at her, she sank to her knees, sure that the Tezzarine saw through everything she had ever been or pretended to be. The Tezzarine's beak opened, pouring song. At the sound, Sara wept, unable to do anything else.

"Don't cry," she heard Bern say beside her. His words sounded stupid. What else was there to do but cry? Why did he interrupt? She needed to finish listening to the song.

But the singing ceased and Bern lifted her to her feet. "Don't you want to free it?"

She wanted to hit him, wanted to make him go away. He'd interrupted the song. She gritted her teeth. This was Bern, the one she loved most. She mustn't succumb to the spells that made her wish she'd never seen him. "Free it?"

"From its cage." Bern gripped one of the bars. "From being a prisoner. A Tezzarine should be free to fly." He spoke with admiration but looked as if he hated the Tezzarine. That was all wrong, of course—no one would hate such a majestic bird. "The Ellowens must have trapped it. We could break the bars and free it."

"Do you think so?"

"These bars aren't real," he said. "They're illusion. They could never hold *you*, my love." Was he flattering her? Sara's head hurt. She looked at the bird, now silent, wings closed, and looked at the cage, seamless, without a gate, reaching up almost as high as the branches of the last sacred ring. Bern must be right—the bars were made of enchantment.

"Free it, Sara."

Sara shut her eyes, sudden anger converging in her heart. How dare the healers capture such a creature and cage it? And how dare they try to destroy her love for Bern? Heat rose in her blood and mounted until it seemed all her veins beat with fire.

"Now," Bern said, and Sara flung the force of her gen at the cage with all the power she could summon.

She heard a rending sound, as if the air had torn. Her eyes opened. She was standing next to Bern in an empty clearing. The cage had disappeared, and the bird with it.

As Renaiya searched the Keep for Sara and Bern, she wished that the ancient Ellowens had not decreed against combining the School of Sight with the Healer's Keep. It was thought that mixing the training of seers and healers could create an overwhelming temptation to turn to the ways of the Ebromal. If one could see the future and heal the sick, it would be too easy to become too powerful. *But I could use a vision now, to tell me where those novices have gone.* Renaiya put the thought out of her mind. Even if she were free to consult a seer, no seer could have a vision within the Keep anyway.

After her midnight meeting with Dorjan, Renaiya had more confidence that she was right about the three novices. Only one who was Genoven-gifted could have seen and done what Dorjan had told her about. But she still had to name the novices to the Council. *How will I get Hester to bend enough to listen to me about her nephew? And Desak has served on the Council for so long, it doesn't occur to him he might be wrong.* Treacherous thought! Dear Desak had helped guide the Keep through the years of King Landen's exile, when they had all lived under the Double Invisibility. *But I fear we are heading for a battle the like of which Desak has never imagined, let alone fought.*

She wanted to hike up the forested hillsides and refresh herself with a sight of the last Tezzarine. But going beyond the seventh ring would take hours and the morning was already half gone.

She found Dorjan sitting alone on a bench near the herb garden. She stopped to ask him if he'd seen Sara or Bern.

"Yes. I saw them both. Early."

"Do you know where they went?"

"They headed into the rings." He pointed toward the forest.

Renaiya took a calming breath. *A Firan with a Charmal? What if Bern recognizes Sara's powers? What will happen to us all if her gift is corrupted before it is trained?* "They haven't come back?"

"No."

Renaiya gazed at the forest. "They'll have to turn back at the sixth ring."

"Respectfully, Ellowen Renaiya—I'm not trained to break your seals, yet you found me outside during the night."

Her breath strangled in her throat. She put out a hand, and Dorjan's steady arm braced her. "I must find them." *Dorjan is the only one in the Keep immune to the Charmal.* She hesitated. "Will you go with me?"

He nodded.

"Thank you, Dorjan. As we go, I'll give you one of the lessons a Genoven learns."

Chapter 9

In the suite given over to Lord Morlen, men surrounded Orlo, men whose temples were marked by scars of squares within squares. Lord Morlen stood in front of him.

"It appears, Orlo, that you retain some muddled sense of loyalty to this Maeve who served with you. No one values proper loyalty more than I, but yours is misplaced. A slave's duty is to his master, and I am your master until the girl is found."

All my years of service, and Lord Indol throws me to this monster as if I were yesterday's stew bone. What does Morlen want me for? He said he would visit her dreams and find out where she is.

"Where would she hide?"

"I don't know, Lord Morlen." Orlo racked his brain for something to say that would satisfy Morlen without giving anything away. "She wouldn't know the streets."

"She knew enough to dress well. She knew what to say to get the boy."

"Her mother must have taught her."

"Did you know she planned to run? A gown is not the work of a night."

"No, sir." Orlo was glad it was the truth. Maeve must have believed it would be easier for him if he didn't know. Otherwise, she'd surely have told him good-bye.

"Did this girl have friends among the privileged?"

"None that I know of, sir." Orlo wanted to add that friendship between slaves and the privileged was unheard of and impossible, but he kept his peace.

"Would she know to head north for Mantedi?"

"I wouldn't know, sir."

Morlen drew his patrier and tapped its handle against Orlo's chin. "You wouldn't know."

Orlo's pores ran with sweat. He wished he could go back two days. If he could, he'd have assigned a different slave to massage this man. Why had he chosen Maeve? Because she was quiet and skillful and there were no complaints about her. Because Orlo had got where he was by knowing how to please Lord Indol's guests. *Because I was a fool, thinking of my master's honor instead of Maeve.* "No, sir."

Morlen sheathed his patrier. He picked up a small flask of orange liquid and opened the stopper. A strange odor, unpleasantly sweet, wafted from the flask. "Do you know what this is?"

"No, sir."

"This is vahss."

"V-vahss, sir?"

"Vahss is the distillation of a rare desert flower, mixed carefully with other substances you know nothing of." Morlen shook the flask slowly. "Perhaps rumors have reached you, Orlo, about terrible powers I possess?"

Orlo didn't want to speak. He wished his heart would not pound so hard, and wondered if it would simply explode then and there, saving Lord Morlen the trouble of killing him.

"Have you heard rumors about me, Orlo?" Morlen repeated.

"Yes, sir. But I didn't pass them on."

"Didn't you? And why not?"

"I didn't want to frighten the bathhouse slaves."

"Very wise. But tell me, what was it you heard that you didn't pass along?"

Orlo longed for a towel to wipe the sweat from his face and neck. "That you can take over the mind of another."

Morlen nodded, smiling coldly. "Not only can I take over the mind of another; I can drive the reason out of another's brain. But you see, Orlo, sometimes I tire of the effort required for me to do so, particularly when the mind I must overcome bores and wearies me. There are far too many fools in the world, and fools bore me to no end. That is why I created this marvelous drink—it does my work for me." He held up the flask. "And you, Orlo, will get a taste of vahss today."

Orlo shook his head. A slight frown appeared between Morlen's brows. "I'm your master now," he said. "And I have chosen vahss for you."

The surrounding men took a step closer to Orlo. If he resisted, what good would it do? He imagined them beating him to the floor, prying open his jaws. No matter what he did, he would be made to drink the vahss.

Orlo opened his mouth. "Excellent," Morlen said. "Perhaps you're not as much of a fool as you appear."

Thick, smooth liquid slid down Orlo's throat. It was as if a beautiful snake had crawled into his chest. His heart slowed, beating calm and even.

"Better now?" Morlen asked. "Good. Tell me everything you know about this Maeve."

Maeve. Orlo saw her in his mind's eye, mixing perfumes and tending to the bathhouse patrons. He knew he felt something special for her but couldn't think what it was. Lord Morlen, who had provided him with vahss, wanted to know about her. That was all right. Orlo would tell him all he could.

Jasper knew it looked odd to be driving an empty buggy through the streets of Slivona without showing a flag to invite fares. Looking odd was a hindrance, but given what he wanted to do, fares would hinder him more. He couldn't put the girl in the blue dress out of his mind. He'd decided to look for her, warn her if he could.

Early as it was, the streets crawled with stripers. They roved singly and in bands, looking everyone over. Several times Jasper was stopped and questioned. He gave the zind his dim look and asked stumbling questions, pretending to be unable to hold more than one thought in his mind. Delivering this buggy to Mister Terrill in the next town west, he told them.

The stripers scoffed at him, making ill-natured jests, but they always sent him on his way. Jasper took side streets and dirty alleys, moving west toward the outskirts of the city to the ungated country tracks leading away from Slivona. It took effort to remind himself to move slowly. He muttered thanks to the emperor that Slivona was not a walled city.

Sun warmed his back as he drove. He found the track he wanted, guarded by a solitary zind. He waited for the soldier to stop him.

"Step out." Jasper did so, and watched the black-and-gray gloves search every cranny of the buggy. "Where you headed?" the striper asked.

"Delivering this buggy to Mister Terrill, lives west."

"How you getting back to the city?"

Jasper scratched his head. "Market cart."

"Let me see your scroll."

Jasper's freedom scroll was getting a bit worn with all the handling. The striper glanced at it with a practiced eye. "If you chance upon a girl wearing a blue dress, or a boy with new marks on his face, turn around and report to me."

Jasper sweated furiously as he climbed back on the box. Once out of the striper's sight, he clicked his tongue to the mare; his wheels turned up dust on the lonely wooded track. His sense of direction said he wasn't far from Lord Hering's property on its northern edge, the other side from where he'd left the girl and boy. As soon as the trees gave an opening, he'd look for the runaways in the woods. It couldn't be more than a matter of hours before Lord Morlen's zind fanned out from the city to search the country.

As Jasper sought an opening in the dense trees, the only sounds were his horse's hooves, the buggy wheels turning, and birds warbling in nearby branches. He drove slowly, around several bends in the track. As he rounded another bend, he suddenly saw the girl. Today she looked like a slave, dressed only in a bare shift, but he knew her by the rich color of her hair. She carried a bundle, and telltale blue peeped out of it. The boy walked at her side.

Jasper stopped, swinging down to the dirt as fast as he'd ever moved in his life. When the girl saw his face, she darted into the undergrowth, pulling the boy along.

"Wait!" Jasper called, running after them. "Wait!" He sped over boulders and through late-summer brush, calling ahead to the girl. "I can help you!" Her bare feet flashed in front of him, running on. "Lord Morlen's hunting you!" he yelled, gaining on her.

She stopped. She spun around. "How do you know?"

"Reward," he said, stopping in front of her. "But I'm not after that."

Sweat stood on her forehead. "If not the reward, what are you after?"

How could he get her to believe him? "To warn you."

"Why would you warn me?" She seemed to be having trouble catching her breath, and her accent had changed. Yesterday she'd talked like the highborn.

"Because you're running. If Lord Morlen owned me, I'd run too."

She grabbed his hand, closing her eyes. Her hands felt soft and strong. "All right." Her eyes opened; she dropped his hand. "I believe you." Again he was struck by how pretty her voice was.

"Whoever you are, there's not a person in the city of Slivona doesn't know you've run, and the color of that dress." He pointed to the blue edge poking out of her bundle. "And how the boy is marked."

"Evan! Come out, Evan. It's all right."

The boy sidled out from behind sheltering trees. Same boy—brown eyes and hair, sturdy bones. Same boy, but no bandages. No bandages and no marks, either.

"They said he was marked."

"He's healed now."

Jasper blinked. "How? Never mind. You have to get away from here. You can't go back to Slivona, and it won't be long before Slivona comes looking for you."

She looked at her feet. "Have you met Lord Morlen?"

"Met him? No. The free know enough to stay out of his way."

He saw relief in her face. "Thank you. For coming to warn us."

"You've got to get away! And leave the dress."

She clutched the bundle. "I can't. My mother made it."

"Doesn't matter. They've seen it."

"She made it so I could get away. It's all I have of her." Tears rose to her eyes.

"She can make you another."

More tears, as she shook her head. "She was dying."

Jasper cast about his mind for something to get her to see. "If she made you that dress so you could escape, you'll break her heart in heaven if you're caught because of it. Leave it, and if you have more gold, leave that too."

She wiped her eyes. Her head came up. "Leave the gold? I can't! It's to buy us food and passage across the ocean."

"It'll buy you back to Lord Morlen. I tell you, he wants to find you. The whole city's on notice for delans like what you gave me."

"It's my price. My freedom."

Jasper sighed. The girl was like a mule, but he had long experience with mules. "It's either your delans *or* your freedom. Do you think Lord Morlen will wait while you gain some wits?"

The girl took the dress out of her scarf. She held it to her cheek, mopped tears with it, kissed it like it was a person she loved. Jasper wished she'd hurry. What if someone came by and found his empty rig?

"I'll leave the dress," she said finally. "You're right. My mother wouldn't want me caught."

"And the delans."

"Most of them. But we need to keep some. We're starving. We have nothing."

"I have bread." Jasper lifted a boulder. He set it aside and began to dig the earth with his hands. The boy, Evan, joined in the digging. The girl folded the dress before putting it in the hole they'd made. She scooped handfuls of big gold coins, throwing them on top of the dress. There must have been near fifty delans. Her price, she'd called it. If Lord Morlen had paid all that for her, there was something about her Jasper couldn't see. She was pretty, but beauty could be bought for much less. He'd known lovely girls to be sold into slavery for a mere handful of besaets. Had Lord Morlen taken a great fancy to this one? No wonder she ran.

She wouldn't give up all the delans—no use arguing with a face set like hers. "How many will you keep?" he asked.

She pitched a leather bag onto the heap of gold shining on the blue dress. She showed him her ragged scarf, nearly empty. Two coins in the bottom. "You said each one would hire and feed you for a year."

"And I didn't lie. We could put them in my shoes. Less likely to be found there." She gave him a long look. He realized he'd only meant to warn her, hadn't meant to do any more than that, but he'd just said "we" as if he meant to stay with her for a while.

She handed him the two delans. He shook out his shoes, wrapping the coins in bits of cloth. The gold felt hard against his toes.

He replaced the boulder, covering the blue dress and stolen wealth. In a few days, the silk would be eaten away by bugs. Jasper was sorry, but there was nothing else to be done, so he tamped the ground, trying to make the place look undisturbed.

"Let's go."

They went back to the track. Still deserted, except for his buggy. Lucky so far. But Jasper never counted much on luck.

He reached into the buggy and brought out a loaf, offering it to the runaways. He knew what hunger was, felt glad he'd brought extra as he watched them tear handfuls of bread, eating until it was gone.

Jasper continued down the wooded track, driving west, away from Slivona. Sometimes the best place to hide was right under the noses of those seeking, but not this time. Stripers were too thorough. It was a piece of luck the boy turned out not to be marked, when the zind were describing him as freshly cut, but as for the girl . . .

Maeve. She'd told him her name, told him about her break for freedom. Jasper admired her spirit. And her pretty face—but her face didn't keep him from understanding that danger surrounded her.

He worried about how quickly she'd told him about herself. What if he'd been a different sort of man? Getting the reward for her would have been easier than scraping a stray besaet off the streets of Slivona. She was too trusting. But she'd run from him at first. What did it mean when she held his hands, then told him she believed him? Had his hands told her something?

She didn't have anything to wear but the slave shift, and he couldn't pass her off as his property—the lowborn free didn't keep slaves. If he'd had a dress for her, she might have pretended to be his wife, except that she didn't have a wife mark, the small triangle at the base of the neck, the only mark the free would consent to.

Jasper didn't believe in magic, or he'd think Maeve had enchanted him. Maybe it was her voice; he'd never heard a voice like hers. Beautiful or not, one instant of bad luck and they'd all be enslaved or dead. Bad odds. Bad odds in a game he didn't know.

Maeve crept through rough underbrush. Jasper had said he needed to get through the checkpoint alone—there was sure to be a sentry, most likely a zind. She and Evan must slip past while Jasper distracted the soldier.

The ground underfoot was full of stones and fallen twigs; the air smelled of dirt and leaves. How different from the heated granite floors and scented towels of the bathhouse. Maeve marveled at how much dirt clung to her, smudging her skin and covering the sad rag her shift had become.

Ahead, the trees thinned. Fields lay to the left, where laborers in broad straw hats shunted beans into baskets. Maeve wanted to steal some beans. They'd been so hungry last night.

But Jasper had given them bread. He'd told them the same thing Lila had said: they must get to Mantedi Bay. There, they might find passage on a ship to Glavenrell and the other free kingdoms across the Minwenda Ocean. Jasper knew the way to Mantedi, but he never said he'd go with them.

Holding Evan's hand, Maeve wondered if he remembered the night and the gray hallways and the Meadows of

Wen, where she'd warmed his cold wounds. When he woke, his pain had gone along with the marks. He didn't speak of bad dreams and she didn't want to remind him. She remembered most of the dream herself, though she didn't understand it. Where were those hallways? Who was the strange young man who somehow seemed familiar? How was it possible for Evan's marks to be taken away?

There wasn't time to think about that now. She heard the slow clop-clop of Jasper's horse approaching and saw the sentry through a screen of leaves. Maeve was used to seeing men wearing silk robes or loincloths. No weapons except patriers were allowed in the bathhouse, a place of relaxation for guests. This soldier wore black and gray leather. A black axe hung from one side of his belt; a long knife was sheathed on the other.

Jasper wasn't as tall as the soldier and had no weapons. What if something went wrong? She should have taken back the gold. If the hulking man found it, what would happen to Jasper?

Maeve hunched next to the last clump of trees before a clearing that stretched between where they were and where they needed to go. As the zind called to Jasper to stop, Maeve wanted to stay where she was, watching over Jasper, as if keeping him in sight could keep him from harm. But he'd impressed on her: "As soon as I stop, move ahead and get as far past the checkpoint as you can."

She tucked up her shift and crept forward on hands and knees, out into the open, motioning Evan to follow. The soldier would only need to look aside to be able to see them. Fifty yards beyond, the woodland grew dense again. Maeve aimed herself there.

She heard shouts. Keeping her eyes on the ground, she crawled on. Small sounds behind her told her Evan followed. More shouts pelted her ears. She tried pretending she was in the bathhouse, early in the day, with Orlo yelling commands. But sun-warmed dirt was nothing like steam and perfumed oils. She could never go back there, anyway. If she wanted to live free, she had to make it to the trees.

As she scrambled forward, tearing skin off her knees, her hands gave out and her face ground into the dirt. Behind her, Evan gasped. The Dreamwen Stone around her neck pressed into her chest. Its hum sang into her heart, impelling her on.

At last! Trees surrounded them. Maeve peered through leaves to the road where Jasper stood beside his buggy, head hanging. The striped soldier yelled and waved his fist; Jasper barely moved. The soldier shoved him to the ground, then laughed while he got slowly to his feet and climbed onto the box.

Once Jasper came to a crossroads out of sight of the sentry, he pulled over on the edge of the dirt road to wait for Maeve and Evan. His shoulders were sore where he'd fallen, but he didn't mind bruises—they healed fast. Jasper knew some moves; he could have taken that striper, except it wouldn't have gained him anything. He never carried a knife—too risky. The lowborn free weren't allowed weapons; Jasper counted freedom ahead of a knife. Pretending to be slow was usually all he needed for protection—and quick fists for the times when acting slow didn't work.

Maeve and Evan scurried up. Maeve's pretty face was streaked with dirt and her shift even more of a rag than it had been before. Evan was just as grimy.

"Why did that soldier yell at you? Why did he knock you down?" she asked.

"Not moving fast enough for him."

"Why did you move so slow?" Evan said innocently.

Jasper put a hand on the boy's shoulder. "Because a witless man wouldn't be smart enough to help out a pair of runaways."

"Thank you," Maeve said. "Thank you."

"Get in," Jasper said. "We'll keep going, find some back country, decide what to do."

A shred of Maeve's shift caught in the carriage's door as she climbed in. "Maeve, do you know how to sew?" Jasper asked.

"I can sew a bit. My mother taught me. She gave me needles—they're in my scarf."

Jasper climbed onto the box, thinking about where he might find cloth. He still had besaets in his wallet.

After finding a place to camp well off the road, Jasper went on foot by himself to get cloth and thread in the closest village. Two rolls of cloth, one undyed muslin, one pale yellow. The most common colors in the land. With the right clothes, they'd have a chance. They might make it to Mantedi after all. He could stay with Maeve and Evan until they found passage to Glavenrell—then he could set up as a carriage driver inside the walled city. Everyone knew there were riches to be had in Mantedi—wasn't it the biggest port in the world? Didn't many wealthy lords live there?

With the cloth, Jasper went on through the village, then doubled back through the woods. Clouds moved across the moon, making the way so dark that he saw only shadows. He knew Maeve and Evan had to be close by. When he'd left them in the afternoon, Maeve was getting ready to dunk in the stream they'd camped near. She wasn't used to being dirty.

The whispers and rustles of night unnerved him; he didn't know why. He'd been out at night hundreds of times before, but tonight even his own feet snapping twigs made him jump. He thought of calling out. *Don't be foolish.* Then he saw a glow of what seemed to be golden light. Mighty odd. The only time he'd ever seen light colored that way, it was near sunset, not after.

"Jasper?" Maeve's voice. How good it sounded—like music. There she was beside him. It looked as if the gold light came from the round rock she wore about her neck.

Jasper touched her arm, just a quick touch. "How do you make a rock light up that way?" He pointed to her chest.

"What?"

Jasper squinted. No light shone from the stone now. It looked ordinary again, just a plain rock tied to a rag. But Jasper knew what he'd seen. "What sort of rock is that? Where did you get it?"

"It's nothing. A memento of my mother." The moon burst from behind the clouds, shedding pale light over their camp.

"That's more than a memento. That rock took the shadows away."

She didn't say anything, and Jasper didn't know what to think. Strange goings-on. The past few days had stirred up his life so that now he was doing things he knew better than to do, and seeing things he'd never thought to see. He'd risked his freedom for a boy and girl he'd met only two nights ago. Now here he was, getting spooked by simple shadows and watching light come out of a plain stone.

"Do you wish you'd never seen us, Jasper?" Maeve stood there like something from a dream, blanket around her shoulders, rock around her neck. Did she know his mind?

Jasper blew out the air he'd been holding. "You going to tell me about that stone?" he said, not answering her.

"Give me your hand," she said.

He did so, liking her smooth, cool skin. She closed her eyes the way she had before when he had first chased after her. She took longer this time to let go of his hand. "It's called the Dreamwen Stone," she said. "It belonged to my father and his mother—back through time."

Good. She was telling him the truth—Jasper always knew a lie. "Dreamwen? I've heard that the Dreamwens stay low, don't let people know who they are."

"This is a secret."

"I can keep your secret."

"It's not only mine. People have been killed to keep this one."

"It's my secret now, too." Jasper meant it. He handed her the bundle, and Maeve unfolded the cloth. She held some up to Evan, nodding. "How long will it take to make clothes?" Jasper pulled spools of thread from his pockets.

"If we all work, a few days."

"I can't sew."

"I'll teach you."

Jasper grinned at the determined slant of her jaw. When he brought out bread and cheese and some corn, Maeve put down the cloth. She might be small, but she had a good appetite.

118

Chapter 10

Sara walked away from the Tezzarine clearing with Bern at her side. The great bird had vanished so quickly that there was no time for one last glimpse of its pearly wings. She who had freed it didn't even have the chance to watch it fly away.

Bern laughed exultantly. "What powers you have, Sara!"

She wouldn't look at him. She ran for the border of the seventh sacred ring, not answering him. She heard him behind her, crashing through the undergrowth, full of careless noise. Her head throbbed and her heart burned. She felt she'd missed something of great importance that she might never come across again. She wanted to outrun Bern, but he kept up with her however fast she went.

When she reached the seventh ring, he grabbed onto her shoulder as she pushed through the seal.

On the other side she caught her breath, daring to look at him again. She felt faint with relief to see the real Bern, the Bern she loved, reaching for her, his eyes alight. She went into his arms. "When we passed the last sacred ring, there must have been a spell. You looked like a sneering, evil person."

"The Ellowens," he said solemnly. "They don't want us to have each other. They know it makes us too powerful. But they can't stand between us, and now with the last Tezzarine gone, they'll be much weaker."

"The last?" Doubt began in Sara's chest. What had she done?

He stopped her doubts with a kiss. She melted into him, forgetting everything but the bliss of loving Bern.

Ellowen Renaiya moved fast for a small woman, Dorjan thought, as he strode next to her through the Keep's forest. The wide path she followed meandered among trees, rocks, and flowers, climbing steadily, moving through the sacred rings. Dorjan listened closely to every word she said as they went upward, about Charmals and about Bern.

"So, a Charmal is gifted but has no conscience?" he asked.

"Yes. Charismatic, but without goodness. Charmals easily gain control over others. They wheedle their way into our confidence; the more secrets we give them, the more power they have over us."

"If Bern is a Charmal, why don't I find him charming? Does his charm work only on women?"

"Oh, no. The charm is felt by everyone. I was taught that the only people able to resist a Charmal's designs are those who have been snared by one and then escaped." She gave him a sideways glance.

Dorjan hoped she wouldn't say anything more in that vein. "Since you know what he is, are you safe from Bern?"

"No. I must exert great vigilance or be trapped myself. But you—though you're young, you must have met with a Charmal before, and somehow seen through him."

"Can a Charmal be female?"

Renaiya nodded.

I did see through her, but what a long time it took. "Is the Charmal's mind diseased?" Dorjan asked, hoping Ellowen Renaiya wouldn't see how desperately he wanted her to answer yes. "Would it be possible to heal one of them?"

"The Keep wisdom says no," she answered gently. "It's been tried. I was taught that any gen expended on a Charmal's behalf would only strengthen the Charmal's capacity for destruction. Charmals are very dangerous, deceptively so."

Dorjan tried to mask his disappointment, blinking rapidly. "Will Bern be dismissed from the Keep?"

"Yes, once I've convinced the Council of what he is. Only Mystives and Genovens are trained to spot a Charmal. I ought to have told the other healers at once, but I doubted myself. As soon as we find Sara and Bern, I won't delay."

"But what will you tell them? What *makes* a Charmal?"

"Charmals have a backward gift—it's close to that of a Mystive. Whatever we want most, Bern can sense. The gift is used to exploit and entrap others rather than to heal."

Dorjan felt sick. He wished he'd insisted on talking to Sara that morning. "What if he 'exploits and entraps' Sara?"

"That's what I fear. If Bern corrupts Sara's gift . . ." Renaiya slowed her pace slightly. "The only thing that can help her is the truth. The truth is better and, for one with her gift, the *only* thing to live by."

"Her gift? What's her gift?"

"Firan. Spirit Warrior."

"Firan. What does it mean to be a Spirit Warrior?"

"A Firan can fight with spirit weapons. It's a mighty gift, Dorjan, one that will take all the Ellowens in the Keep to train well."

A sudden change in the light made Dorjan glance up. He didn't see any clouds, yet the sky had dimmed, as if the sun were a lantern that had sputtered and not regained its full radiance. Impossible. Yet the colors of the flowers at his feet were fainter somehow, and branches above him drooped, their leaves pallid.

"No," Ellowen Renaiya whispered. "It can't be."

"What is it, Ellowen?"

"No," she said again. "Impossible that the last Tezzarine could leave."

"Tezzarine?"

"The great birds of the Keep. For centuries they lived wild in the high places here, communing with the healers, linking us with Ellowenity." She looked absolutely forlorn, wilting like a plucked flower. "They began disappearing a few months ago. Finally there was only one left. The Ellowens worked together to form a protection around it to keep it here." She lifted a thin arm. "The light! See how it falls, like an echo of what it should be. I'm afraid the last Tezzarine has left."

Not waiting for him to reply, she redoubled her pace. They walked in silence for a time. As they rounded a bend in the trail, they saw Sara and Bern coming toward them. Sara was gazing devotedly at Bern.

"Hello, Ellowen. Dorjan." Bern spoke pleasantly, as if it were a normal day. Sara seemed startled.

"Where did you go?" Ellowen Renaiya sounded flustered.

"We've taken a journey, Ellowen," Bern answered. "Exploring the Keep. Sara wanted to see if your rings were truly strong."

Sara took a step back.

"But you—you couldn't go past the sixth ring?" Ellowen Renaiya asked.

"I'm afraid so, Ellowen. The sixth, and the seventh," Bern answered, eyes gleaming.

Ellowen Renaiya gulped air, staring at Sara. "Did you see the Tezzarine—the bird?"

"Yes," Bern said. "But it's gone now."

"No," Ellowen Renaiya cried. "Please, no."

"Why was it caged?" Sara asked, her voice quavering.

"For protection."

Bern stepped forward, grasping Renaiya's hands, looking into her crumpling face. "You knew she was trouble, didn't you, Ellowen?" he said softly. "The granddaughter of Kareed the Invader. She has the same seed of conquest he carried. She should never have been trusted within the Healer's Keep."

Bewildered, Dorjan looked from Ellowen Renaiya to Bern to Sara. What was Bern talking of? *King Kareed's granddaughter?*

Even in far-off Emmendae, Dorjan had heard the famous tales of Kareed, warrior king of Archeld. But Kareed had only one child, a daughter named Torina. That daughter had married Landen, the Bellandran prince who had once been driven from his kingdom by Kareed's conquest. It was a romantic story, beloved by the bards.

And Landen once saved the life of a Sliviian conscript named Cabis, by pulling him from the ocean during the battle for Glavenrell.

Sara—the daughter of Landen? Was it true? How did Bern know?

"I would have stopped her, Ellowen," Bern was saying. "But I didn't know how."

It looked as though something had blotted away the healthy color in Sara's face. Even her lips were pale. Dorjan mastered his confusion, tried to send her some of his gen. *It will be all right, Sara. It will be all right.*

"How tired you must be, Ellowen Renaiya," Bern said. "May I offer you my arm down the trail? Please."

Ellowen Renaiya looked tiny, even shrunken, as she put her small hand on Bern's elbow. Dorjan wanted to say something to shake her out of the Charmal's web. No words occurred to him.

In another minute, Bern and Ellowen Renaiya were out of sight. Dorjan had the urge to run after them, throw himself on Bern, wrestle him to the ground, beat the false sincerity from his eyes. But he stayed with Sara. He couldn't leave her now; her face was too stark. Afraid she might fall, he put a hand on her shoulder. At his touch, she sank to the ground, covering her face. Dorjan sat beside her, wondering what he might say.

The woods were oddly silent and the light still dim. Finally she lifted her head. "How could I have told him all my secrets? I told him everything—all about me. He *knows*."

"Sara. Bern has a . . . backward gift. It makes everyone near him act witless." He winced, for that wasn't the way he meant to say it.

A tinge of color came into her face. "What backward gift?"

"Ellowen Renaiya told me only this morning. Bern is what they call a Charmal—his gift isn't a healing gift, doesn't belong to the Keep. It lets him charm others and get them to do what he wants."

She chewed her lip. "I'm so ashamed."

"Don't be."

"You don't understand what I've done."

"I understand you seem to have escaped a Charmal after a few days. It took me years."

"Years? You?" She stopped sniffling.

"Years." Dorjan didn't want to give Sara his secret, but Ellowen Renaiya had said truth was the only thing that would help her. "What will you do when Bern comes to you and says he never meant any harm?"

"I won't believe him." Her hands clenched into fists.

"Is what he said true? Are you a princess?"

She nodded fiercely. "Princess Saravelda. I didn't want anyone to know. I *told* him it was a secret."

How odd life is, shuffling kings and conscripts, princesses and commoners, to land next to one another. "Ellowen Renaiya said Charmals want secrets. The more secrets they know, the more power it gives them."

"Ugh." Sara looked as if she'd like to spit.

"She found your gift, and mine. She told me you're a Firan."

Sara frowned. "Firan? A warrior? But I wanted to learn to dance like the Trians." She seemed crestfallen, shaking her head and muttering, "Firan."

"She said it would take all the Ellowens to train you."

"They won't train me now. Don't ask me what I've done."

Dorjan got up and offered her a hand. "We'd best go back."

The light was still lackluster as they started down together. "What's your gift, Dorjan?" she asked.

He hesitated. "Genoven."

"Is that what you hoped?"

"I didn't believe it would be any of the others. Walking in dreams is something I've done since I was small. My father's from a Dreamwen family."

"Dreamwen?"

"It's a Sliviian word. I think it might mean the same thing as Genoven."

"Sliviia! The pirate country? But I thought you were from Emmendae."

"My father sailed here eighteen years ago as a conscript with the great Sliviian invasion."

"A conscript. What happened to him?"

"Rescued from the ocean." Dorjan took a big breath. "By your father, King Landen." A chill raised hair on his arms. If it hadn't been for this girl's father, his own father would have died, and he himself wouldn't exist. And now, against custom and chance, he and she were both in the Healer's Keep.

"Wait." Sara paused on the trail. "I might know this story. My father told me about the night of the pirate invasion. And how they took a man from the sea . . ."

"My father," Dorjan said. "Cabis Denon."

"Cabis." She sounded guarded. She started walking again, avoiding a root that crawled across the path. "Yes. He served with my father for a while. Then he left."

"Yes. He was lured away." Dorjan brushed aside a branch. "By a Charmal." He didn't want to tell her anything more.

"What Charmal?" When he didn't answer, she asked again. "Who, Dorjan?"

He stared at the way the light struck the dirt dully. His throat hurt. *I can't be sure she's a Charmal. She fits the description: gifted, but without conscience. But she isn't evil, not like Bern.*

"What Charmal, Dorjan?"

He looked at Sara. "My mother," he said.

"Oh." She put a hand on his shoulder and changed the subject again. "So you think a Dreamwen and a Genoven are the same? What *is* a Dreamwen?"

"Dreamwens can be awake in dreams and visit other . . . places while they sleep."

She grabbed his arm, almost causing him to stumble. "That's how you were in my room at night?"

He shook his head. "I don't know."

As they continued down the path through the sacred rings, he told her what Ellowen Renaiya had said about Charmals, and about Tezzarines. Her eyes grew puffy when he mentioned Tezzarines.

When they got near the border of the trees, Bern was waiting for them. He opened his arms to Sara, pulling her to him. Dorjan was suddenly sure that Sara would forgive Bern his betrayal. He remembered the way she'd looked at him that morning.

But Sara was stiff in Bern's arms. He drew back from her. "What is it?"

"You touched me. Don't do it again." She spoke with command. *Like a princess.*

"Sweetheart, you didn't take amiss what I said to Ellowen Renaiya? The Ellowens don't want us to be together. I had to distract her. Don't be sad—Renaiya won't disturb us tonight." He moved closer to her again, ardor in his eyes.

"Don't come near me," she said, pushing him away.

"You have to believe me!"

"I don't." She turned her back.

"You don't know what I can do," Bern said. "I can get them to dismiss you from the Keep."

Dorjan smiled grimly to himself. *A mistake.* If Bern had continued to feign wounded love, Sara might have relented.

She spun around, advancing on Bern. Every line of her shrieked menace as she stood in front of him, raking him with her fierceness. "You're nothing, Bern, nothing but the sneering shadow I saw today. From now on I'll see you that way whether I'm past the seventh ring or not." She walked away.

Bern stared after her, then turned on Dorjan. "You." His eyes roared with hate. When Dorjan didn't answer, he stalked off.

At the edge of the lovely gardens, Dorjan stood irresolute. Should he go to the Council? Tell them what he'd seen? Repeat Ellowen Renaiya's warnings?

The Charmal was headed toward the Meeting Hall. He'd get there first. The bells for supper sounded, and soon Ellowens and students moved on the pathways. They walked with their customary uniform step, but the sunlight fell dimly across their faces. They looked washed out, as if they inhabited a painting, and the painter had mixed too much water with his colors.

Dorjan shivered. Why did everyone seem to be following the ordinary routine, as if nothing had changed? Ellowens were supposed to embody heightened perception. Just what was the connection Ellowen Renaiya had touched upon, between Ellowens and Tezzarines?

The last Tezzarine has left the Keep, and it seems that not only has the light been dulled, but also the awareness of the Keep's members. Dorjan wondered how much of his own perception was affected. And Sara—what had she done?

Chapter 11

"What is it, Dorjan?" The white-haired woman in the flowing blue dress looked both concerned and happy. "As always, it's wonderful to see you. You seem agitated, my dear. Why have you called me into your dream?"

"I need to ask you, Grandma. Do I have a sister in Sliviia? Did my father have a daughter?"

Marina's wise eyes, deep blue like his own, like his father's, like the girl he'd guided to the Meadows of Wen, widened in surprise. "A sister? If you do, Cabis doesn't know of her existence. Tell me why you ask such a question."

Dorjan told her.

"The Dreamwen Stone? Missing all these years, buried in the ground?"

"Yes, Grandma. I *believe* she's my sister. My heart recognized her."

"Your heart has the gift of truth, Dorjan."

"I must find her again."

"Did you ask her permission to visit her dreams?"

"No. There wasn't time before I woke."

"Then you must wait," Marina said sternly.

"I can't wait! It could be years before we meet by chance

again. And she lives across the Minwenda Ocean, in Sliviia. I can't meet her face-to-face to ask her permission."

"You know that Dreamwen law says invading the dreams of another without permission is the way of the Ebrowen."

"But I don't mean her any harm. And she's your grandchild, too. Help me find her."

"Dorjan." Marina brushed his cheek with her hand. "I long to see her. But nothing can make me break the Dreamwen law."

"Isn't there anything to be done?"

"Have you sent out the message that she may come to you?"

"I've tried, but she's untrained. She doesn't seem to receive it."

"Keep trying, my dear. It's the only thing you can ethically do."

Maeve lay quiet, next to a sleeping Evan. Jasper slept on the other side of the boy. Each night, they moved cushions out of the buggy to give their heads something soft, and spread Jasper's blankets underneath. The ground wasn't any harder than Maeve's old pallet in Lord Indol's garret, but here the air smelled sweet and free. Maeve wished her mother could have come with her.

If she's dead now, she's free too. We're both free, except I'm alive and free on earth. I hope she can see that I have the Dreamwen Stone. Maeve's hands were crossed over it. She felt its hum close to her skin.

She looked from Evan to Jasper, thinking about the resemblance between them. Both had brown hair, brown eyes, sturdy bodies. It seemed to Maeve that their bodies matched their souls, for both behaved as sturdily as they looked.

Odd to think that a short time ago she'd been a slave who didn't know her father's name and had never heard of the Dreamwen Stone. Evan had been her new friend in the bathhouse, Jasper an unknown carriage driver. Now Evan and Jasper were her companions in fleeing Lord Morlen, and she was free.

Freedom! Maeve knew those who hunted her could crash through the moonlit peace where the three of them lay and drag her back to drudgery. But oh, how wonderful it was to wake in the morning and choose her own tasks. Until her escape, freedom had been to lie on her pallet after a day of work and listen to Lila tell stories of the world she never saw. Maeve had labored in the steaming bathhouse almost since she could walk. When she was small, she'd carried towels, washed and folded silk robes. As she grew, she'd learned to render perfumes from herbs and flowers. At fifteen, Orlo had taught her how to knead the muscles of the Sliviite upper classes. Through it all, he'd been both her protector and taskmaster. Orlo. What was he doing now? She imagined him checking the fire on the kettles, goading the slaves to work faster.

Yesterday, she'd sat an hour near the stream, letting her feet play in and out of the water while she dreamed of sailing across the ocean and meeting her father. Cabis Denon. He had a star carved on his chest. If he lived, she could find him.

She looked up at the moon-streamed trees. Their leaves seemed to hear the song from her stone as they danced and waved. She let her drowsy eyes close.

As soon as she did, the world of dreams cast her into a building where the ceiling was torn off. She saw rocks rolling and crashing; the walls were crumbling.

The young man she'd seen in the gray hallways was beside her. He pointed to a wild-haired girl running toward them.

Then Maeve saw a huge bird, so dark it seemed to blot out the stars, flying low over the running girl. The young man grabbed the girl. Maeve looked down at the Dreamwen Stone; its center shone with golden light. She held it out.

The unknown girl reached toward Maeve with both hands. Without touching the Stone, she gathered its golden brightness into herself, until she, too, glowed. She turned to face the bird. Bursts of gold shot from her fists as she danced with mystic power.

The bird beat the air with loud wings, flapping away.

The young man turned to Maeve. "Please," he said. "I must ask you—"

But Maeve woke to the woodland grove, clutching the Dreamwen Stone. Evan and Jasper slept on, while she gasped quietly, trying to calm herself.

She thought of how for seventeen years she'd lived under Lord Indol, going only from his bathhouse to his garret, dreaming often, but never a dream such as the one she'd just had. Now she traveled distances while asleep and hid from Lord Morlen when she was awake.

Lord Morlen. Why did he want her? What did he see? *He has command over as many men as he cares to hire, and I have only myself and these two friends.*

But Maeve had something Lord Morlen didn't have. She had the Dreamwen Stone, and maybe that would be enough.

Chapter 12

Jasper liked watching Maeve's deft hands as she sewed. "Measure with your thumb," she told him. "That way the seam won't waver. Hold your wrists like this." She had one hand over and one hand under the cloth, while he turned his cloth over and back with every stitch.

"Doesn't help," Jasper said. "My hands were never meant to hold something as small and sharp as a needle."

"You hold fishhooks."

He chuckled. "Even a small hook's bigger than a needle, the same way my thumb's bigger than yours."

They sat on boulders in their camp. Evan was at the stream fishing. The buggy was wedged into a space among the trees close by. Jasper had gone over the ground from the road and hoped he'd erased the traces of their passage. It was a back road, yes, not much more than a track, but he knew stripers. He kept one ear open for any unusual sounds.

"I like to sew. Evan likes to fish, and you're handy with the hooks and the coals," she said, smiling at the cloth as she worked.

"The free know how to make the most of a fire."

"I don't understand how you lay it so it doesn't smoke. Every time I touch a fire, it starts to smoke."

"That's because you dunk yourself in water every day. Fire hates water," Jasper said, grinning and turning his cloth over.

"You could do with a bath yourself."

"That so?" He set down his work—a trouser leg for Evan—and carefully stuck the needle into the fabric. He stretched his arms.

"That's so."

"Maeve, sometimes I think you know everything I don't and I've seen everything you haven't. Put us together and we know the world."

She kept sewing. "But where we're going, neither of us has been."

"If we get there." No sense pretending it was a foregone certainty.

Her forehead puckered a little as she leaned closer to her sewing. "Will you come with us across the Minwenda?"

"Wouldn't know what to do in the east. I'm Sliviia born."

"If you didn't like it, I'd give you what's left of the gold to return."

"Maeve, you've got to see we can't keep that gold with us. If they ever search me, those two delans won't buy us anything but slavery. Or death."

"I'll carry them, then."

She was always stubborn with him about the gold. He wanted to throw it in the stream, watch the water bury it in mud. He'd lived his whole life without delans, often without even besaets. There were other ways.

"I'm done with this length," he said, standing up. "And here's Evan." The boy was waving two fat fish. Jasper clapped him on the shoulder. "I'll help you gut them. Then I'm going for a wash."

Maeve smiled. "A wash?"

"Yes. For you, I'll brave the cold water."

"Will you sing, Maeve?" Evan said, plumping the fish onto a rock.

Maeve held a length of yellow cloth against her leg.

"I have lived on the borders,
My real face unseen,
but where I go now
has no boundary but dreams.
Walk with me, walk with me out of this night,
For you are my love, and you are my light. . . ."

Jasper pulled out his biggest fishhook to gut the fish Evan had caught. Maeve's voice took away all trouble. This tune seemed to be a favorite with her. He wasn't quite sure of the meaning in the first two lines, but he liked "you are my love, and you are my light." She said she'd learned the song from her mother, who had learned it from the father Maeve never knew, but Jasper enjoyed pretending to himself that it was written for him.

Jasper sauntered down the dusty road toward the small village near where he, Maeve, and Evan were camped. He scuffed up puffs of dust, wearing his dull face, cap pulled low. He entered the store, where a sharp-eyed woman greeted him, the same one who'd sold him cloth.

"See you patched your trousers," she said.

Jasper scratched his head, wondering what she'd say if she could see the big pocket Maeve had sewn on the inside of his shirt. "Need fishhooks. The big ones."

She pulled three large steel hooks from a basket. "One besaet will get you three, and a small hook thrown in."

Jasper dug in his pocket for a coin.

"Where you going fishing?" she asked.

"Where the fish are."

"Ha! Where the fish are." Her quick smile vanished. "Good fishing to you, then."

"Not many people about," he said, looking around the empty store.

"Not since those stripers come through. I had to stand here while they rummaged through my goods. As if I'd hide a pair of runaway slaves!" Jasper couldn't stop the sweat from breaking out on the back of his neck. He wondered if Morlen's mercenaries had had wits enough to ask about any cloth being sold. "Wanted to know, had anyone seen a girl wearing a blue gown, and a boy with new marks. Ha—a pair like that wouldn't get through this village without being spotted."

"Reward," Jasper said.

"Two delans, more than I'll see in ten years." She fussed with her apron. "Stripers wouldn't listen to me—took me hours to straighten the shambles they left. No one knows when they'll be back."

When Jasper left the store, he ambled out of town in the opposite direction from where he'd entered. Once alone and out of sight of the meager village, he doubled past it to get back to Maeve and Evan.

Maeve looked good in her newly finished dress, the yellow cloth against her skin like sunlight meeting a field of ripe wheat. Evan's trousers and shirt suited him, too. Both were still without shoes, but the poorest lowborn free often went barefoot. They'd pass.

Jasper squinted at the buggy, hidden behind the leaves of late summer. The rig, which had captured all his dreams a week before, seemed full of risk now. He was sure that every road to Mantedi would be blockaded and all buggies searched.

While they ate, he thought the problem over. When the light grew dusky, he spoke. "We've got to leave the buggy here."

Maeve looked up at him, her mouth full. She swallowed, choking a little. "Leave your new rig?"

"Can't take it with us to Mantedi. We won't ever get there if we go by the road."

Her eyes glistened. "You could go back to Slivona yourself," she said. "You'd be safe without us."

"But you wouldn't be safe without me." The words fell from his lips before he knew he would say them. *It's the truth.*

She stared at him across the coals, blinking. "It's dangerous for you."

True. Jasper shrugged. "More dangerous for you."

Evan moved a little closer to Maeve. She put an arm around the boy. "Won't it take a long time to walk?" she asked.

"The longer we keep hidden, the more the chase will lose heart. We'll take turns on the horse, go the byways. If we shove the buggy deeper in the trees, maybe no one will find it."

"You'll teach me to ride?"

He grinned. "Pay you for teaching me to sew."

Her eyes were still watering. "I suppose we'd best get some sleep," she said.

"No. Got to leave tonight."

"Tonight! But it's getting dark."

He didn't want to tell her about the stripers in the village. "Maeve, my bones tell me to go, and my bones are what's kept me alive and free until now—nothing else. The moon will be out." She put a hand to the stone around her neck. "But first," he said, "you got to muss your clothes. New clothes get noticed. And if anyone spots us—Evan, you're my brother, and Maeve, you're my wife."

"Wife?"

"I'd call you my sister, but who'd believe it? You don't look anything like me and Evan."

"I'm not marked like a wife. I lived seventeen years as a slave and was never marked. I'm not going to be marked now that I'm free." She had that stubborn look.

"It's a tiny nick at the throat. New hooks are sharp. I know how to cut so it won't hurt."

"No." She tilted her chin. "No scars."

"What if we meet a patrol?"

"I'll be your cousin."

He shook his head. "My way's better. Safer."

"Your way cuts me."

He saw he'd never persuade her, but he wasn't happy about it. And he wasn't happy about the gold.

They made everything ready. The buggy was hidden, the blankets and a cushion tied on Fortune's back, the fishhooks neatly folded into a scrap of cloth and stowed in the big pocket Jasper had inside his shirt. Maeve and Evan went down to the stream for a last drink while Jasper sprinkled dirt on the fire. When they returned, he decided to visit his favorite spot near the stream to get a drink himself.

Kneeling by the stream, Jasper shook water out of his

eyes, muttering to the moon. "Maeve's right. A wash is a fine thing." It felt good to rinse away the sweat that had dried on his skin. *Am I wrong to keep the news of stripers to myself?*

A chill grabbed the back of his neck. Noises in the night that shouldn't be there. Jingling spurs. A man's voice.

Jasper glided through the trees, back toward the camp.

Moonlight banded on light-and-dark stripes and glinted off shining steel knuckles. A zind! One man. He was swinging down from a great stallion, his gloved fingers holding the reins. Maeve and Evan were staring at him as if they had no legs. Then Maeve shoved Evan, telling him to run.

The zind drew his long knife, the steel singing as though glad of the chance to be out of its sheath. Evan tugged at Maeve. She pushed him away. The zind stepped closer. "Well, this pairing is one we're all searching for. A girl, seventeen, with a young boy. The boy was said to have marks, but maybe, Miss, you shed the marked boy and picked up a stray. *You* look to be seventeen." The man had fine teeth; they flashed white. Maeve backed away from him, pleading with Evan to run, while the boy clung to her arm. "Gold hair, Lord Morlen said," the zind went on, "and unless the moonlight deceives me, your hair is gold."

Jasper knew he could melt into the night, return to Slivona and live on. He knew where a ransom in gold was buried in the north woods of Lord Hering's woodlands. Hadn't he done all he could? Maeve's luck had run out.

May as well ask the water in the stream to run back to where it came from. I can't leave now. He felt in his pocket for the fishhooks. He unwrapped the two biggest hooks with shaking hands.

"That's far enough, girl. You seem to be fond of this boy. Take another step and I'll gladly slit his throat." The zind caressed his knife.

Jasper moved with all the stealth he could manage, working his way to the trees behind the zind, listening to the man's tormenting words. Hating him.

"Maeve," the zind said. "That's your name, isn't it? I'll gain more than the reward for finding you. Morlen never said you couldn't be touched. All he said was bring you to him alive." He dropped the reins of his horse. "But once you're his, pretty bird, I won't have the chance to pet your feathers."

Jasper darted forward. He plunged a hook into the stallion's haunch. The animal reared and ran. As the zind whirled, Jasper was already behind him, slamming a foot into the soft place in the back of the man's knees. The zind went down but was instantly twisting to get up, slashing with his knife. Before he could rise, Jasper dived on his neck, pounding his well-shaped nose, driving at his eyes with the other fishhook. The zind yelled and let go of his knife to grab at his face.

Jasper took up the knife. He planted it in the zind's chest, then rolled to get away. Away from the dreadful sights and sounds of death.

"There's your reward," Jasper said. He lay against the hard pillow of the earth, pressing his cheek to the ground, gasping, wondering where his breath had gone to, hearing Fortune's terrified snorts and stomping hooves, Maeve's quivering voice calming the horse, Evan's voice saying, "Is he dead?"

A trembling hand smoothed Jasper's hair. "Jasper. It's all right, Jasper. Here, put your head in my lap. You'll bruise your face. Evan, dear one, get some cloth and dip it in the creek."

He rolled onto his back. He let her put his head in her lap, let her dab at his face with her sleeve. She kept smoothing his hair. "Thank you, Jasper. Thank you."

Evan came back with a dripping rag. "Give me your arm, Jasper," Maeve said. "No, the other arm." He looked at the arm she wanted him to give her. A long gash, black in the moonlight, dripping ink.

"More water, Evan," Maeve said, sponging the gash. Jasper's flesh awoke—a fierce pain began in his arm.

"When it's clean, you must bind it tightly," he said.

"I will."

"Had to stop him," Jasper whispered. "Had to."

She went on wiping his arm.

"We need to go," he said. "Right away."

"We'll go. Soon." She patted him. "It's quiet now, Jasper. No one around."

He listened to the night, straining for any sound of danger. He heard trees whispering, heard the light bubbling of the stream, the rustle of an animal. The world had broken in upon them, but now it seemed peaceful again. "Sing to me, Maeve?"

She began softly singing:

" . . . *walk with me, walk with me out of this night,*
for you are my love, and you are my light."

Her voice steadied his heart, lifting away his anguish.

Orlo felt fine, though his stomach was empty and his body sore from riding. Lord Morlen's soldiers had taught him to ride by putting him on a horse and telling him to keep up. The first few days of traveling to Mantedi, Orlo had fallen to the rear of the line of zind. Now he was proud that he could sit a horse well enough to stay close to Lord Morlen.

There was plenty to see from horseback as they went north. Orlo enjoyed watching the changing terrain during the days: forests, farms, rolling hills. And now there was rocky desert ahead, stretching west like an orange blanket, and a salty smell in the air, with a glimpse of ocean to the east.

Orlo hoped the search for Maeve would be over soon so Lord Morlen would be happy. Every day when the zind captain reported her still missing, Lord Morlen looked angry. Luckily, he was good to Orlo—he gave orders that Orlo was to have as much vahss as he wished. The first day, when the vahss had worn off, Orlo's heart had pounded against the bars of his ribs as if it wanted to get out. He didn't remember why—it was something to do with Maeve. Since then, they'd given him enough vahss to keep his heart steady all the time.

Today the flow of travelers on the road had been thickening since morning, and now it was late afternoon. Very few people were heading south, away from Mantedi— mostly farmers hauling empty carts, walking beside silent, weary-looking beasts. Orlo noticed with surprise that the foreheads of these freeborn farmers had been branded. Each of them must have met the same iron, a design that looked like a sheaf of grain.

As for those moving toward Mantedi, Orlo had never seen such a collection of humanity. Men, women, and children of every skin color, from lightest pink to velvet black. A few were well-dressed lords and ladies, looking down haughtily from the high saddles of their splendid horses. Scores of slaves plodded behind them, clad in the simple garments of their class, necks and faces studded with scars. Some of the horde was made up of lowborn free, their clothes fluttering raggedly as they hurried along on foot.

When lords, ladies, or nobles saw the line of zind, they guided their mounts to the side of the road, calling to their slaves to give way. The lowborn free tumbled into the ditches beside the road, waiting for the zind to pass. With everyone making room, Lord Morlen's group reached the gates of Mantedi quickly. The wide gateway bristled with soldiers wearing maroon uniforms, weapons glinting at their belts, faces marked with squares inside squares. Orlo stared curiously—he'd never seen soldier slaves before. Lord Indol used mercenaries, as did most of the other lords in Slivona.

"Captain Lorv!" Morlen shouted. A dark-haired man in his prime stepped forward with a salute. "Did you receive the message I sent by courier, Captain?"

"Yes, my lord. We've not let anyone into the city fitting the descriptions of the runaways you seek."

"You've detained no one?" Morlen frowned.

"There weren't any boys with fresh marks, sir, but we sifted out a group of lowborn lassies. They're in the guardhouse, waiting your inspection. The rabble began to gather, asking for their daughters and sisters back. As you ordered, I gave them vahss, and they became quiet."

Morlen nodded. "I'll see the girls in a moment. First, I've brought reinforcements to patrol the wall and to aid you here at the gate." Morlen barked a command and the leader of the zind urged his horse forward. "Captain Lorv, meet Captain Fahd. He commands these zind troops. You will answer to him."

Orlo had often noticed that Fahd never changed expression. And no matter where he slept or how far he rode, Fahd's striped doublet always looked clean and new. "Don't gape like a fool, Lorv," Morlen said. Lorv closed his mouth and stood blinking at the zind. "Now, show me who you have detained." Lord Morlen dismounted and stalked after Captain Lorv. Orlo watched them disappear into a solid wooden building a bare twenty paces away.

They soon returned, Morlen shaking his head. "You're more of a fool than I knew, Lorv. Not one girl matched my description. Did I say fair? I said *gold* skin, gold hair, *deep* blue eyes. Did you think I put in such words for your amusement?"

"N-no, sir, I only wanted to be certain—"

"You can be certain you have served your last day as captain, Lorv."

Lorv instantly fell to his knees. Sweat ran over his face as if his pores had become waterfalls. "I obey your will, Lord Morlen."

"No, you have ignored my will. You have wearied me long enough."

Morlen signaled Fahd. The zind leader leaped from his horse. He drew the black axe from his belt. Lorv bowed to the ground. The zind captain chopped the kneeling man's head from his neck, like taking melon from a vine.

Orlo's mouth went suddenly dry; he could feel his heart pounding all the way into his fingertips. He wanted to pull his stinging eyes out of his face so he wouldn't have to see what was in front of him. A furious desire grew in him, to run at Lord Morlen and trample him.

"Thank you, Captain." Morlen's glance flicked to Orlo. "Have one of your men give this slave some vahss. Now."

A striped glove extended an orange flask. Orlo seized the vahss and downed it in one long gulp, then clasped the empty flask to his chest. His angry thoughts faded as his heart beat slow and quiet.

"What do you want done with the girls who have been detained in error?" asked Captain Fahd.

"Do what you like with them, Captain. Most are comely enough to be sentesans. From time to time a lovely flower springs from an untended bed of manure. Those girls would have been sold long since if their families had a particle of sense. They'll be better off as slaves."

Captain Fahd showed no expression. "Shall I compensate the fathers, sir?"

"Offer them more vahss or ten besaets. See which they choose." Lord Morlen swung back on his horse. "You know your duty, Captain. I leave you with the gate. If you can make use of my soldiers, by all means do so." He headed up the main street of Mantedi, and Orlo followed.

With the zind left behind, they were a smaller company—only Lord Morlen's retinue and Orlo. They rode through wide streets lined with rich estates. At first Orlo thought that Mantedi must be populated only by the wealthy, but as they went farther into the city, he caught glimpses of alleyways where grubby children played, their bones sticking out of rags and tatters. As they approached the waterfront, he was astonished by the numbers of slaves and free streaming through the streets. Many of the free looked pitifully thin. Lord Morlen was right—it was better to be a slave.

The sun had nearly set when they arrived at the ocean. A great network of piers jabbed from the shore into the water. Every pier swarmed with men, loading and unloading ships, shouting to one another. When Lord Morlen dismounted, handing his reins to a dockhand, the pier where he stood went quiet. Orlo gave up his horse, too, and followed Lord Morlen, who strode down the long wide pier, his cloak snapping darkly in the wind. All the other men on the pier moved out of his way.

Lord Morlen rapped on the door of a wooden house built onto the pier. A bald man with a bull neck stepped out. He shook Lord Morlen's hand.

"Evening, Warren. I trust you received my message?"

"Certainly, sir, and the docks are well posted. I've notified all the piermasters. No sign of the runaways thus far."

Lord Morlen beckoned Orlo forward, put a hand on his shoulder. "This man stays with you," he told Warren. "He'll help you look for them—he can ride the waterfront for you. And he can identify them once they're caught."

Orlo looked at the ocean, at the way the sun's dying rays dappled it orange. His heart beat a slow tempo, like the waves.

Chapter 13

As Sara went into the dormitory, she didn't talk to any of the other students. She didn't see Ellowen Renaiya and was glad—she despised the Ellowen for letting herself be taken in by Bern, when she knew enough about Charmals to tell Dorjan of their ways.

It seemed so long since the morning. Sara looked back disgustedly on her former self, the one who had met Bern and taken him through the sacred rings. She'd been tricked by a deceiver; she'd let him kiss her, kissed him back. Her lips were forever defiled. She remembered exactly how Bern had appeared past the seventh ring. Why, oh why, had she ignored the wisdom of that place?

She climbed into bed. Thoughts of the exquisite pearly-winged bird whose cage she'd broken filled her mind. How could she have listened to Bern and done what he said? She wanted nothing more than to go back to the clearing past the seventh ring and see the Tezzarine again. But now, because she'd been a dupe, the beautiful creature was gone. She tried to remember its song, but she kept hearing Bern's gloating laughter. Every place he'd touched her seemed contaminated.

She wrestled with her pillow, wishing she could begin the day over. But that could never be. Tomorrow she might become the first student ever to be dismissed from the Healer's Keep.

Ellowen Renaiya found it so difficult to set the seals on the dormitory doors that she almost gave up, almost called Ellowen Mayn to help her. When she finished, she followed the walkways to her own place.

A simple well-made cottage greeted her—healers had no need for sumptuous quarters. She sank into her chair, her eyes resting on the pristine altar in the corner. On the wall hung a painting of a group of Tezzarines, done ten years before by Ellowen Desak: his gift to her in celebration of the attainment of Ellowenity. When Renaiya looked at the painting, she could almost hear the song of the Tezzarines, the mingled ecstasy and sorrow of pure compassion.

Gone now! What will become of us? Oh, Lars! Why didn't I die with you? I wish I could go back to the time before the invasion, when we were happy. I wish I could tell you not to go to Bellandra's court. That way, you wouldn't have been there when Kareed's soldiers stormed the palace. You'd still be alive. What do I live for, if the Keep can be undone by one reckless girl with a powerful gift?

The Council meeting with Bern had been grueling. When he'd told them how Sara had broken through the seventh sacred ring, and what had happened with the Tezzarine, Hester was eager to dismiss the girl at once. But the rituals for such a proceeding were unknown. Hester and Desak had argued protocol until Renaiya's head ached. Renaiya had been quiet through most of it, very tired. When she reached for her gen to strengthen it, it was like trying to coax a dying candle whose wax was nearly at an end. She sat gathered into herself, glad for Bern to do the talking.

The Council had finally decided to hold a hearing with Sara on the following day. Why draw in the rest of the students and faculty, disturbing the harmonies more? Better to attend to the matter quietly.

Feeling ill, Renaiya had formally named Bern Draden-gifted, and seen Hester's haughty smile. She had decided to wait on naming Sara and Dorjan.

Now, looking at Desak's soaring Tezzarines, Renaiya sighed. Not feeling strong enough to get on her knees, she prayed from her chair for guidance. *Help me to lay aside everything but the truth.* Gradually, she was able to feel a trickle of harmony.

She remembered that when she had started up the trail with Dorjan, she had gone for some purpose. Something to do with Sara—and Bern. Why couldn't she remember? All her years of mindfulness and now she couldn't recall something as simple as her purpose at the beginning of the day. *Bern.* Renaiya shifted uneasily in her chair. Some unknown and unwelcome presence seemed to hover near her. Her mind was so cloudy. What had she been thinking about, just now? Perhaps it would be best to go to sleep. She always felt better in the morning.

She made one more try. *Bern.*

She remembered! *Charmal.*

Bern must have guessed he could persuade Sara to break through the seventh ring and destroy the Tezzarine's protection. Then he used my grief for my beloved Lars and my bitterness against the invasion to bring me into his web. And now I've named him Draden-gifted.

What now? She alone among the Ellowens understood what Bern truly was. No one but a trained Mystive or Genoven would be able to recognize a Charmal.

Perhaps it would be best to go to Sara tonight. They could leave together, ask King Landen and Queen Torina for assistance. Renaiya dared not face the Charmal again. She'd seen how futile her defenses were. *And I'm far weaker now than I was at the beginning of the day.*

Renaiya yawned. Yes. That was what she'd do. Leave that very night, in a few hours, with Sara. No sense subjecting the girl to a hearing before the Council, which would surely condemn her. Before she left, she'd talk to Ellowen Mayn— the Sangiv would hear her out. Someone else at the Keep needed to know the truth.

Wearily, she moved about the room. Her bed looked wonderfully inviting. She sat on its edge to think through her plans.

Sara ran through the Keep. Everywhere she went, the walls tumbled into choking dust. Students stood transfixed while she tried in vain to get them to move. "Run!" she yelled. They looked at her with vacant eyes as the walls fell around them.

A dark shape swooped toward her. She ran on while a cold grayness seeped around her, slowing her, squeezing her lungs. Enveloped by shadow, she doubled over. A sharp, cold claw touched her back.

Someone grabbed her arm with a warm hand. Dorjan. "Fight," he said. "Fight." A strange girl stood beside him, holding a stone that gave off golden light. "Use the light," Dorjan said. "Use it to fight with."

Somehow, Sara understood him. She reached toward the stone, pulling its light into herself. Strength filled her; light poured from her hands. She clenched her fists and began to dance, punching the dark sky, facing the deadly, dark bird. When she shook her fists, fiery bursts of gold flew toward the bird. With a hideous cry, it flapped away.

Sara woke lying in her rumpled sheets. She sat up to breathe better. Moonlight streaming through the small window in an unbroken wall shone on a shape at the foot of her mattress. Dorjan. Slowly he sat, resting against the bedstead, panting, covered in sweat.

"Dorjan," she whispered, "don't go away."

He shook his head, a faint movement. Sara crept close to him, leaning against the comforting solid wood of her bedstead. Dorjan looked spent. He must be as tired as she was, perhaps more so.

"Did you see it, too?" she asked. "The Keep falling, becoming dust?" He nodded, his eyes full of moonlight. "What does it mean?" She hoped he would know, would be able to explain the dream. "Did we dream of the future?" She wanted to run to the window, look outside, assure herself the Keep still stood firm. But it was all she could do to stay upright on the bed—and there were no sinister rumbles, no sign of cracks in the wall.

"I think we were shown what will happen if the dark birds win," Dorjan said softly.

"Win? What are they trying to win?"

"I believe they serve the Shadow King." His breath sounded uneasy. "They seem to be quite interested in the Healer's Keep, and especially interested in *you*, Sara."

"Wait. Shadow King? Who's that?"

He sighed. "King of Shadows. The Dreamwens have seen him, and so have the healers of the Keep."

"I don't understand."

"I don't understand, either." He rubbed his forehead.

"But—tell me what you know."

"I can tell you the Dreamwen lore my father taught me."

"Please."

"*When anger is your highest good,*" Dorjan chanted,

"And greed what you hold dear,
When truth is hated for its pain
Or crushed so you won't fear—
The Shadow King is smiling,
The Shadow King is near."

He stopped. She was holding on to the bedpost. "Sara? Are you all right?"

"I think Bern makes this Shadow King smile, and that I do also."

"Sara," he said gently, "Bern's a Charmal. He took you in. You didn't know."

She told him about the seventh ring and Bern and the Tezzarine, afraid that Dorjan would despise her.

"How did Bern know you could break the cage?"

"I don't know." Restless, Sara tested her legs against the floor. "All this talk of shadows! We need a candle." She found one and went into the hall, taking flame from one of the lanterns and bringing it back to Dorjan. "How dare the Shadow King send dark birds into my dreams!" she said. "Next time, I won't let the bird get away. I'll kill it."

Renaiya was looking for someone, but couldn't remember who it was. Someone young, with a fierce spirit. The person she looked for could protect the Keep, stop its fall. Who was it? Shadows trailed through her mind, smudging every thought.

She heard the swish of powerful wings. For a moment, hope lifted her head. Perhaps the Tezzarine had returned. But when she looked up, she realized this was nothing like a Tezzarine. This creature was darker than darkness, canceling all other sight. As it flapped close, she didn't understand why her feet were so heavy. Though she tried to run, her legs made no headway. When she looked behind her, the bird was gaining fast. She must get to a door before it seized her. If she could slip inside, she could shut out the bird. Why were her legs so useless?

A freezing talon brushed her neck. Renaiya tried to scream. She knew, then, who it was she needed to call on, whom she searched for. Sara, the girl with the warrior gift, the granddaughter of Kareed the Invader. And Renaiya understood that she herself was asleep, caught in a dream and unable to wake.

A swirling circle of blinding light opened before her. She knew at once that it led to her physical death. She looked away.

To her left the air thickened, congealing into a gray hall-way. A figure stood inside the gray, a winged man waiting behind a thin barrier of silver. He smiled at her, beckoning. "If you step through the Boundary, you can keep your place in the world," he said.

Two doorways. But no one called to her from the dazzling light.

"Come, Renaiya. Only one step," said the winged man. "You don't need to die. Come through the Boundary to me. I've been watching over you, and you belong to me."

"No," Renaiya answered. "No. I have never been yours."

The great claw tore at her back. There was no time to regret what she might have done or what she might still do if things were different. No time to mourn the abrupt end of the healer's life she'd led for so long. She wouldn't be able to pass on all she'd learned, say good-byes, make apologies, or give good wishes. Her life would have to stand just as it was. Renaiya put aside pain and desire and regret. She stepped forward and gave herself to the bright light.

Chapter 14

Dorjan felt more and more awake as he and Sara talked on. When he told her about the dream in which he'd met the girl with the Dreamwen Stone, she questioned him excitedly.

"The girl with the light! Your sister?"

"I believe so."

"And this . . . Dreamwen Stone—you say it enhances the gifts of anyone who holds it?"

"That's the lore. A legend among Dreamwens. It's supposed to have been made in the Seed Void."

"Seed Void?"

"A place in the center of all the realms: *'A particle within the Seed Void / More fertile than all the fields of earth.'*" The verse rolled off Dorjan's tongue. "Very few ever travel to the Seed Void; it's full of danger."

"But someone went there, and made the Dreamwen Stone?"

"Yes. Made it, and brought it back."

Sara passed her finger back and forth through the candle flame until Dorjan was sure she would burn herself. She raised her eyes to his. "If the Shadow King is attacking our sleep, and the Dreamwen Stone has power in dreams, couldn't it help us fight *him?*"

Dorjan couldn't quite believe that she was suggesting they fight the Shadow King head on. "Renaiya must have it right about your gift," he said. "Spirit Warrior."

Her tangled hair fell around her shoulders while she put her finger in the fire again. "He's attacking *us*. Why shouldn't we attack *him*?" She stood, looking resolute. "Whatever I am, Firan or Trian, I can't stay here." She reached for her pillow and shook it from its case. "I'm leaving the Keep. Tonight." She dropped the pillowcase and put a hand on his arm. "Come with me. We'll find your sister and the Dreamwen Stone."

"Sara," he said, "Dreamwen lore says the Shadow King can never be defeated altogether, that each soul must decide whether to follow him."

She bit her lips. "You won't even try—because of some dead lore? Isn't that what's wrong here at the Keep?"

"Maybe so. But if we go, we should warn the Council before leaving."

She began stuffing a blanket into the pillowcase. "They won't listen to us. They might teach forgiveness, but they haven't forgiven what my grandfather did to Bellandra. They hate me; they're planning to throw me out—I know it. After what I've done, they have good cause now. And you—you're not Bellandran. Draden Hester is Bern's aunt—she'd believe anything he said even if he wasn't a Charmal." Candlelight danced with the shadows beside her, reminding Dorjan of the way she'd danced while fighting the dark bird of their dream. "We won't get help from the Council. We need to go to Sliviia and find your sister."

"My father grew up in Sliviia. It's a dangerous land. Nothing like here, where kings such as your father are merciful and just—Sliviia's ruled by a corrupt emperor."

"Your sister's there."

She had struck on the unanswerable truth. Now that he believed he had a sister, he wanted to find her. She was being hunted by an Ebrowen, and no one had taught her the Dreamwen ways. She needed help, desperately.

But Sara? How would she weather a long journey and a land like Sliviia?

She took her Keep jacket from its hook. "We can't let the Shadow King prevail." She looked around the small room. "Now I'll never learn to dance like a Trian." She pushed her hair back from her face defiantly. "I'm going. Will you come with me?"

He nodded slowly.

When Dorjan returned to his room for his things, the seals on the dormitory seemed weak. He was glad of it, for he still felt weak himself—the dream journeys that moved his body from place to place tired him out far more than anything he'd ever done. He dressed in the clothes he'd worn to the Keep, but brought along the warm jacket given to him by the Dradens when he arrived. Summer wouldn't last forever.

Sara was waiting for him just outside her dormitory, wearing the clothes he'd first seen her in—a wrinkled red blouse and plain skirt. Like him, she carried her Keep jacket. The stuffed pillowcase was slung across her shoulder.

She walked without hesitation toward the back gates. They wouldn't be guarded; the seals set by an Ellowen were considered unbreachable. The Halls stood whole and sound as ever—no cracks, no roaring clouds of dust and rubble. The dream had been just that—a dream.

As they passed the little circle of cottages where the healers lived, Dorjan hung back. He looked at Ellowen Renaiya's residence, remembering her kind face. He rallied his gen, directing it toward her, wondering if it would be safe to ask her to join them.

The emptiness he sensed inside her cottage made fear rise in his throat. He pushed it down. He must be wrong about what he felt. Surely, with all her training, Ellowen Renaiya would not be harmed. He hurried after Sara to the gate.

There, neither of them could break the seal. *Too depleted.* Dorjan set down his bundle. "Give me your hand?" Sara slid her fingers into his. He reached toward her with his gen, feeling for the bright edge of her spirit. There. Warm and sharp. Dorjan joined his own gen to hers to cut through the seal. The gate opened.

They tramped down the dirt road outside the Keep, heading for the sea. "It's dark," she said, brushing close to him, taking his hand.

"If I fall, you will too," he said, smiling.

It was easier to move than to think of how tired he was. They'd decided to go to the little town of Tanyen, only five miles from the Healer's Keep. There they might find a carriage to take them on to the port of Iduna, where they could find passage on a ship crossing the Minwenda.

Dorjan wondered what the queen of Archeld and Bellandra would think of her daughter going to Sliviia with the son of Cabis Denon. But Sara was right—they couldn't let the Shadow King stand unopposed. If anything could defeat him, it would be a Firan, with the Dreamwen Stone. And if they were to ask permission, who would grant it?

"How does it feel to be a princess about to leave your kingdom?"

"How does it feel to be a Dreamwen?" she retorted.

"Being a Dreamwen is an easy secret to keep."

"I liked having no one know I was a princess—while it lasted."

"Where we're going," he said lightly, "you'll get another chance." As the thin rim of dawn pushed into the east, Dorjan breathed deeply, and the smell of the sea uplifted him.

Dorjan and Sara arrived at the wharves of Iduna by mid-morning. Afraid to sleep, they had stayed awake during the carriage ride from Tanyen.

"The light looks right again," Dorjan said, gazing at the shimmering ocean as they emerged from the carriage. *Whatever was wrong must be confined to the Keep.*

"Brighter than it needs to be," Sara said, squinting. She looked tired, but seemed eager to take in the sights and sounds of Iduna.

Throngs of sailors moved along the landings. Sara stopped a skinny man and asked where to find passage to Sliviia.

"You're not in your right mind," the sailor answered gruffly. "Sliviia's no good place for a sailor, let alone a lass like yourself." He didn't wait to hear any argument. The next five men she talked to said the same, some more coarsely than others.

In the end it was Dorjan who found the name of a ship bound for Sliviia. The *Lanya,* and her captain was Navar.

They wove through the crowd to the pier where the *Lanya* was said to be. They found the ship; she lay in the water like a tired duck with no ambitions to swim.

Captain Navar reminded Dorjan of a piece of driftwood, as if his years at sea had worn down all his edges. "You don't have a notion of what you're after," he said, shaking his head at Sara. "Sliviia's a land where girls like yourself can be sold into the worst sort of slavery." He nodded at Dorjan. "And young men beg for a berth on a ship going away from there—any ship, going anywhere."

"Do you take them?" Sara asked.

"If I did, the piermasters would never let me dock again."

"Why sail there at all?" Her eyes accused him of being worse than the piermasters of Sliviia.

Captain Navar blinked. "It's a living, miss. Bellandra has the best wine makers in the world. We fill the gullets of the Sliviite lords, and they fill our pockets. But you—no need for *you* to see what's across the water."

"We're going for his sister," Sara said, pointing at Dorjan.

"Even if I would agree to take you," the captain said, "this is a poor season to be crossing the Minwenda. A man never knows when storms will seize his ship."

Sara held her ground; kept waving her gold under his nose. Finally, he shrugged his stout shoulders. "I can give you the aft cabin but I can't nursemaid you. Hope you have coats for the rain." And he muttered on, all the while counting the coins she gave him.

A dour-faced sailor showed them to a tiny cabin. Two narrow bunks were stacked on top of each other, the lower one bolted to the floor. A small porthole let in murky light. Dorjan bumped into an old sea chest. When he opened it, it was empty.

"At least this ship is clean," Sara said.

"It's also old," Dorjan said, noting the floorboards, bleached with age. "It doesn't look as if it would hold up through a storm. I hope the captain was overstating the weather."

Sara kicked off her shoes and flung herself lengthwise on the lower bunk. "I need to sleep."

Dorjan climbed into the bunk above her. He tried to think of the words to ask her permission for shepherding her dreams. Something about her gift had attracted the attention of the Shadow King; she needed to be taken to a safe dreamscape. But what could he say? She was proud. She might refuse. *Sara, may I move you in your sleep to a place I've made, where you'll be safe . . .*

"Dorjan?"

"Sara—"

"Do you think I helped the Shadow King?" Her question floated through the boards underneath him.

"If you did, you never will again."

"I'd give anything to change what I did, go back and finish listening to the Tezzarine's song." He heard her sigh. Then she spoke again. "I'm glad it's you here with me, Dorjan, and no one else."

Now was the time to ask her about the dreamscapes. Dorjan leaned over the edge of his bunk to look at her. She was already asleep, one arm hanging off the bed along with a curling tangle of hair.

He turned back to stare at the ceiling, which was little more than a foot away. If he let Sara sleep unprotected, the dark birds would surely find her. She didn't know about dreamscapes and wouldn't know how to wake herself when needed.

The other times he'd met her in dreams, he hadn't been looking for her—they'd happened to meet when he went prowling the dream terrain of the Healer's Keep. But now, if he went deliberately into *her* dreams without her permission, wouldn't he be taking the way of the Ebrowen? *And if I don't help her, and the dark bird seizes her mind, won't that be worse than breaking one of the Dreamwen laws?*

No time to think about it longer. He shut his eyes, focusing on Sara, guiding his awareness into her dream.

He found himself on a smooth beach in bright sunshine. Beside him danced Sara—arms gracefully floating, feet skimming the sand as the ocean creamed against the near shoreline.

Recognizing Dorjan, she clapped her hands.

"Sara, there's somewhere else I want to show you. Will you go?"

Her dancing feet on the sand made a swishing sound, like the beat of mighty wings. "I love the sand here, and the sound of the water. Don't you?"

"Yes." Dorjan looked warily at the open sky. "Will you go?"

"After I've finished the dance." She leaped and spun.

Dorjan heard a loud rush, and it wasn't from the waves running up the beach. He saw a shadow on the sand, a wide wingspread closing in. He raced to Sara. He caught her hand. Wrapping her with his dreaming strength, he moved with her off the sparkling beach, hurtling out of her dream to the gates of his own protected grove.

He pushed her through his gates and ran in after her, pursued by fiercely beating wings. He spoke the word to galvanize all the Dreamwen protections embedded in the gates as he closed them. A great wall of light flew up. Just before the dark bird vanished, Dorjan caught a glimpse of its raging gray eyes trained on Sara. The eyes seemed to say that the bird would never stop hunting her.

Too close. Dorjan looked at Sara. *Firan,* Ellowen Renaiya had called her. Spirit Warrior. Dorjan had no doubt anymore that whatever power Sara carried, the Shadow King knew about it and wanted it for himself.

"Welcome," he said shakily, "to the grove of sycamores."

The peace of this dreamscape glowed in every leaf and seed cluster, in the white and yellow shades of the sycamore bark, and in the quiet sky. One gigantic tree stood guard over the rest, rising up and up, spreading its branches, the scent of its wood filling the air. Dorjan went to the great sycamore, touching it. He slid down to rest against it. Across from him, Sara leaned against another tree. She laid her cheek against the wood.

Chapter 15

Lowen Camber met Bern outside the Boundary House of the Healer's Keep. She looked nervously at the surrounding grounds.

"No need to be furtive, Cam," Bern said, waving a Draden key. "I'm a sanctioned Dra, named by Ellowen Renaiya herself. Now that she's dead, my standing can't be revoked." He grinned gleefully.

Camber wished she could glare openly at Bern, wished she alone could have been chosen to subvert the Silver Boundary. She would have been capable—hadn't she always excelled in everything she turned her hand to? But, as usual, she'd been passed over. Now she must put up with this arrogant young man, who seemed to believe he already knew everything. Gave her no respect.

No doubt Bern had been well prepared. After all, he'd been fortunate enough to be discovered by a prominent Ebromal when he was quite young. She herself had not met a single Ebromal until she'd spent half her life in the Healer's Keep. Half her life! Years of misery, during which she'd learned as many of the Keep's secrets as the Ellowens would give her. *And even though I mastered herbology faster than any other student, even though I outstripped others in all my studies, no one wanted to acknowledge me as the equal of an Ellowen.*

Camber was sure they wouldn't have allowed her to teach if they'd had a Phytosen Ellowen to replace Camber's own teacher, Ellowen Brogan, when he died. Shorthanded and needing to train a new generation of the Phytosen-gifted, the Keep's faculty had taken her on. And still they wouldn't grant her the status of Ellowen; still they smiled condescendingly each time she brought it up. *"Ellowenity is an experience. When you have that experience, we will know it. Meanwhile, it cannot be rushed."*

Camber hated their patronizing ways, hated being kept out of the most important meetings, excluded from Boundary House teachings, left on the fringes of the Keep no matter how many times she proved that her knowledge and talents were extraordinary.

But there was one important teaching, usually given only to Ellowens, that Camber had received. On Draden Hester's orders, Ellowen Mayn had reluctantly taught her how to create Invisibility, so she might do her share in helping to disguise the Keep. *What a mistake he made.*

Using her knowledge of Invisibility, Camber had invented the method for creating *Dark* Invisibility—a smoky illusion that deluded even the Ellowens. *That* had earned the notice of Bellandra's Master Ebromal! He'd pressed her to develop her skill, until she could exert the Dark Invisibility around a living creature—even if seen from afar—around a Tezzarine, no less.

Once marked with her Dark Invisibility, the Tezzarines could be taken from the Keep by Ebromal adepts who never set foot there—the birds were drawn directly into the Shadow realms and there bound over to the Shadow King. *I'd have won them all, but the Ellowens noticed—and banded together to seal the leader inside a protection. Now this upstart, this* seventeen-year-old pip named Bern, steals my glory by wrecking that protection. Now I'm Bern's subordinate, by order of the Master Ebromal.

Camber could hardly stomach it. She promised herself she would work on perfecting the Dark Invisibility until it could be used upon a human being—a student, a Draden, even an Ellowen. After that, she wouldn't take anyone's orders ever again.

I'm more talented than all the Ellowens put together. Without her work, what Bern did to overcome the protections wouldn't matter. It was a mark of her skill that neither Ellowens in the Keep nor seers outside it could perceive the way the Invisibility had shifted. Enough to let Bern enter the Keep. He was there through Camber's efforts—and now the Master Ebromal puts him above me.

Camber's resentment rose as Bern put his Draden key into the keyhole of the Boundary House. Only Ellowens and Dradens were allowed into it. This was the only building on the Keep having a door that locked, instead of the seals that were commonly used. Dradens were expected to keep the Boundary House clean, but Dradens weren't able to create seals or to break them—hence the keys. And she, Lowen Camber, a Keep member for so many years, had never seen inside it!

Bern clicked his tongue and smirked. "Building a place like this, and setting no one to guard it! The Ellowens are inconceivably childish."

"It wasn't the Ellowens of this generation who built the Keep," Camber said, frowning as she realized she was defending the group she hated.

Bern laughed. "But it is the Ellowens of this generation who leave a mere lock to guard their most important treasure."

He didn't wait for her to precede him but went straight through the door. He paused at the threshold, so suddenly that Camber bumped into him. "Sorry, quite sorry," he said sarcastically. "I'm simply overwhelmed. The silence, you see. A silence that shouts of power. And the floor! What a wonder."

Near the entrance, a carving of a sword inlaid with gold and silver glimmered in the shining marble floor. Beside the sword was a round etching, set with diamonds. The entire floor made an elaborate painting of stone and jewels, which caught the light from the stained glass windows. Camber had to admit that the sight was enough to make anyone stop short.

"Beautiful," she answered sourly.

Bern removed his shoes. "As any faithful Dra would do," he said, sneering. He took three running steps and slid a few feet along the floor. He looked up, spreading his arms. He twirled around to face Camber.

"Do you think the Ellowens might still save the Boundary if they band together, as they did to save the last Tezzarine?" she asked.

He chuckled. "You've lived too long at the Keep, Cam. You don't see the Ellowens as they truly are; you see only what you've been taught they must be. You hold them in too much respect, I fear."

"They do have power," she said. "You'd be wise to remember that."

"Oh, I do remember—I would never be so stupid as to forget. But as for wisdom—no, I'll leave wisdom to them. For it's this so-called wisdom, you see, that will be the downfall of the Ellowens."

Camber did not enjoy being talked to as if she were uninitiated. She refused to ask him what he meant.

He didn't notice. "The Ellowens will keep to their virtues," he said. "Kindness, generosity, reliance on goodness. Quite convenient for my purposes—they won't believe that someone within the Keep plots its ruin. You know this. Even with their Tezzarines vanishing, they aren't suspicious of one another."

He sat in the middle of the floor. "A shame you can't see the Boundary as I do, Cam. Secret structures: bright circles within circles, suspended inside pyramids of light. Each balanced upon the others! And silver force flows through the shapes and spreads from them out across the world."

Camber was silent. She saw nothing beyond the extraordinary etchings on the floor and the clear colors of the stained glass. *I'd be able to see, too, if the Master Ebromal would train me.* "This room is suited perfectly to me," Bern said. "Those ancient Ellowens *designed* it to enhance the prayers and enlarge the gen of whoever enters here." He snickered. "They failed to consider that it enhances *any* word spoken. Enlarges *my* power along with theirs.

"I'll summon the power now," he said. Camber knew he was asking her to stay quiet. What he was about to do would take enormous concentration.

Watching him as he closed his eyes, Camber couldn't understand why she'd thought of Bern as an irritation before. It was a great thing he undertook here, to prepare the way for the Shadow King. She should honor him. And why hadn't she noticed how very handsome he was?

His body grew taut. He spoke words Camber didn't know, and somehow as soon as she heard them, she forgot them. He continued that way for what seemed a long time. Camber stayed motionless in the entrance.

At last, Bern picked himself up. He looked about, nodding solemnly. "It's done," he said. "I've pushed the central pyramid just enough. Now all the shapes that touch it will slowly collapse."

Camber bowed devotedly. "What now?" she whispered.

"Tonight the moon will be full. When it's full again, the Shadow King will walk the world of form." He came close to her. "But now is when *your* powers are needed," he said. "You can lay a Dark Invisibility over this House?"

"Ellowen Mayn himself will not be able to find the Boundary House, will not remember that he ought to look for it," she answered proudly.

Chapter 16

Maeve trailed after Jasper as he led Fortune. Evan lay along the mare's neck, face resting against her mane, asleep. Jasper tilted his head back for a moment, checking the sky. Maeve followed his gaze. It had been a cloudy night with few stars to be seen. Now day was just beginning—a gloomy light only a shade brighter than darkness.

When the moon shone and the deer trails didn't wind too much, they made fair progress. But on nights like this one, with clouds screening the sky and trails that doubled back over each other, their headway was slow. Jasper always kept going, saying they must stay ahead of the cold. He was right, for the days were getting shorter and the nights cooler.

Maeve caught up to Jasper at a spot where the trees ended abruptly. An expanse of wild grasses rippled under a circle of lowering sky. She smelled mint. Running forward, she fell to her knees on the soft ground, hands searching for feathery leaves. She crushed the fresh herb between her fingers, breathing in the bracing scent. All about her were fragrant clusters of plants. She rubbed her cheek against their fronds, loving them.

Jasper sank to the ground beside her. "Fortune's happy."

He gestured at the mare munching grass a few paces away, with Evan still sleeping on her back.

Maeve showed Jasper the clumps of mint. She put a sprig in her mouth. "I'm happy, too."

He pulled handfuls of long grass. "I know how to make a garland," he said shyly.

She watched while he wove stalks together. She tried her hand at it. As the cloudy dawn gradually erased more of the night, they found flowers hiding close to the earth. Soon they were twining blossoms into their garlands. Maeve set her creation on Jasper's head. She jumped to her feet and gave him a lady-of-the-court curtsy, just as Lila had shown her how to do long ago. "Prince Jasper, flower of the land," she said in her best highborn accent. She dropped to the earth again, laughing.

Jasper grinned, but he sounded serious when he asked her where she'd learned to talk that way.

"My mother. She was born a high lady." Maeve stopped laughing.

Lila's story poured out: how her father had promised her to a man she despised, how she'd lost everything to love, how her beloved had sailed away and never returned. How Lord Hering had ordered her to tell him the name of her child's father. When she wouldn't, he had cut her himself—slashed her lovely face into ugly welts so that no man would want her. Cast her into slavery, where she had lived out the rest of her days. "But she didn't hate me for costing her so much misery," Maeve finished. "She loved me. And she taught me almost everything she knew."

"She made the blue dress," he said softly.

"Yes. In secret." Maeve pressed her eyes with her fists, as if her knuckles could send back her tears. "And I couldn't be there when she died."

"If she sewed a dress like that in secret, she must have wanted very much for you to escape. She's happy now when she sees you, you can be sure."

"Do you think she can see me?" Maeve wiped her eyes with her sleeve.

He braided a blue flower into a wedge of yellow grass. "I know when I die, I'll look for you, Maeve."

A wave of warmth ran over Maeve's chest and into her face. She hoped Jasper wouldn't notice her blushing. "Do you think it's possible to meet a real person in a dream?" she asked, trying to change the mood.

"In a dream? Why do you ask?"

Maeve told him her dream of the gray hallways and the young man who had guided her to a magical meadow.

"And when you woke, Evan's marks were gone?"

"Vanished."

Jasper whistled; he told her that if she ever went to that starlit place again, he'd be glad to go, too. "That way, maybe I wouldn't have a scar on my arm." His fingers brushed her hair as he settled his garland on her head. "And your mother taught you to sing?"

Maeve nodded. "But she said I must never let on that I could." His face was so close, she could see every hair of his brown whiskers. "She believed that if Lord Indol heard me, he would make me a sentesan."

"So," said Jasper, and fell silent as Evan shuffled across the grass.

The boy leaned against Maeve. "I like your hat," he said.

"Evan," Jasper said. "See that tree over there, the one with the big knot?"

Evan beamed. "I see it."

"Will I hit it?"

Evan nodded vigorously. Maeve watched Jasper gather a few rocks. He threw with great force, his stones hitting the far knothole with a *thwack* and bouncing off. Soon Evan was bounding through the clearing, picking up rocks and throwing them. When the sky began spattering them with rain, Jasper and Evan kept going, bending and throwing until the shower became a downpour.

They ran for cover, pulling the blankets off Fortune. They stood beneath dripping trees, waiting for the cloudburst to blow out. It didn't move on for a long time. When the rain finally stopped, the sun was still hidden. Soaked and shivering, they tried to make a fire. Nothing had escaped the wet.

"Jasper," Maeve said, "do you think we dare find a farmhouse? Dry ourselves?"

Jasper touched the sodden crown of grass and flowers she still wore on her head. "No, Maeve, I don't think we dare. The stripers haven't found you. That means they're still searching."

Rascide, Supreme Seer of Bellandra's School of Sight, stood at a window overlooking Bellan Bay, staring out at the breathtaking view of water and sand.

"Have you ever seen the queen?" his assistant, Chandra, asked.

Rascide turned from the window. Chandra's green robe was a mass of rumples. Why couldn't such a gifted seer manage her appearance? Whenever he admonished her, she always showed the desire to improve. Yet here they were in

Bellandra's palace, about to have an important interview with the queen, and Chandra looked like yesterday's laundry. Not that he cared what impression they made on the queen, a barbarian pretender. "Once, from a distance, many years ago, when King Landen first brought her to Bellandra as his bride. I was young then, Chandra, near the age you are now."

"Why doesn't she ever visit the School of Sight? I thought she was the Great Seer?"

"Chandra, you're quite a child at times."

The young woman's pasty forehead furrowed. "Sir?"

"The queen holds that title, yes, but only because she married King Landen. She had the Great Seer's crystal because her father, Kareed the Invader, stole it from Marla, our last Great Seer. He took it during the *sacking* of this palace."

"But—do you mean to say she has no visions?" Chandra looked scandalized.

"Oh, indeed she does. She's gifted, after a fashion. However, she's had no training, and her powers are exaggerated by her position."

"Respectfully, sir, couldn't she learn from us?"

Rascide coughed dryly. "None of the Supreme Seers, myself included, have thought it fitting to invite an imposter to our school. If she'd insisted, we would have been forced to admit her. Fortunately, it never came to that."

"But if you believe she's not the true Great Seer, who is? Bellandra needs the rightful Seer, surely. If not her, who does the crystal belong to?"

Rascide sniffed. "Since it was stolen, there hasn't been a way to conduct a formal examination."

"Sir, I've heard it said many times that the only way to gain recognition as a seer is to See." She looked down at her lumpy hands.

Yes, Chandra. You sit beside me with your frowzy hair and wrinkled robe because you're a gifted seer. I lead the School of Sight because time and again I have Seen further and faster than the others. "Don't you see, Chandra, she's the *queen*."

Chandra's moonface was still. "There must be a way to test her."

"Indeed," said Rascide. "That's the very thing I intend."

Torina was still uncomfortable in the stately hall of Bellandra's palace. High on the vaulted ceiling, a mark showed where the magical chandelier of Bellandra had once hung. Though she had never been told what happened to it, she knew anyway, from looking with her seer's eye. She'd watched the chandelier crash to the floor, its crystal lights exploding into shards, by the command of her father, Kareed.

Now the Supreme Seer requested her presence. Torina seethed, wondering why, after more than fifteen years, the seers had come with such ceremony to beg an audience with her. They'd invoked every ritual they had to press for this meeting.

When she'd first come to Bellandra, she'd wanted to commune with these men and women who were kindred to her because they, too, could See. She'd traveled to the School of Sight and stepped through its doorways with anticipation and great joy.

They had rebuffed her. Zeerd, then Supreme Seer, had accused her of holding a stolen stone. He would not listen when she explained that Marla had *given* it to her father, Kareed, and asked him to take it to his red-haired daughter.

No, Zeerd had insisted, if she wanted to be a friend to Bellandra, she must return the Great Seer's crystal. And that she would not do.

Two other Supreme Seers had come and gone. Each time, Torina had made hesitant advances, sending messages of goodwill. She had received only icy replies. The current Supreme Seer, Rascide, had been particularly frosty.

Now Torina sat beside King Landen, two steps above the rest of the room. She wore a soft cream-colored gown, her braided hair her only crown. As usual, she was without jewelry. Bellandra had some of the finest gems in the kingdoms, but she preferred to be unadorned. A supple leather pouch containing the Great Seer's crystal rested in her lap.

A swish of fabric heralded the seers—men and women in embroidered green robes. Torina rose to greet them. They bowed formally, then sat on cushions on the carpeted floor.

Their spokesman, a tall man wearing the insignia of the Supreme Seer, remained standing. Torina looked coolly at his smooth black hair, smooth robe, smooth angular face.

"Good evening, Your Majesties. I am Rascide, Supreme Seer."

Torina nodded, hiding impatience.

"We would not disturb you, my queen, if it were not important," he continued. "We have encountered a disruption."

"Of what nature?" she asked.

"Then *your* visions have not found anything of note, Your Highness?" He managed to convey disrespect even as he gave her the title.

"I confess, I haven't looked in the crystal for a day or two," she answered.

His black eyes expressed doubt. "Would you honor us by gazing now?"

Honor them. The way a jackdaw might honor a nightingale by trying to sing. They don't believe in me. Then why are they here?

A round-faced young woman sat in the middle of the first row of seers. Torina decided to ignore the spokesman, focusing instead on the soft face of the young seer before her. "Certainly, Rascide."

Rascide joined the other seers, taking a cushion. Torina wished her uneasiness would go away. It increased. According to Bellandran custom, Seeings were to be done in private. If she asked to be left alone, would they be offended? If she gazed then and there, would they scorn her lack of refinement?

Something's wrong. I need to find out what it is. She took out the crystal.

Quietly seated, Rascide watched. He had trapped the queen. She was about to be stripped of her ridiculous claim to being the Great Seer. All the top-ranking seers in Bellandra would witness her degradation. He had wanted this moment for years.

Rascide knew that many seers hoped Queen Torina would be able to shed light on their predicament. Suddenly, the day before, many of them had become unable to See. Others saw only cloudy visions, impossible to decipher. Rascide's powers were diminished, but he could still See. Oh, yes, he could still See, and the rest of the seers knew it. When this upstart foreigner could not find any visions, she'd be forced to turn Marla's crystal over to him. Even her husband, King Landen, whom she had some-how bewitched, wouldn't be able to stop it.

The queen withdrew the shimmering Bellandran stone while Rascide controlled his fury. He, the Supreme Seer, had never beheld Bellandra's most important crystal before!

Without an invocation, without discretion, without waiting for the seers to lower their eyes, the queen gazed. Rascide did not look down. Why should he? He owed her no courtesy.

She took on stillness that would credit a promising novice. Rascide saw the color leave her skin. Her slender hands tightened on the crystal.

"Torina." It was the king speaking. "What is it?"

The queen looked at the seers. "Many of you are Sightless? Gray fog shrouds your visions?"

Rascide frowned. Who had betrayed the seers by send-ing a message to the queen?

Chandra bowed her head. "Yes, my queen. We don't know why."

The queen spoke to Chandra. "What do you know of the Shadow King?"

Someone had told her everything. Rascide fought to govern himself while Chandra gave her answer.

"I can say only what I've been taught," Chandra declared. "The Shadow King abides in a different realm from ours but seeks control over all souls. Once his influence overtakes a soul, that person loses sight of love, succumbs to greed, is full of lies. Since the Shadow King cannot enter this realm himself, he depends on servants to work his evil here."

What an excellent student Chandra is, Rascide mused. *I could not have explained the Shadow King better myself.*

The red-haired queen turned to her husband. "It's as she

says. And this Shadow King has been thwarted for centuries from walking in our world with a form of his own."

The king's expression made Rascide remember that the peaceful Landen was also a famous warrior, a man who insisted that Bellandrans be versed in martial skills. "Thwarted?"

"What holds him back is a special Boundary that forms a protective shield around our world." She paused. "Made out of the resonance of all the souls who live, but kept in balance by the Ellowens of the Keep." As she looked at King Landen, Rascide thought he saw unspoken words flying between the two. Both looked extremely worried. "One of the Keep Houses is dedicated to the Silver Boundary," the queen went on, "protecting us all from the Shadow King. He can't walk in the physical realm so long as the Boundary is in place."

"And now?" asked the king.

"Somehow, he is gaining strength to overcome that Boundary," she said. "And the weakness in the Boundary is the reason the seers' visions are fogged."

"And if the Boundary *is* overcome?" King Landen asked urgently.

The queen shivered. "If the Boundary falls, we'll hardly know our earth—the heartwood in trees will turn gray and thin, and blood will run cold and merciless in the human heart. . . ." Her mouth twisted as though she held back horrified cries. "The Shadow King will be triumphant."

"How is the Boundary being weakened?" the king prodded.

"I'm not certain."

Everyone was silent. Rascide struggled to net his thoughts, which flew about in chaos. King Landen's glance found him. "As Supreme Seer," he asked, "how much of this did you understand?"

"Most of it, sir." Rascide didn't bother to note the reactions of the other seers.

"Why not tell what you knew?" the king demanded.

Rascide coughed. "The teachings of the Shadow King and the Silver Boundary are only for healers and seers."

"By whose decree? Didn't your student say 'seeks control over *all* souls'? Are the souls of those who are not seers or healers unimportant?" the king challenged.

"No, sir. Of course not. But this knowledge might not safely reside with untrained people."

"If that is what you believe, why, then, are you here?" asked the king.

"It's customary to consult the Great Seer during a catastrophe."

"And do you know now, who this is?" The king lifted his wife's hand. Rascide didn't answer. The king stood. "Do all of you know who this is?"

Chandra got to her knees awkwardly, tangled in her rumpled robe. "I know, my king." Other seers followed. Soon all but Rascide had acknowledged the queen, but he couldn't humble himself to her. *She's nothing but a crudely gifted sham, shored up by a spy, and I will find out who the spy is.*

"Landen, I have something more to tell the seers." The king waited as Queen Torina stood beside him, speaking to the group. "If you do your gazing in pairs, your visions will have more light."

It was wrong, Rascide believed, this cavalier mingling of gifts. The interference of another's mind would merely scatter a vision.

180

"Working together," the queen said, "we may have a few more hours of Sight. We must begin now, lending strength to one another."

The seers stared at her with blank faces. "Now," the king ordered. His voice rang through the room.

As Chandra scooted in front of another seer, Rascide held himself aloof.

"Every one of you is needed," the queen said. She descended the short stair. Rascide sat rigid as she folded gracefully to the floor in front of him. "You and I will gaze together," she told him. "We'll use your crystal to begin with."

To begin with. Her words contained a promise—he would have his chance with Marla's crystal. Rascide was sure that once he did, he would know every secret of the future.

He set his crystal, the finest the School of Sight had to offer, between them. He muttered a brief prayer of invocation. The queen didn't seem to notice, for she had gone into stillness.

Rascide suspended all personal thoughts and feelings, disengaging from the anchors of ordinary time and place. As the stillness removed his indignation, he sat in the quiet that was only to be found outside of time. When the surface of the crystal expanded in his vision, he let himself be drawn into it.

He sensed that he was above the grounds of the Healer's Keep, though he couldn't see below him. *The Invisibility prevents more Sight.* Cold shadows swirled. The air beat rhythmically. Dark, fearsome shapes floated close to him. *Birds. Birds belonging to the Shadow King.* Rascide's mind wanted to get away from the cold and the shadows. He did not allow his thoughts to be turned.

"Ebes," he heard someone say. "Birds that fly through the realms of sleep, serving the Shadow King."

Rascide's concentration broke. He was aware of being on the floor in Bellandra's palace, dazed by what he'd seen. "Yes," he said. "Ebes." He'd just echoed Queen Torina. She had Seen before he had! And his own vision had been clearer and more far-reaching than those he'd had recently. Somehow, her presence had increased his sight.

Rascide peered into his crystal again. Nothing came to him. Nothing but smoky gray mist, denser now than it had been earlier that day. He'd been able to see through it before—now he could not.

"Landen," the queen went on, "this attack is like nothing we've faced. The healers and the Boundary they keep are being weakened from someone or something *inside* the Keep. Whatever it is has enlisted these Ebes."

"It's true," Rascide said. He put his head down, bowing to the queen. "I was wrong. Accept my apologies for doubting you."

Astonishingly, she bowed to him in return. "Accept my thanks for combining your gift with mine, allowing me to see what was hidden from me."

"But the Ebes?" the king asked. "Tell us exactly what they are and how we may fight them. Where do they live? How can they be killed?"

Queen Torina inclined her head toward Rascide. "Let the Supreme Seer speak."

Rascide faced King Landen. "It appears they don't live in our world at all, sir," he said. The queen nodded. "They dwell in the Shadow realm, and move through the worlds of sleep." He paused. "I don't know if they could be killed, sir."

"If not killed, can they be defeated?"

The quiet in the room was very loud as Rascide considered what to say. "Perhaps a dream warrior could defeat them, sir."

"Dream warrior? Where might a dream warrior be found?"

"If one exists, the Ellowen healers would know."

"Draft a message," the king said shortly. Then he burst into action, striding from the room, calling for Captain Andris.

Chapter 17

As Ellowen Mayn opened the seals on the main gate of the Keep, he greeted the day with the same ritual he'd performed thousands of times before, thanking God for the glory of the morning.

The familiar words didn't bring him joy. When he looked at the fountain and beautifully placed rocks and plants of the welcoming garden, he felt only sadness. He struggled with Ellowen Renaiya's death, made worse by the disappearance of the last Tezzarine. For days, grief had affected his perception until even the sunrise seemed lacking, as if some of the light had gone out of the world. The Ellowen's funeral had been very difficult. Healers normally lived to an advanced age. Impossible to explain how Renaiya had died. She'd been found in her bed without a trace of sickness or injury anywhere on her.

Mayn felt tired through and through, and a new stiffness made his joints ache. Soon the day's work would begin, but the harmonies seemed disarrayed. It wasn't for Mayn to monitor how things were going at the Keep—that lot fell to the Council trio. With Ellowen Renaiya gone, another Mystive had been sent for. In the meantime, no one wanted to wrestle with Hester. The Chief Draden had all the earmarks of the rest of the Draden tribe: unbending with regulations, full of self-importance. But that was the way of the Keep—Dradens attended to all the details of worldly life, leaving the healers free to work their art. Mayn, for one, had never missed tangling with the world. He much preferred his duties as the Keep's most knowledgeable Sangiv.

He started for the infirmary. He would tell the Draden who served there that he wouldn't be able to teach today. His mind wasn't clear enough. It was high time he spent a day in contemplation. He needed to get some peace and comprehension again.

As he headed along the walkway threading the gardens, a student approached from the opposite direction. Bern.

"Health, Ellowen Mayn." Bern radiated abundant gen. "May I walk with you, sir?"

"Certainly. I was about to inform Draden Dale that I won't be supervising in the surgery today."

"Not ill, I hope?" Bern fell into step beside Mayn.

Mayn fought a gray fogginess that seemed to penetrate his head. "Sorry, Bern. Yes, I have allowed my gen to become depleted. Would you deliver my message to Draden Dale?"

"Of course, Ellowen. But first, let me see you to your cottage."

"Thank you. Considerate of you." Mayn leaned on Bern's supporting arm. Wretched timing to fall sick now, but at least he knew how to rejuvenate. He'd be well again before the end of the day. All he needed was a little rest.

After seeing Ellowen Mayn to his door, Bern headed toward the Boundary House. All the Ellowens were in decline—the leak in the Boundary muddled their minds, while dream visits from the Ebes drained their gen. Cam's Dark Invisibility was apparently completely effective—Bern had not seen a single Ellowen go near the Boundary House since she had put the Dark Invisibility in place.

It wouldn't be surprising if Mayn, like Renaiya, did not survive the night. The Sangiv! What a stroke. Legend put Mayn head and shoulders above the other healers, the oldest and best in the Keep. Yet he'd been defeated, without ever seeming to guess he was in a fight. Bern almost wished it were possible to battle openly with someone who had a chance to defeat him. Sara flashed into his mind. *"You're nothing, Bern."*

She was wrong about him; he was much more than nothing. He'd been right about her power to knock down seals and protections. The last Tezzarine gone! He had known from the moment of Ellowen Mayn's first lesson, when forceful bursts of gen had betrayed Sara's gift, how the Tezzarine's protection could be done away with. Bern remembered how difficult it had been that day to let Mayn believe he was only a dull, Draden-gifted novice.

Bern spoke the word Camber had taught him to dispel the Dark Invisibility. The Boundary House, which had appeared as a simple pile of stones, sprang into view. He entered it, using his key. He kept the door jealously locked. Cam was a faithful Ebromal, but she had no right to this place. It was too powerful for anyone but him.

He'd brought the knife with him today, the one sent by Bellandra's Master Ebromal. Draden Hester had innocently delivered it to him. Seals set on the gates, enormously weakened since the departure of the last Tezzarine, had registered a faint warning when the knife entered the Keep, but the Dradens had given all their attention to a suspicious bunch of herbs, sent in a separate package with the same delivery to throw them off the scent. No one had given a second thought to the innocuous box for Bern.

Sitting in the middle of the Boundary House floor, Bern reverently took out the Ebromal knife. Short and sharp, its thin blade could cut through stone. When Bern was done with what he meant to do here today, it would cut through *more* than stone; it would penetrate all the layers of magic arrayed in this room.

He was still dazzled by the potency the Ellowens had built into this place. When he spoke, he could feel rays of power gathering around him, answering his will, infusing the knife with a killing force that went far beyond matter.

When he was done, he rested for a while.

He'd gone over every inch of the marble floor. By examining the inlaid carvings, he'd come to understand that the Ellowens of old had taken a great risk—they had assembled symbols for the most important mystic objects in Bellandra and then made otherworldly pathways to those objects from this floor! *To give themselves a way to watch over Bellandra's magic wealth, no doubt.*

Maybe they'd never thought of what could be done here by someone who used their work against them, never thought of how the powers held inside the mystic objects they had connected to the Boundary House could be stolen. *Without a hand being laid on them.*

Bern knelt on the floor beside the intricate carving of Bellandra's famous Sword. He let Shadow force build in his hands. When it pulsed through him, he sent it through the knife, plunging its blade to the heart of the Sword. He spoke the charm that would open the pathway to the Sword and bleed its magic into the realms of the Shadow King.

After he pulled the knife free, there was only a single fine line to show what he had done. If anyone looked closely with the eyes of an Ellowen, they would see much more. But the Ellowens would never look at this floor again.

Next to the Sword was the circle of diamonds representing the crystal of the Great Seer. A smile played at Bern's lips. He put the knife away. He would allow the queen of Bellandra a few more days before he struck again, before he sliced the crystal and drained its power, too.

Let her see the king's health fail, before her own health is taken.

In the palace of Bellandra, in a small room outside King Landen's sickbed, Queen Torina and Supreme Seer Rascide sat with the Great Seer's crystal between them. Though they drew upon their combined gifts, they saw only shadows, thick and gray.

"Rascide, there's no more we can do as seers. Not only am I unable to See; the crystal itself seems dim, as if it were made of poor glass."

He nodded, looking like a different man from the haughty Supreme Seer she had met, his black hair rumpled, his robe twisting. "Has there been any word from the Healer's Keep?"

"Not yet." What could be keeping Andris? It wasn't like him to be late with a message. And *this* message was of such importance—warning the Ellowens of the weakening Boundary, asking them if a dream warrior could be found, telling Sara to come home.

Rascide sagged like a stalk snapped off from its roots. "If only I had acted sooner! Half a day might have made a difference. Now Bellandra pays the price for my pride, and with my gift blinded, I can give nothing."

Torina looked around at the rich furniture, the ornate lamps holding golden flames. If beauty could be traded for truth, she would have all the answers. "Though our gifts are gone, we still have hearts and minds. We don't need our gifts to know that the king is ill and the Sword of Bellandra has lost its light. We must do something, Rascide. We cannot let the king die."

Rascide's head fell lower; Torina stared at the crystal. A strong chill passed over her. The crystal, too, looked gray, with no sparkle deep in its heart.

She stood, but it seemed as if the darkness at her feet thickened, wrapping her legs. Dizzy, she staggered, sinking to the floor. She heard Rascide shouting, as though from a long distance away.

Orlo rode a big gentle horse along the waterfront. Warren, the master for Pier Five, had set him riding lookout for Maeve. Orlo didn't like Warren much; Warren begrudged him all the vahss he needed. It seemed to take more and more to keep his heart steady—Orlo always knew when the vahss was wearing off, because his heart began thumping loudly again and his mind wasn't easy.

Though the sun had gone down, so many dock lanterns shone that no one had to stop work because of darkness. The shift was changing; waterfront slaves poured off the docks, replaced by more slaves surging from the other direction. Shouts of foremen and ship captains carried over the constant roar of Mantedi.

Orlo headed up the main road to give the piers a chance to settle into the new shift. He wasn't allowed to roam far, just a half-mile west of the water, because his task was to look for Maeve. Warren and Lord Morlen had told him Maeve would likely make for the ships and try to leave Sliviia.

The miners were trooping home. Many of the free lived in camps out past where the waterfront streets ended, between the city and the great wall that hemmed it. Orlo knew many free died every day trying to get over the wall. He wondered if Maeve would die. But if she did, Lord Morlen wouldn't be happy. He wanted her alive.

Part
Four

The
Dreamwen
Stone

Chapter 18

Sara and Dorjan stood at the guardrail of the *Lanya*. The horizon flashed lightning, and a rough wind buffeted their faces. "Odd, isn't it," Sara said. "Last night was clear enough to see the moon."

"Nearly full," Dorjan added, nodding. "Now the whole sky is cloudy."

"This boat is too slow." Sara hunched against the wind. Confined to the ship almost a month, and Captain Navar said they were still seven days from shore. She wished she had her mother's gift and could look into a crystal to see *where* in Sliviia Dorjan's sister was. Vasex, her tutor, had said Sliviia was almost as large as this great water they traveled over. How were they to find one girl, without knowing so much as her name?

Fat drops began spattering their faces. A sailor running across the deck yelled as he passed, pointing at the sky. "Storm will be upon us in no time!" Another sailor rushed by. "Best get below!" he shouted.

Surprised by the sudden fierceness of the rain, Sara and Dorjan ducked for their cabin. There they dried themselves hurriedly. They put on their Keep jackets—cream-colored, thick-knit and warm, with snug hoods and mufflike pockets for their hands. The floor of the little cabin sloped steeply as the ship tossed. Rain pelted their porthole. Sara heard the wind howling.

"That wind sounds as if it could tear this ship apart," Dorjan said.

Sara felt uneasy as the walls of their cabin groaned. "How did the weather change so fast?"

The ship plunged violently, slinging her into a corner. She inched along the rising floor toward Dorjan, who reached a hand to her, but the ship threw her backward. She landed against the wall. Dorjan and the old sea chest came tumbling at her. She pushed out of the way just before the chest crashed into the wall, its wooden sides splitting with a loud crack. Dorjan scrambled toward her as she grabbed the edge of her bunk and managed to pull herself up. He sat next to her.

"Remember the small boat near the stern?" he asked, nearly yelling to be heard over the shrieking timbers of the ship. "We should get to it. The *Lanya* won't live out the storm." He clasped her hand. "Can you swim?"

Sara nodded. They pushed across the pitching floor to the door. By the time they reached the deck again, the ship had rocked so far over that the deck was nearly sideways to the ocean. The *Lanya* rolled back upright as they clawed their way to the guardrail and hung on. Violent bursts of spray drenched them. One moment Sara was looking at a wall of water; the next moment her stomach lurched as the ship plunged into the steep trough between two waves.

The *Lanya* seemed no more than a mouse in the paws of a giant cat. The ocean yowled and spit, shaking the ship mercilessly. "The boat!" Dorjan cried in Sara's ear. Though he was so close, she couldn't see him, blinded by sheets of salty spray. When she tried to pull herself along the sharply tilting deck, the wind roared against her. The rail, slippery with rain, dipped into the sea. She clung to it, a rush of ocean filling her mouth. The rail lifted out again. She squeezed her eyes frantically, trying to clear them.

Glassy, gray-green water rose cliff-like in front of her. The *Lanya* yawed far to the starboard, and the guardrail went under again. Sara lost her grip on the rail. As the ocean swept her up, she heard a booming crash. For a moment, she caught sight of the ship's mast, snapped like a stick by the ocean's power.

Sara's lungs burned as she searched for a spot of air. The air had disappeared, abandoning her to a world of water.

She pushed against the water, making her legs kick, making her arms stroke. She burst through the ocean's angry surface to snatch a breath of air. A plank hurtled into her. She clutched it. The ocean seemed determined to wrest it from her grasp, but she hung on. She'd have no chance without something to float her. She kicked madly, tossed on swells so steep the troughs were liquid valleys. Just as she would catch a breath, a new wave would slap her in the face.

On and on she fought, caught in the seething ocean, buffeted by whirling debris. Over and over she stole enough air from the grudging sky to stay alive. After hours of battling, her body felt as if it were made of bruised stone, stone that wanted to sink. And still the rain lashed on, and still the ocean churned, while Sara clung to her plank with numb hands.

She wouldn't allow herself to be drowned by a storm. She needed to reach Sliviia and find the Dreamwen Stone, stop the Shadow King. She wanted to live so she might one day hear a Tezzarine again.

And she had to find Dorjan. He couldn't have drowned.

"Mantedi." Jasper pointed.

Maeve looked down a steep ravine. Finally, after weeks of journeying, below them lay a vast, walled city, close against a large bay. To the east stretched the Minwenda Ocean, and to the west the plant life dried up and the land looked rusted. They had been catching glimpses of the western desert from the ridges of the forest they traveled through. Now it was near.

A network of roads led into mounds of bare slag, heaped almost as high as foothills. All around the city, a tall wall extended, the same rough orange color as the desert. The top of the wall looked wide enough to walk upon and had sentry turrets spaced along it. Maeve wondered why the wall needed to be so thick, broken only by a single wide gate. And why did it continue into the ocean? The line of rusty rock went out into the sea a long way. Mantedi's waterfront bulged into the bay, a jumble of piers where ships and boats anchored by the hundreds.

Evan peered at the city, his eyes round. "So many," he said.

Mantedi looked like a dirty, roiling river, moving in graceless streams from the piers in the east to the ugly heaps of slag westward. The road leading to the gate was full of people and animals waiting to get in. Maeve saw groups of zind, their black and gray stripes made tiny by distance, checking each arrival.

"Not safe for you to enter by the gate," Jasper said.

She looked at the wall. "How will we get in?"

"Evan and I will go ahead of you. We'll meet you by the wall when it gets dark. I'll string Fortune's harness and halter into one rope, and throw it over the wall." He studied the wall, narrowing his eyes. "I might need to tie the blankets in, too, to get past all that height. Then you can climb it."

"I don't know how to climb, Jasper."

"Prop your feet against the wall and pull on the rope. It's no harder than anything else."

Maeve looked at him affectionately. He made it sound simple. "Look how the sun glances off the top of the wall," she said.

"They must have mortared pieces of glass along it." He pointed. "See the long stretch of wall there between those two sentry turrets? That's where I'll throw the rope. An hour after dark."

Maeve looked the spot up and down. Her heart beat the way it had in Lord Indol's study when she had stolen her price. "All right," she said softly.

"Good, then," said Jasper.

"I'll keep the gold. They might search you at the gate." She didn't want Jasper killed.

"Leave the gold. What runaway ever got out of Sliviia by *buying* passage across to Glavenrell? They did it by stowing away or getting service on a ship."

"Because what runaway ever *had* gold?" She didn't like arguing with him, but she wasn't going to leave the gold outside Mantedi after they'd carried it so far.

Jasper shook his head, but bent to his shoes. He handed her the gold, warm from his feet. She put it into her fraying scarf and tied it around her waist.

"Evan," Jasper said, "you ready to be my brother?"

Evan gave Maeve a tight hug. She kissed his cheek. "I'll see you when it's dark."

Jasper handed her a blanket. He checked Fortune's harness and helped Evan onto the mare's back. "So, then," he said.

"So," she answered.

"It may take us a while to get to the road. We'll have to pick our way carefully and go back a distance to get around this ravine." Maeve watched as he took the halter and led Fortune a few steps. It was odd not to follow him. It would be very odd not to see his sturdy shoulders in front of her. She blinked.

Then Jasper dropped the halter and marched back to her. He threw his arms around her. She kissed his face. "We *will* see you when it's dark," he said into her neck.

"Yes, Jasper. You will."

He took up Fortune's halter again. Evan waved.

Maeve looked intently at the road until Jasper and Evan finally came into sight, part of the human snail inching through the gates of Mantedi. She gritted her teeth when her friends got near the front of the line, but the zind didn't pause for them. They went into the city.

She lay in the bracken behind a screen of trees, on the blanket Jasper had left with her. She was comfortable there, against the ground. There wasn't anything more to do until night came. She might as well sleep.

She held the Dreamwen Stone, wishing she could understand its music. Soon now, they'd find a way to get on board a ship. They'd cross over to the eastern kingdoms and look for Cabis Denon. Her father might be able to tell her how to use the treasure she carried.

Chapter 19

Sara lifted her head from the wide plank that supported her. She ached all through and there was a hideous taste of salt water down her throat. Around her, the sea was calm, the sun just west of the midheaven, and glaringly bright. The storm had blown off at last.

Searching the horizon, she saw plenty of debris she took to be from the wreck of the *Lanya*, but nothing that looked like a boat or a person. She bit her chapped lips. "Dorjan," she said aloud. "Dorjan, where are you?" She cupped one hand around her mouth, calling, "Dorjan!" Her throat hurt. The sea looked horribly vast and deep, the sky endless.

Only the lapping water answered.

"Dorjan!" During their journey together, she'd grown used to having him near. She liked to see his smile flash across his face, just as the sun at dawn would flash across the water. When he smiled, the remoteness that usually filled his eyes went away.

"Dorjan!" He couldn't have died. She couldn't be drifting on the ocean without him.

A bigger piece of wood floated nearby: several curving, painted timbers, snapped raggedly on the ends but still pinned together. They made a shallow bowl—must have come from the side of the ship. The bowl looked like a better raft than Sara's single plank. Awkwardly, she paddled toward it with her hands. She had to dunk in the cold ocean again, but succeeded in climbing onto it.

She hauled in the plank that had saved her; it might serve as a rough oar. She urged her makeshift boat toward bits of drifting debris, hoping to find something to take away the sickening taste of the raw ocean. But all she saw was more scattered pieces of floating wood. She wished she had wakened soon enough to capture some rainwater before the hot sun took it all back.

"Dorjan!" she cried. Again nothing answered her.

She spent the afternoon drifting under the merciless sun, calling for Dorjan. When the sun was a red mass on the ocean's rim, she was too hoarse to yell anymore.

She shivered. Her clothes had dried salt-stiffened and rough. The hooded jacket seemed a pitiful defense against the chill of evening. It would get colder. It would get dark.

She thought of her mother, and the Great Seer's crystal. "See me," she prayed. "Oh, see me." But even if her mother found her in the crystal, it would take weeks to get to her in a ship.

As the stars began to twinkle, Sara lay on the timbers of her refuge, looking up at the great dome of jeweled light above her. Its beauty was too big to give any comfort. Fear, wide as the ocean, pushed at her, like the dark water pushing at her raft.

She prayed for Dorjan, bringing up the image of his face as close as she could.

A fat moon moved in and out of clouds as Maeve set out for the Mantedi wall. She suddenly wished she could call Jasper and Evan back. Mantedi frightened her. Perhaps it would have been better to go west into the desert, or continue on north—find some hidden land where the zind never went.

But Lila had believed Cabis Denon was alive. If Maeve didn't find him, he'd never know he had a daughter. She needed to get to Glavenrell. If only there were another way, besides Mantedi Bay, to start across the ocean.

Maeve slipped on pebbles. She fell, sliding. When she stopped, she was close to the wall, her heart thudding. Would the noise she'd made bring anyone? But city sounds were all she heard: muted human shouts blending with the cries of animals.

The wall loomed above, three times her height, made of rock without a handhold anywhere. Who had built such a thing? Maeve hoped she was in the right place. The clouds were thickening and when she tried to see the sentry turrets, all was shadowy. What was it like on the other side of the wall? What if Jasper wasn't able to throw her a rope? She groped along the wall, her hand feeling for a dangling halter. Prickly shrubs grew next to her; she had to reach across them.

There! A knotted rope. Had Jasper's hand tied those knots? She gripped the rope, sensing through its fibers. Her fingers told her there was an echo of Jasper there.

Maeve tied the blanket around her shoulders. She wedged herself between two bushes, ignoring their prickers. She wrapped her hands around the rope, pulling on it to help her feet take a step up the wall. Her arms had always been strong and she remembered Jasper's words: "It's no harder than anything else."

She progressed, moving upward. It was slow going and the darkness pressed in on her. The darkness! Suddenly she longed for its protection—as it was broken by swinging lights along the base of the wall. She saw shadowy stripes grouped inside circles of lantern light, and heard the steady tramping of boots.

Panic pumped through her. She scrabbled and clawed up the wall. When she reached the top, something sharp gashed her palm—she'd forgotten the glass embedded there. Never mind. She swung her body up, hauling the rope after her with desperate speed.

The top of the wall was easily three feet across. More lanterns now, but these were on the wall itself! Stripers advancing toward her, along the walkway made by the top of the wall. They marched with precision, gray boots made visible by the lanterns they carried. In moments, they would be upon her. She needed to tie her rope to something in order to climb down the other side of the wall, but she didn't have time.

She tossed the whole knotted harness over the wall. She scrambled to hang at the wall's edge, cutting her hand again, not daring to call to Jasper. She let go.

A pair of arms caught her and then she and Jasper were both on the ground. He clutched her, whispering her name. "Lie low, Maeve. Shhh. Wait for them to pass."

She lay as still as she could, listening while the zind went by above. She could feel Jasper's heart racing next to her own, could feel his overwhelming relief at seeing her again.

"They'll be back." Jasper rose, reaching for her hand. "What's this? You're bleeding."

"It's nothing. . . . The glass."

"I'll tie it up." Jasper rummaged in her scarf and found the last strips of cloth they hadn't used for clothes. He tied a bandage around her palm.

"Evan?" she asked.

"Beside the building yonder, with Fortune." He gathered up the wad of rope and blankets she'd thrown down. He set to work untying them. "You were lucky," he said.

"You're my luck," she answered.

He led her through the shadows to where Evan stood waiting, hands twined in the mane of the patient mare. When Maeve put her arm around the boy, he clung to her while Jasper harnessed Fortune.

"Shall we head toward the docks?" Jasper whispered. He took Maeve's right arm; Evan held the hand that wasn't hurt. Jasper wrapped Fortune's halter around his wrist.

Hurrying away from the wall, they were soon making their way through a network of dim alleys. Gaunt, ragged women and children extended thin arms, asking for food. They must be free, for they weren't marked. Maeve had never mixed with the free in Slivona, because her life had been contained by the bathhouse and Lord Indol's mansion, where free were never seen. Now she wished she had a bushel of loaves to give.

They came to a wider street where lanterns hanging on high posts cast shallow light. Maeve wondered if Mantedi ever slept. People milled about, mostly men, a few women, the occasional child. Many had scars on their faces—the most common mark seemed to be squares within squares.

Evan kept tight hold of Maeve's hand and Jasper squeezed her arm from the other side. As they went farther on toward the sea, the crush of people got denser; the city seemed louder and more awake the longer they walked. The mixture of odors was overpowering—unwashed bodies, garbage, and lantern oil overlaid with a fishy smell. Maeve didn't see any trees in this stretch of Mantedi, only buildings of stone and wood.

Many of the men passing by had soot smearing their faces. Miners. Lila had told Maeve about mines—how it was always night inside the earth. Maeve saw no marks on the blackened faces. The lowborn free. Was she one of them now? Cabis Denon had been lowborn free, and from a Dreamwen family.

"The grandson of the last great Dreamwen, the only son of an only daughter. . . . You may be a Dreamwen, Maeve."

A man rode toward them on a brown horse. Something about him made Maeve look at him closely. And although the rider was thinner than she remembered him, she recognized him at once. It was Orlo.

Chapter 20

Sara knew she was dreaming. It wasn't a good dream— a flock of dark birds was hunting her, searching her out, wheeling nearer and nearer. She tried to waken but nothing she did released her from the dream. The birds circled in, about twelve of them, getting closer. Closer and closer.

A splash and a shower of spray shook her awake. She was lying inside the curving raft under shining stars. She heard coughing and spluttering.

"Dorjan?" she said hoarsely.

"Yes." He coughed and blew.

"Grab the wood!" she cried. He did, rocking her raft. She edged to the far side of the molded timbers. "I'll balance you while you climb up."

He tried; she could see he tried. "Sorry," he muttered. "No strength."

"Hold on." Sara plunged into the sea on her side of the raft and swam around to Dorjan through numbingly cold water. He hung on to the boards next to her. "Dorjan, I'm so glad you're alive." She put a hand on his shoulder, needing to touch him. "I'm so, so happy to see you." She noticed that her voice was grainy. "I'll help you."

His smile flashed. "Sara, I know it's not far. Just now it might as well be a hundred miles." His voice sounded parched, too.

They hung in the water, shivering. When he was a little recovered, they worked together until he was in the raft. Sara got herself up into it, too.

"Thank you," he whispered.

"I searched for you. Where did you come from? The bottom of the ocean?"

"Nearly."

"Look, Dorjan, aren't the stars bright?"

"Very. A shame we can't use them to start a little fire."

"That's a fine moon."

"Very fine." His face in the moonlight was the picture of exhaustion.

She lay down next to him, nestling up beside him for warmth. There wasn't much warmth to be had. He slid his hand into hers. He closed his eyes.

Dorjan was soon asleep, but Sara was slower. She wondered if she were dreaming, though, as unearthly light gathered around the raft. The light had a pearlescent quality; in its rays was an echo of the Tezzarine's song. Sara didn't move, afraid that if she stirred, she'd break the moment. And indeed, when a small swell rolled under them, rocking the raft, the pearly light faded and the song was gone.

More than anything, Sara wanted that song to come back.

When she recognized Orlo among the great crowd of strangers in Mantedi, Maeve felt overjoyed. Orlo had always been kind to her, as kind as he could be under slavery. A good man, a man she'd known all her life, the closest she'd come to having a father.

"Maeve! Evan!" His booming voice threw her memory back to the bathhouse. But how thin he was. What had he been through since she'd last seen him? Had he, too, run away? He drew his horse even with her. "What good fortune to find you."

She took a step toward him. A group of men and boys with soot-circled eyes streamed between her and Orlo's horse. She waited for them to go by.

Orlo leaned down in his saddle. "I know a dock man," he said. "Has me a berth on a ship to Glavenrell, working as a deckhand."

"That's wonderful, Orlo." Maeve's spirits lit with hope.

"I can get you on, too. Ship's due to sail at dawn."

"*This* night's dawn?"

"This night's dawn. We'd best be on our way. Don't want to miss it."

Jasper was looking doubtful. She nodded to him, smiling, ignoring the cautious shaking of his head. He didn't know Orlo as she did, didn't understand. He shrugged then, putting Evan up on the mare.

"I'm so glad I found you, Maeve." Orlo turned east.

The street possessed them again, swallowing any chance for more speech. Maeve fell into step beside Orlo's horse. Every now and then, she looked over her shoulder. Jasper plodded behind, guiding Fortune through the crowds.

After a while the street opened onto a waterfront laced with long piers. So many lanterns were strung that their light seemed to make an eerie twilight. Many ships stood at anchor. Gangs of men, most of them deeply marked, loaded and unloaded cargo, the crates they lifted hitting the boards of the docks while foremen shouted without letup.

Jasper pulled Fortune up next to Maeve, pointing at a water trough that sat on one of the smaller piers. Maeve waved to Orlo. He stopped next to the trough, dismounting. His horse bent to drink, Fortune nudging in beside. Orlo nodded to a ham-handed man standing on the pier. "Evening, Anson. Wonder if you might carry a message for me. Tell Warren I'll be bringing some cargo."

Though hundreds of men moved up and down the pier, Anson slipped away so fast it was as if he'd never been there. Maeve stood on the boards at the pier's edge, out of the way of the rush and the roar. She looked over the side, where rugged pilings disappeared into deep water. Lantern light flickered off the ocean's uneasy surface.

Beside her, Orlo smiled in a way she'd never seen him smile. "The word was, when you left, that a heap of gold left, too," he said.

Maeve remembered the gold lying loose inside the scarf knotted around her waist. Her heart beat too fast. Was he asking for passage money?

He took her hand. "Little Maeve. Lila the Fair's daughter."

At his touch, a gray chill slithered up her arm. She tried to shake it off. Orlo had given her many reassuring pats over the years, and they had never disturbed her before. But the *knowing* that spoke to her through her sense of touch had always told the truth. "Need to rest a moment," she murmured. She dropped his hand and sat on the weatherworn boards, letting her feet dangle off the pier, trying to catch Jasper's eye. Jasper, next to Fortune, was splashing his face.

Wrong. It's all wrong. If Orlo were a runaway, would he be riding a horse through the streets of Mantedi? She played with the knots of her scarf, loosening them. She balled the scarf into her hands. She leaned toward the water, letting the scarf slip away. The soft plop it would have made landing in the ocean was lost in the din of the docks.

Orlo heaved his body into place beside her. "After tonight, no one will hunt you." He took her hand again. Cold shadow covered her, stifling and gray. She was suddenly sure that Lord Morlen had found a way to Orlo.

Lord Morlen. The Dreamwen Stone at her breast vibrated. The Stone! If Lord Morlen caught her, he must not find the Dreamwen Stone.

"Let's go on," Maeve said. "Don't want to miss your berth." She stood. In the moments it took Orlo to get to his feet, she unfastened the Dreamwen Stone from around her neck. She got behind him as she turned to go. She dropped the Stone into the ocean and watched it sink. Her heart keened with immediate loss.

She ran toward the teeming road. If she could lose herself in the maze of people, maybe she could avoid Orlo and Lord Morlen. The boards of the pier thudded under her feet. She had to dodge right and left, left and right, elbows jabbing her, her breath coming in sharp gasps. *Please, let the dockworkers hide me. Please, let Jasper and Evan get away. Without me, they stand a chance.*

She bumped into a big, bald-headed man, who seized her arm with such violence that she came to a wrenching stop. "Please, sir. Please let me go." She twisted in his grasp.

He looked over her shoulder. She didn't like the way he smiled. "No, no. I won't be letting go." She turned and saw Orlo, sitting his horse, bearing down on them. "This the cargo?" the bald man asked.

"Yes, Warren. That's Maeve." Orlo's face was not a face she knew. His broad smile was empty.

Chapter 21

Maeve fought her captor with all she had, but it made no difference. As the bald man dragged her along, Orlo slumped on his horse next to them. Though she tried to catch the attention of the dockhands, they worked on impassively.

She was hauled to a wooden house built on another pier. Once inside, the bald man slammed her against a wall. She sank to the floor, crying. She cried for her lost days of freedom, and for Evan and Jasper, her friends. Cried for her mother, whose patient and terrible toil had ended this way. For Orlo, who had betrayed her. And for the Dreamwen Stone—she yearned to hear its song.

"Be silent!" the man shouted. He moved about, lighting lanterns.

Orlo wandered in, looking confused. "Don't cry, Maeve," he pleaded.

She wished she could stop crying. It wasn't right for these men to watch her weep. But deep sobs rose up and broke through her throat, unstoppable as waves on the shore.

"It's time for my vahss," Orlo said. He was sweating. "My chest hurts."

The bald man grunted. "First tell me how you found her," he said.

"I chanced on her, near the waterfront where you told me to look."

The bald man squatted next to Maeve. He picked up her bandaged hand. "Climbed over the wall, I see." He turned to Orlo. "What about the boy?"

Orlo sweated more, though it wasn't very warm in the room. "Where's my vahss, Warren? I need some vahss."

"Answer me. Did you see the boy?"

Orlo's mouth moved. No words came out. In the lamplight, the skin of his face mottled into purple and red, except for the slave marks. He poured sweat.

"Did you see the boy?" Warren repeated, yelling this time.

Orlo looked from Warren to Maeve. "Maeve," he said. "Oh, Maeve, you shouldn't be here. You've got to run."

Warren stood between her and the door.

"Run, Maeve," Orlo urged. "I can hold him back." He lunged for Warren. Maeve stumbled to her feet to dodge around them. She heard a sickening crunch and turned to see Orlo doubled over, holding his chest. She dived for the door. Her trembling fingers turned the knob.

She was seized from behind and flung backward across the room. When her head hit the wall, the light went out.

Maeve stood under the full moon on a deserted beach. The colors of sand and ocean, muted by moonlight, seemed heartbreakingly dim.

Her head hurt. She was looking for something. What was it? She turned slowly, scanning the lonely terrain. Wind rippled the sand and brushed at her hair.

She bent to the ground. Pebbles lay in the sand at her feet, reflecting the moon. Pebbles, ordinary pebbles. But perhaps they weren't ordinary—after all, the Dreamwen Stone didn't appear to be unusual.

The Dreamwen Stone. That's what she searched for and needed to find.

She closed her eyes against the wind. When she opened them, a young man stood in front of her, the same young man she'd seen at the beginning of the journey to Mantedi. *In a dream.*

Beside him stood a girl with wild brown hair. Maeve remembered her, too. She had fought with a dark bird in another dream.

"Dream," Maeve said.

The young man nodded, his deep blue eyes fixed on her with a passion she didn't understand.

"Who are you?" Maeve asked, looking from one to the other.

"Dorjan," he said. "Son of Cabis."

Son of Cabis! Maeve stared at the young man. He looked to be near her own age. How was it possible? Cabis had loved her mother, Lila. Could he have fathered a son so soon, while Lila sacrificed her beauty and her future to spare him discovery? Maeve's heart hammered in two directions. How happy she was, to think she had a brother, and how unhappy, remembering the scarred face of her mother.

"My name is Maeve," she told him.

"Maeve. I've been wanting to ask you—"

But as suddenly as they had appeared, they were gone.

Dorjan's parched lips had cracked. When he licked them, it only made it worse. His eyes felt as if sand had been ground into them. Stiff with cold, he tried to ease his shoulder, where Sara's head was pillowed. Moonlight showed her face, chapped and blistered, her lips scabbed. But she was alive! How desolate he'd been during the long day alone, searching for her.

She stirred, opening her eyes. She sat up slowly.

He propped himself on an elbow, feeling the cold air on his damp jacket. "Sara, do you remember where we were?"

"Where we—" She grabbed his shoulder, almost tipping him into the water. "Yes! We found your sister. Maeve, she said. Her eyes are like yours." Her voice sounded as if she'd swallowed sand.

I tried to find her—to find her and bring you with me. I broke the Dreamwen law again.

He still hadn't told Sara that since her first dream aboard the *Lanya* when he'd found her dancing on the sand, pursued by a dark bird, he'd taken her to his sycamore grove every night. He'd wanted to tell her, but somehow never did. Why? Because in the daylight hours, her eyes when she looked at him were bright with affection. He feared her warmth would be replaced with cool disdain if she learned he'd been helping her without her knowledge.

"Dorjan," she said eagerly, "do you think you might be able to travel to her, the way you've done with me?"

"I'm wondering the same," he said. "But—"

"It uses up your gen, doesn't it?" she asked. "You're already exhausted."

"And I can't think of leaving you here."

"How do you travel . . . that way?"

"I'm only beginning to understand. To go where I want to, I seem to need to aim for something I know or have seen."

She looked as if she'd like to ask more questions. She also looked disturbingly tired. "See, the sky is lighter. It'll soon be dawn."

He could see her dark-circled, sunken eyes more clearly. Worry knotted his stomach. They needed fresh water.

Determination rose in his heart. "I'm taking you with me."

The little raft bobbed as she shifted her weight. "Can it be done?"

"It *must* be done. I won't leave you alone to drift." *If I'm breaking another Dreamwen law, so be it.*

She leaned in to embrace him. He touched her sun-blistered cheek gently.

"I'll aim for Maeve and the Dreamwen Stone as soon as we can fall asleep again," he told her.

She snuggled in beside him. "Thank you."

"Don't thank me yet," he said, shutting his eyes.

"Dorjan, what if you leave and I stay?"

He put both his arms around her. "If I can go, I can come back. And I will."

When Jasper turned from the watering trough on the pier and saw Maeve pulling the Dreamwen Stone from around her neck, he knew there was trouble. Her scarf was missing, too, he noticed instantly. She'd never give up the gold unless something had gone terribly wrong.

Then she ran.

Orlo got on his horse and started after her. Jasper mounted Fortune in front of Evan, blaming himself. They should have stayed hidden once they arrived in Mantedi.

When he saw Maeve captured by the bald man, Jasper wanted to trample him, grab Maeve, make off with her. But that would just get him turned into a slave—then he'd have no chance of helping her. Instead, he slipped from Fortune's back, lifting Evan down, too. Now that Maeve was taken, Orlo would remember Evan, wouldn't he? There were dozens of horses on the pier, but a horse stood out more than a person on foot. At the first signs of a search for Evan, Jasper was ready to melt into the passersby, even give up Fortune if he had to.

But Orlo didn't look back for them, which Jasper thought strange. Orlo had called Evan by name; he must know who he was. He'd seen that Evan was unmarked— how long before he gave that secret away?

"Where are we going?" Evan cried, hanging on to Jasper.

Jasper bent down to speak in the boy's ear. "We're following those men to see where they take Maeve."

With Fortune's halter wound in one hand, holding Evan by the other, Jasper edged after Maeve's captors. Orlo rode with his head down, body slumped low, never turning to look for Evan. Mighty strange.

A great crew of dockworkers streamed off one of the piers, blocking Jasper's way. They looked straight ahead, carrying boxes on their heads, giving no room for anyone to cross through them. When Jasper could go on, he'd lost Maeve. He mounted Fortune again, Evan behind him, and went all the way to the end of the wharves, searching for Maeve's gold hair.

Where the piers ended, sand began. Jasper continued along the sand. He thought about making a life in Mantedi, thought about trying to forget Maeve. He had a mare, and some besaets left, which was more than he'd had for most of his life before.

He shook his head. *Might as well ask this sand I ride upon to become rock again. I can't forget her.* He saw her in his mind's eye, all decked in flowers, rubbing petals against her cheek, softly smiling. He had to clench his jaw to keep from bawling aloud. Once Lord Morlen claimed her, she'd never smile that way again. She'd get marked as a slave, or worse— she'd told him what had happened when Morlen looked in her eyes.

Jasper wished he'd pushed Orlo off the pier.

Soon they began to pass camps of lowborn free. Some slept; some were awake beside flickering fires. Asleep or awake, every camp had someone standing watch. Jasper pulled up beside a small fire where a gray-bearded man sat gazing at the ocean alone. He dismounted and lifted Evan down.

"Evening," he said quietly.

"Night," the man answered. Soot streaked the lines of his face.

Jasper pointed to himself and the boy. "Jasper," he said, "and Evan."

"Carl," said the graybeard, searching his face. "Good color you have. Don't drink vahss, do you?"

"Vahss?" Jasper asked, puzzled.

"Where you from?" Carl asked.

"Slivona. Just arrived."

Carl shook his head mournfully. "Better off there than here. But every day they come to Mantedi, lured by the tales of our riches. Riches!" He spit in the sand. "Once here they discover that they can't leave."

"Can't leave?"

"The only way for the free to leave Mantedi is to die or to be a farmer."

"Farmer?"

"Come now, young man. You came into the city with all the other rags and tags, did you not? Didn't you notice that many of those you passed coming the other direction had the sheaf of grain burned into their foreheads?"

Jasper *had* noticed. Plodding men leading horses and empty carts, their eyes on the ground, the distinctive brand on their foreheads.

"They supply the city with grain and goods, and for the privilege they bear the brand. Freemen! Taking a brand so they can do commerce in Mantedi." Carl spit again.

"They take the brand even though they're free?" Jasper's stomach turned.

Carl nodded. "Every night more free die on the wall, trying to get out of this cursed city." He motioned at the waves. "And more free drown trying to escape by way of the ocean." He put a stick of driftwood on his fire. "But not the ones who drink vahss. They don't try to leave."

"Vahss?" Jasper asked again.

"Vahss. The best hell brewed on earth. Takes the soul right out of the man or woman who drinks it. Anyone offers you orange liquid, don't take it, and keep the boy from it."

What new evil was this? A drink that took the soul from a man? Jasper took a long breath.

"Morlen's poison," Carl said, speaking low. "Vahss. The orange flasks. Morlen's doing. Those who drink vahss cease to care for anything but what Lord Morlen wants." He ground one bony fist into his other open palm. "Some drink it again and again, until it stops their hearts."

Shuddering, Jasper fumbled in his pocket. "Do you have any bread or water to spare? I'd gladly trade for besaets."

Carl nodded, taking a besaet. He gave Jasper a loaf and a lump of cheese.

"Water?"

Carl rose. He dug in the sand for a moment and brought forth a leather bottle. He handed it to Jasper, who took a long drink. The water, though slightly brackish, tasted fine to his dry throat. He tore off a hunk of bread, and offered Evan the bread with some water. He put the rest of the food away. They would need it later. "Thank you." He rose. After taking another swig of water, he slung the bottle over his shoulder. He lifted Evan onto Fortune's back and mounted again himself.

He turned back toward the piers. Soon, Evan's sleeping weight sagged against him. Jasper rode to where the posts supporting the wharves began to rise out of the sand. He got off the horse. He stared out over black waves rolling toward him from far away. The clouds had thinned, and a distant moon, nearly full, looked down.

He woke Evan. "We're going back to get the Dreamwen Stone. Maeve wouldn't want it to be lost."

The boy looked at him with awe. "You going to jump off that pier?"

"No. Going under the wharves." He pointed into the blackness below the long docks.

"How you going to know which pier?"

"Been counting."

Jasper looked into the space beneath the waterfront wharves. Too low for the mare to walk under. He tied her to a support post, knowing she might not be there when he got back. "Don't let anyone steal you." He rubbed her nose affectionately.

He and Evan went in under the low-hanging beams. The boards of the waterfront over their heads made the sound of waves crashing on the shore echo loudly. Footsteps of people and animals tramping above them boomed and shook.

It was a long way to go at a crouch. Jasper envied Evan being able to walk upright. When the ocean started looking eerie and gray, Jasper knew dawn would come soon. He saw signs that the tide would rise underneath the waterfront docks. They'd better hurry if he wanted to find the Stone and get back to the end of the wharves before the space beneath them filled with water.

He counted the piers faithfully; when they arrived under the one where Maeve had been captured, the first rays of sun shot across the water. Jasper crept out from under the beams, Evan behind him. The pier rose high above, its massive pilings anchored with mortared rock at the open sand.

Stripping down to his loincloth, Jasper hugged the sand with his bare feet while a chilly breeze raised goose bumps on his skin. He wasn't looking foward to putting his whole body in the cold ocean. He wasn't much of a diver—didn't like holding his breath. "Watch for me, Evan. I'm going in."

He struck into the waves. The cold pushed at him, telling him he belonged on land and would stay on land if he knew what was good for him. He could touch sand with his feet for most of the distance, but by the time he got near where he guessed Maeve had dropped the Stone, the bottom dropped away.

He dove. Salt water pricked his eyes as he searched the murky ocean bed. There seemed to be hundreds of small rocks; he felt them with his hand more than saw them with his eyes. He brought some up, but none was the Dreamwen Stone. His teeth chattered, and goose bumps covered his skin. He wished the sun would show some strength. His wish wasn't answered. He took another deep breath, made another dive, and another, groping the ocean floor, straining to see through the blind murk.

His hand caught hold of a waving bit of what felt like cloth. His grip tightened. Bringing it to the surface, Jasper gulped back a sob when he realized what he had. Maeve's ragged, dripping scarf, weighted with two gold delans.

He looked again at the ocean, marking the place with his eyes. The Dreamwen Stone was down there somewhere.

He swam back to Evan. He wrung out the scarf, tied it awkwardly and tenderly around his arm. He placed the gold inside his shirt pocket on the shore, then prepared to try again for the Dreamwen Stone.

At the water's edge he saw a sight that froze him: two people wading out of the surf. One of them, a tall young man, leaned on the other, a girl. Both wore dripping, hooded jackets over their drenched clothes and looked as if they were having great trouble staying upright. The young man held something up high, something tied to a familiar, sodden rag. The Dreamwen Stone.

How dare these strangers take Maeve's treasure! Jasper ran at them, barreling into them with his head. They fell to the sand, fighting for air. Feeling ready to kill, Jasper grabbed the Stone from the young man, who did nothing to stop him. The girl, gasping loudly, got unsteadily to her feet. She swung a fist at him. As Jasper dodged her, a small body hurtled into him from the side, knocking him flat with surprise. Evan! Evan was trying to fight him.

"Stop!" Evan cried. "Stop, Jasper."

Jasper jumped up, seizing the boy. "What are you doing? This is Maeve's stone. They can't have it." He backed away from the girl, who came at him, blazing fury in her eyes.

"But I know him!" Evan shouted. "He knows Maeve."

"You know him?" Jasper yelled. He stared at the girl, who had stopped in her tracks, gaping at Evan. Behind her on the sand, her companion was trying to sit up.

Evan's head bobbed up and down. "He's good, Jasper. He helped me and Maeve."

"When? When did he help you?"

"In a dream!"

Shaking his head with the effort to understand, Jasper looked from Evan to the brown-skinned young man. Could this stranger on the beach be the same young man Maeve had talked about, the one she'd met in a dream? Maeve wouldn't want him to hurt these people if they were her friends. Were they? Jasper looked harder at the strangers.

The girl's skin was sunburned, her lips badly cracked. Deep-circled, fierce eyes filled her face. "Who are you?" Jasper asked.

"I'm Sara," the girl said in a peculiarly rough voice. "He's Dorjan." She bent to help the young man; Jasper bent with her, putting a hand around Dorjan's wrist and pulling him up, dismayed to feel how cold his skin was. Too cold. His eyes were badly bloodshot. Their color startled Jasper— exactly the same deep shade of blue as Maeve's.

Dorjan staggered, almost falling, his breath coming in heaving gasps. The girl put her shoulder under his; Jasper supported his other side. They got him under the docks, where he collapsed. Reluctantly, Jasper handed him the

Dreamwen Stone. He felt somehow that it was what the young man needed.

Evan had picked up Jasper's clothes and brought them to him. The racket from the docks above was so loud they couldn't talk. Jasper started yanking off the other young man's soaked jacket, gesturing to the girl to help him. Together, they dressed the cold stranger in Jasper's dry things. The pants and shirtsleeves were short. When they were done, the girl said something Jasper couldn't hear. "What?" he bellowed.

She pointed to her mouth.

Of course. The deep-circled eyes, the grainy voice, the exhaustion. Jasper ran for his water bottle. When he gave it to her, she poured some into Dorjan's mouth before taking a drink herself.

As the tide crept up the beach, Dorjan revived slowly. Jasper twisted the seawater out of Dorjan's clothes. He rolled up the pant legs, shimmied the shirtsleeves and put them on himself.

They had to go or the tide would trap them under the wharves. Besides, moving was the best way to get warm. Jasper yelled to make himself heard, asking if Dorjan had any injuries. Dorjan shook his head.

"We've got to go!" Jasper shouted. He pointed to the tide.

Sara nodded. She and Jasper helped Dorjan to his feet.

Tired and edgy, Jasper forged ahead as fast as he dared. The strangers looked ready to drop, especially Dorjan, but he went on without complaining. Before long, they were all wading through ankle-high water, the tide buffeting their knees with each wave. Jasper gave a hand to Evan, for the boy was struggling.

When they reached the end of the wharves at last, Fortune whinnied a greeting. She was still there! Maybe they had some luck left over. It was a relief to be in the open, where they could speak and be heard. Jasper gathered Fortune's reins and led the way higher up the sand, past the tide line.

They all sat, except for Evan, who stretched out on the sand and went to sleep instantly. Jasper tried to remember the last time he'd slept. He and Maeve and Evan had moved through the night on their way to Mantedi. Was that only two nights ago?

He looked from Sara to Dorjan. "How did you find that stone and bring it out of the ocean?"

Sara glowered at him. "We need more water," she said hoarsely. She looked as if she suspected Jasper of being a crazed ruffian. *Well, it's not as if the greeting I gave her could make her think wonderful thoughts of me.*

Jasper handed them the food, too, watching as they ate and drank with shaking hands. When he judged they wouldn't starve or die of thirst, he asked again. "The Dreamwen Stone? How did you get it?"

Dorjan looked at him with interest. "How did you know its name?"

Jasper cursed his carelessness. Maeve didn't want the secret spoken of. His enormous fatigue seemed to be making him stupid. "Maeve told me," he blurted out. "Your eyes. They're like hers." He pictured Maeve: her skin somewhere between the colors of melted butter and the brown crust of new bread, her hair like a mix of all the ripe grains they'd passed on their journey to Mantedi. And her eyes, deep blue like this stranger's.

The tall young man leaned toward him. "You know Maeve?"

Jasper decided to trust Dorjan. He told everything from that first carriage ride to his last sight of Maeve on the piers. As he talked, Sara's expression slowly changed from hostile suspicion to great warmth. She and Dorjan listened avidly to Jasper's tale, horrified when he revealed that Maeve had been a slave and was now a runaway. "I tried to watch where they took her," he finished bleakly.

"Jasper," Dorjan said, "if my eyes remind you of hers, it's because we may have the same father. Sara and I came to Sliviia to find her. I thought she carried the Dreamwen Stone, so I aimed for the Stone, and ended up in the ocean."

Same father! "She never told me," Jasper said.

"She didn't know." Dorjan looked at Sara.

Since she'd had water to drink, Sara's voice wasn't as dry and strained. Jasper listened quietly as she told of how she and Dorjan had been shipwrecked, then traveled over miles of water by *dreaming*. Jasper wiggled his fingers and toes, wondering if he could lift them just by using his mind. He tried to pick up his arm that way. It didn't stir. How had they done it? Was *he* dreaming, or were they lying? He could spot a liar as easy as he could sniff out a bad fish. These two didn't have that smell about them. The girl's skin was badly burned—her skin wouldn't get that way unless she had been somewhere she couldn't get out of the sun, like the ocean. Strangest of all, they'd found the Dreamwen Stone.

"I have to go to her," Dorjan said.

"But you don't know where she's being held," Jasper protested.

"I can find her."

"But you're half dead," Sara said. "How will you do it?"

How could Maeve's brother find her without knowing where she was? *He found the Dreamwen Stone, didn't he?* "Take me," Jasper said.

"I can't take others. I'll have to hope she's alone when I reach her. Alone and asleep would be best."

"Wait," Jasper said. "What if she's *not* alone? I can fight. What if you have to fight?" His question hung in the sunny air.

"I've only tried bringing someone else along once before. I *know* Sara." Dorjan turned up his hands.

"You know me now, too," Jasper said.

"Not enough to find you in a dream and persuade your spirit to bring your body along wherever I go."

Jasper wondered if he might be going a little mad. This talk of spirits and bodies and dreams didn't make sense. "What will you do if there's a guard? I'm not afraid of a lord or his guards. I'm saying I'll fight for Maeve." He wanted to take Dorjan by the neck, show him what he could do—in case Dorjan didn't remember having the wind knocked out of him back on the beach. Dorjan *had* to see it would be better to take help.

"He's right, Dorjan," Sara put in. "And you'll need me, too."

Dorjan looked hard at Jasper. "If I try to bring you, it could go wrong. I may not be able to bring any of us back, because I might not have any strength left to return with."

"Better odds with me there," Jasper persisted.

Dorjan sighed. "All right, Jasper. If I can. But I don't want to bring you, Sara. The danger's too great."

Sara glared at him. "The danger's less for me than for you. Besides, if you can't return, how will I find you?"

Dorjan shook his head.

"Please," she said, making the plea sound like a command, "let me help you."

Dorjan finally nodded, his eyes troubled. He sighed. "All right, then. We'll need to find some shelter for while we sleep. You need to get out of the sun, Sara."

"I wish I had skin like yours," she answered.

They both turned to Jasper. "Where can we go that has shade, where we won't be bothered?" Dorjan asked.

Jasper wondered what it would feel like, to be taken through a dream to another place. "I don't know," he answered, casting his eyes across the beaches of Mantedi, the scattered camps of the lowborn free. "We'll need to look for something."

He got to his feet along with the others, trying not to stumble. Much good he'd be in a fight just now, too tired to know his own direction. He lifted the sleeping boy onto Fortune and persuaded the mare to move again.

They scouted the beaches, moving wearily. There were many scrawny stands of trees—some had people encamped in them; some were deserted. They found an empty one within sight of the Mantedi wall.

Jasper tied Fortune's reins to a branch. He tried to wake Evan to let the boy know what they were about, but Evan was so deep in sleep that even when Jasper stood him on his legs, he didn't waken. Jasper worried about him possibly waking up alone, but it couldn't be helped. They had to find Maeve. His bones told him they mustn't wait. Evan was smart. He would know to stay beside Fortune. Jasper laid the boy along the mare's back—the two of them were used to sleeping that way.

He spread the blankets. Lying down beside Sara and Dorjan, he heard Dorjan say, "Think of Maeve as you go to sleep." Jasper threw a corner of blanket across his eyes and thought of Maeve.

Dorjan's whisper was warm in Sara's ear. "He's already asleep."

"Yes," she murmured, and laid a hand on his chest. "You did it, Dorjan. We made shore."

"The best part of shore is the drinking water."

"I owe you my life."

"You don't owe me."

"Are you all right from the journey? Can you do this again?"

Dorjan didn't answer her. Lying on his back, he brought out the Dreamwen Stone, rolling it around in his long hands, smoothing the frayed, damp cloth it was tied to.

"It looks ordinary," Sara said.

"Doesn't feel ordinary." He handed it to her. "When I hold it, I feel the world of dreams."

She hefted it lightly, hand to hand, put it to her ear, peered at it closely. A smooth brown stone about the size of her palm. She gave it back. "When I hold it, I remember fighting the evil bird and I want to fight it again."

"That's because you're a Firan." His grin flashed. "Remember, the Dreamwen Stone will enhance the gifts of whoever holds it."

Sara gazed around. Even the sky looked unfamiliar here. She closed her eyes.

Chapter 22

When Maeve woke, the beach she had dreamed of still seemed to surround her for a few moments. Then she realized she was lying on a hard floor in a place without any lamps or candles to relieve the chilly darkness. She heard gasping and moaning, but couldn't see anything. "Who's there?" she asked.

"Maeve?" *Orlo's voice!*

"Yes, Orlo. It's me."

"Maeve! I thought I heard someone, but—can't move." His breath wheezed like steam from a broken kettle.

"I'll help you."

"Maeve, how can you bear to help me? I led them to you."

"That wasn't you, Orlo, I know it. Lord Morlen did something . . ."

"Yes . . . he took me. Took me from myself. Vahss. Don't let him give it to you."

She didn't understand him. She scooted to him, touched his face gently. The foulness she'd felt in him on the pier was gone, but there was something else on his face besides tears. "Blood?"

"He crushed me inside, Maeve," Orlo moaned.

She laid her hands on his chest. "Shhh."

"I'm sorry, Maeve, so sorry. You were like a daughter to me, and now because of me, look where you are."

"Not because of you, Orlo." She kept her hands on his chest.

"We're in his house. He'll be here soon."

She hummed softly. Though she didn't have the Dreamwen Stone anymore, she tried to sing its song.

The whistling air from his lungs came slower. "Don't let them give you vahss." His chest moved up and down under her hands. She went on humming. "Didn't know you could sing, Maeve . . . wonderful tune. I could almost believe in heaven, listening to you."

When Orlo slipped into sleep, she stayed beside him, singing on.

How quiet he was—no snoring or sighs and even his chest was still. Maeve stopped singing and put her ear near his mouth. No breath.

She didn't shake him, didn't cry out. She lifted her hands away, her fingers trembling. She clasped them together, trying to get them to stop shaking. The rest of her body began to shake, too, like one of the autumn leaves she'd seen on the journey to Mantedi, fragile and futile, soon to land on cold ground. What would she do when Lord Morlen came for her? She wanted to say something to Orlo, something he could hear. But he was gone.

At least now he didn't have to face Lord Morlen.

"Good-bye, Orlo," she said. "Good-bye." Crawling to a corner, she whispered frantically to herself. She mustn't think now of her grief. If she did, she'd remember her mother, would know that Lila was dead, too, with her hopes buried like the blue dress that lay in Lord Hering's woodland.

She must not disappear into weeping madness; she must not. She would think about something else. What had become of Jasper and Evan? Had they gotten away? Probably so. Jasper would know what to do, how to lose himself and Evan. Hadn't he been right about the gold?

Her weeks of freedom rushed through her mind, filled with memories of Jasper. His strong hands moving a needle back and forth. Teaching her to skip rocks over water, how to cook, how to bank a fire, how to ride Fortune. Trudging patiently through the long, dark nights, following deer trails. Weaving garlands. Arguing with her about the gold. The kindess, *the love,* in his eyes. Maeve hoped with all her heart that he'd ridden away without looking back. He and Evan could live safely together.

Footsteps sounded outside the door. *I won't tell Morlen about Evan and Jasper.* Morlen could cut her until Jasper wouldn't know her again, but she'd never speak.

The door opened. The bald man who had hurt Orlo came in, followed by a marked slave holding a lantern. The slave set the lantern down and stood aside. Lord Morlen swept through the door, gray eyes catching the lantern glow, shoulders nearly as wide as the doorway.

Morlen went straight to Orlo's body, bending to it. "What's this, Warren?" His voice was cold, as it had been the last time she'd heard him, in Lord Indol's study. "This man's dead."

"Not dead, sir. I hurt him, didn't kill him."

"He's dead."

Maeve cowered in the corner, eyeing the closed door.

Bald Warren squatted next to the body. "I've done that move a hundred times, Lord Morlen. It's never killed anyone."

Morlen straightened. "His death will come out of your pay."

As Morlen's feet approached her corner, Maeve wished she could follow Orlo from the world.

He knelt on one knee in front of her. "My lovely runaway. Wouldn't it have been easier to go with me from the beginning?" She didn't answer. "Not talking?" He ran a finger down her cheek. "That will change soon, Maeve. I have everything I need to unlock your mind and all its secrets." She concentrated on her hands in her lap. "What an unusual spirit you have," he went on. "Soft on the surface, yet underneath there's defiance. But you can't escape me. We are joined by destiny."

"W-what do you want with me?" She wouldn't look at him, but the question that had been tormenting her burst out.

"I see things about you that no one else can see. Things not even *you* can guess."

"That's no answer."

His hands went to both sides of her head, pulling her face up. She shut her eyes. "Clever girl, aren't you, Maeve? Much more clever than anyone guessed. Fooling the matron, in my name. Taking the gold." The horrid grayness in his hands seeped inside her head, cold and shadowy, stealing through her mind. She tried to hold herself limp, tried to pretend she didn't hear him. "But taking the boy along—that was foolish." Some foreign force pushed on her eyes from the inside. She squeezed them shut tighter. Morlen chuckled. "Good, Maeve. I see you're resisting. That makes it more interesting. But you won't be able to resist much longer."

Maeve felt the truth of what he said as he tightened his grip around her head. Cold seared her, worse than fire. She summoned her will, but it was like calling up a ghost. The coldness in her head spread through her body. She kicked out with her legs but nothing happened. She tried lifting her hands; they lay lifeless.

"If you open your eyes," she heard, "I'll drop my hands."

She thought of her mother and how she must have suffered, being cut again and again. *At least blood is warm.* Maeve didn't decide to open her eyes, yet they opened, and there was his stare as before, steel-colored and sharp. "You said you'd let go," she said, gasping.

He held up two hands, but she could still feel them on the sides of her head. She wanted to touch her face, but her arms would not move. Though she meant to look away from his gaze, she couldn't. His eyes drove her down, down, down, into shadow. As she descended, she could no longer see anything in the room where they were. Freezing fog filled her body, making it impossible to move.

She could still hear Lord Morlen's voice. "It's better to accept what happens, Maeve. And I have questions for you, my dear."

She conjured up bits of her life to hold on to, made herself remember the flowers and fragrant grasses of late summer, her mother's voice, Evan's face, Jasper's warm hands. Even the bathhouse courtyard, where she'd basked in the sun.

"Yes, Maeve. Show me all your memories. The more you show me, the more I know of you." *Show him?* Could he see, then, what she remembered? "You still believe you can get away from me? But that's an idle fancy, Maeve. You can't. Which brings me to ask: How did you elude me during sleep? How did you prevent me from entering your dreams?"

The Dreamwen Stone. No, she must not think of it. Anything, anything else. She brought Lila to mind, going over every scar on her mother's face. Lord Morlen couldn't do anything to Lila now.

"Clever to show me a dead woman's face. Clever, but not clever enough. The Dreamwen Stone? Hidden all these years, and *you* had it? Tell me where it is."

She clung to the image of her mother, but felt as if Lord Morlen were peeling back her mind, exposing the secret fruit of her thoughts. He clicked his tongue. "Ah now, what have you done? Thrown away the greatest treasure of the Dreamwens. Never mind. When you're an Ebrowen, we'll take back the Stone together."

I'll never be an Ebrowen. Though her mouth refused speech, he answered her as if she had spoken. "Hush, now. You don't know your own destiny. You are a Dreamwen. That means you can be an Ebrowen, soar with an Ebrowen's power."

Dreamwen. "*The grandson of the last great Dreamwen, the only son of an only daughter . . . you may be a Dreamwen, Maeve.*" She had wanted to know if she was a Dreamwen, but not from him, not ever from him.

He chuckled in her ear. "Yes. Tell me about your family. I want to know everything about you."

Panic-stricken, Maeve searched for a way to hide her thoughts, but wherever she turned within her mind, Morlen followed. "A father across the ocean . . . perhaps a brother, too!"

Mother, Mother. Help me. Take me from here.

Morlen continued. "See through *my* eyes, Maeve; get a taste of what it means to be an Ebrowen."

Horrified, Maeve realized that her own sight was being replaced with Morlen's. She tried to stop herself from looking where he wanted her to, but it was like trying to keep a dead leaf from being carried on the wind. Her awareness spun suddenly upward, out of the room where they were, over Mantedi. She could see the walled-in mass of streets and buildings, the welters of wretched alleyways, the tired motion of people and animals. Higher she whirled, out toward the bay and beyond, where she saw the surf tossing against the horizon. Then she and Morlen sped across the Minwenda.

In moments they had arrived on the shores of an eastern land, where wide beaches embraced the water. A marble palace seemed to grow up from the shore, the lines of its turrets and windows as fluid as the peaceful bay it overlooked.

Glavenrell?

"Bellandra," Morlen answered.

He ushered her into a grand room where shafts of sunlight lay across the velvet blankets of a bed. A man and a woman rested there. The man's noble face was thin and still; the red-haired woman held his hand as her eyes fluttered feverishly. A soldier with a scarred face stood by them; in his dry eyes Maeve read overwhelming grief. She realized he wasn't able to see her or Morlen.

"The king and queen of Bellandra," Morlen said. "They don't have long to live."

Why?

The royal room disappeared. She felt as if she were going from a mountaintop into an abyss, falling too fast, too far.

At last her feet touched something solid. Dizzy and sick, she looked about her, reminding herself that her true body wasn't there to feel sickness; it was far away in Sliviia, frozen in the windowless room where Morlen held her in his eyes.

A hallway. She had seen one like it before. Gray stone, lit by cold gray light. Morlen led her out of the hallway into a great dome. He crossed the dome with a sure stride and opened a door in its far wall. Maeve heard water dripping. Following him reluctantly, she wondered why the sound of those falling drops filled her with despair.

Approaching the door, she looked into a small square room. Four gray, wide-rimmed vessels, each as high as Lord Morlen's chest, stood in the middle of the floor. Something was dripping into them from holes in the ceiling above.

Light. Drops of colored light. Each time a drop fell, its light went out.

"You're fortunate, Maeve, to see this," Morlen said, sounding reverent. "This is Ebe Elixir."

Ebe Elixir?

"Look closely, Maeve. You see how the light falls into these vessels? That light is being drained out of the world, from objects of bright magic. Here, at last, the Shadow King is able to reverse light; to turn it into darkness. Ebe Elixir. It grants untold powers to those fortunate enough to drink it."

His eyes told her he had drunk the elixir.

Maeve didn't understand. And she couldn't forget the king and queen lying inside the palace of Bellandra. *Why must they die?*

Morlen shrugged. "They were too close to objects of bright magic. The reversal of light from those objects has made them ill." He smiled.

"One day, Maeve, you will come here yourself. You'll crave the powers this elixir gives." He seized her hand. The dome blurred as he lifted her with sickening speed to another place.

When her eyes cleared, she saw a stone building with colored glass windows, sitting next to a forest under a sky that seemed to be missing its full share of sunlight. "The Boundary House of the Healer's Keep," Morlen said.

Looking at it with Morlen's vision Maeve felt sure that to most eyes the building would appear to be nothing more than an uninteresting heap of stones. A smoky tissue of dark magic disguised it to others, but Morlen's vision seemed to penetrate the magic easily.

"Soon this place will be gone," Lord Morlen said.

The building sent ribbons of shining silver light past the smoky darkness surrounding it. For an instant Maeve envisioned a sheen of silver enclosing the entire world in a membrane of light.

"The Silver Boundary still holds back the Shadow King," Morlen said. "But not for long. When it falls, the Shadow King will walk the world."

He turned to a group of buildings nearby.

The foundations are cracked.

"True," he said. "But the healers don't see."

Maeve saw people dressed in simple robes and tunics, walking sedately along fine pathways, unaware of her and Morlen. *Look around you!* she tried to scream, but of course they couldn't hear her. They didn't see when a dark bird flew across the grounds, a fragment of night winging past them.

"An Ebe," Lord Morlen told her. "The Shadow King has all of them now."

Much as Lord Morlen frightened her, the bird, the Ebe, terrified Maeve even more. She fought to run away from it, to get back to the room in Sliviia where Morlen had caught her in his eyes. Compared to the bird, he seemed a haven of safety.

"Coming to me for protection, Maeve? How touching. I agree, you and I should be side by side. But first you must let the Ebe take your spirit."

If only she could reach her body, she would run, run until her breath was gone forever, run until her heart ceased to beat. But this was not the ordinary world—she couldn't seem to find her body, and Lord Morlen moved her mind at his whim.

She heard a faint thump; Lord Morlen's voice changed, muffled as though he talked through a scarf. "What's that noise, Warren?"

Warren. Maeve tried to see what Morlen meant, but she couldn't. She had thought she was already as chilled as life would allow, but now the cold intensified. For a moment it hurt like a thousand patriers piercing her, and then numbness took the pain away.

Nothing mattered anymore. Lord Morlen was right. It was better to accept whatever would happen.

Chapter 23

When Dorjan's hand touched the bark of the great sycamore in his peaceful dreamscape, he remembered his mission clearly. He must go to where Maeve was, bringing Sara and Jasper with him if he could.

He reached for Sara's essence, for the bright core of her spirit. When he found it, he launched some of his gen toward it in a blend. He gathered her surging vitality and courage close to him, and soon she stood next to the sycamore.

Going after Jasper was more difficult. What was the essence of this young man? Dorjan sifted through pieces of what he'd seen: Jasper attacking him and Sara for the Dreamwen Stone, then returning it on the word of a child; Jasper giving his own dry clothes to help a newcomer he knew nothing of; Jasper watching out for Evan. And most important, Jasper's love for Maeve. That love had to be there—why else would he risk slavery and death for her?

Dorjan sought the beacon of Jasper's love for Maeve and blended with the nature it revealed until Jasper stood beside Sara.

Instantly, Dorjan moved his focus to concentrate on the soul of his sister. Her essence seemed feeble and distant. He was tired, his gen still low from the journey to Mantedi. The Dreamwen Stone was helping, though—he knew he'd be useless without it.

He tried again, cast some of his gen toward Maeve. When his gen found her, it fastened to the place where she was. Dorjan blended with both Sara and Jasper, then sent the rest of his gen after, tugging his companions along.

He felt the now-familiar sensation of transport, like sliding through mounds of sand to land against a wall.

Jasper woke when the floorboards hit him, instantly aware that he was in a different place. A windowless room. A lantern stood near him on the floor, and a marked slave stared down, surprise and fear in his face.

Jasper felt a strange sluggishness. He shook it off, getting to his feet in one motion. Dorjan lay on the floor like a stranded fish, seemingly unable to rise. Sara crouched against the far wall. Close to the door lay Orlo, not moving. Next to him was the bald man Jasper had followed along the piers and lost sight of, the one who had dragged Maeve so cruelly. And in the opposite corner sat Maeve, eyes locked with a large man kneeling beside her. Had to be Lord Morlen. "What's that noise, Warren?" he asked calmly, without turning away from her.

The bald man stood gaping. Jasper didn't wait for him to come to his senses; the advantage of surprise lasted only as long as the surprise did. Grabbing the lantern from the floor, Jasper threw it at the bald man, catching him in the face. The glass broke; flaming oil spattered. The man put his hands to his face, screaming. Jasper didn't care about his pain—he deserved worse for stealing Maeve and taking away her freedom.

Flames fed the lantern oil that ran along the floor, trailing smoke. Jasper crashed his heel into the man's knee. The man went down, twisting and shrieking. Jasper stomped on his chest.

The slave stood, seemingly rooted, gibbering.

"Gart, go get help." Morlen turned his head. As the slave moved toward the door, Sara flew to block his way. Jasper looked at Morlen as the lord stood up.

This was the man who'd sown fear in so many, made his name something the free hated, used his patrier on hundreds. A broad, tall, well-muscled man. But Jasper had taken on bigger men and come away the victor. He remembered what Maeve had told him—don't look in Morlen's eyes.

Head down, Jasper rushed Morlen. A powerful set of arms caught him and spun him down. He landed on Maeve. How cold she felt! She didn't seem to realize he was there. He rolled across her to his feet. He grabbed her wrists. It was like handling someone dead or asleep; she wasn't any help to him. "Maeve! Get up!" he cried wildly. Morlen was bearing down on them.

He saw Sara leave the door and run toward Morlen's back. Morlen whirled to face her as Jasper struggled to pull Maeve up.

From the floor, Dorjan saw it all. It happened very fast. Sara had the scarred slave cowed, but as soon as she went for Morlen, the slave darted out the door. A haze of smoke from the broken lantern hung in the air. A small blaze crept toward the wall, burning next to the two men on the floor. One of them was completely still; the other twitched and groaned.

Jasper had said he could fight, and he hadn't lied. In the first minute, he'd changed their odds, while Dorjan lay helpless, while Maeve sat unmoving. Dorjan needed to get to Maeve, to touch her with the Dreamwen Stone—she seemed to be in the clutches of an Ebrowen spell. He tried his utmost to move and only flopped against the floor. Jasper had Maeve by the wrists, pulling on her, pleading with her to rise.

When Morlen turned to face Sara, Dorjan feared that she would fight head on. She wouldn't stop to wonder if Morlen was too strong for her—she'd lock into battle, unaware of the immensity of what she fought until it was too late. But Dorjan knew. He had touched Morlen's essence with a fragment of his gen. Morlen was no fledgling Ebrowen—no, he was terribly powerful.

Sara would lose.

In the next few minutes, Sara would be taken, the sister he'd wanted to rescue would be beyond help, and the brave young man who'd joined this quest would be enslaved or killed.

Lord Morlen grabbed Sara by the shoulders and threw her back into thickening smoke. Grief racked Dorjan. To come so far, only to fail. To be born with the Dreamwen gift and have it end this way, of no use to anyone. Ellowen Renaiya's words drifted through his mind: *"You can walk in dreams, and dream in daylight."*

That was the worst of it. Before he could transport them away from here, every one of them would have to be asleep. By then it would be too late—by then he'd probably be dead, or fighting with the last of his gen to fend off the Ebrowen.

Dorjan put his hand around the Dreamwen Stone. Warm, peaceful strength flowed from the Stone through his palm and into his breaking heart. *Asleep. Stop. Maybe we don't have to sleep. Maybe all that's needed is to dream.* "Dream in daylight," Renaiya had said. *What is dreaming in daylight? If I can wake while dreaming, could I dream while waking?*

What about the others?

Dorjan stopped thinking. If he thought further, he'd go mad. Morlen had Sara's face in his hands. Everything was escalating: the fire was a little higher, and there were sounds of approaching feet. Reinforcements.

No time to stop and think. Shutting his eyes, Dorjan clasped the Dreamwen Stone more tightly. He pulled for the sycamore dreamscape. There was the great tree, strong and quiet, just as it appeared when he was asleep. Dorjan molded himself to the shape of dream travel. He borrowed energy from the Dreamwen Stone and sent it into a blend. First Sara. Next Jasper and Maeve. He went straight to the core of essence in each one. Maeve seemed lifeless, but he blended with her as best he could.

He tugged at them all with every bit of force he had left, acting as if they were asleep. He aimed for the stand of trees where the boy, Evan, slept.

Sara sat up slowly. She touched her head, then put her hands against the ground. Nearby, a spindly tree grew. Sand, harsh and real, left grit under her fingernails.

She sighed with relief to see Evan, still sleeping deeply on the back of Jasper's horse. *Mantedi Beach. This is where we went to sleep.*

Jasper was coming around, too. He put his hands on the ground, groping the sand. A few feet away from him, Maeve lay pitifully still. He crawled to her, lifted her head. "Maeve," he said. "Maeve." She didn't move at all, her face looking like cold wax. "Come back, Maeve. Come back."

Sara stared at the motionless young woman they'd crossed the Minwenda to find, the one they'd met in dreams. *Maeve.* Was she dead?

Next to her, Dorjan gulped air as though he couldn't remember how to breathe, his lips a horrible blue color. Sara jumped for the water bottle that hung on Jasper's horse—jumped, but her legs wouldn't hold her. She fell heavily, stumbled to her feet again, grabbed the water. She held it to Dorjan's mouth—some of the water was lost as he choked and spit. She patted his shoulder. "Slowly," she said. "One drop. Then another."

He seemed to be trying to say something, but she couldn't understand him. "Another sip," she urged.

Gradually, his lips got some color back. "Dreamwen Stone," he said. "Maeve. She needs it."

Sara understood. She took his hand and pried the Stone from his stiff fingers. She passed it to Jasper.

"Her forehead," Dorjan said, gasping. "Put it on her forehead."

Jasper did so. "Maeve, it's all right. We have the Dreamwen Stone. Come back, Maeve."

Maeve couldn't see, but she could hear a little. Weren't there voices? Faint voices, distant as if calling from another world.

She couldn't tell what they were saying, and even if she had wanted to get nearer to them, she couldn't move.

Beloved voices. She idly wondered whose thought she heard. Not Lord Morlen's. He would never say such a thing. Or would he?

One of the voices wouldn't stop, a soft urgent murmur rising and falling. She knew that voice but couldn't place it. What did it say?

A point of warmth stabbed her forehead, breaking the numbing chill. Sharp light burst in her eyes; she felt tears on her face. *Warm. Tears are warm.* Heat spread into her head, her chest and arms, her legs—a slow fire nearly killing her with pain.

"Maeve, you're all right. We have the Dreamwen Stone. Maeve, come back. Come back, come back. . . ."

Jasper's voice.

She could see again, through her own eyes. Sky. She lifted a hand. She could move! Jasper knelt beside her, his face more precious than all the gold she'd buried in Lord Hering's woodland. Close by, a young man lay on the sand—the young man from her dreams. *Dorjan, son of Cabis.* Beside him was the girl with windblown hair, who took her hand, offering her water. "I'm Sara," she said. "Drink."

A delighted squeal pierced the air. Fortune tossed her head and stomped as Evan slid from her back. "Maeve, Maeve, you're here, you're here!"

"Yes, Evan. Yes, I'm here." With an effort, she sat up to hug the boy. She looked around at the others. "Thank you," she said. "Thank you all." Her eyes spilled tears.

Sara was helping Dorjan to sit against a tree. He waved at Jasper. "You're quite the hand with a lantern."

Jasper chuckled.

"Dorjan," Sara asked, "how did we get away? We never went to sleep. I thought we had to be asleep before you could move us."

"I didn't know it could be done," he answered, "but when we were losing the fight, I tried dreaming in daylight."

"You're a marvel." Sara rubbed his fingers.

Then Dorjan gazed directly at Maeve. "My father's name is Cabis Denon," he said, his voice quivering a little.

"Then the dream was true," she said. "You're my brother."

Part
Five

Missing

Chapter 24

Half lying, half sitting against a tree, wrapped in blankets, Dorjan realized he'd used up too much gen. He'd hardly been able to summon the energy to swap clothes with Jasper again. Maybe there was a way to replenish himself after such an outpouring, but he didn't know what it was, other than rest, and rest had its dangers. He dreaded the fast-approaching night.

Sara had prodded Jasper and Evan to take Fortune a short way down the beach with her. Dorjan was grateful for her understanding that he and Maeve had things to say to each other alone.

"I'm sorry to be so tired," he began. "How I've wanted to meet you."

"No, no," said Maeve. "Don't say you're sorry. What you did—I can never thank you enough. Not only for tonight, but for Evan." Her eyes were wet, her voice startlingly beautiful.

"Then you remember."

"I could never forget."

"You must have questions about our father." He knew he was right by the hunger on her face. "I'll tell you all I can, but it must wait. I can't stay awake much longer," he confessed.

"There are things I need to tell you now—the Dreamwen Stone will keep you safe in the realms of sleep, but not the others. If anything should happen to me, I want you to know how to help them."

"Happen to you?" she asked anxiously.

"Lord Morlen—" He stopped at the fear in her face.

"Did he look in your eyes?" she asked.

Dorjan shook his head. "Sara's." He paused.

"Can't you use the Dreamwen Stone on her, as you did on Evan?" she asked.

"Undoing the trace of an Ebrowen must be done in the Meadows of Wen," he said, fighting his weariness. "I don't have the strength to get there tonight."

"What will we do, then?"

"Sara's also being hunted by other servants of the Shadow King." He paused. "I've been taking her to a safe dreamscape every night. I'll do it again."

"Dreamscape?"

"Every Dreamwen learns to build a refuge in the realm of dreams. Mine takes the form of a sycamore grove. Another day, I'll teach you to make one of your own. For tonight, let me tell you how to reach the one I've built."

Dorjan couldn't read her expression. She hugged her knees, speaking softly. "Before you do, I have to tell you— Lord Morlen wants to make me an Ebrowen. Because he caught me, he *knows* about the Dreamwen Stone now. And you. And Cabis." Her lovely voice shook. "All that my mother suffered, to keep the Dreamwen secrets, and now he knows. He'll be looking for all of us, and looking for the Stone, too. He'll hunt us; he'll never give up."

Dorjan made himself sit a little straighter. "All we can do is what's in front of us, Maeve," he said gently. "Let me teach you how to protect Sara. If Morlen can't find her, he won't know where the rest of us are."

She took a long breath. "Yes. Tell me."

She listened avidly and her questions revealed keen understanding. Dorjan began to relax. As he did, the crushing fatigue in his body made it even harder to stay awake. "Something else to tell you . . . ," he said. "I should have gotten Sara's permission to enter her dreams. I never did . . . afraid she'd say no."

"She'd surely say yes now, Dorjan. And I hereby give you my permission, always—to find me in any dream I have."

Evan woke needing to pee. He heard the ocean sighing; everything else was quiet and still. He left the circle of his sleeping friends, walking on sand, not making a sound. He could see well enough by the big moon.

He heard a noise behind him. Before he could turn, someone grabbed him and covered his mouth. He struggled—tried to yell but couldn't make a sound. The arms that held him wouldn't let go.

When Maeve opened her eyes, it took a moment to comprehend where she was: lying on the beach of Mantedi. Not quite dawn. Around her neck, the Dreamwen Stone hummed gently. A few feet away, her brother slept.

She hadn't told him about Morlen showing her the peril the world was in. Maybe today she'd find a way to talk about it, and Dorjan could tell her whether it was real.

Maybe there would be time for him to tell her about Cabis Denon, too.

She'd been able to follow Dorjan's directions to his dreamscape. The sycamore grove had made her feel more refreshed than she had felt since her visit to the Meadows of Wen. But as she glanced over the other sleepers, her heart stuttered. Where was Evan? Not where she'd seen him last, wrapped in a blanket beside her.

Small footprints led her along the sand. She heard a sound behind her. She whirled, but it wasn't a stranger.

"Jasper." Relieved, she put a hand in his. Jasper was a haven, steady and sound. "Evan must have wandered."

"I'll go after him, Maeve. Lord Morlen didn't get a good look at me."

"I'm going, too."

He shook his head. "You can't let them find you again."

"I can't go back without Evan. And here we're among the free."

He sighed. "Stay next to me, then."

Evan's tracks were soon lost among others crisscrossing the way. In the other camps of free, people were beginning to move about. Maeve and Jasper approached the nearest camp, where an old man warmed his hands at a small fire, and a bony woman rattled pots. "Wondered if you'd seen my brother," Jasper said. "Strong boy—about eight years old. Looks like me."

They shook their heads. "Got to watch the children," the man said. "More free getting snatched. Girls taken for sentesans, and boys get sent out of the city in closed carriages, heading west. They don't come back."

"What's in the west?" Jasper asked while Maeve clutched his hand tightly, her palms suddenly wet.

"Desert."

"But what's in the desert?"

"No one knows. There's talk of a fortress Morlen's built there."

Maeve and Jasper walked on frantically, circling the surrounding camps, asking after Evan.

Dorjan wondered how many nights of sleep it would take before he felt strong again. He was slow to prop himself up on an arm, slower to stand. Walking was full of effort; he was glad no one asked him to run. He noticed that Maeve, Jasper, and Evan weren't around, and Sara was only beginning to wake up. Close by, Fortune was tethered to a scrubby tree. Dorjan staggered into the stand of trees to relieve himself.

He sank back onto the sand, watching the whitecaps rolling. "I wish it was night again, time to sleep among the sycamores," he said to Fortune. The horse blew. "And I wish I had oats for you."

When Sara rose, she came to sit beside him, her hair a mass of tangles, her face peeling, lips cracked. He decided he had to tell her about the dreamscape. He couldn't let another day go by. "Sara—"

But she was getting to her feet. "Something's wrong," she said, pointing along the sand to where Maeve and Jasper came at a run, their faces strained with worry.

"Evan," Maeve said, panting. "Is he here?"

Dorjan shook his head. "We thought he was with you."

Jasper kicked at the sand. "The free tell us that children are being stolen. They say he's likely been taken to the western desert." He looked up and Dorjan saw him grip Maeve's arm. "Stripers," he said.

Dorjan turned, following Jasper's gaze. Two men, wearing doublets striped black and gray, marched purposefully along the sand. Their boots were gray, and they bore axes at their belts.

"They've seen us," Jasper said. His brown eyes looked nearly black.

"Morlen's men?" Sara asked.

Jasper nodded. "They've seen us," he said again.

Dorjan wondered if it would kill him to dream-travel again.

If I must die, I must die. He shut his eyes, reaching within, embracing Maeve and Sara with the last of his gen.

When Dorjan shut his eyes, Jasper dared to hope. *Use my strength*, he said silently, wondering if Dorjan could possibly hear his thought. Whether he did or he didn't, he and the two young women disappeared.

When the zind arrived, Jasper pretended he belonged here, pretended he'd grown up on this beach.

The stripers looked about them. "Where did they go?" one said.

"Who?" Jasper asked.

"Saw them a moment ago. Lord Morlen has them posted. Where'd you hide them?"

"Sun phantoms," Jasper muttered.

The zind who'd spoken drew his knife.

Jasper stepped forward. If he acted witless, he couldn't help Maeve. Every other time he'd talked to a soldier, his spine had slouched while he looked at the ground. Now his back was straight. "Sun phantoms," he said again.

The zind put his knifepoint to Jasper's throat. "I saw them," he said.

"I've seen food when I was hungry." Jasper met the man's eyes, didn't flinch as he felt the blade prick his skin, felt blood trickling down his neck.

The zind took a step back. "Did you see them?" he asked his companion.

The other man shook his head confusedly.

The first zind pushed Jasper to the ground. But he sheathed his knife, and he and his companion left.

Jasper brushed the sand from his clothes as he stood up. He searched his pockets for something to dab the blood on his neck. His hand found the two gold delans.

"Fortune," Jasper whispered, stroking the horse, "I'm glad Maeve brought this gold into Mantedi." He took the mare's halter and made his way along the beach to where he remembered talking to the graybeard who'd sold him food and water. When he found him, Carl had his things packed into a bag, ready to make the walk to the mine.

"I need to leave the city," Jasper said.

Carl shook his head. "I told you. Can't be done."

"There must be a way."

"If you had gold, and you were a farmer, you could get the farmer's brand and move in and out as you like. But you ain't got gold by the looks of you, and you ain't a farmer or you'd be tending your harvest."

"But if I *were* a farmer?"

Carl shook his head. "A brand lasts a lifetime."

"I need to get out of Mantedi today. The rest of my life is a dead thing if I don't."

Carl picked up his bag. "A woman?"

Jasper wasn't ashamed to say yes.

"You'd be branded for her?"

"I would face a patrier."

Carl slung the bag over his shoulder. "It's half a delan to get the brand. Anyone daft enough to pay for a burn deserves a scar."

"Show me where it's done."

Carl began walking. "I'll show you. But no woman's worth a brand."

Jasper trudged beside him. "This one is."

Chapter 25

Maeve found herself with a mouthful of grit, lying in a rutted road, looking after a closed carriage as it sped away. Next to her Sara coughed and spat. A few feet away, in the middle of the road, Dorjan lay on his back, motionless, eyes closed.

Maeve gathered herself slowly to sit. The land around was strewn with small rocks, as if a giant who played with boulders had thrown down his toys and stomped away, leaving thousands of pieces of broken orange stone behind him.

Sara tugged on Maeve's sleeve. "We have to get Dorjan out of the road," she said, "without waking him. If we leave him there, another carriage could crush him."

She was right. They mustn't wake him. Dorjan had said it was important not to interrupt a Dreamwen's sleep. Was he sleeping? He looked like death.

Maeve got shakily to her feet. She bent to Dorjan's ankles. Sara took the weight of his shoulders. Together, they carried him to a patch of sandy gravel in the shade of a tall outcropping of rock. Maeve's hands told her that Dorjan's life force was nearly gone. She was so afraid he was dying, she could hardly stagger the few steps it took to get him out of the road.

Sara sank to the ground. She leaned back against the rock, swearing and praying with the same breath—chiding Dorjan for using the last of his strength, blessing him for saving them, calling on God for help.

Maeve took the Dreamwen Stone, still tied to the fluttering threads of what had once been the hem of her slave shift, from around her neck. She laid it on Dorjan's forehead. Dorjan was still breathing—faint and slow, but breath was life. Maeve wanted to put her hands on his chest, wanted to sing to him. But she remembered Orlo. When she had sung to Orlo, he had quickly died. What if she only helped Dorjan to die?

Sara was looking around. "I wonder what Dorjan would aim for that would land us here?"

Maeve put a hand to her head. "Evan!" she cried. "That carriage must have had Evan in it." She jumped to her feet.

The outcrop they had taken shelter by was the tallest thing she saw. Finding handholds, she hoisted herself up it. From its height, she scanned the terrain. The desert glared back at her, heat waving in all directions across rock and sand, running from yellow to orange. Though it had seemed lifeless at first glance, from her vantage she saw skittering lizards and patches of hardy cacti. The road cut the land like something made by a child learning to whittle—a jagged, rough line going west and east. Far to the east, she could make out a blue edge, which she took to be the Minwenda. Westward, the road led over a small hill. Just past the hill, a fortress loomed, rust-colored like the desert surrounding it. It wasn't very far away—Maeve could see a carriage stopped in front of it, and men pulling boys out of the carriage. She gasped as she recognized Evan's sturdy walk and his pale yellow shirt.

The desert fortress.

Except for the road, the building was the only sign of humankind to be seen. Maeve wondered how far they were from the city of Mantedi. Her relief at seeing Evan alive mixed with fear that he would be made a slave again. She wished all the slave owners in Sliviia could be put inside a walled city of their own, and have to serve one another.

She climbed down. Dorjan still lay, unmoving except for his thin, uneven breathing. She told Sara what she'd seen.

"Whoever took Evan must plan to put him to work," Sara said. "They wouldn't bring him all the way out here to kill him."

Maeve nodded. She couldn't help noticing how blistered Sara's skin was. Thankfully, their rock gave shade. But without water, what would they do? Would the brother she had met in waking life only yesterday die at her side today? And how could she help Evan?

"We need water," Sara said, echoing Maeve's thoughts. "But I don't want to leave Dorjan."

Maeve didn't want to leave him, either. "I didn't see any water, though there's sure to be some in the fortress."

Blood welled from Sara's cracked lips. "From the open sea to the open desert," she said ruefully. "The sun follows me. I used to believe going hungry would be the worst hardship, but now I know it's going without water. Even so, I'm hungry enough to eat a lizard if they didn't scuttle so fast." She squinted. "When the sun goes down, we'll find water."

Dorjan didn't have the strength to stand, and sitting was agony. All around him stretched ground as bare as bone.

Hills rose in the distance, bald and lifeless, and an angry sun stood on the horizon, unmoving. Hot wind scoured precious drops of moisture from his skin as he scanned the wasteland for any sign of water, any growing thing. A dried-up streambed lay next to him, its clay baked into wide cracks.

Memories sparked in his skull like cinders. *Sara. Maeve. I pulled them with me. Where are they?* He made himself turn in a full circle, ignoring the pain that blistered him with every movement. Scorched desolation stared back at him, empty, completely empty.

But wait—far away, near the chalky hills, a small wave of heat stirred steadily. Dorjan's mind clung to it as if it could save him, because it moved apart from the wind. He waited, afraid that what he watched would turn out to be only a puff of ash. But it kept coming, until he could see that it was a woman, her dress trailing scarves of silky blue. Her hair, long and white, flowed in the wind like her scarves. She came nearer. When she stood in front him, he searched her face with burning eyes. Her bronze skin was etched with many lines, her eyes blue mirrors of his own.

"Grandma." He bowed his aching head, touching the hem of her dress. "How did you come to be here, in the desert?"

"The prayers of those who love you have brought me here." She reached her hand to him. "You must come with me."

He took her hand. It felt soft and cool. "I'd gladly go," he said, "but I'm unable to stand."

"You must. You can't stay here any longer."

His mouth felt drier than dust. "Do you have any water?"

"There's water where we're going. Here, no water is left. You've used up every living drop." She tugged at him gently. Flames of pain rolled over him as he tried to stand.

"Used . . . but I've never been here before."

"You have lived here all your life. Now you must leave, for there's nothing left."

Fire licked through his lungs. "I don't understand. Where are we going? Is Sara there? And Maeve?"

"The place we must go is beyond that hill." She pointed.

Getting through each breath was all Dorjan knew— that, and the cool hand guiding him. He breathed in, beset by stabbing fire, then breathed out and took another step. At last they reached the hill Marina had come from. She led him past its base. He hadn't thought his pain could grow, but it did, towering over his mind, an inferno.

A short stairway, sculpted of stone, rose before them. Dorjan crawled upward, each step a long agony. When he finally ascended the top stair, the scene transformed. In front of him was a pool lined with shining stones, where the clearest water lightly danced. Around the pool, lush plants and large flowers swayed; beyond it stood healthy trees, footing a skyline of majestic mountains.

Marina gestured at the pool. "Drink," she said. "Bathe."

He slid headfirst into the water, gulping, immersing, soaking.

When he came out of the pool, Dorjan sat quiet among the flowers, his grandmother watching him. She seemed older, somehow, than she had when she first appeared—the lines in her face looked deeper; her frame was slightly stooped. Dorjan looked again at the pool, startled to see that it was nearly empty.

"Where did the water go?" he asked.

"You needed it," she said softly.

"But—I didn't drink so much as that." The trees that had looked so tall and green moments before were leafless now. The flowers beside him dropped petals. "Where are we?" he asked.

"This is my life. Yours was used up."

"But why is this place drying out?"

She turned away from the pool, ignoring his question. "We can't stay here much longer, either one of us. Come."

Dorjan followed her as she walked slowly away from the pool. She stopped beside a stand of trees that had kept their leaves. She turned to look back, clasping her hands. She bowed with great dignity. "Thank you for my life," she said, speaking out across the dry land, holding the bow.

She seemed to be saying good-bye. What did it mean? She gestured at the near trees. "We must go forward now."

Dorjan hung back. "Forward to where?"

She smiled a little. "Come. You can't stay here." She stepped into the trees, and he couldn't see her anymore.

The ground where he stood began crumbling underneath him. Withered plants blew past him, and gathering dust whirled about his head. Dorjan strode into the trees after Marina.

"He's breathing better," Maeve said.

The worry in Sara's face smoothed out a little. "He'll wake up soon," she said.

To pass the time and push their spirits, they talked: Maeve told the story of how she'd met Morlen, how she'd escaped him and then been captured. Sara listened with rapt attention, prompting with questions. Maeve related all that she remembered. When she came to the part about the visions Morlen had shown her of the land across the Minwenda, Sara suddenly gripped her wrist. "He showed you Bellandra's king and queen? You saw them?"

"Yes. Lying still. He told me they didn't have long to live."

Sara's hand tightened, trembling. "Not long to live? Not long to live? Why?"

In Sara's touch, Maeve felt an intensive, latent power. What was it? *Overwhelming force, yet she doesn't seem to know she has it.*

"It had something to do with being close to mystic objects," Maeve answered, reeling from what she'd sensed in Sara. "The next place he took me was a chamber. I don't think it's part of our world—part of a place I'd seen before in a dream. I saw light being changed into something else."

Sara dropped her wrist. "Tell me," she ordered grimly.

Maeve went on with her story, while Sara hung on her words.

"The Healer's Keep! What did you see there?"

Maeve described the building that pulsed with silver light, the cracked foundations of the other buildings. "A great dark bird flew toward me. Morlen called it an Ebe. He said the Shadow King had all of them now."

"Ebe? The dark birds are called Ebes?" Sara's eyes snapped. She stood, muttering breathlessly to herself, "All the Ebes. Ebes." She paced, heedless of the sun's heat. After a while, she dropped to the ground next to Maeve again. "We have to stop them. We'll use the Dreamwen Stone. I can fight them." She grabbed Maeve's shoulders. "Tonight. We'll hunt them together. If you stand by me, I can kill them."

Maeve stared, almost frightened by Sara's ferocity, but admiring her.

"You can help me; it has to be you. I can't ask Dorjan—he's too tired." Sara let go of Maeve's shoulders. "Will you stand by me?"

"I—I suppose."

Satisfied, Sara told her about meeting Dorjan and what had followed. She finished her extraordinary tale by saying, "You and Dorjan are the only ones I've told about what happened with the Tezzarine."

"Birds with feathers like pearl," Maeve said wistfully. "Bellandra must be a land of marvels."

"Yes," Sara said. "We mustn't let the king and queen die."

As the sun dragged unremitting fire through the sky, Maeve began to wonder if they'd get out of the desert alive. The air burned with each breath. Her tongue felt dead and dry; she and Sara didn't talk anymore.

Following his grandmother, Dorjan emerged from the trees into a meadow. Instead of a blazing sun, stars shimmered in a midnight blue sky—close stars, trailing silver light over softly waving grass. Marina stood waiting for him, her face shining.

"The Meadows of Wen?" he said, bewildered. "How did we get here?"

"Yes, Dorjan, the Meadows of Wen." She smiled.

A figure wearing Ellowen robes approached them, treading lightly over the grass.

"Ellowen Renaiya?" Dorjan asked, not trusting his eyes, drawing closer to be sure. "I thought—you might be dead."

"I am," she said.

"Y-you are?" He looked along the expanses of silver grass. "Am *I* dead, then?"

She raised a hand.

Another figure appeared. *Ellowen Mayn.* "Welcome, Dorjan," he said.

"You're . . . not dead, are you?" When Ellowen Mayn nodded, Dorjan didn't know what to think. "Am *I* dead, too?"

"Not quite. You're still alive because of what your grandmother has given you."

"What she has given . . ." Aghast, Dorjan looked at Marina. "No. You're not—?"

Marina's face was calm and happy. "I couldn't let you die, Dorjan," she said.

"But—"

"It's best," Marina assured him. "I had a long life."

Before Dorjan could reply, Ellowen Renaiya stepped forward. "We have something to show you," she said.

She touched his head with gentle hands. All at once he seemed to be floating with the bright air, part of it, wafted high, his view widening, increasing, looking out across the world—a living globe jeweled with plants and animals, water and fire, birds and fish. He saw humans, their souls visible, some glowing faintly, some shining like small suns, some lightless and gray. He saw something else, too—a resplendent sheen of silver enclosing it all. "The Silver Boundary," Ellowen Renaiya said.

"Look closely," his grandmother told him.

Dorjan noticed points of dreary gray in the gleaming silver. "The world of form is no longer safe," said Ellowen Mayn.

Dorjan's vision changed. A gray pall descended over the world. Even the water ceased to sparkle. As for the people, though Dorjan sought for the bright souls he had seen moments before, he couldn't find any. Instead, there were great numbers of lightless ones.

"No," he said. "This can't have happened."

"It hasn't happened, not yet," he heard Marina say. "But the Boundary is in peril."

The vision left suddenly. Dorjan could hardly grasp what he'd seen. His grandmother—dead? The Ellowens, too? He felt enormously uneasy even though he stood in the Meadows of Wen. *The greatest refuge of peace throughout the realms—and I feel uneasy.*

"The Silver Boundary holds back the Shadow King," Marina said. "And it's collapsing."

Dorjan didn't know what to do. "Why did you show me?" he cried. "And why don't you keep this . . . Boundary from falling?"

"The Boundary can only be brought down, and can only be mended, by the living," Ellowen Mayn said. "We can't return to the world of form, Dorjan, but *you* can."

Mayn continued talking—about the Silver Boundary and the Healer's Keep, about something known as the Boundary House and how it had been used by Ellowens for centuries to tend the Boundary—while Dorjan hoped Marina would break in and tell him this was not a truthful dream but an ordinary nightmare.

But she didn't, and Ellowen Mayn went on. "Tonight, Dorjan, the Boundary will fall. Unless someone in the world of form prevents it."

Dorjan was feeling more and more uncomfortable.

Renaiya patted his shoulder. She brought a tiny vial out of her robes. "Take it," she told him. "Drink."

The vial was clear; the liquid inside it sparkled and glowed. "What is it?"

"The essence of Wen," she answered. "It will heal you of the effects of your dream travels."

Dorjan hung his head. "I can't take it."

"Take it. You need more healing."

Dorjan remembered how spent he had been after Maeve's rescue. He remembered the dry, cracked streambed of the place Marina had found him. He looked longingly at the sparkling liquid. "I don't deserve it. I broke the Dreamwen law. Many times."

Ellowen Mayn stepped close to Dorjan. "Even as you broke the law of spirit, you were upholding the spirit that formed the law. You didn't act out of greed, or anger, or lust for power. If you had, we couldn't offer this to you now."

Dorjan looked at his grandmother. Marina nodded.

Reverently, he took the vial from Ellowen Renaiya. He opened it, tilting his head to take the precious drops. A dazzling taste filled him, as if the silver light shining over these meadows had been distilled into liquid. He felt able to do anything.

He bowed very low. "Thank you all." He straightened. The three of them were looking at him silently. He sighed. "Tell me how the Boundary can be saved."

Ellowen Mayn began describing the secrets of the Boundary House and told of how Bern and Lowen Camber had conspired to destroy it. "But there's still a chance it can be renewed—if you get there in time."

"I must go back to the Keep?"

"Yes. Here is what needs to be done." And Mayn launched into long, involved instructions.

"But before you go, Dorjan, listen carefully." He sounded even more serious than he had while talking of the Boundary. "You have made seven dream journeys in which you have used your mind to transport your body. You'll be allowed three more. If you attempt a fourth, you will die instantly."

"Three more?"

"Such journeys are unnatural to the world of form; only someone with a great affinity for other realms could travel in such a way. You know the costs to your body. You have been healed here; that healing will extend to only three more journeys. Use them wisely."

"What about the others who traveled with me? Are they injured? Will they be hurt if they go with me again?" *Please say no.*

"Each traveler incurs depletion of gen, but theirs is not as severe as yours. So long as the journeys are few, they will recover. Remember, only three more," Mayn said. "And now you must return. Many hours have passed while you visited us. It's evening in the desert, and nearly midnight at the Healer's Keep."

Chapter 26

Sitting propped against a rock, burning with thirst, Maeve marveled at the desert sunset—not only the west, but the whole sky flamed with color. She heard hoofbeats. She could make out a rider coming toward them. "Jasper," she whispered. She waved her hands, trying to call out, but her throat was too dry.

When Fortune came abreast, "Whoa!" came a soft command. Jasper jumped down. He grabbed a leather bottle. He knelt beside Maeve, pouring water into her mouth, and then into Sara's.

He wore a white scarf wound over his forehead. Maeve wondered how he'd come by it—it looked like a bandage, but it must be to protect him from the sun. "Thank you," she said. She gripped his hand. His touch held a burning pain. "What is it?" she asked. "Jasper? You're in pain?"

He shrugged. He looked at Dorjan. "Shall I wake him and give him water?"

"We think he's on a Dreamwen journey. If he is, it's best to let him sleep," Sara said. "Anyway, he looks better now than he has since we left Bellandra."

"But Jasper, how did you get out of the city?" Maeve asked.

"I spent half a delan to do it," he said.

He'd told her the day before about how he'd gone diving for the gold. "Was it a bribe, then?"

Not answering, he handed her the water bottle. He stood up. He took a saddlebag from Fortune. "Food," he said, grinning.

They sat and ate together, bread and cheese and apples. Maeve told Jasper about seeing Evan beyond the small hill. The news made him look grave.

"I'll go look for him," he said.

"Alone?" Sara asked.

"Alone," he said firmly. "The night will hide me."

"I'll go with you," Maeve told him, though she felt so exhausted she could hardly move.

"No." He put a finger on her lips. "I'll never risk you again."

She wanted to argue, but had no strength for it.

He gave them two blankets and left the water bottle and a loaf. "There's more," he said when Maeve protested. He lifted her to her feet. "I can't let Evan stay there. I'll be back." But he hugged her as if he might never see her again.

He mounted Fortune and went on down the moonlit channel of the road. Maeve watched him climb the hill and disappear from sight. Why hadn't he told her how he got out of Mantedi? And what was his pain from?

"I'm glad to be so tired," Sara said. "Ready for battle with the Ebes." She spread a blanket on the ground beside Dorjan. "I know Lord Morlen will be hunting me. You said once an Ebrowen looks in your eyes, he can follow you into your dreams. I don't know why he didn't find me last night when we slept on the beaches of Mantedi."

Maeve forced herself to consider what was at hand. "Because of Dorjan's safe dreamscape," she said. "We can begin there tonight. He told me how to get there, how to bring you, too, as he has done. Maybe he's there now."

"As he has done?" The sharp edge in Sara's voice was startling.

She doesn't know. Dorjan didn't tell her, didn't ask. "As he's done every night, to protect you."

"Protect me?"

"He said the dark birds were hunting you," Maeve said, faltering. "He meant to tell you."

"As he's not here, perhaps *you* should tell me?"

So Maeve explained what she could about Dorjan's sycamore grove. "We can leave the grove once we know we're together in our sleep," she promised nervously. "These Ebes seem to be hunting you, so we'll likely see them as soon as we leave Dorjan's dreamscape." Gently, she lifted the Dreamwen Stone from Dorjan's sleeping body and put it around her neck. When she touched him, her hand told her that he was well. Wherever he had gone, he'd recovered from bringing them out of Mantedi.

Dorjan, Dorjan, if you can hear me, please come with us. She lay a blanket next to Sara under the bright round moon. "Think of the great sycamore," she murmured. Sara didn't reply.

When Maeve saw the peaceful sycamore rising majestically in Dorjan's dreamscape, she sought Sara's spirit as Dorjan had taught her, but didn't find it. She felt so safe and serene here, she wanted to stay. Maybe Dorjan would arrive. But if she waited and he didn't come, Sara would be left to fight the Ebes without help.

Maeve found the gateway leading out of the dreamscape. She pushed it open and found herself on the edge of a moonlit cliff, ocean waves below. When she turned from the cliff, she saw Sara hurrying down a path that led away from the sea. She ran to catch up.

"If I can reach them, I can tell them what's wrong," Sara said.

"Tell who?" Maeve asked.

"The king and queen of Bellandra. I know this place— we're close to the palace."

An unbearably piercing call sounded in Maeve's ears. She looked back and saw a black shape looming above the cliff, winging toward them. An Ebe.

Sara turned to face the Ebe. "Stand by me," she said.

Maeve whisked the Dreamwen Stone from around her neck, holding it up, watching as golden light poured from its center. Sara stood, arms outstretched, gathering in the Dreamwen luster. The Dreamwen song, stronger than Maeve had ever heard it, echoed across the cliffs. It pushed aside all her thoughts, dived deep in her heart, looked out of her eyes.

Everything was before her in absolute shades: Sara's expression, nearly mad with battle lust, poised to kill; the hunting Ebe, trained on Sara, talons ready. The dark bird was so near, one of its wings brushed Maeve's shoulder. She tried to draw back from what she knew then, but could not.

She knew what the bird was.

Immediately, she drew the Dreamwen Stone away from Sara's sight.

Too late.

Swollen with powerful light, Sara blasted the Ebe. The creature shrieked and dropped to the earth, blazoned with burns, one eye gouged with fire. Sara raised her fists again, leaping foward. Maeve crashed into her, trying to knock her over, but Sara seemed made of granite. She didn't budge.

"The Stone!" Sara cried. "Hold out the Stone so I can finish it!"

Maeve turned and ran. Footsteps pursued, crunching over the ground. Sara was upon her, shaking her, shouting. "Why are you running? Give me the Stone. I can kill the Ebe!"

"No. No. You won't ever forgive yourself. Stop!"

"I can't stop now!"

"I'm sorry," Maeve said. "I'm so, so sorry. I didn't know."

"What didn't you know?"

"That bird is a slave to the Shadow King. Not a willing servant."

"But it's still an Ebe! It's still doing the Shadow King's work."

Maeve nodded. "Yes. Yes, it is. But Sara, it's a captured Tezzarine."

Bern liked the night, when he could prowl the Keep at his ease without making excuses to the Ellowens who remained.

He thought it amusing that routines at the Keep carried on as if nothing had changed. How did the healers explain the death of Ellowen Mayn? He'd been an old man, but in perfect health. No, they couldn't explain it, any more than they had been able to explain the loss of Ellowen Renaiya. But they went on, teaching and practicing. The Dradens provided meals and kept everything scrupulously clean. Some of the novices had left but not a single Lowen, though many of them complained of nightmares.

The sick had continued to visit the infirmary. Many improved during their stay—especially those treated by

Lowen Camber. The herbs she administered alleviated her patients' pains, even as she cunningly weakened their gen. Now she was on her way to Bellandra's palace to bring "medicines" to King Landen and Queen Torina, who had both been struck by an unknown malady. Bern smiled to himself.

He had visited the Boundary House every night, enjoying the slow collapse of the Silver veil. Tonight was the full moon. By morning, the Boundary would have slipped enough to make it impossible to repair. The forces holding sway over the world of form would shift to the Shadow King—the Keep itself would crumble, and the new reign arrive.

On the steps of the Boundary House, Bern muttered the word for overcoming the Dark Invisibility. He mounted the steps.

Sara fell upon Maeve, determined to get the Dreamwen Stone from her. "You're wrong!" she cried, looking back to where the broken Ebe flapped feebly on the cliff top. "You've never seen a Tezzarine. You don't know what they are."

"It brushed me. That's how I know—I don't know why, but it's true." Maeve huddled against the ground, her body covering the Dreamwen Stone.

"It can't be true!" Sara couldn't bear the idea that the Ebe would get away from her again, would live to haunt her dreams over and over. "Give me the Stone or I'll take it from you." She fought against Maeve.

Strong hands pinned her shoulders from behind, lifting her away. When she twisted to see who was there, she saw Dorjan. "It's true, Sara," he said, pointing to the Ebe.

She felt as if the Ebe had its dark claw in her chest. "You knew this?"

"No. I believed they were the enemy."

"They *are* the enemy!"

"Yes. But no. You said you'd give anything to see a Tezzarine again." He gestured at the evil-looking bird. "There. All that's left of a Tezzarine."

She hated the thoughts creeping across her mind: if this were indeed a Tezzarine, enslaved to the Shadow King, its insight corrupted, what creature could be better for invading the dreams of the gifted? And if captured, as Dorjan and Maeve declared, perhaps it was the very one whose protection she had done away with.

No. They had to be wrong. She'd been on the verge of victory and they had stolen it from her. If Maeve had stood beside her as promised, the Ebe would be dead, not trying brokenly to fly. And even if the dark bird had once been a Tezzarine, it wasn't one now.

Unwillingly, she heard a stanza of the Dreamwen lore chanting in her mind.

When truth is hated for its pain
Or crushed so you won't fear . . .

Her anger gave way to sudden shame. How Dorjan must detest her. "I'm sorry," she said.

"Sara," he said gently. "You didn't know. I didn't know. None of us knew."

"Where did you go?" she whispered.

"I'll tell you everything, I promise. But just now, there's something urgent. You and Maeve and I—we need to go to the Boundary House of the Keep; Bern has—"

"Look there!" Maeve interrupted, jumping up, pointing.

On the cliff beside the fallen Ebe, a tall, broad figure could be seen. As it ran toward them with frightening speed, there was no mistaking Lord Morlen.

"Will you come with me?" Dorjan cried.

"Yes!"

A streaming wind whirled around Sara, batting at her, harder and harder, until she landed against it, and it wasn't a wind at all, but a solid, circular room.

She was fully awake, breathing hard. Stained glass windows shed faded moonlight across an inlaid floor. Under her hand, a depiction of a sword was carved into marble. It looked familiar somehow.

Beside her Maeve blinked and gasped, clasping the Dreamwen Stone, and Dorjan lay panting, his deep eyes wide. Sara peered across the room, waiting for her eyes to get used to the dim light. In the middle of the floor, twenty feet away, a young man sat facing her. *Bern.* The eerie light played across his handsome features.

He ignored her. Instead, his eyes were on Maeve as he rose. "I closed my eyes alone," he said. "I open them and see a vision of beauty. My name is Bern. And you are—? Not a dream, I hope."

Maeve stared up at him, looking entranced. Slowly, she stood.

"What is that stone you bring?" Bern advanced with soft steps, hand outstretched. "May I touch it?"

Maeve cradled the Dreamwen Stone in both hands, moving toward Bern.

"No!" Sara screamed, scrambling to her feet.

Bern took the Dreamwen Stone. Maeve's hand touched his and her smile changed into a grimace of revulsion. She stumbled backward, falling. As she fell, Sara heard a rumbling, as if great rocks slid into one another. She squeezed her palms against each other. Was she dreaming after all? She seemed to be awake, but the rumbling sound was like the dream she'd had, of the Keep collapsing into dust.

"Too late," Bern said. "The Keep is falling, and the Boundary with it." Something crashed loudly outside, while Bern smiled triumphantly, holding the Dreamwen Stone in a tight fist. With his other hand, he drew out a thin-bladed knife. He brandished it at Sara. "I know you'd rather not see me this way, my sweetest Sara—not with the taste of defeat in your mouth." He put the knife to his lips. "This blade has killed your parents."

He's lying . . . couldn't get near them with a knife . . .

"True, sweetheart, so sadly true. I stabbed the Sword of Bellandra and Bellandra's crystal. Now all the light they had is reversed into the Shadow King's power. The king and queen will not live to understand how they died, or for what."

Will not live. . . . Then they are still alive. . . . Stabbed the Sword . . . crystal . . .

Bern opened his fist, held the knifepoint against the Dreamwen Stone. "And this pebble that you are all so fond of—I have it now."

Looking at him, Sara felt as if an enormous fire burned within her. *I won't let you keep it.*

She bowed to Bern as if he had won. She held the bow, watching as a gloating sneer covered his face. Coming out of the bow, she leaped, clean and swift, plucking the Dreamwen Stone from his hand. She tossed the Stone to Maeve, then aimed a sudden kick at Bern. A coil of silver light rolled from her foot, and his knife clanged against the floor.

He charged. She dodged him, dancing out of his way. Then she feinted left, skipped back. Again. Forward, feint right, back, forward again, *strike*.

He landed return blows, many of them, but it didn't matter to her. She must not think of quitting, must not retreat at all. She wouldn't stop until he was defeated, would never stop unless he killed her. She fought on, while Bern's fists battered at her and the air shook with the sound of falling rocks.

She had him midway between the center of the room and the door before she began to feel the pain of all the blows she'd taken. His hard knuckles beat against the bruises he'd already inflicted. How strong he was; fighting him was like fighting more than one man. Though she locked every bit of her gen against him, she couldn't hold him. Couldn't hold him, and he knew it—his eyes baited her. "Now who's nothing?" he said.

She risked a glance, looking behind Bern. Dorjan and Maeve sat together in the middle of the floor, the Dreamwen Stone between them. Their eyes were shut, their hands flowing in ornate patterns. What were they doing?

Bern's knife lay close. Before Sara could get to it, he swooped, picking it up. This time, her weak kick didn't dislodge it from his grip. He sliced through her jacket, running the knife along the edge of her collarbone. She felt a piercing cold, as though the blade were made of sharp ice. She shivered violently, while Bern flourished the knife in front of her.

"Who shall be first?" he said. "You, my lovely Sara? Or those others, sitting foolishly in the doorway of my king?"

Sara jumped back. The floor shook. Rumblings from outside roared higher. Bern swiped at her again and she dodged, stumbling, trying to keep him away from Dorjan and Maeve.

"Sara, I would dance with you till dawn," he said, panting only a little. "But you're not much of a dancer, and there are other partners waiting. Time for you and me to say farewell."

She wove in and out, between knife thrusts, giving ground. She stumbled, righted herself, stumbled again. The cold in her chest seemed ready to freeze her heart.

She sidestepped Bern's slashing arm. "You're nothing, Bern, and you will never be more than that." She slid backward on faltering feet, toward the entrance, leading him away from Dorjan and Maeve.

He let her get near the door, let her get a small distance away from him. His lips drew back from his teeth, and his arm drew back, too. He threw the knife. Desperately, Sara ducked its force. She heard it whine past her head, saw it drive into the wall.

She grabbed the hilt and pulled. It was like trying to pull a tree from the ground. Behind her, she heard Bern's jeering laughter. She hung on to the knife with all her weight. It came loose from the wall with a sudden jerk that landed her on the floor. She flopped over, only to see Bern running at her.

"Nothing," she whispered. She threw the knife.

The blade met his chest. He kept coming, but only for a few steps. Then he sprawled across the landing. He twitched a few times, and stopped moving.

Sara lay gasping, overcome by what she'd done. She, a princess of Bellandra, had killed Bern in battle for the Boundary House of the Healer's Keep.

Across the floor in the center of the room, Dorjan and Maeve didn't seem to notice. Their hands went on gliding.

Though both brother and sister had their eyes closed, their hands agreed movement for movement.

Leaning against the wall, Sara gazed at Bern's body. A trickle of his blood ran slowly across the floor, toward a circular engraving that sparkled next to the splendid engraved sword she had noticed when she first arrived. The circle reminded her of her mother's crystal, and the sword was very like the legendary Sword of Bellandra.

Why wasn't Bern's blood drying up? It was flowing faster, dripping into thin crevices in the engravings.

"No!" Sara cried. "You can't have them. You're dead. Dead!"

She peeled off her knit jacket and flung it over the spreading stain of his blood on the floor. Where the blood seeped through, the crystal's diamonds turned smoky gray, and the sword's silver faded to the color of lead.

Sara shivered furiously as an idea formed in her mind: *It was here, in this room, that Bern stabbed Bellandra's treasures. This place must connect somehow to the real Sword and crystal . . . and to my parents.*

The Boundary House, Dorjan had called it. Sara looked again at Dorjan and Maeve, at their hands weaving patterns above the Dreamwen Stone. *Boundary House.* What had Bern said? *"Too late. The Keep is falling, and the Boundary with it."*

Did this have something to do with the silver net Maeve had seen during her "journey" with Lord Morlen?

Sara wanted to ask Dorjan a hundred questions, but he and Maeve worked on. Whatever it was they were doing, she mustn't disturb them. Bruised and hurting, her wound like stabbing ice, Sara picked herself up. She stepped past Bern's body. She went to the door and looked out at the rest of the Keep.

How long had she fought with Bern? Long enough for dawn to arrive. She could see many of the Keep's buildings fallen into rubble. The bell tower leaned at a crazy angle. People walked dazedly here and there, faces as uncomprehending as they had been in the dream Sara and Dorjan had shared the night they left for Sliviia. No one seemed to notice her standing there. It was as if they *couldn't* see her. Why? She was quite sure she was awake.

She turned away from the ruins and went back inside. Bern's dead eyes confronted her with unblinking malevolence, the knife hilt protruding from his chest.

Shivering from the cold in her wound, Sara spoke the vow that rose in her heart. "Though the world breaks around me and everything I love is taken from me, I will find a way to turn back this evil."

Chapter 27

Jasper tried to focus his thoughts on the moon shining in a clear desert sky, making the road visible as he rode away from Maeve and Sara. With each beat of his heart, the brand on his forehead burned anew. He didn't like leaving Maeve again, but told himself she was safer resting where she was than she would be if she came with him into more danger.

Ahead, lanterns winked. Jasper left the road when he neared the fortress. He tied Fortune to a rocky projection and continued on foot.

Light escaped from the fortress roof, but only narrow, high windows showed in the walls. Lanterns were strung from the entrance to what seemed to be a large carriage house, and men moved about in the lantern light, stacking crates, grunting and shouting. The noise showed they felt no fear of being attacked; no one seemed to be serving sentry duty.

Jasper circled around to the back. He climbed to the roof of the fortress. He looked down through a ceiling of glass, more glass than he'd ever thought to see in one place. The glass topped a room full of orange-leafed plants growing up dozens of trellises. A few lanterns lit the place, but Jasper saw no people. He crawled farther across the roof, to where a skylight showed another room bigger than the first. Here, too, lanterns cast light, showing several men and twenty or more boys, wearing kerchiefs over their noses, tending vats over low fires. Jasper's eyes searched the boys. None of them was Evan. The thought of Evan trapped somewhere inside made him want to throw something.

Flasks stood on shelving against the wall in the room below. A thousand or more, all filled with orange liquid. Jasper remembered the Mantedi graybeard's words. *"Morlen's poison. The orange flasks."*

Vahss.

A plan began forming in Jasper's mind. He climbed down from the roof and checked the front of the fortress again. The men he'd seen outside seemed to have finished their work and gone back inside, leaving their lanterns burning. Stacks of crates stood unattended.

He started collecting rocks from the desert floor. He took off his shirt to make a rough sack so he could climb the roof with rocks tied to his back. He worked doggedly for hours until his hands and arms burned like the brand on his forehead, and there was a large pile of rocks on the roof.

Finally, he took a big boulder and carried it to the back wall of the fortress. He fashioned a sling for it by taking off his pants and knotting them around it, then tying the pants to the sleeves of his shirt. He put the sling over his shoulders and climbed the wall once more. On the roof, he lay the boulder by the ceiling of glass.

He dressed himself and perched next to his pile of rocks on the edge of the roof, overlooking the entrance. The first rock he threw crunched into one of the flimsy crates stacked outside. Glass shattered. Orange liquid seeped onto the ground.

It was like playing with Evan on the journey to Mantedi. Jasper enjoyed it—the heft of the rocks, deciding his targets, hearing the crates smash and the glass tinkling into bits. Soon the lantern light glancing off shards of broken glass shimmered on a pool of orange. A clotted smell rose from the mess, strong and sweet.

Jasper threw his rocks more and more savagely. When nearly all the crates were demolished, a man poked his head out the door. Seeing the destruction, he gave a yell. Jasper felled him where he stood.

Another man peered out, but before he could finish hollering, he joined the first man on the ground. Jasper picked off three more in the same way. Then a group of five came out the door together. Three went down. The two remaining dodged inside.

A few minutes later, perhaps twenty men surged through the doors. Jasper slung two rocks and picked up two more. Some of the men crumpled, groaning. Their fellows looked for handholds in the wall, and while they looked, Jasper pelted their heads. He imagined each man stealing Evan—it was easy then to hit them squarely in the forehead and watch them drop to the ground.

He heaved another rock at a light-boned man who was outpacing the rest, climbing the wall, getting much too close. The man ducked, the rock only glancing off the side of his head. Squirrel-like, he scurried up the wall. He had his hands on the rim of the roof. Jasper kicked at his face and he went down, just as another man's blond head rose past the wall.

Jasper aimed a rock, and the blond man tumbled.
Quiet.

Looking cautiously over the roof, Jasper saw that there were no more attackers on the wall. He waited, panting, watching the door, getting his breath. No one came out.

He crawled over the roof, looking down into the big room through its skylight. All he saw was guttering lanterns. The men and boys had left. He scrambled to the ceiling of glass, checking to be certain no one was below.

He picked up the boulder and heaved it against the glass. With a shattering crash, it plummeted. Jasper leaped through the gash in the ceiling made by the boulder, catching hold of one of the vine-covered trellises to slide to the floor.

The room he landed in caught him fast with amazement. The first thing he noticed was the water, so thick in the air that it stood in drops on the wide orange leaves of the strange plants that grew from great pots on the floor and up the trellises.

Water in the desert. Water so plentiful it almost seemed he might sip the air. Where could it be from? The plants gave off an oppressive, cloying smell as he made a quick search. Jasper wondered what species of plant this was. Not one he knew.

In a corner, he discovered a large spring-box, full to the brim. He dipped a cautious finger into the box, tasting. Sweet and pure. Morlen had caged an oasis for himself! Even the innocent water, he used for his corruption.

Jasper hurried around the trellises, making for the door of the room. He felt dull and dizzy as he slid through it. On the other side, he flattened himself against the wall. Pits in the floor smoked tiredly, but the place was deserted except for the shelves of orange flasks.

Remembering the men and boys with their kerchiefs, he took off his shirt and tied it around his face.

Sweeping an arm along the top shelf, he knocked twenty flasks to the floor. Most shattered. A few simply spilled open, their stoppers loose. He lifted whole shelves, pitching them violently aside. Even through his shirt, he smelled an odor so overpowering he wanted to retch. By the time all the flasks were thrown down, he felt light-headed.

He moved on to the opposite door. It led to a narrow corridor lit by a single lantern. He shuffled forward, the smoky air stinging his eyes. His legs seemed heavier than they should be, but he kept inching his way along.

The corridor branched into two hallways. Jasper took the one to the right. He came to a door made of bars. Peering through the bars, he saw a room full of bunks. A narrow window high in the wall let in very little moonlight, but Jasper's eyes had grown used to the dark. He could make out sleeping shapes on the bunks, and here and there a face. Young faces. Boys, at least fifty of them.

"Evan," Jasper called softly. "Evan, are you there? Evan!"

A head lifted. "Evan?" Jasper had his hands on the lock, trying it.

"Jasper?"

"Over here, Evan. By the door!"

Then something knocked Jasper's feet out from under him, and hard hands gripped his arms.

Dorjan concentrated as hard as he could on remembering everything Ellowen Mayn had said about restoring the Boundary. He could see the pyramids, hoops, and spheres of light, the way they were slipping into collapse. Linked with Maeve, he worked to lift them up, to bring them into rightful balance again.

Time had never been so precious. Even when he heard Sara cry out, he compelled himself to ignore her and keep going. Another careful balancing, another nudge to a circle of light—on and on until the Silver Boundary flowed evenly once more.

At last Dorjan opened his eyes and saw Maeve sag to the floor, her golden skin covered with sweat.

Something was wrong in spite of the mended Boundary. A gray coldness crept through the room. Dorjan tried to banish it, but it grew.

Sara shuffled over to him. She sank to her knees. Her face was badly bruised, and along her collarbone, the faded red fabric of her blouse had been slashed, revealing a long, painful-looking cut. She pointed to the entrance. Bern lay there, quite still. "He's dead," she said. "Dead, but he isn't." She sounded angry and shaken. "Did you finish what you were doing?"

"Yes. The Boundary is in place again," Dorjan said. The sight of Sara's bruised face and the blood on her blouse cut into him. He stared at the entrance, at Bern's body, at the stain of blood covering part of the floor. The grayness and cold seemed to proceed from there.

"The Sword and crystal," Sara said, tugging at his sleeve. "Look. On the floor. Carvings of Bellandra's Sword and crystal. Bern cut them." She pointed. "Somehow, he cut through the true Sword and crystal when he sliced through the carvings of them here on this floor. Do you see?" Dorjan nodded. He did see. "Their magic is being taken. We have to get that magic to come back. We have to follow Bern, Dorjan. His blood ran into the crevices—*after* he died."

How like her, to be ready to go where it was most perilous. He looked again at the ugly wound in her chest, and at the trail of Bern's blood with its gray shadow.

Follow Bern.

"We have to," Sara said again. "We *must.*"

"To follow him, we'll need to sleep," he said. "Here, on this floor, with Maeve to guard us."

"I'm going with you," Maeve said.

Part Six

Ebe Elixir

Chapter 28

Boz, Lord Morlen's desert overseer, dismounted his weary horse and sped up the stairs of Lord Morlen's mansion in Mantedi. His body shrieked for water and the chance to rest, but thirst and fatigue were the least of his worries. Bad enough that he carried ill news; he also had to wait while the louts who guarded Lord Morlen verified that he could enter. Because he worked in the desert, tending the vahss harvest, these minions with their crossed spears didn't recognize him. Boz had been here only once before, and then he'd remained in the courtyard.

The soldiers made him remove his spurs. Lord Morlen's rules—he liked his floors unscratched. Another guard led him farther into the mansion. Boz noticed that almost every wall he passed was hung with weapons; all looked ready for use, polished and sharp. The more halls he walked, the more Boz wished he were back in the desert and the more he cursed the vandal who had destroyed the vahss harvest.

They arrived at an inner door. "News from the desert for Lord Morlen," Boz told a giant of a man standing guard.

"Lord Morlen's sleeping," the guard said brusquely. "Your news must wait."

"He'll want this news, and he'll not want time wasted,"

Boz said, hating the way his voice quavered in the presence of the brawny soldier.

"He's not to be wakened," the soldier insisted. Boz was pointed to a hard chair. He fell into it, wondering if he could stay awake until Lord Morlen rose from his sleep.

Sara stood next to Maeve and Dorjan in a great dome. This place might have been beautiful, with its high, vaulted ceiling, except that its windowless walls were an unrelieved gray, its floor gray and cold. Harsh light from an unknown source fell heavily on the three dream travelers, as though weighted. Sara heard a dripping sound. "Where are we?" she asked.

"Somewhere in the Shadow King's domains," Dorjan answered.

"I've been here before," Maeve said. "Lord Morlen brought me here." She turned to Sara. "The place I told you about, where light drips away."

"Then we're on Bern's track," Sara said.

Dorjan advanced toward a narrow door in the back of the dome. Sara and Maeve followed.

"Wait," Maeve said. "That door—Lord Morlen said I would come back here. I don't want to go in there."

"This is where Bern has gone," Dorjan answered. He opened the door and went through it.

Sara felt colder. She stepped after Dorjan, and Maeve brought up the rear. The door closed with a dull thud.

Sara looked about at the square room they were in. Far smaller than the dome, empty except for four plain gray vessels standing close to the center of the floor, each as high as Dorjan's shoulder. Empty cups hung on hooks at the rims of these vessels. Despair washed over her as she saw bright colored droplets dripping into the vessels from holes in the ceiling.

Dorjan went forward. He reached up and caught a yellow drop on his fingertip. When he turned to Sara and Maeve, the end of his finger shone.

"What is it?" Sara asked.

He peered into one of the vessels as another drop fell into it. "Light," he said. "Light falling . . ." He watched again. "Doused. But not like a flame. The light goes in and *becomes* whatever is in these vessels."

Sara approached one of the jars. Gray liquid nearly filled it. As a bright bead of red light fell into it, the red dissolved into empty gray. She shivered. She looked up at the ceiling, at the trickling light. "This is where the stolen magic from the Sword and the crystal must be going."

Dorjan nodded. "And from other things as well."

"If the light can be brought here," Sara said, "then there must be a way to return it."

"Clever," said a voice, so near that she jumped. "But you need more than cleverness to enter this room and live, Sara."

Bern stood beside her. Bern, or a likeness of Bern, dressed in shadowy gray. He gave her a mocking bow. "I must thank you. You've given me immortal favor with my king. You helped me complete his collection of Ebes."

"You're dead!" she cried. "You're nothing but a dead shadow."

Bern smiled. "Why did you follow *nothing?*" he asked. "Why follow me into the very place that can make you, too, a *nothing?*"

Sara shivered more. The hideous cold of this place ate away all warmth. Bern chuckled. "You want to leave, don't you? Because you can do *nothing* here. But you can't leave." He pointed. "The door is locked, and one such as you would not carry the key."

But as Sara looked at the door, it opened and Lord Morlen appeared, looking more formidable even than he had in waking life. Though she wanted to run, her feet wouldn't move. Dorjan and Maeve also stood rigid, and the door banged shut.

Morlen gave Bern a curt nod. He bowed to Maeve, as if he were lord of a castle welcoming a guest. "How good of you to bring your friends here, Maeve. I have wanted to meet them again." He bowed to all of them. "Your stamina is impressive. Impressive, but soon gone, I expect." He unhooked a cup from the rim of one of the vessels. He dipped it. He tilted his head for a drink. "Ahh," he said.

He offered the cup to Maeve.

"No," she said.

Morlen shook his head. "Poor unwitting child. There isn't any way to leave this place without drinking the Ebe Elixir. You might say you're trapped, my dear." He drained his cup. "When you drink, you will become allies of the Ebes." He dipped once more. He raised the cup. "That is the choice I wish for all of you. And unless you drink, you die."

He went nearer to Maeve. "If you drink, you'll learn to use your gift. You'll never be a slave again, not even to me."

She looked as if she wanted to pull back from him, but she didn't move.

"The Dreamwen Stone," he said softly. "You've recovered the Dreamwen Stone? Clever girl. Give it to me." He opened his palm. "I'll take it back to the world of form for you. If it stays here too long, its power will be drawn into the Elixir, merged with the Ebe shadows. It won't be special in the way it is now."

Maeve shook her head weakly.

"When you drink the Elixir," he said, "you can return to the world of form. I'll share the Stone with you then."

He reached for the Stone, and Maeve didn't resist him. He lifted it from around her neck, while Sara watched, aghast. *No! Don't let him have the Dreamwen treasure!* Sara leaped at Morlen, but he clasped the Stone, shoving her away so hard that she hit the wall behind her. He bowed to Maeve once more. "Thank you. I'm glad the time is near when you will stand beside me. It is *your* voice, Maeve, that will bring many more into the service of the Shadow King."

Sara rushed at him again, but before she reached him, he tapped his forehead with the Dreamwen Stone and vanished.

She stared at the spot where he'd stood. "So we *can* leave this chamber. We need only to wake ourselves."

"Not so," Bern told her.

Sara moved closer to Dorjan. "Help me wake up."

He shook his head. "It can't be done, or we'd be gone. When Morlen entered, I tried to move us."

Bern stepped in front of Sara. She wished he'd quit smiling. "Which shall it be?" he asked. "Elixir or—" She struck at him with all her force. Her fist merely passed through him, a useless hand passing through smoke. He laughed at her. "You forget, I am *nothing* now—and you can do *nothing* to me."

Drawing back, she looked at Maeve, who stood, her face a ruin of grief, seemingly too stunned to move or speak. What hell was this, where the evil dead gloated over the living? *Where I asked my friends to go, and where I thought to save my parents.* Sara imagined her mother and father, lying ill, unable to defend anyone or anything.

Tears rushed into her eyes and she thought how odd it was to feel tears and know she dreamed and know she could not waken.

There was only one thing to do. Sara bent to the cup Lord Morlen had left behind. She dipped it into a standing vessel. As she lifted it to her lips, she heard Bern's taunting laughter.

Someone shook Boz's shoulder. Through a haze of sleep he saw Lord Morlen standing over him, asking for his news. Instantly, Boz was fully awake.

In the desert, his meetings with Lord Morlen had been brief—the lord had been cool and brisk, had let him know his orders, then dismissed him. This time, the gray eyes had a triumphant glint so ferocious that Boz could hardly speak. Perhaps he shouldn't tell his news about the entire vahss harvest being destroyed, about the fortress gutted from above. He should leave here and never return, hide himself somewhere in the alleys of Mantedi.

"Speak up, man. My guards tell me you come from the desert with a message that couldn't wait? A message you carried through the night, nearly killing a good horse?"

Boz's tongue felt ungainly in his mouth. "Yes, sir." He looked hopelessly at the racks of well-oiled weapons on the wall. Perhaps he could reach one of the knives and stick it into his own throat before the guards could prevent him. A quick death.

"The message?"

"I—that is—a man broke into the—" Boz glanced about, afraid to speak of things that were meant to be secret.

"These guards are loyal, man—they watch while I sleep. A man broke into the vahss works? Is that what you're telling me?"

"Yes, sir."

"One man—and the news couldn't wait? I will need to question him. I can do so when I visit the fortress again."

Boz was thankful for one thing—he had no children to receive Lord Morlen's vengeance. He gathered himself and mastered his tongue. "There's more, sir."

Draden Hester wandered the rubble of the fallen Keep with Dra Jem, looking for the injured. She stumbled a little, but refused to let Jem support her with his arm. She was Chief Draden—she wouldn't become a sniveling weakling just because an unforeseen earthquake had destroyed most of the buildings on the grounds.

She and Jem had worked diligently, roving through the ruins, rallying dazed students and healers. The dining hall had been demolished. Some of the rooms in the infirmary stood firm. Most of the Healing Halls, with their spacious classrooms and priceless collections of art, were destroyed. The bell tower listed as though blown by a hard wind. The student dormitories leaned badly, the beams in their ceilings poking through crumpled roofs like fingers reaching for aid. Thankfully, many of the students had been spared, suffering only contusions. But others were missing, including the one Hester searched for most intently—her nephew, Bern, the promising new Dra.

Hester noticed a heap of stones on the outskirts of the Keep's gardens up against the forest. Puzzled, she turned to Dra Jem. "What place is this? I don't recognize it."

Jem shook his head. "Sorry, Draden. I don't know."

"We'd better look, to be sure there's no one trapped." Hester noticed a peculiar reluctance to making the inspection here. Annoyed, she tried shifting one of the stones. It didn't budge. Very odd. And her feet seemed to be standing on a flight of steps. *Who has been practicing illegal enchantments?*

Mounting the stairs, she and Jem passed into a room far too large to be contained by the stones they had seen from outside. Dim light made it difficult to see, and Hester nearly tripped over someone sprawled across the threshold.

"Bern," Jem said tonelessly.

"No," she said. "It can't be."

"It's Bern," he repeated. "And there's a knife in his chest."

"No," she said again, but her eyes had adjusted and there was no mistaking now. She saw a smear of blood, much of it covered by a fraying jacket. More blood trailed along the floor, ending abruptly at a spot where artists of long ago had carved emblems of Bellandra's Sword and crystal.

In the great room beyond the entrance, three more people lay motionless, their heads close together. Draden Hester knew she should investigate, but that would mean stepping over Bern's body. "What can have happened here?" she asked, bending to her dead nephew. The expression on his face shocked her—death had caught Bern in a ghastly grimace.

Dra Jem didn't answer. "Help me carry him out," she said. "Then we'll come back for the others."

Obediently, Jem helped her carry the body. Bern's open eyes disturbed Hester so greatly that she asked Jem to close them, and was ashamed by how much better she felt when he did so. Her nephew! How could Bern be dead? And how, in death, could he appear almost evil?

"We'd better go in for the others," she said.

"Maybe they're not dead, Draden."

"Humph. I doubt they're asleep."

They started up the steps of the derelict structure that unaccountably housed a large, ornate room—a room where Bern had died with a knife in his chest.

When Dorjan saw Sara drink the Ebe Elixir, his thoughts swirled chaotically. Her eyes were turning gray, as if smoke filled them from inside. She still held the cup, and looked to be suspended, unmoving except for the color changing in her eyes. Then all of her began to fade and the cup dropped to the floor. When Dorjan reached for her, she was gone.

Smiling, Bern positioned himself on the place where she had stood. "Accept my apologies for leaving you here," he said, "but I must follow Sara. She will need my advice in her transformation. I wouldn't want her to become lost." And he, too, disappeared.

Urgency pounded Dorjan. "Maeve," he said, "I have to go after them."

"The Dreamwen Stone, Dorjan. I let him have the Dreamwen Stone."

"You didn't give it to him, Maeve. He took it."

She didn't answer.

"I'll do everything I know to return to you." He picked up the cup that had dropped from Sara's hand. He plunged it into the nearest vessel. Standing where she had stood, he drank the Ebe Elixir.

He was snatched into darkness so fast he didn't know where he was. Looking for Sara, all he saw was trailing smoke. A crushing pressure mounted around him, squeezing from every direction.

Then suddenly everything was gone.

Dorjan put out a hand. He wiggled his fingers, relieved to find that they moved. But they moved within a formless emptiness.

A flutter to his left made him turn.

"Dorjan?" Sara said.

Very glad to hear his name, he whispered yes, and it sounded like wind blowing through a canyon.

"Where are we?" she asked. "Why did we come here?"

"I don't know."

He heard a small chuckle, and Bern's shade appeared in front of them. "True," Bern said. "You *don't* know. But I do. You're here because you serve the Shadow King now."

Sara frowned. "I do *not* serve him."

"You have." Bern turned. He gave a dismal call. The sound crackled through the space behind him. With a rush of wings, a crowd of enormous dark birds emerged out of the void. "The Ebes welcome you," Bern said. He motioned, and the birds came closer. "It was you, Saravelda, who gave the Shadow King the leader of his Ebes." He pointed at the lead bird. A livid scar showed on its wing. One of its eyes was missing, half its head scarred and featherless. The remaining eye glared, deep gray and raging.

Dorjan saw doubt and pain taking over Sara's face. Her outline began to change, turning gray. The slash at her collarbone left by Bern's knife opened like a grate. Shadow, like dark water, poured through the gash into her form.

No, Dorjan thought. *She was tricked.*

"You've found your destiny, Sara," Bern said gleefully. "This is what was meant from the beginning. You have followed the Shadow King's plan for you."

As if agreeing with his words, the shadow filling her deepened.

What is this place? Not an ordinary dream world. Not even the halls of the Shadow King would give every word Bern speaks that kind of power.

From somewhere in his mind, Dorjan heard the chant of the Dreamwen lore.

> *A particle within the Seed Void,*
> *More fertile than all the fields of earth,*
> *A word spoken there*
> *More potent than a thousand seeds.*

Seed Void. The legendary realm where the least action would reverberate across all realms.

We're in it. In the Seed Void.

But how had they come to be here? And now what could be done?

Dire warnings in the Dreamwen lore about the Seed Void said that the inner nature could also be shaped and recombined here.

Few ever travel to the Seed Void—
Those who do risk lingering madness.

No wonder Bern had tried to cast them as the Shadow King's servants here. For if they believed him, his claim would be true.

Bern in the Seed Void! What evil might such a creature wreak upon the realms if he were to contaminate this ground? Dreamwen lore said the Void contained the beginnings of all creation.

As Dorjan watched the Shadow filling Sara, he knew he had to do something. He must name her essence before it was lost.

"You're wrong, Bern," he said, deliberately infusing his words with gen. "Saravelda is not a servant of the Shadow King. She is his enemy. You made a mistake, bringing her here, for she is a Firan, a Spirit Warrior!"

As he spoke, a billowing light surrounded Sara. The dark grate in her chest reversed, rapidly pouring shadow. Her wound closed. Fierce vitality began to radiate from her.

Her essence.

She spoke to Bern. "I will not serve him—ever again."

"You *will*," he answered.

She lifted a hand, and a thin thread of gold split the Void behind the flock of Ebes. The thread lengthened, spinning out a shimmer of light that widened into a doorway through which more light rolled. Sara took a step forward.

Bern waved a hand, too. A suffocating gray mist descended. Dorjan heard wings flapping and saw nothing but creeping fog, a cloudy weight dragging against him.

I should tell Sara where we are.

But Dorjan hesitated. Maybe the Dreamwens who had

visited the Seed Void had been hindered by the tales they brought with them. Maybe the danger now would be less if he left her innocent of everything others had said.

"You will serve him," Bern demanded. "It is what was meant from the beginning."

"No, it isn't." Sara's words sent back the mist, and Dorjan could breathe again, could see her facing Bern. In her hand was a curving knife! Its blade was the color of ashes, but ash was without light, and this knife shone with deadly brilliance. "We're free," she said.

Free.

Though she didn't know where they were, she had already drawn on the Void to make the ash-colored knife. In moments, she had created an essence weapon!

Waving her knife, she rushed Bern. "Nothing!" she cried. "You're nothing."

The Ebes clustered together, but to Dorjan's surprise, they fluttered silently and didn't advance. Bern bore back before Sara's attack, his form rippling unsteadily. "You serve him!" he cried, but his words wailed thinly.

Sara didn't answer. Instead, she began to dance.

As she danced, she slashed smoothly with her knife through the space surrounding Bern. She cut underneath his feet, beside his upraised arms, above his head. Where she cut, the Void curled around him like torn skin, and though he tried to beat his way out of the hole she was making, it only widened. A rumbling sound began.

"Nothing," Sara said, her voice louder and clearer than the rumble. She danced, gathering the ruptured edges of the Void, pulling them across Bern's figure. "Nothing!" she yelled, drowning his cries.

The edges she held merged together, seamless and blank. "Nothing," she whispered into a sudden silence.

Bern was gone. Sent, Dorjan was certain, into nothingness forever. Bern had tried to make the Seed Void a tool of his designs, but he'd met with Sara instead.

How did we get here?

Morlen had said that if they drank the Ebe Elixir, they would become allies of the Ebes. But the Ebes were really Tezzarines, captured by the Shadow King, and the Ebe Elixir was made of what had once been light. Did the elixir's power change according to the mind of the one who drank it? *When Sara drank it, she didn't do so to further the Shadow King. And I? I drank it because I love Sara.*

Dorjan realized he might never know how they had come to be here, but gratitude overwhelmed his heart as he watched Sara.

Knife in hand, she dropped to her knees in front of the Ebes. The birds filled the Void with their massive wings, sharp beaks, and bitter eyes.

She spoke to the leader passionately. "You don't belong to the Shadow King."

The scarred leader opened its beak. Its cry shook the Void.

"You're free. You're Tezzarines!" she told it.

The leader lifted on wings of night, and all the other Ebes rose, too. They turned in a circle. They flew through the doorway of light, their flight stirring a wind that roared across Sara and Dorjan. Dorjan closed his eyes against the wind. When he opened them, the bright doorway beyond wavered like a heat phantom, vanishing.

Gaping at the now-quiet emptiness, Dorjan knew there

was something more for him to do. *He* must heal the light that belonged to the world.

"The Shadow King and his servants are barred from this place," he said, speaking into the Void, putting all his passion into the words. "Forever! And the Ebe Elixir is no more. The light that has been taken by the Shadow is returned where it belongs. Forever!"

Chapter 29

Maeve tried the door to the chamber of Ebe Elixir, but it was like trying to open a slab of frozen granite.

It's no use. Lila's love, my escape, our journey. I've given away the Dreamwen Stone, and now I'm alone.

Cold. So cold. It's the cold that will kill me.

She glanced at the cup Dorjan had used to drink the Elixir. If she drank, she could leave this freezing chamber. But she remembered too well what she had seen through Lord Morlen's vision when he'd caught her in his Ebrowen eyes. She wouldn't drink the Ebe Elixir. She wouldn't risk being part of defiling the world of form: the dear, lovely world where, for a short, enrapturing span of time, she'd had the chance to live—to breathe, to move, to sing, to love.

To sing.

Maeve concentrated on remembering the Dreamwen song. Its tune murmured through her, faint yet powerful.

She raised her chin. Death might come quickly, or it might be a lingering wait, but while she waited for death, she would sing of life. She would not give her last moments over to despair.

She lifted her voice and poured out her song. She sang as if nothing else mattered but singing—as if the light beside her did not drip into grayness, as if she stood on the earth making garlands with Jasper and Evan, as if she still had the Dreamwen Stone, as if her breath didn't form frosty clouds that drifted toward the vessels of Ebe Elixir.

Hester didn't know how to explain what was happening. As she and Jem prepared to reenter the enchanted outbuilding of the Keep, she could suddenly see all of it. A whole and graceful structure. What's more, she knew she'd been here before, many times over many years.

"The Boundary House!" Jem cried.

"So it is."

Light poured out of vivid stained glass windows, so brilliant it was as if the sun itself dwelt within the House. With trepidation, Hester opened the door. The landing, where she had seen a smear of blood only moments before, was clean. Sparkling jewels in the floor hurt her eyes. She gaped at the empty spot where three people had lain.

"They're gone," said Jem.

"So they are."

Maeve opened her eyes to scorching sun. To her left, Sara and Dorjan stirred, beginning to wake from sleep. Maeve sat up to the sight of orange sand and rocks extending all around her. "We're back in the desert!"

She thrilled to the truth of it. Not trapped in the Shadow King's domains. Not alone on a cold gray floor waiting for death. She rolled from the blanket, reveling in the gritty earth.

Sara and Dorjan woke fully. They, too, rolled in the sand, laughing unreasonably.

"What a dream that was!" Sara said when they'd calmed themselves.

"More than a dream," Dorjan answered softly.

He pointed to where a curving knife lay on the blanket, its ash-colored blade glinting with a sharp and haunting light. Sara picked it up. The smooth, simple shaft fit her palm exactly, and the blade matched her astounded eyes.

Gray eyes!

Maeve stared. Sara's eyes were close to the same color as Morlen's, though the gray was softer, like crumbled ashes. *Is she an Ebrowen now, too?*

Turning to Dorjan, Maeve couldn't believe what she saw. His eyes, staring back at her, were gray also.

"It's all right," Dorjan said. But Maeve shrank back, doubting him.

They drank the Ebe Elixir.

She needed to touch them, needed to know. But what would she do if she found that they'd become like Morlen?

She stood. She bent to put a hand on Sara's shoulder. Touching her was like handling seedpods on the journey to Mantedi; Maeve had been awed by the life within them waiting to burst forth. Sara gave off tremendous vitality, like the seeds. But she was different, too: the seeds of most plants felt innocent and harmless—Sara had an edge of danger in her. *As if she could be poison or medicine, either one.*

Maeve reached for Dorjan. When she touched him, all she felt was love. "I don't understand. What's happened? Where did you go? What's that knife? Where did it come from?" Sara's torn blouse showed only a faint line along the skin under her collarbone. And the bruises that had been on her face and neck were scarcely noticeable. "You're healed."

"We went into the Seed Void," Dorjan said. "That knife is Sara's essence weapon."

Maeve didn't know what he meant. He was looking at Sara.

"I'm sorry, Sara," he said.

"Essence weapon?" Sara traced her blade with a finger.

"Dreamwen lore says there are only three others in existence," he said. "Sara, I'm sorry."

"Essence weapon?" she said again.

"We were in the Seed Void," he repeated. "And you made an essence weapon. Look at it, Sara. It's *you*. The blade of a Spirit Warrior."

"Seed Void?" Sara asked. "We were in the Seed Void?"

"Yes. That's where we were. Sara, I'm trying to tell you I'm sorry."

Sara lay the knife in her lap. "Sorry, Dorjan? What are you most sorry for? Are you sorry for keeping me from being taken by an Ebe in those first days at the Keep? Sorry for not letting me die on a raft in the ocean? Or sorry for healing me in the Seed Void?" She looked regal as she put her hands together and bowed her head for a moment. She lifted her eyes to his. "Yes, Dorjan," she said. "I know what you've done for me." She grinned. "But I forgive you."

Maeve felt a stab of sadness. Sara's eyes had been a special color, like the ocean, and now they were gray. But Dorjan smiled. "Thank you. I don't regret those things. But it was wrong of me not to get your permission when I brought you to the sycamore grove for all those nights on end. That's what I regret."

"You have my permission now. Now and tomorrow and all the days that follow. Yesterday and all the days before that. Truly."

Looking at Sara's knife, Maeve remembered that she'd given away the Dreamwen Stone. It did not lie softly against her heart, humming to her. Lord Morlen had it now. If, as Dorjan had told her, the Stone enhanced the gifts of anyone who held it, what uses would Morlen find for it?

An intrusive blur of sound interrupted her thoughts. "I hear something." She put her ear to the sand, sobered to hear a loud drumming of hooves. "Riders."

Sara grabbed her knife and jumped up. Dorjan snatched the blankets, kicking sand over the smooth patch where they had lain. Maeve slung Jasper's water bottle over her shoulder and picked up the loaf he had left. They all ran behind the rocky projection that had sheltered them the day before. Dorjan peered around it. He pulled his head back quickly. "It's Morlen himself with a retinue. Riding hard."

Maeve crawled up the side of the overhanging rock and looked out. Morlen's cloak fluttered as he rode at the head of a group of soldiers toward the fortress. Some of those who followed him were zind, about ten of them, their striped doublets standing out. The rest, another ten men, wore maroon uniforms. "Jasper," Maeve whispered. "He hasn't come back."

Lowen Camber had an easy journey to Bellandra's palace. The insignia of the Healer's Keep earned her the respectful courtesy of passersby and innkeepers alike. When she arrived at the palace gates, she was bowed through by attentive soldiers, and met by a man with a hideously scarred face who introduced himself as Bangor. He asked after her needs.

"I would like to refresh myself from my journey, but will only need a brief time to do so, for I'm anxious to attend the king and queen."

"Certainly. A bath can be made ready in moments. May I bring you anything besides food and drink?"

"I will need a kettle of steaming water, a jar of cold water, a basin, and two goblets delivered to my room, so that I may prepare a restorative tonic for Their Majesties."

Servants hastened to fulfill her requests. Camber bathed in a marble pool sprinkled with lily petals. She dried herself with luxurious towels, and then dressed in her robes. She dined on harvest fruits, fine bread, and delicious cheeses. Wine was brought, but she refused it, taking only a cup of tea.

Alone in the room she had been shown, she opened her bag of herbs. She poured hot water into the basin Bangor had provided and added a pleasant extract of cherries and poppies to steep. A liberal sprinkle of sugar. A large pinch of arsenicum poison—the sugar and cherry extract would disguise its bitter taste. Enough cold water to cool the mixture.

The good-smelling potion filled two goblets. Camber put the goblets on a tray. She called for Bangor.

She was surprised to hear that Queen Torina would receive her in one of the open halls. She'd expected to find the queen lying in bed. The messenger who had come to the Healer's Keep to beg assistance had reported both the king and queen to be gravely ill. Now Queen Torina was recovering? What did it mean?

Bangor led her through wide corridors to an elegant hall. There, Queen Torina presided over a small gathering of soldiers and a smooth-faced man in the embroidered robes of a seer. Camber looked curiously at the queen. Her face was only a little pale, her eyes alert. Her red hair contrasted with the creamy brocade of a curtain behind her.

Cam curtsied. "Good day, my queen. I am Lowen Camber, Herbalist from the Healer's Keep. I've come here because your messenger said your health suffered with some mysterious ailment that your healers were not equipped to treat."

"Welcome. I'm glad to find that the Healer's Keep has responded to a need from the palace." Camber wasn't certain, but she thought she heard irony in the queen's courteous words.

"Certainly. I've brought a broad pharmacopoeia with me, in hopes of healing you and the king. To begin with, I have prepared a tonic for you." Camber indicated the servant behind her, holding the tray of goblets. But as soon as she spoke, she realized her position. *Since the queen is well, it won't be possible to pretend that my potion was insufficient to ward off her death. They might guess she's been poisoned!* Camber cursed silently.

"Tonic?" Again that tone, as if the queen knew what Camber was about. She beckoned the servant who held the tray, and took one of the goblets. "Tell me, Lowen, what news of the Keep? Did our messenger, Captain Andris, reach you? For though he left a good while ago, he hasn't returned." She raised the goblet, sniffing the mixture.

"Yes, my lady." In fact, she had intercepted the royal messenger—a hugely proportioned, blustery man—before he could take his message to the healers—his message about a leak in the Boundary, along with a demand for Sara to leave the Keep. He was now confined to a bed, for Camber had looked after him personally. She prided herself on her knowledge of herbs: the man would not die, but he would not be able to rise until his message was no longer relevant, and when he did recover, he would not remember what he had been sent to do.

The queen held the goblet but did not drink. "Has the Silver Boundary been restored?" she asked brazenly.

Camber glanced about at the men standing nearby. Bangor stood as still as the statue of a krenen beside him. The mythical beast's large head and wide ears had been rendered with uncommon detail. "I'm sure you understand, Your Majesty, that these matters cannot be discussed in the presence of soldiers."

"These men are discreet, Lowen. Has the Boundary been restored?"

Camber looked at the polished floor. "The restoration was incomplete when I left, my lady, but there are many skilled and talented healers in the Keep."

"Such as Bern?"

Startled, Camber looked up. "Bern? Yes, he is talented, but he isn't a healer. He's Draden-gifted." She began to feel agitated.

The queen watched her as if she were a disgusting yet fascinating creature, one who merited study. "Bern is dead. Did you know?"

Camber's hands bunched in front of her. She ordered her fingers to relax. "Not possible, my lady. When I left the Keep, Bern was in good health."

"I don't doubt the truth of that." The queen had her hand on a leather pouch attached to her belt. "But since then—there have been changes at the Keep. When you left, it was still standing; now it lies in ruins. When you left, Bern was at work destroying the Boundary that protects our world. Now he's dead and the Boundary has been mended. When you left—"

"Impossible!"

"Is it? Yes, perhaps my crystal is mistaken."

"Your crystal! But—the Invisibility—"

"There is no Invisibility now. It has been lifted and not replaced, though I believe something will be done by the end of the day." She leaned forward. "You've made a journey in vain."

Camber glanced again at the soldiers. "Is there no one in the palace, madam, who might need the services of a healer?"

"Of a healer, yes, but not *your* services."

Camber drew herself up. "How dare you? I am a Lowen!"

"You come bearing the insignia of the Healer's Keep, expecting the welcome and the reverence that a true healer would command, while planning to use poison to overcome Bellandra's king and to end Bellandra's legacy." The queen set down the goblet. She stood with a rush of silk. "I accuse you, Camber, of treachery. I accuse you before Supreme Seer Rascide, before Captain Bangor of King Landen's guard, before the guard, and before the king!"

Before the king?

The curtain behind Queen Torina moved. Out of it strode a tall man in a wine-colored mantle. He carried a naked sword, its blade more iridescent than a thousand jewels.

"King Landen?" Camber could hardly speak the words. He nodded. How was it possible for him to be whole and well? Bern had assured her that the king and queen would both be very weak. He'd also said Bellandra's Sword and crystal would not be impediments ever again. Here stood a healthy king with a luminous Sword. And a raging seer queen, who had seen Bern's death in her crystal.

Camber tried to assemble her thoughts. *The Dark Invisibility. I must weave a Dark Invisibility around the goblets. If no one can see them, the poison won't be discovered.*

First, she needed to summon the Shadow. She reached for it, but somehow it seemed faint and far away. There wouldn't be enough of it to make a Dark Invisibility quickly!

She would have to use her wits. "Since you accuse me," she said, "I must submit to the law. I will withdraw my medicine and await your justice."

"There is no need to withdraw your medicine," Queen Torina said. "Medicine is the very thing you need." She picked up the goblet again. "A restorative will set you to rights from your tiring journey here."

Camber strained again for the Shadow, but this time it seemed even weaker and farther away. Her trembling knees made her feel foolish. "I am perfectly well, Your Majesty."

"But I want to see you feeling as well as your tonic will allow. No need to be afraid, Camber. Your own potion—you know what is in it."

Camber appealed to the king. "Everyone calls you the most merciful king in all the kingdoms."

King Landen's steady gaze unnerved her almost as much as the queen's relentless stare. "The merciful have no need to ask for mercy from me. Here you have the chance to vindicate yourself before the charge of treason. Why not drink what you have brought to us?"

Camber looked wildly about her for a sympathetic face, but all were hostile. "I am innocent!"

"Then drink," the queen said.

Camber took the goblet from Bangor. She lifted it to her lips. She tasted the flavor of cherries all down her throat.

Part Seven

The Silver and the Gray

Chapter 30

Jasper's ribs complained with every breath. His branded forehead burned and his nose itched. That was the worst part of being tied—couldn't scratch an itch. But all his discomfort was nothing next to seeing Evan beside him, hands bound, trying to put a brave face on captivity in a desert fortress. What kind of men would tie a child's hands?

He knew the answer. *Morlen's kind.*

He and Evan lay awkwardly at Morlen's feet. The only light in the big stone room came from one narrow window and a wide skylight too high to jump for. Perhaps twenty armed men were in attendance, half of them zind. Another forty men, many with foreheads purpled by bruises, stood against the walls empty-handed.

"Help these prisoners, Pel," Morlen said.

Hearing the same voice that had spoken so calmly in the place where Dorjan had taken them with his dream magic, Jasper shuddered. He remembered what Maeve had told him about avoiding Morlen's eyes, so he looked at the henchman, Pel, instead.

A red rash on Pel's face was broken by slave marks. "Help them, sir?" He didn't hide his bewilderment.

"Help them to sit. Untie their hands and feet."

Jasper forced his face to show nothing as Pel removed the rough rope around his wrists and ankles. He raised his unbound hands to scratch his nose. Evan, too, was released.

"Now restore the man's weapons, Pel."

"W-weapons, sir?"

"Weapons. The weapons with which he overcame the sentries, the fortress guards, and the workers."

"H-he had no weapons, sir. He's a freeman. He used rocks."

"Surely, Pel, you don't mean to tell me that this man, armed with desert gravel, overcame this fortress and destroyed the vahss harvest? How many of his men escaped you?"

"I—don't know, sir. Never saw any others."

"No others? No one else?"

"N-no, sir."

"Impressive, isn't it?" Lord Morlen's boots approached Jasper and Evan. "One man. In search of a boy?"

A ghastly silence grew until Jasper longed for a noise, any noise, anything but this threatening quiet.

"Kill them." Morlen's tone was conversational.

Jasper's first thought upon hearing his death sentence was that he'd fight all these men with his bare hands before he let more harm come to Evan.

"A-aren't you going to question them first, sir?" Pel sounded flabbergasted.

"Ah! You thought I meant the prisoners? No, Pel, I need more time with them. They have much to tell me." His boots turned, heels facing Jasper. "No, I meant kill *them*. The guards." Jasper looked up. Morlen was pointing at the battered men standing against the walls. "The so-called sentries, who didn't keep watch. The fools who let my vahss harvest be destroyed. *Them.*"

Zind sprang into motion ferociously, quickly followed by Morlen's soldier slaves. They leaped on the hapless, unarmed men. Jasper put an arm around Evan and hid the boy's face against his chest.

Twice in his life before, Jasper had seen unarmed men fight to defend their lives. Now he saw again what desperate strength it gave them, as the fortress laborers battled frantically, meeting axes and knives with naked fists. Amid the melee, he recognized the wiry squirrel-man who had nearly scaled the fortress roof. Squirrel was smart enough to band together with a tall blond man and another dark, burly fellow. The three of them wrested an axe from a zind. They killed him with it and took his knife.

As the room rang with shouts and the noise of blades meeting bone, Lord Morlen stood aloof, watching as though this combat were a theater for his entertainment. Jasper didn't want to see any more blood, but it was all around him. Maybe it would be better to die from plain steel than to find out what Lord Morlen meant to do with him and Evan once the battle was over. He wasn't tied. He could run into the path of one of the zind.

But that would mean leaving Evan alone.

Maeve was glad when she came across Fortune. The mare's affectionate nose against her face let her forget for a moment that she was about to give herself up to Lord Morlen.

Pretending to give up was Sara's idea. She'd pointed out that the fastest way inside the fortress was to be taken through the doors rather than trying to break them down. "If we pretend we're here to deliver Maeve, his guards will let us in," Sara had said. "I'll hide my knife in the waist of my skirt, against my back. When we get next to Morlen, I'll use it."

"The guards will surely search us," Dorjan had said.

"They'll search *you*," she answered. "I won't threaten them—I look like a desert waif. And when Morlen sees we're alive in the world of form, won't he believe we must be his allies? He'll see by our eyes that we drank the Ebe Elixir."

"Except me," Maeve said.

"Keep your eyes cast down, or he'll know at once that something's afoot." Sara had spoken with great verve, as if she looked forward to meeting Lord Morlen and his zind. "Then, when we're close to him and ready to attack, show him your eyes. It will put him off guard."

"But what if he already knows—about everything we've done since he left us?" Maeve asked.

Dorjan frowned in concentration. "Bern is truly gone now, and who else would know anything about what we've done? And Morlen woke himself with the Dreamwen Stone. Then he rode here from Mantedi. He hasn't been back to sleep since then."

But Maeve remembered that when Morlen captured her in his gray eyes and pushed her mind across the Minwenda and into other realms, he'd been awake. He might not be able to move his physical body with his mind as Dorjan could, but . . .

"He went into my mind while he was awake," she said. "He took my secrets. He'll know we lie."

"Morlen was sure we couldn't escape without drinking the Elixir," Sara said, "or he'd never have left us. When he sees our eyes, he'll believe." Her unnerving gray eyes softened. "It's a risk. But by tomorrow Morlen will certainly have slept again. We'll have lost our chance."

And Maeve had agreed to Sara's plan. For Evan, and for Jasper.

They untied Fortune. Maeve dribbled a little water into the mare's mouth. They went on. Soon the fortress loomed close to them, reminding Maeve of a great orange lizard, the high narrow windows staring like reptile eyes.

Outside, a grizzled soldier in a maroon uniform stopped them.

"We're here to see Lord Morlen," Dorjan said.

The man's slave marks were old and faded. He prodded Dorjan with the blunt end of his knife. "And what would Lord Morlen want with *you* while he's finishing executions?"

Executions? The sand seemed to swim nauseatingly under Maeve.

"We've brought him a prize," Dorjan said, shoving Maeve forward.

"Well, now. If someone took the grime from your face, little Miss, Lord Morlen might take to you. But I'm not witless enough to disturb him now. It may be that I'll keep you to myself," the man said greedily. He caught hold of Maeve's shoulder and she felt his fear and lust—fear of Lord Morlen and lust for herself. The fear of Lord Morlen was greater.

"Her name is Maeve," Dorjan said. "And we expect the reward."

The man frowned. "Maeve? The selfsame Maeve he's been chasing for so long?"

"The same."

He looked her up and down. "Come with me, the lot of you."

Jasper tried to shut his ears along with his eyes, but they wouldn't close. He heard a hundred and more blows and yells and groans.

When the fighting was over, half of Lord Morlen's soldiers were dead along with the group they'd been ordered to kill. Many of those left alive were wounded. They began wiping the blades of their weapons on the clothes of the men who had fallen.

Barely acknowledging the zind captain, Morlen commanded Pel to bring him Jasper's freedom scroll. When it was in his hand, he waved the scroll slowly.

"Jasper Thorntree."

Jasper didn't want to look at his freedom in the hands of Lord Morlen.

"Jasper," Morlen mused, "do your deeds impress me or anger me more?"

Jasper sighed guardedly. It looked as if his prayer for a quick death wasn't going to be answered. Prayer was an odd thing, for most times what he asked for didn't come his way, and oftentimes the best things in his life had landed in his path without him even knowing that he wanted them. *Like Maeve.*

"You'll have no need of this scroll again." Morlen beckoned to a soldier and handed him the scroll. "Burn it," he said casually.

Jasper felt sweat on the back of his neck and blazing heat in his face. He must still be cursedly alive or he wouldn't care about the scroll being burned.

Morlen tapped Jasper on the head. "Don't pretend to be witless. It's a dangerous thing to try playing me for a fool. What you did here could not have been done by a witless man. Look at me." Jasper looked reluctantly, not meeting Morlen's eyes, hating the thin lips and neat hair. "I suppose someone told you not to look into my eyes. Would it be Maeve? And would you be one of the mysterious visitors who spirited her away?"

At the mention of Maeve, Jasper tried to breathe normally but it seemed that his chest had locked out the air.

Morlen turned to Evan. "And you, Evan. Did you think I wouldn't remember you, boy?" Evan was silent. The blue veins in his neck throbbed visibly. Morlen bent and touched his cheek. "Maeve," he said softly. "Even more of a marvel than I guessed."

He straightened. He drew his patrier. He ran its edge against his forearm. Short hairs from his arm drifted to the floor. Evan huddled closer to Jasper.

"I left Maeve in a place no meddlesome friends can take her from," Morlen said. The patrier flicked out, nicking Jasper's neck. "Yes, I caught her, and no one can interfere this time." The calm, almost friendly voice continued, while blood began soaking the collar of Jasper's ragged shirt. Morlen reached into his own shirt, bringing out a pendant—a smooth, ordinary-looking stone—hanging on a gold chain. Jasper gasped. *The Dreamwen Stone.*

Morlen paused, then went on talking. "I admire you, Jasper. Ungifted though you are, your determination has led you to do things gifted people can't manage. Destroying the vahss harvest! How many free must have dreamed of it. But none of them could even leave Mantedi. How did you do it?" Morlen's tone changed, suddenly harsh. "Pel, remove the scarf from his forehead."

Jasper didn't fight as Pel pulled off his bandage, exposing the brand. Unprotected from the air, it flamed anew.

"Ah," said Morlen. "The farmer's brand." He bent close to Jasper. "You must love her very much," he said in a mocking whisper.

The boots moved away again, two steps, while Evan stared at Jasper's forehead.

"I wonder," Morlen went on, "what is fitting? Slavery, of course. But first, I think, you should taste vahss yourself."

"You have no vahss," Jasper said through his teeth.

Morlen answered him by producing a flask of orange liquid. He removed the stopper; Jasper smelled the overpowering, sweet scent he remembered from the night before. "The boy will drink first," Morlen said.

"No! He had nothing to do with it."

"He had everything to do with it." Morlen took hold of Evan's shoulder. "You have a choice, boy. You can drink this without a fuss, or I will cut off your friend Jasper's throwing arm."

Evan's lips went pale. He wriggled out of Jasper's grasp. He reached for the flask, but Jasper put a hand on his wrist. Morlen's patrier flashed again, cutting Jasper's forearm. Evan scooted away and took the flask. He put his mouth around the rim, tilting his head back. Morlen seized the flask as soon as Evan gulped a swallow. "Clever boy," he said. "But you'll want to leave some for your friend."

Evan's frightened face changed. His eyes dulled. His empty smile reminded Jasper of another's. *Orlo.* So vahss had been behind Orlo's betrayal.

"And now, Jasper." Morlen shook the flask. "Your turn."

Jasper clamped his teeth together. *Kill me, Morlen. You'll have to kill me.*

Behind Morlen, one of the doors was flung open. A weather-beaten old soldier stepped inside. He murmured to the men standing guard. Morlen turned around. "I ordered that no one disturb me."

"Perhaps this news will please you, sir," the grizzled soldier said, pushing Maeve into the room.

She looked as though she'd bathed in sand, her hair and skin dirty and smudged, eyes cast down. Behind her were Dorjan and Sara, just as disheveled.

As Morlen's boots advanced on Maeve, Jasper didn't think—he only knew what he was going to do as he did it. He bounded to his feet and ran at Morlen. Morlen might be evil and he might have powers Jasper couldn't fathom, but he still had to use his legs to stand on. Jasper bowled into the back of his knees.

It was like hitting a hardwood tree. Jasper came to rest flat, with two stripers pointing knives at his throat.

Chapter 31

The first thing Dorjan noticed when the old soldier brought them into a big stone room was the stench of fear. Next, the sight of armed men wiping blades on bodies that lay around the walls. Then Lord Morlen, carrying a double-edged knife, advancing on them too fast. And behind him, Jasper and Evan. Jasper's forehead had a livid mark on it, and his neck and arm were bleeding. Evan sat with a peculiar smile on his face.

When Jasper threw himself on Morlen only to land helpless against the floor, Dorjan wished he could summon the forces of Shadow just this once, to overcome Lord Morlen. Jasper had hit the back of his knees, but Morlen didn't even spill his flask.

"Lord Morlen," Dorjan said, steeling himself to show no passion, hoping to gain Morlen's attention before anything more was done to Jasper, hoping his gray eyes would say what his tongue refused to speak.

Morlen's eyes darted over all of them. He sheathed his knife with a smooth, practiced movement. He gave a slight wave of his hand, and Dorjan, Sara, and Maeve were instantly seized by soldiers wearing striped doublets. Already, Sara's plan was undone. Gray eyes were not supposed to earn them rough handling by burly soldiers smelling of blood.

"I didn't know you were so near." Morlen's thin lips curled as he took in their clothes. "Or that you were such friends to the desert. Do you know, we haven't been properly introduced." He put a finger to Maeve's cheek. "But Maeve can tell me who you are." He stroked her dusty skin. "I bid you welcome, Maeve. Didn't I say we were joined by destiny?" He spoke softly, like a lover.

Maeve bowed her head farther and he stooped to see her face. He tapped her forehead. "You see I have the Dreamwen Stone."

A flicker of startling blue as Maeve's eyes fluttered.

"What's this?" The welcome left Morlen's face. "You didn't drink the Elixir? How, then, did you get out of the chamber where I left you?"

Dorjan realized that until now he'd never truly been afraid. Even the storm that had nearly drowned him hadn't frightened him the way Morlen's voice frightened him now. "When she wouldn't drink, we brought her out of the chamber," he said, but knew as he spoke that Morlen would not believe him.

Another signal, and more soldiers moved in. Gloved hands drew long knives. Dorjan felt steel against his throat. Everything was going wrong. He had one more dream journey left. Should he use it now?

But even as he closed his eyes, harsh fingers pried his eyelids up. Morlen held his eyes open. "Fahd," Morlen said. "I need strong string." As he waited for it to be brought, he talked. "You," he said to Dorjan. "A dream traveler. Oh yes, I have studied the Dreamwen annals. Unfortunately for you, I studied them thoroughly. I know how to prevent you from doing what you want to do." Through aching eyes, Dorjan saw a striped glove extended, holding string. "Use the string,

Captain Fahd. While I hold his eyelids, bind him so that he cannot close his eyes."

The soldier tied string tightly around Dorjan's head, drawing his eyelids up. "Good," Morlen said. "Now watch him." And with mounting fear, Dorjan found that it was true that with his eyes forced open he couldn't find the sycamore grove, couldn't shape himself to dream travel.

Morlen paced in front of his new prisoners, halting before Maeve. "You and I were about to come to an understanding, weren't we?" he said. "But we were interrupted. No matter. We will not be interrupted again. I will see your friends drink vahss, and then I will decide whom to keep and whom to kill." He shook his flask, the orange liquid inside it sloshing. "Once they have tasted vahss, I will learn how you left the chamber of Elixir."

"V-vahss?" Maeve said. She looked as if the only thing holding her up was the strength of the two soldiers who gripped her.

Morlen whirled about. He beckoned to Evan. "Come closer." Dorjan's eyes tried painfully to blink as Evan, still wearing a glazed smile, walked up to Morlen.

"Tell them, Evan." Morlen shook the flask again. "Tell them how you like vahss."

The boy showed no fear of Morlen. "I like vahss."

"Now tell me, Evan, which of these prisoners despises me?"

Evan seemed unconcerned. "They all do."

"Do any of them wish me dead?"

"They all wish you dead."

"And you? Do you wish I were dead?"

Evan shook his head.

"Would you like to help me?"

The boy nodded.

"It's Jasper's turn to drink," Morlen said. "But first there's something I want to change about his face. I want you to help me change him, Evan." He took out the wicked-edged knife again. He put it in Evan's small hand.

"I don't like the brand on his forehead," he said. "You must cut it off."

Evan wrapped his hand closely around the haft. He braced his other hand on Jasper's head. He put the knife's edge against Jasper's forehead.

Jasper didn't look at him. Instead, his eyes found Maeve's.

It was then that Maeve began to sing.

There weren't any words to her song, and there weren't any words to describe the way it tore through the room. The soldiers stood transfixed. Maeve's guard dropped his arms, setting her free. Dorjan shrugged out of his own guard's grasp, and Sara did the same. Jasper's guards let him go. The knife in Evan's hand clattered to the floor. Even Lord Morlen stood stock-still. Dorjan ripped the string from his eyelids.

In that moment of confusion, Sara leaped, her curving knife shining in her hand. She jumped on Morlen, slashing at his throat.

Pouring blood, Morlen batted Sara away with his arm. She fell heavily, clutching her knife. Dorjan sprang to help her.

Could anything but a knife forged in the Seed Void have made Morlen bleed?

Morlen dropped his flask. It shattered at his feet. He grasped his throat with both hands, slowing the flow of blood. "Kill her." He spoke in a rasping rattle. "Take the knife from her and kill her."

But the soldiers didn't lift their weapons. They stood listening to Maeve's song, and they wept like hungry children. Dorjan pulled Sara to her feet. She menaced Morlen with her knife. He sank to the floor, holding his throat. Blood trickled through his fingers. "You'll never be safe from me."

"You're dying," she said, standing over him, while Maeve's song wove around them all.

It's true. She cut through him with her essence weapon. "Don't look in his eyes," Dorjan warned. "The moment of death will have great power, and he will take you with him if he can."

"I know who you are and where to find you," Morlen said, gasping. "Death cannot stop an Ebrowen. Not one of you has the barest understanding of my power." One of his hands went to the chain around his neck. He clutched the Dreamwen Stone.

Close by was the knife Evan had dropped. Jasper picked it up, but Morlen's hand shot out, grabbing his wrist. Dorjan heard bone snap. Sara brought her blade down, slashing Morlen's hand. He let go of Jasper, his hand flopping.

Jasper grabbed Morlen's knife again with his good hand. He used it to cut through the chain that held the Dreamwen Stone. He rubbed the Stone on his shirt, wiping away Morlen's blood.

He got to his feet. He wove unsteadily toward Maeve, holding out the Dreamwen treasure as her song ended. Maeve took the Stone, then opened her arms to Jasper. The two of them embraced as if holding each other was all that would ever matter.

"Maeve," Morlen said, his croaking voice carrying over the sobs of his men. "I would have made you an Ebrowen . . . given you the world . . ."

"Don't meet his eyes," Dorjan warned again.

"The world!" Morlen said, rasping.

"The world," Maeve answered, "isn't something I want."

"Fool," Morlen said. "Your gift is wasted . . . the legacy you could have had, thrown away."

Maeve lifted her chin. "I have the legacy of my mother, whose courage will live forever."

Sara brandished her unearthly blade. "And you, Morlen, have nothing. No pathways leading away from here for you to corrupt with your blood."

He closed his eyes. "I will seek you through death and beyond," he whispered.

Maeve gave a sudden gasp. "Evan!"

The boy was shuffling toward Morlen as if pulled by an invisible leash.

Maeve dodged in front of Evan. She scooped him up, turning his face to the wall. Dorjan stepped between them and Morlen.

A shadow rushed at Dorjan. He heard his own breath, and was puzzled to find that though the shadow thickened and spread for a long time, only one breath was slowly filling him. He wanted to speak—to tell Sara she must use her knife again, cut through the shadow that grew before him— but the slow air filling his lungs wouldn't allow him to say anything.

The shadow pushed him, a wall of cold against his heart. His own words reverberated inside him. *The moment of death will have great power.* And still he had not finished one breath.

Help me, Sara.

Another figure appeared, not quite human, with long, dark wings, standing in a gray hallway just behind a sheen of silver.

Cabis had said the Shadow King appeared to those who were dying. *Am I dying, then?*

"You have come to me, as I knew you would," said the winged man.

Dorjan felt a clean, sharp point graze his side. The pressure lifted from his heart. He saw Morlen's shadow passing by him with a gust of cold. It crossed through the Silver Boundary into the gray hallway beyond.

Dorjan exhaled a long whistling breath. Sara stood beside him, her blade poised, eyes vigilant. "He's gone," she said.

"Thank you." Dorjan put all his feeling into the small words.

Maeve set Evan on his feet. The boy looked from one to another of his friends with steady brown eyes. "Is he dead?" he asked.

"Yes, Evan," Dorjan answered. "Morlen is dead."

Chapter 32

Captain Andris, the king's messenger, woke with a grim-faced woman bending over him, snapping her fingers. "I see you're awake," she said. "I'm Hester, Chief Draden. And you are well now, Captain Andris."

Andris raised himself. The room he lay in was missing a wall. "Have I been ill, then?"

"What else but illness would keep you in bed through an earthquake? But the healers tell me you've recovered."

Earthquake? Andris put his feet on the floor, feeling quite well. He tried to remember what his illness had been, tried to remember his message, without success. "Then I shall not trespass on your kindess any longer," he said.

"You haven't delivered your message." The Chief Draden looked at him accusingly.

Andris tried again to remember, but it was as if someone had opened his head and shaken out his wits. "How is the Princess Saravelda?" he asked, bluffing.

"Regretfully, Saravelda is missing. She has not been seen within the Keep for some time." The Chief Draden folded her arms.

Andris stood up. "Missing? I will leave at once, and tell the king and queen what you have said."

No one wanted to stay in the room full of carnage where Morlen had died. With Maeve's comforting arm supporting him, Jasper staggered with the others into the fierce desert sun. He slumped to the ground in the meager shade of the fortress wall, looking at his wrist. His hand pointed the wrong way. It had swollen to nearly twice its normal size and turned an interesting shade of purple. An injury like that should hurt, surely, but it didn't.

Dorjan knelt beside Jasper. "I know a little bone-setting," he said. "Will you let me do what I can?"

Jasper held out his arm. Dorjan's large hands probed gently. "Is the pain bad?"

"The truth is, something's wrong. I don't feel it."

"Nothing's wrong," Dorjan said reassuringly. "You've had enough pain."

The small surviving band of Morlen's former soldiers hovered around Sara. She wiped her sunburned face with the grubby edge of her sleeve and pushed back her tangled hair. The knife in her hand glinted. "Stop cringing as if you were my slave," she said, frowning at Pel.

"He *is* your slave, Sara," Jasper said. "You killed his master. By law he's yours."

She rounded on Pel. "The law says you belong to me?"

"Yes, my lady."

"The stripers, too," Jasper said.

"Stripers?"

"Zind. We free call them stripers." Jasper pointed with his good hand at the black-and-gray doublets of the six zind who had lived. He didn't like seeing the sharp black axes at their belts—they could easily kill him and his friends. But he didn't believe they would, not after Maeve's song. "See the double-lined scar from temple to jaw, with the emperor's crown? Mercenaries. Usually serve the emperor, but Morlen began using them to help find Maeve. Since their contract is unfulfilled, they must serve it out under you."

Sara called to the zind. "Do you have a captain among you?" A great-shouldered fellow with several wounds on his arms and neck stepped forward. "Your name, sir?"

He cleared his throat. "Fahd, my lady."

"Captain Fahd, is it true what Jasper says?"

"Yes, my lady." He shifted his feet. "And there's the matter of the song. I can't forget it."

"No need to forget it, Captain." She turned to Dorjan. "You know how to set Jasper's hand, Dorjan?"

"Maybe. I listened to Ellowen Mayn." Dorjan smiled. "Best lie flat." Jasper let himself slide to the ground. "I may need some help—someone to hold his arm steady."

Sara nodded to the striper called Fahd. "Help Dorjan."

The big zind instantly got on his knees in the dirt. Dorjan showed him what to do. Jasper didn't watch them. He looked at Maeve and Evan instead. "Boys," he said. "There are other boys still locked inside."

Sara whirled on the men standing by. "Show me these boys." She marched back to the door. Pel bowed her through. The rest of the soldiers followed.

Jasper felt a strong pull on his wrist, and several tugs. He risked a glance. His hand faced the right direction again. But then the pain started, severe and grinding.

"We'll need to make you a sling," Dorjan said, "and we'll need to wash that burn and cover it if we can find anything clean to wrap it with."

Jasper told Fahd about the spring-box inside the fortress. Fahd brought water and found clean sackcloth. By the time Sara and the soldiers came back with over fifty boys, Dorjan had washed Jasper's brand and wrapped it. Maeve sat quietly beside him all the while, one arm around Evan. Jasper didn't ask how Dorjan's and Sara's eyes had turned gray. He didn't ask anything. It was enough to savor freedom and to see Maeve and Evan nearby.

The rescued boys squinted fearfully at the zind. Many looked undernourished. "Feed these boys," Sara ordered the soldiers.

Jasper grinned to see the men saluting the gray-eyed young woman. They scurried back into the fortress. When they brought food and water out, Sara gave them more orders. "Make sure each boy is fed. Feed yourselves. Then feed and water the horses. When you're done, remove the bodies from inside and bury them—all except Lord Morlen. Don't touch him. We wouldn't want you to become ill."

She accepted only water herself. Jasper was glad of water, but he didn't want to eat, either. All the blood he'd seen had left spatters across his mind.

While the soldiers worked shoveling sand and rock, boys ran and jumped, tossing rocks at the fortress. Evan didn't want to let go of Maeve, but Jasper persuaded him to join the other boys so that Dorjan and Maeve could go a little apart and talk privately. Jasper watched as they sat together in the shade of a rock. Maeve kept wiping her eyes—must be talking about her mother. And father.

Sitting beside Jasper, Sara asked what had happened since he'd left her and Maeve the night before. As the sun crept past the midheaven, Jasper told his story.

"You're a brave man," she said when he finished. "You risked everything."

Jasper shrugged. *I had to.* "Your eyes . . . what happened?"

She told him. Some of her tale got lost in the searing throb of his forehead and the wrenching ache in his wrist. *Seed Void?* He wasn't sure he'd ever understand.

Fahd and Pel and the other men presented themselves, dripping with sweat, the burials done. Sara sighed. "Must I order you to drink?" She waved them away. "And wash yourselves. Find something to cover your wounds."

They tramped off as Maeve and Dorjan rejoined Sara and Jasper. Maeve rested against the wall, tucking her warm hand into Jasper's.

"Dorjan," Sara asked, "do you think Morlen *could* follow us through death and beyond?"

The tall young man shook his head. "The Silver Boundary is mended. I don't think he can cross back, now that he's dead."

Jasper was too tired to ask what he meant. Morlen was dead, and the dead didn't return. That was as much as he wanted to know.

"I wanted to defeat the Shadow King!" Sara sounded very disappointed.

"Perhaps it's true that it can't be done, that each soul must decide alone." Dorjan's gray eyes looked almost silver. "But you vanquished Bern and Morlen, Sara."

She stroked her knife. "We all did. But I hope I've atoned for helping the Shadow King before." She sounded suddenly hoarse again, as she had when she first arrived in Sliviia.

Dorjan nodded, and now Jasper could have sworn his eyes were pure silver.

Maeve rubbed the Dreamwen Stone hanging on a length of sackcloth around her neck. "I wonder if the Dreamwen Stone will ever sing again."

"Again?" Dorjan gave her a puzzled look.

She lifted it from around her neck and handed it to him. "Lord Morlen must have done something to it. It doesn't sing anymore."

Dorjan covered the Stone with his large brown hands. "It has as much power as it ever did," he said. "The power to enhance the gifts of whomever holds it. The power to protect the traveler in the realms outside the world of form." He laid the Stone in her palm. "Did it ever sing to anyone but you, Maeve?"

"I don't know."

"It sang to you as long as you didn't know your gift."

"My gift?"

"Your voice. You defeated Morlen with the same talent he must have wanted you to use in his service. Your talent became a weapon against his power."

Jasper remembered Maeve telling him how she'd spent most of her life hiding the fact that she could sing. "Weapon?" he asked.

"Didn't she cut away the killing hatred in Morlen's men with her song? No, Maeve, the Dreamwen Stone hasn't lost anything." Dorjan smiled keenly at her.

Cut away the killing hatred . . .

Leaning forward excitedly, Jasper jarred his broken wrist. "Would her voice overcome *anyone*? What about other lords? What about the emperor?" He didn't wait for an answer. "Sing to the emperor, Maeve! Make him free the slaves!"

He watched his thought enter, watched the deep blue of

her eyes deepen more. "Free the slaves," she said. "Free the slaves?"

Dorjan and Sara stared at her, their eyes mirrors of one another. "Free the slaves?" Sara echoed reverently. "Free the slaves," Dorjan repeated.

The shouts of the pack of boys playing bounced against the fortress wall. Maeve put her head back, looking at the vastness of the desert sky. *She's thinking of her mother,* Jasper thought. "Could it be done?" she said.

"Yes," Jasper said. "Yes, Maeve."

Maeve looked at Dorjan. "If I stay in Sliviia, will you tell Cabis about me?" she asked softly.

He gazed across the desert. "I have only one dream journey left, Maeve. Sara and I will be returning to the Healer's Keep tomorrow by way of dream travel. You could come with us. If you stay here this time, I'll never be able to bring you or anyone else across the Minwenda by dreaming. If you decide to meet our father later, you'll have to find a ship across the water."

Maeve bowed her head. Jasper saw her fingers tremble as she clutched the Dreamwen Stone. "Tell him," she said. "Tell him about me."

"I'll tell him," Dorjan said gently. "About you, and about your mother."

"Thank you," she said. "Thank you for coming to Sliviia."

Somehow, Jasper vowed to himself, *I'll see to it that she gets the chance to sing before the emperor.*

Just then the soldiers returned, their hair slicked with water, wounds neatly bound with sackcloth.

Sara spoke. "You're certain, Maeve? You want to sing before the emperor?"

Maeve nodded warmly.

"Captain Fahd," Sara said, and it occurred to Jasper that it had been a long and tiresome day for Fahd. Perhaps he was near to falling from exhaustion, but if so he gave no sign. "You have served the emperor of Sliviia?" Sara asked.

The captain bowed. "I have served Emperor Dolen personally."

"Can you gain admittance to him?"

"Yes, my lady."

"How long was your term of hire with Lord Morlen?"

"Until the winter solstice."

"Then I have only a few more orders for you," Sara said. "First, you will escort Maeve and Jasper and the boy, Evan, to the palace of the emperor." She flourished her knife, eyes glowing as if bits of the ash-colored blade looked out of her face. "You will watch for their safety and let none of them come to harm. You will arrange for Maeve to sing before Emperor Dolen." She sounded like a queen.

An escort of zind! I never thought to return to Slivona under the protection of zind. Jasper squeezed Maeve's hand; she squeezed back.

Captain Fahd bowed to Sara again, then to Maeve and Jasper. "It will be my honor to protect the singer."

"Thank you, Captain. You and your men may rest yourselves now."

The zind bowed and took themselves away. Sara beckoned Pel. "How many carriages are stored here?"

"Eight, ma'am. We were making ready to carry a harvest of vahss to Mantedi."

"And horses?"

"Yes, ma'am. Two horses for each carriage, and then all the horses the soldiers rode."

"You, Pel, and the other slaves will use the carriages to

take these boys, who are lowborn free and have been wrongly made captive, back to Mantedi to rejoin their parents."

"Yes, ma'am."

"After that, you may do as you like. I don't expect to call on you again."

Pel scratched the rash on his face. "Do you mean to say we're free then?"

"Once you fulfill these orders, yes, you're free."

Pel touched his slave marks. "But how will we live, ma'am?"

Sara gaped at the men, at the hopelessness hardened into their faces. Not a single one showed joy at the idea of freedom.

Jasper spoke up. "Give them carriages and horses. They can set up as carriage drivers inside Mantedi."

And as Jasper explained the ways of a carriage driver, the men who had once been slaves looked slightly more cheerful.

When Queen Torina's health had so miraculously returned, she and Rascide had used the Great Seer's crystal to receive visions of the Healer's Keep. But Torina had looked in vain for Saravelda.

She wasn't in the habit of asking for visions of her children—the independence of their souls seemed to her a vital matter. But this time, she needed to know. Saravelda was not at the Healer's Keep. Where, then, had she gone?

After the scene with Lowen Camber, Torina and Landen went alone together to a private section of beach by the Bellan Sea. They sat on the sand, watching the easy waves roll toward them from the west. Torina took out her crystal again, asking for news of Saravelda. She was too eager and had to wait what seemed a long time to find stillness within herself.

When the visions finally came, she saw an odd succession of images, and wondered, at first, what connection they might have to her daughter.

A rock-strewn desert, the sun low in the sky creating a red sunset. A sturdy-looking young man with a recent brand on his forehead was building a fire.

Sliviia.

A group of people sat around the fire, singing, their voices carrying into the desert evening. A beautiful young woman wearing a tattered dress led them, and as she sang, she met the loving glance of the man who'd made the fire.

"I have lived on the borders, my real face unseen,
but where I go now has no boundary but dreams.
Walk with me, walk with me out of this night,
for you are my love, and you are my light."

A young boy leaned against the lovely young woman, his head drooping in sleep. Soldiers wearing striped doublets stood watch.

Then Torina saw her daughter among the group around the fire. Saravelda looked as if she hadn't combed her hair since she'd left the palace for the Keep, and her face was badly sunburned. In her hand she held a luminous, curving knife, and her eyes above it were no longer the color of the Bellan Sea—they were the color of ashes.

Before the queen could wonder how Sara's eyes had changed and how she had crossed the Minwenda and how she would get back again, a powerful message from the future overrode the vision of Sliviia.

She came out of stillness. She replaced the crystal in its pouch. She turned to the king.

Maeve spread a blanket under the desert stars so Jasper could lay the sleeping Evan down. No one wanted to use the bunks inside the fortress. She could hear Captain Fahd arranging a watch through the night. Pel and his fellows were gone—they'd settled all the other boys into the carriages and left for Mantedi.

The air had cooled when the sun set, and now the temperature was pleasant, the air fresh. The stars seemed to smile over the deserted fortress. "I suppose it will be a while before that spring takes back this part of the desert," she said.

"Thanks to you, one day the place where Morlen brewed his vahss will be an oasis."

"Thanks to *you*, too, Jasper."

"I'm glad I'll be with you when you sing before the emperor."

"I'm glad you've been with me all this way, Jasper." She took his good hand. "Did you ever think—"

"No, I didn't, ever." He stepped in very near. "I know now how much more there is than what I used to think." Moonlight fell softly over him, illuminating his kind face. His arm went around her.

Maeve's lips met his. It was as if his kiss united all the separate flames of each fire he had lit along their journey into one blaze of steady warmth.

A quick step nearby made them turn. Sara and Dorjan approached.

"Sorry to interrupt," Sara said. She stood in her rags as if she wore a gown as fine as the blue silk Lila had sewn.

"You'll be going to sleep?" Maeve asked. They nodded. "And you won't be here in the morning," Maeve said sadly.

"You know how to get to the sycamore grove," Dorjan said, his voice husky. "And I give you permission to visit there as often as you like."

Maeve looked from one to the other. "I wish your eyes could turn back," she said impulsively. "Won't they ever be the way they were before?"

"I don't think so," Dorjan answered.

"It's all right," Sara said. "We can't change what we've seen and where we've been. It's the same with you—everything is different now."

Maeve saw Jasper's face, Evan's sleeping form, the vigilant zind close by, and knew it was true. Everything *was* different. She wasn't running from Lord Morlen anymore, trying to leave Sliviia in hopes of seeing her father. She was getting ready to go back to Slivona, with the ambition to sing before the emperor, and Lord Morlen was dead.

"I don't want to say good-bye," she said. Tears pricked sharply.

"This isn't good-bye," Dorjan said. "Far from it."

But they all embraced as if it really were good-bye. And the zind looking on bowed as they might once have bowed to the emperor.

Chapter 33

When Sara woke in a grassy clearing, she thought at first that she was still asleep. But no, she knew now how to recognize the difference between dreaming and waking; this place had the steadiness of being awake in the world of form. When she turned her head, Dorjan was there, watching her. In his smile, she saw all that they had been through, from their first meeting at the Healer's Keep, to the Seed Void, to now.

Trees surrounded the clearing where they lay, leaves glistening in a way Sara remembered from another day that seemed long past. "Where are we?" she asked.

"The Healer's Keep," he said. "Within the seventh sacred ring."

Sara heard a fluting call. She stood, raising her eyes to the sky. Great birds came into view, wheeling slowly above. Their pearly feathers split the sunlight into rainbows.

"The Tezzarines," Sara breathed. "They've come back."

The birds had new markings—the tips of their wings were shining black. Somehow it added to their beauty. One of them descended. It hopped along the ground. Burn scars marred its plumage, and a scar covered one of its eyes.

Sara approached it. She knelt in the grass before it. And

this time, as the Tezzarine opened its beak to sing and her tears began, she knew that no one would tell her not to cry.

Draden Hester faced a large pile of parchments. Only midmorning, and already she had been interrupted several times with questions from workers.

Another knock sounded. Dra Jem opened the door before she could ask him to wait. It seemed to Hester that Jem had become quite forgetful of etiquette. In only a short time he'd changed from a reliable Dra into someone who burst into rooms without ceremony.

His timing could not have been worse. Hester had just spattered a great spot of ink on the account sheet she was writing. A spot! She blotted the ink, then realized she would need to begin again—the smear was intolerable.

"What is it?" She shuffled other parchments to hide the one with the spot.

"More news, Draden."

"What now?" As if there weren't enough for her to do, overseeing the rebuilding of the Keep.

"King's messenger."

"Good. He can carry a message to the palace," Hester said crisply, glad she'd now have a simple way to send the king and queen the message that their daughter had been found.

Saravelda had come strolling out of the Keep forest, along with that tall foreigner, Dorjan. Both had been dressed in the most filthy clothes imaginable, a mere collection of rags. Neither had shown proper respect to Hester when she'd told them that a hearing would take place as soon as it could be arranged, to address their wrongdoings. They'd asked, rather discourteously, for baths, and then demanded a meeting with all of the Ellowens. When Hester would not agree to such an assembly, Saravelda had said that the meeting *would* take place, and *without* the Dradens. Her eyes had looked quite wild—Hester noticed what a freakish color they were, like ashes; Dorjan's, too.

Hester had met with Ellowen Desak and Ellowen Claire, the new Mystive on the Keep's Council, and insisted there must be a hearing. Though they had agreed, they had said they could see no harm in meeting with the other Ellowens and the two renegade students. Over Hester's objections, the meeting had taken place, *without a Draden present*. Afterward, Hester had not received a report, except a brief notice that Sara and Dorjan had consented to staying at the Keep until the hearing.

Consented! How dare they?

"Draden?" Jem was looking at her oddly.

Hester roused herself. "Yes?"

"The messenger says the king and queen will be here tomorrow afternoon."

"Tomorrow afternoon! But that's when the hearing is to be."

"Perhaps the time could be rearranged."

Perhaps. But then Hester thought of Queen Torina squirming as she watched the humiliation of her daughter. "Or perhaps the king and queen can observe. Yes. That's what will be done, Jem. See to it." She rapped her knuckles on her desk. "Is there anything more?"

"Yes, Draden. There have been reports of Ellowens catching glimpses of Tezzarines. Ellowen Wrena and Ellowen Claire will be climbing to the seventh sacred ring today to find out if they've returned."

❖ ❖ ❖

Landen, king of Bellandra, arrived at the Healer's Keep in the afternoon of a golden autumn day. With him rode his wife, Torina, and a small group of well-armed soldiers. Captain Andris had met them en route and the king asked for his company back to the Keep.

The front gates of the Keep were flung wide by four Dradens. The travelers' horses were led away, the travelers themselves led into the Keep.

Though Torina's visions had prepared him, Landen was shocked by the appearance of the grounds. The buildings looked as though they'd been kicked by an angry giant. Many of the roofs had fallen in, leaving great mounds of rubble through which broken beams reached forlornly. The fountain that had stood in the welcoming garden lay in pieces. Even the walkways had been scrambled into haphazard mixtures of dirt and flagstones.

But Landen also saw evidence that the work of restoring the Keep had begun. Some of the walkways had been neatly laid again; one of the buildings had a new wall. And the bell tower stood straight, its silver bells gleaming.

The Dradens ushered the king and queen into a hall that had escaped damage. Food and wine were put before them. There they waited for Draden Hester to join them.

The Chief Draden looked sour when the king asked if there was any news of his daughter. Torina had assured him that Saravelda was heading for the Keep, traveling from Sliviia by some unknown, rapid means.

"Saravelda is here," Draden Hester said. "You will see her shortly, Your Majesty, at her hearing, which is scheduled to take place within moments."

"Hearing?"

"Hearing," said Draden Hester firmly. "Your daughter has involved herself in activities that are highly suspicious. All the Ellowens and Dradens are prepared to attend."

Landen smiled, turning to Torina and catching her eye. "How fortunate we are, to be invited to witness this hearing. Ordinarily, the Keep does not allow the outer world to mingle with its inner functions." He watched as sweat formed on Draden Hester's forehead.

"Yes," Torina said. "Thank you, Draden. Please don't delay."

Seated among the gathering of Ellowens and Dradens, Landen waited eagerly to see his daughter. The room chosen for this hearing had all four walls standing; the paintings on the walls were well placed, the incoming sunshine muted by elegant drapes. Two simple chairs at the head of the room stood empty. A door behind the chairs opened. Sara entered, followed by a tall young man. They bowed and took the chairs.

Landen leaned forward, looking intently at his daughter. He tried to pinpoint what it was that made her look as if she were grown up. Was it the place? The situation? Her hair, though not absolutely smooth, had certainly been combed. She wore the standard tunic of the Healer's Keep. She didn't fidget. Her face had seen too much sun, and her eyes, as she gazed out at the gathering, startled her father. Torina had warned him that Sara had been on a voyage so transformative it might even have changed the color of her eyes, but this! Soft gray eyes, shot with silver, holding an expression both fierce and compassionate. When she found her parents among the small crowd of people observing, Sara didn't jump up and run to them; she only smiled quietly.

Draden Hester introduced the tall young man. Dorjan. He reminded Landen of someone the king hadn't seen for many years—Cabis Denon, the conscript he'd rescued from the ocean after a sea battle during the great Sliviite invasion. Dorjan's nose and chin had the same shape as Cabis's, and his skin was similar, too. But his eyes were like Sara's—gray and silver, and looking as if they'd seen many things that could never be told.

Landen listened to Draden Hester denounce Sara with a tale involving a broken seal, a protection destroyed, a bird sacred to the Keep lost, and other mysterious and suspicious events Hester believed Sara to be connected with—the death of her nephew, and an unauthorized enchantment on the Boundary House.

When Sara was given leave to talk, she asked if Dorjan might speak on her behalf. Draden Hester begrudgingly granted her request.

Dorjan rose. "I'm glad none of you are hungry." An odd way to begin. "This story is long, and needs to be told from the beginning. You may be hungry before I finish."

The Ellowens looked at one another.

"It starts eighteen years ago, before my father, Cabis Denon, was conscripted into the Sliviite navy and forced to sail to Glavenrell with an invasion."

Landen sat farther forward.

"What nonsense," Hester interrupted. "This hearing—"

"Let him speak!" Landen could easily make himself heard over a crowd much larger than this one when he wanted to, and though he knew that the Keep did not recognize the governance of a king, he used his royal voice.

Hester did not interrupt again.

Landen didn't miss a word of the extraordinary tale. The Dreamwen lineage, Cabis and Lila's love, the Dreamwen Stone, the daughter Cabis never knew. Ellowen Renaiya's revelations to Dorjan about his and Sara's gifts, and about the Charmal, Bern. Bern's use of Sara; the Ebes who had attacked the sleep of the gifted; the Silver Boundary; and the Shadow King. Crossing the Minwenda, Maeve's rescue, the battle for the Boundary House in which Bern had died. The journey to the chamber of Ebe Elixir and into the Seed Void. The return of the light that had been draining from mystic objects. The essence weapon that had killed one of the Shadow King's foremost servants, Lord Morlen. The parting in the desert, Maeve's ambition to free the slaves. And finally, the Tezzarines.

When Dorjan finished speaking, he gestured at Sara. "She may have destroyed the protections on the last Tezzarine," he said, "but it was she who freed them all from bondage to the Shadow King, by reminding them of their essence while she was in the Seed Void. And though she killed Bern, if she had not, he would have killed her and much more than her— he would have succeeded in bringing down the Silver Boundary so that the Shadow King could walk the world."

Dorjan sat down to thunderous quiet.

The next person to move was a tall, plain woman in the silvery robes of an Ellowen. She stood, facing the assembly. "I am Ellowen Claire. As a Mystive I can vouch that this young man has told the truth. The Ellowens gathered here are grateful for the return of the Tezzarines. We mourn the passing of Ellowen Renaiya and Ellowen Mayn. And we have agreed that it is time to name two more Ellowens." She lifted her hands, and the seated Ellowens all stood.

Ellowen Claire turned to Sara and Dorjan. "Please rise."

They stood, looking surprised.

"Dorjan and Sara, you have healed the light. You have saved the Silver Boundary and listened to the song of the Tezzarines. We recognize you as Ellowens. Welcome."

And if Landen had thought the healers too contained and staid, he revised his opinion as they embraced and laughed and raised their voices. Their rejoicing made no room for Hester's flustered protestations that if she had only known, if Ellowen Renaiya had simply told her, there would have been no misunderstandings.

Sara and Dorjan waded their way past the congratulations and kisses of the members of the Healer's Keep to the king and queen, to be kissed and congratulated some more.

"Thank you, young man," Landen said, "for all that you have done." He looked into Sara's face. "A different gift, Sara? We thought you'd be a dancer, but you're a Spirit Warrior."

"I want to see your knife," said the queen.

"She may be a Firan," Dorjan said quietly, "a Spirit Warrior with an essence weapon. But she danced to save the Silver Boundary, and she danced to vanquish corruption in the Seed Void. Saravelda *is* a dancer, sir, a mighty dancer."

Landen saw an otherworldly depth of light in his daughter's smile. *Not long ago, she left my household a willful child. Now she stands before me, a young woman who has traveled distances I will never go.*

"Yes," Landen answered respectfully. "Yes, she is a dancer." He clasped hands with Dorjan, and gave thanks for the day he had pulled Cabis Denon from the ocean.

Glossary

Avien Artistically gifted healer. Aviens study at the Healer's Keep, learning to create art that will enhance and harmonize the health of those who view it.

Boundary House A round building at the edge of the forest in the Healer's Keep, where the Silver Boundary is tended. The Boundary House was designed and built by powerful Ellowens; it enhances the gen of anyone who steps across its threshold and gives added power to any word spoken and any action taken within its walls. Its windows are stained glass, inlaid with precious jewels of every color. The floor is marble, and the marble has been carved into symbols and signs, also inlaid with jewels and precious metals.

Charmal Charismatic, charming person with no conscience. Charmals can see into others; they use their insight not to benefit people, but to get what they want.

Double Invisibility A field of protection generated by Ellowens at the Healer's Keep. Double Invisibility hides the Keep completely from inner vision of every sort and from normal physical eyesight, too. It is only used during times of extreme danger.

Dra Draden in training.

Draden Worker at the Healer's Keep. Dradens study and enforce Keep law. They also see to functions such as cooking, cleaning, scheduling, and general upkeep.

Dreamwen A person who is able to visit realms beyond the world of form via conscious travel during sleep. Dreamwens live by a strict code of ethics that forbids them to enter the mind of a dreamer without permission.

Ebe A very large bird of Shadow. Ebes dwell in the Shadow realms, and are in bondage to the Shadow King. They fly through the unseen worlds and attack the souls of sleeping people.

Ebromal A person who is dedicated to the service of the Shadow King.

Ebrowen A Dreamwen who has fallen under the sway of the Shadow King. Ebrowens are not bound by the Dreamwen code of ethics; however, they cannot invade the dreams of any person they have not made eye contact with at least once. An Ebrowen can also overpower the minds of waking people by looking into their eyes.

Ellowen An advanced healer who has completed training in one of the disciplines taught at the Healer's Keep and who has also experienced Ellowenity. Ellowens have a high level of vital force, which enables them to do things such as set seals, generate Invisibility, and practice their gifts with extraordinary skill.

Ellowenity A personal experience of spiritual love and unity.

Firan A person with an extremely rare gift. Firans study at the Healer's Keep, learning to cultivate spiritual warriorship.

Gen The mysterious, animating flow of life. Vital force.

Genoven Genovens study at the Healer's Keep, learning to walk consciously in dream states and heal the minds of those oppressed by melancholia or insanity. (The Bellandran equivalent of a Dreamwen.)

Great Seer The foremost Seer. There is one Great Seer born every fifth generation, and only one for all the kingdoms.

Great Seer's crystal A Bellandran crystal of exceptional purity, traditionally used by the Great Seer to bring forth the clearest possible visions.

Healer's Keep The place in Bellandra where healers study. The Keep grounds include an infirmary, study halls, a dining hall and kitchen, meeting halls, dormitories, cabins, gardens, cliffs edging the Bellan Sea, and the forest of sacred rings.

Lowen One who has completed training in one or more disciplines at the Healer's Keep. A Lowen is a respected and effective healer.

Lyren Musically gifted healer. Lyrens study at the Healer's Keep, learning to create music that will enhance and harmonize the health of those who hear it.

Mystive Psychically gifted healer. Mystives study at the Healer's Keep, learning to perceive the inner essence of others.

Phytosen A healer who is gifted with plants. Phytosens study at the Healer's Keep, learning the uses of plants and how to grow them, how to distill plant extracts and mix them to create medicines.

Sangiv A healer who is gifted with power. Sangivs study at the Healer's Keep, learning how to remove malignant growths from the body in bloodless surgery; Sangivs are also very able bone setters.

Seal An invisible lock or barrier woven by an Ellowen or Ellowens.

Seven Sacred Rings Seven concentric rings formed by ancient trees within the forest at the Healer's Keep. The rings are protected with various levels of seals. Each ring occupies a higher elevation than the previous. Inside the last or seventh ring is the high clearing where the Tezzarines make their home.

Shadow King King of shadows, lies, greed, and anger.

Silver Boundary A protective boundary around the world, made of the resonance of all living souls. The Silver Boundary prevents the Shadow King from entering the world of form directly. It is tended by Ellowens at the Healer's Keep from inside the Boundary House.

Single Invisibility A field of protection generated by Ellowens that guards the Healer's Keep from outside interference, including the vision of seers.

Tezzarine Large, sacred bird with iridescent pearl-colored feathers. Tezzarines live in the clearing within the seventh ring at the Healer's Keep. Only Ellowens have actual contact with Tezzarines.

Trian A gifted dancer. Trians study at the Healer's Keep, learning to create dances that will enhance and harmonize the health of those who view them.

Wen Spirit.

Genealogies

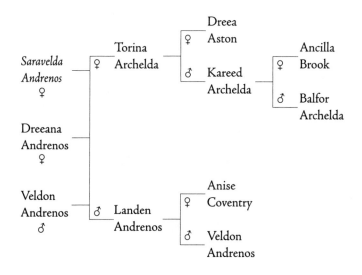

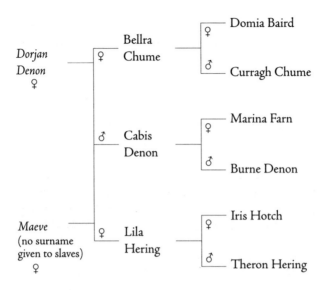

Dorjan Denon ♀

Bellra Chume ♀
— Domia Baird ♀
— Curragh Chume ♂

Cabis Denon ♂
— Marina Farn ♀
— Burne Denon ♂

Maeve (no surname given to slaves) ♀

Lila Hering ♀
— Iris Hotch ♀
— Theron Hering ♂

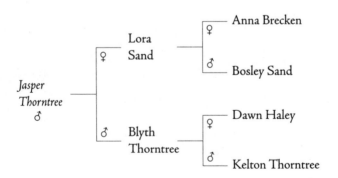

Jasper Thorntree ♂

Lora Sand ♀
— Anna Brecken ♀
— Bosley Sand ♂

Blyth Thorntree ♂
— Dawn Haley ♀
— Kelton Thorntree ♂

VICTORIA HANLEY grew up without a TV, and learned to love books at an early age. "Writing for young adults is a joy and an honor," she says.

Victoria is a certified Montessori teacher and a certified massage therapist. Born in California, she has also lived in Massachusetts, Wisconsin, New Mexico, Oregon and Colorado. She has two young adult children—a son, Emrys, and a daughter, Rose—and is married to a young-at-heart husband, Tim.

To learn more about Victoria Hanley, go to her Web site:
www.victoriahanley.com

Also by Victoria Hanley

THE SEER AND THE SWORD
A companion book to *The Healer's Keep*

Princess Torina lives a charmed life, nurtured by loving parents in the mighty kingdom of Archeld. But her father, King Kareed, has a hunger to extend his boundaries. He seizes the peaceful kingdom of Bellandra—and its legendary sword, rumored to defeat any enemy. On his return, he offers Torina two gifts: a beautiful crystal and the defeated king's son, Landen, as a slave. Both prove to be more precious than she could ever imagine, for through them Torina makes two magnificent discoveries: She is a seer, able to view the past and future in her ball, and Landen is not a servant but a peer, a noble spirit who matches her in wits, bravery, and strength of character.

Yet beneath the seemingly orderly surface in Archeld lurk greed, revenge, and mutinous plots. Fingers point at Landen, but Torina cannot believe he would harm her or her family. Can she use her new-found powers to save her beleaguered kingdom? Or must the seer take up the sword?